1636
THE VIENNESE
WALTZ

31 December
2014

1636
THE VIENNESE WALTZ

ERIC FLINT
PAULA GOODLETT
GORG HUFF

1636: The Viennese Waltz

This is a work of fiction. All the characters and events portrayed in this book are fictional, and any resemblance to real people or incidents is purely coincidental.

A Baen Books Original

Baen Publishing Enterprises
P.O. Box 1403
Riverdale, NY 10471
www.baen.com

ISBN: 978-1-4767-3687-7

Cover art by Tom Kidd
Maps by Gorg Huff and Michael Knopp

First printing, November 2014

Distributed by Simon & Schuster
1230 Avenue of the Americas
New York, NY 10020

Library of Congress Cataloging-in-Publication Data

Flint, Eric.
    1636 : the Viennese waltz / Eric Flint, Paula Goodlett, Gorg Huff.
        pages ; cm. — (Ring of fire ; 18)
    "A Baen book."
        ISBN 978-1-4767-3687-7 (hardcover)
1. Time travel—Fiction. 2. Seventeenth century—Fiction. 3. West Virginia—History—
Fiction. I. Goodlett, Paula. II. Huff, Gorg. III. Title. IV. Title: Sixteen thirty-six.
    PS3556.L548A61869 2014
    813'.54—dc23
                                                                    2014027151

10 9 8 7 6 5 4 3 2 1

Pages by Joy Freeman (www.pagesbyjoy.com)
Printed in the United States of America

To Virginia DeMarce, for all the persnickety details we would have gotten wrong without you and even for the ones we got wrong in spite of you. You have made this a better series and a more realistic world.

Contents

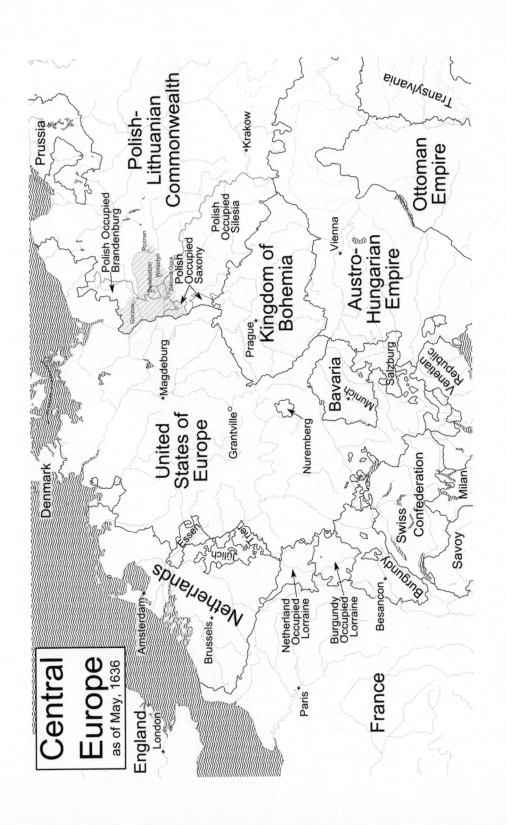

Central Europe as of May, 1636

England
London

Denmark

Prussia

Polish-Lithuanian Commonwealth

Polish Occupied Brandenburg

Poznan
Swiebodzin
Zielona Gora
Wolsztyn
Gorzow

Krakow

Polish Occupied Silesia

Polish Occupied Saxony

Transylvania

Ottoman Empire

Magdeburg

United States of Europe

Grantville

Prague

Kingdom of Bohemia

Vienna

Austro-Hungarian Empire

Salzburg

Venetian Republic

Netherlands

Amsterdam

Brussels

Essen

Trier

Jülich

Nuremberg

Bavaria

Munich

Netherland Occupied Lorraine

Burgundy Occupied Lorraine

Burgundy

Besancon

Swiss Confederation

Milan

Savoy

Paris

France

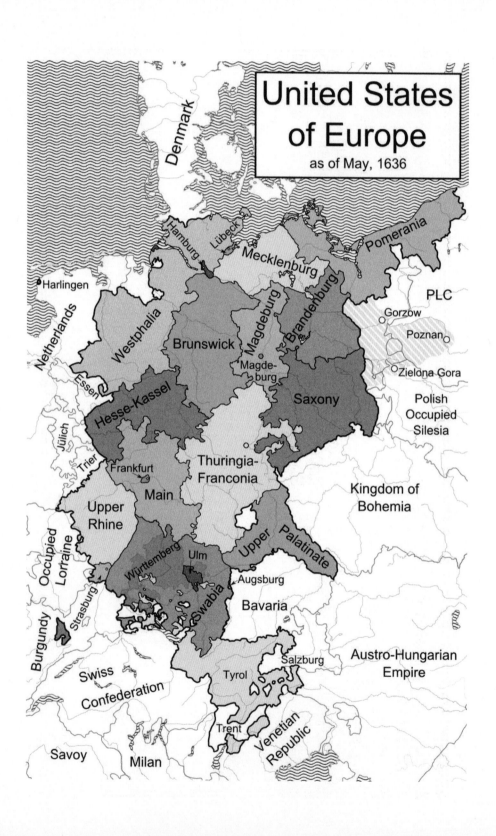

United States
of Europe
as of May, 1636

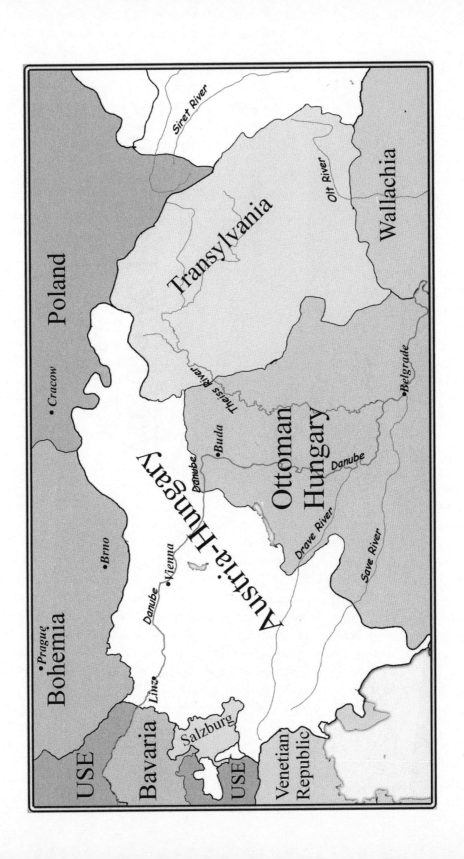

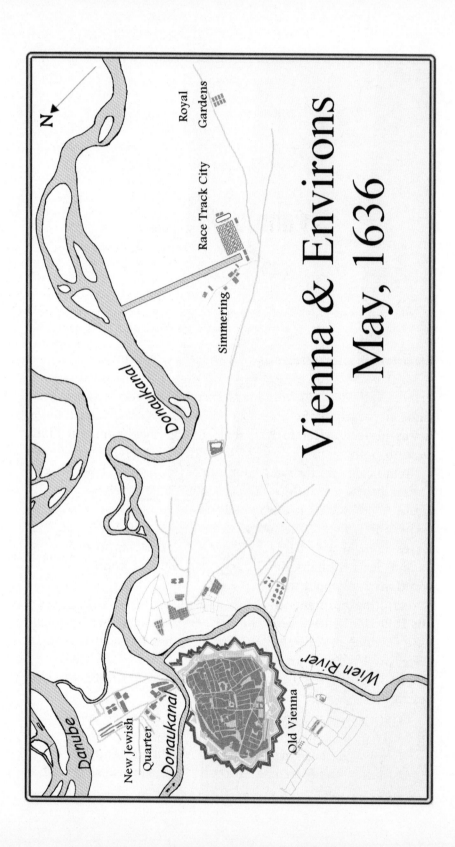

CHAPTER 1

ꜰꜳmily Issues

June 1634

Liechtenstein House, outside the Ring of Fire

Prince Karl Eusebius von Liechtenstein watched Istvan Janoszi smile nervously as he was ushered into the oak-paneled room. It was perfectly clear to Karl that Janos Drugeth's minion didn't want to be here.

"What can I do for you, Your Serene Highness?" Istvan asked.

Karl held up a cut-crystal glass with a light yellow bubbling liquid in it, swirled it around for a moment, sniffed, took a sip and made a face. "The latest attempt at producing Sprite still leaves something to be desired." Karl waved Istvan to one of the padded leather chairs he had in his study and continued. "But you don't care about that. Nor should you. What you care about is recruiting up-timers to go to Austria. And yet, at last report His Imperial Majesty Ferdinand II doesn't believe that up-timers have anything of real value to offer the world. Or has that changed since last I heard from my uncles?"

Karl waited to see if Istvan would lie. He ought to know better but he was probably a bit off his game.

"Prince Ferdinand would like an up-time car and someone to take care of it."

So. Not a lie, but not the whole truth either. "And?"

"And what, Your Serene Highness?" That was a weak response.

1

"And does his imperial father know? And why the Fortneys? And what happens to the Sanderlins and Fortneys when they arrive in Vienna under Ferdinand II's eye? For that matter, what happens to Prince Ferdinand when they arrive?"

"That's a lot of ands."

"I have more, but start with those." There was nothing at all soft or gentle in Karl's voice. He didn't appreciate people playing games with his friends.

Istvan was a reasonably brave man but he swallowed, then began to explain. "No. As I understand it, the emperor doesn't know. He is very ill and not expected to last more than another couple of months."

"Less than that if they bleed him, which they probably will," Karl agreed. "Go on."

"His Imperial Highness, the prince, does not wish to distress his father."

"But he wants to get them there as soon as he can, without upsetting the emperor. His Imperial Majesty is quite unreasonable about the Ring of Fire and all that it implies, I know. I have gotten chapter and verse on that from my uncles in Vienna," Karl said.

"Yes, Your Serene Highness. As to the Fortneys, they will be hired because Ron Sanderlin insisted." Istvan seemed about to continue but didn't. Karl noticed, but wasn't sure what it meant.

"And aside from the car, which I don't doubt Ferdinand does want," Prince Karl said, "he also wants all the technological transfer he can manage. I take it from your comment that there is no great rush to get them there."

"Not exactly, Your Serene Highness. I think most delays will happen on the road before we reach the Danube. So I would like to have them at the Danube and waiting before the emperor . . ."

Karl moved to a seat across the coffee table from Istvan and sat down. "And then have them wait where until he dies?"

"Regensburg."

Karl nodded. Regensburg was a good stopping point. "My interest, which you should feel perfectly free to put in your next report to Janos, is mostly in the Fortney family because of business connections. They asked me what they should take to Vienna and I wanted to know what their situation was likely to be before I advised them. Given what you have said, I will advise them to take as much as they can carry. That will be all."

Istvan got up and started to leave, but Karl thought of something else. "No. Not quite all. Another of those 'ands' I mentioned. How much is Ferdinand paying for the cars? For that matter, how much is he paying the mechanics?"

Istvan winced, then said, "One million American dollars for the car. They insisted on American dollars."

The prince snorted a laugh. "I imagine they did. You didn't try to get them to take HRE reserve notes, did you?" There were two new versions of HRE reichsthaler that had been tried since the Ring of Fire. The first were Holy Roman Empire notes based on the principles of the federal reserve notes that the up-timers issued, commonly called American dollars. Those notes had been rejected by anyone who had any choice in the matter at all, and had lasted only about eight months. While they had never actually been recalled, they were effectively out of service by mid-1633. Prince Karl Eusebius von Liechtenstein had never found it necessary to take any, but his uncles had found it unavoidable. The second notes, the silver-backed HRE reichsthaler, had been more successful and had some value even in the USE. It was, in theory, a note issued on a full reserve depository, exchangeable on demand for 0.916 up-time ounces of silver, the equivalent of a Bank of Amsterdam guilder. However, a lot of people in the USE seemed to doubt that claim, or were simply unwilling to take HRE silver-backed reichsthaler to get the silver. So the HRE reichsthaler was trading at about half the value of a Bank of Amsterdam guilder.

"Welcome, Mr. Sanderlin, Mr. Fortney, and company," Prince Karl said graciously as the gaggle of up-timers arrived in his foyer. "I would greet you all as you deserve, but it would probably take too long." Karl ushered them all into his larger sitting room and motioned them to the conversation area with its delicate chairs and tables.

"Thanks for talking to us, Your Serene Highness," said Ron Sanderlin. "I didn't know you were involved with this."

Karl waited as people found chairs then answered. "I'm not, or at least I wasn't until Judy Wendell called me about it. After that I called Istvan Janoszi to find out what was going on. I understand you're selling your car, or at least *a* car, to His Imperial Highness."

"Yes, to Prince Ferdinand," Sanderlin agreed. "And he hired me and my uncle to look after it. Frankly, it seems pretty weird.

One car and two mechanics, unless Janoszi finds another car to buy. They didn't even squawk too much when I hooked Sonny in on the deal."

Karl noticed the slightly shifty expression on Sanderlin's face when he mentioned Sonny Fortney, but made sure his expression stayed politely curious. "And why did you invite Mr. Fortney in on the deal?"

"Well, partly it was because Ron knew I was looking for a different job," Sonny Fortney said, in a sort of slow drawl that suggested he wasn't the sharpest tool in the shed. But Karl had met his daughter Hayley and couldn't believe that the father of a girl like that was slow-witted. "Partly it was because Ron was a little nervous about taking his family so far from Grantville all by themselves. Like I'd be able to do anything if your folks decided to roast us all on spits."

"I assure you, sir, we'll not roast you on spits," Karl said with great dignity, then added, "Deep frying, that's the way to prepare up-timer."

Sonny Fortney gave Karl a slow grin. "See, Ron? I told you they was civilized."

"What sort of job are you looking for, Mr. Fortney?"

"I'm a steam-head, Prince Karl. And interested in railroads."

"I'm sure that Prince Ferdinand will find use for your skills, Mr. Fortney. But you're here to learn about Vienna and what you might want or need there?"

"Yes, Your Highness," Ron Sanderlin said.

They spent the next few hours chatting about what might be of use to the two families who were moving to Austria.

"My parents are kidnapping me!" Hayley Fortney wailed over the phone. Hayley wasn't quite fifteen.

Judy the Younger Wendell, who had just turned sixteen a month ago, held the phone away from her ear for a moment but she still heard in the background, "Hayley! It's nothing like that and you know it. Your father got a good job. That's all!"

"Like I said," Hayley continued. "My parents are kidnapping me. I need to know what to take to freaking Austria!"

"I don't have any idea, but I think I know who to ask."

"Who?"

"Prince Karl." Karl Eusebius von Liechtenstein had been the

Barbie Consortium's main financial backer since his return from Amsterdam at the beginning of the year.

"The Ken Doll?"

"He's from there. He should know what they have and what they need."

"Okay," Hayley agreed, sounding less panicked. "But he's the Ken Doll. You know, stands around looking pretty and giving us money."

Which was a patent untruth. Prince Karl Eusebius von Liechtenstein was anything but a Ken Doll. He was, in fact, the head of his family—his rather wealthy family—in the Holy Roman Empire, an acquaintance of His Majesty Ferdinand II as well as His Royal Highness Ferdinand, who would probably become Ferdinand III in the near future. Prince Karl was indeed rich, and smart enough to let others with more financial acumen manage that wealth.

"Sure, but he was a royal prince before that. Besides, I think Sarah has the hots for him." Sarah was Judy's older sister and the source of Judy's information when back in late 1631 Judy had organized her friends on the Grantville Middle School cheerleading squad into the Barbie Consortium.

"What about David?"

"She's still dating him. Too. I didn't think Sarah had it in her."

Apparently even juicy gossip about Judy's older sister wasn't enough to distract Hayley for long. "Never mind that. I know he's a prince and you know that just means one of his ancestors was a successful crook."

"His dad, actually," Judy explained unnecessarily. "And both his uncles, one way or another. Don't you pay attention to anything but nuts and bolts?"

"Nope," Hayley said proudly. "The rest is just paperwork so I have the nuts and bolts I need." Which was another patent falsehood. Hayley was the Barbie Consortium's mechanical "genius" though she wasn't in the same class as Brent and Trent Partow in Judy's opinion. But she was not really ignorant of what the rest of the Barbies did.

Judy wisely let it pass. "Karl will know what opportunities there are in the sticks." It didn't occur to Judy Wendell that there was anything odd in calling the capital of the Holy Roman Empire "the sticks." To her, civilization had arrived on Earth with the Ring of Fire and she lived in its center. As soon as she was off the phone with Hayley, she called Karl.

CHAPTER 2

Send Money

June 1634

Liechtenstein House, outside the Ring of Fire

"It's a letter from your Uncle Gundaker." Josef Gandelmo, Karl's tutor, financial manager, and companion, handed him the letter across the desk.

Karl opened it and read. "The family wants me to increase their allowance."

"That's hardly fair, Your Serene Highness." Josef's voice held quite a bit of censure, but at least a touch of humor as well. He moved over to the sideboard and gestured to the drink bottles.

Karl shook his head. He still wasn't happy with the down-time version of Sprite and had never been all that pleased with beer or wine. "I know. But it does seem a bit strange how the world works. Gundaker wants five hundred thousand guilders in silver. Which is insane. Granted, silver is worth more in Vienna. It might even be profitable to ship silver to Vienna and dollars back here. If they had any dollars worth mentioning in Vienna. But they don't."

"I suspect His Imperial Majesty is putting considerable pressure on your family and if your family's access to its wealth is problematical, His Imperial Majesty's lost two-thirds of his tax base. The wealthier two-thirds," Josef said.

Karl nodded. "Somehow, I don't think my neighbors in Grantville are going to be all that thrilled with me if I start sending silver to fund Ferdinand's armies. For that matter, Wallenstein—who is King Albrecht now—won't be thrilled and he can cut off access to the better part of my assets. Frankly, it would be better politically if I didn't have the money...at least not in cash."

Josef snorted. "You should do more business with the Barbie Consortium. I'm sure they would be happy to relieve you of your cash...Ken Doll."

Karl looked at Josef, then leaned back in his swivel chair and grinned. "You know, that's not a bad idea."

"I was joking, Your Serene Highness."

"I know, but I'm not." Karl gave Josef a serious look. "Josef, that letter was delayed. I didn't receive it for at least a week from now. A month would be better. Meanwhile, get in touch with both Judy Wendells, the younger and the elder."

Seeing his look, he added: "No, Josef, I don't intend to defy my family and my emperor. But I'm walking a tightrope here, with Ferdinand II on one side and Wallenstein on the other. I can't send cash. It would raise too many red flags. If I don't send anything, it will raise red flags on the other side. I will send an authorization for the family to borrow against family assets in Bohemia and Silesia. Those assets will have considerably more value if they are the planned recipients of up-timer sweet corn, new plows, stamp presses, sewing machines, and anything else I can think of or learn from Mrs. Wendell. For the rest, I can't send it if I don't have it, and the Barbies might be just the group to invest those funds in ways that will make them temporarily unavailable. Go, Josef. Make your phone calls."

Wendell Home, Grantville

Judy the Younger, irrepressible as always, said, "I don't know how you do it. Somehow that outfit works on you."

Karl smiled, gave her a little bow, and followed her into the living room where her mother and sister waited. She waved him to the couch. Karl was wearing dark-red calfskin riding boots with a bronze down-time made zipper replacing the laces. Zippers had become all the rage since the Ring of Fire; at least, for those who could afford them. Tucked into the boots were dark brown pants with embroidery in red and gold. A white linen shirt was covered by a gold lamé waistcoat and a dark green morning coat with the same red and gold embroidery. Both the vest and the morning coat had zippers as well. This was all topped with a beaver cowboy hat, which Karl took off and set on the end table once he was seated.

"So, what's so important, Prince Karl?" asked Sarah Wendell. She was wearing the down-time version of a woman's business suit, a divided calf-length skirt and a matching jacket, with a high-collared blouse, all done in various shades of blue.

"I find myself in an unusual position," Karl admitted. "For complicated reasons, I find it would be much better if I temporarily had a great deal less cash on hand."

"I have to ask." Judy the Younger grinned. "What complicated reasons?"

"My uncle wants me to send him five hundred thousand guilder in silver."

Judy tut-tutted. "You people don't know anything about money."

"Be nice, Judy, or I'll send you to your room," Judy the Elder told her daughter.

"I note, however," Karl said, "that you didn't disagree with her."

"Well..."

"It's perfectly all right. I have come to believe that, to a great extent, our knowledge of money is on a par with our knowledge of medicine." Karl sighed. "The truth is that three years ago my family knew more, or at least as much, about money and finance as anyone in Europe. And Kipper and Wipper were, I believe, less the result of avarice than of ignorance."

Judy the Elder was giving Karl what he could only describe as a doubtful look.

"It's true, ma'am," Karl said. "I'm not saying that avarice played no role, but my family minted money using less silver and after only a short while, no one trusted it. You people mint money out of *no* silver and everyone trusts it."

Sarah cleared her throat. "Ah...why does your family want you to send them eighteen to twenty million dollars in silver? I mean, well, extravagant lifestyle or not, that's a lot of money."

"It's not lifestyle," Karl said. "It's politics. Most of my family's lands are in Bohemia, Moravia and Silesia. When Albrecht von Wallenstein declared himself the king of Bohemia, he effectively conquered my family's lands. We hold those lands in fief from the king of Bohemia.

"King Albrecht must let us collect our rents and taxes from our lands. To do otherwise would be to declare before all the world that he doesn't respect the rights of his nobles. But, with my uncles in Vienna and serving in Ferdinand II's court, he is pointing out that he is not required to allow those monies to go to people who are actively at war with him."

"But you're not actively at war with him," Judy the Elder said, nodding.

"Quite right. I am living here in Grantville, a prince in name, but acting as a businessman and not holding any government post for any state. I can collect family rents, tithes and taxes. My uncles can't, not for lands that are in Bohemia or Silesia. Then there is the matter of my Aunt Beth. She is the duchess of Cieszyn, a duchy in Silesia. Aunt Beth is involved in two lawsuits in the Holy Roman Empire, one with the empire itself and one with my uncle, her husband. Aunt Beth is living in her duchy and daring Uncle Gundaker to come see her there. She appealed to King Albrecht on both cases and he has found for her in both cases. She, in return, has sworn loyalty to King Albrecht."

"What are the cases about?" Judy the elder asked.

"In a sense both are about her being a woman. There was a privilege granted by King Władysław II Jagiellon to Duke Casimir II of Cieszyn in 1498, under which was secured the female succession over Cieszyn until the fourth generation. Aunt Beth is the fourth generation or her older brother was. Ferdinand II insists that she was disqualified by her gender. The lawsuit with Uncle Gundaker involves the wording of the marriage contract and who is the duke or duchess of those lands. And, as I said, when King Albrecht took Bohemia, she appealed both cases to him as her new liege. Albrecht confirmed her as duchess of Cieszyn. She swore fealty to him and has dropped all persecution of non-Catholics in Cieszyn."

"Good for her," Judy the Younger said.

"I agree, though I prefer not to say so in my uncle's hearing," Karl said.

"Makes sense. There's lots of stuff I don't like to talk about in front of Sarah, because she gets all high and mighty."

"Judy," Judy the Elder said, warningly, but Judy the Younger just grinned.

"Still, it seems simple enough," Sarah said. "You appeal to King Albrecht about your rights and collect your rents."

"Would that it were so simple. There are other issues. Among them that some of our lands are in the Holy Roman Empire—what's left of it—and openly giving fealty to King Albrecht would be an act of treason against the empire. Not to mention the fact that both my uncles are in the service of the emperor."

"Would it be taken that seriously?" Judy the Elder asked. "I'm no historian, but I seem to recall that it was...is...pretty standard practice to have part of the family on one side and the other part on the other, to cover all the bets, so to speak."

"Yes, we do, so to speak, cover all the bets and the kings and emperors know it. But we are expected to be as discreet about it as we can. More importantly, we are expected to pay our taxes. By each side."

"How unreasonable!" Judy the Younger said. Then laughed.

"My thoughts exactly," Karl agreed. "Ferdinand is bringing considerable pressure on my family to support the government. And the family, in turn, are asking me to send them the money to do it with. It would be very convenient for me to not have that money available.

"It has always been my intention to invest in the family lands in Bohemia and Silesia. However, my plan was to do it gradually, in a systematic way, once the armies were out of the area. Now I need to rush things a bit and I am in need of advice."

"What sort of advice?" Judy the Elder asked.

"What should I buy? Who should I buy it from? Understand, it's not necessary that everything I buy be shipped immediately. In fact, it would be better in some ways if it were delayed. It will be more likely to get there if it waits till some of the armies have moved out of the area. At the same time, I have no desire to spend a great deal of money and then have the company I'm buying these products from go broke."

"Part of that includes areas where it would be illegal for me to help you," Mrs. Wendell said. "I can tell you what you need to buy but not which company to buy it from. It's simply too easy for a conflict of interest to rear its ugly head if I recommend specific companies. This is a case where public officials have to be like Caesar's wife, because any suspicion that we were endorsing a company for personal gain, or even for the general gain of Grantville, would endanger the whole industrialization project.

"The Grantville Better Business Bureau maintains a list of

companies and their reputation. Beyond that, Sarah and Judy can probably tell you quite a bit about the economic health of most of the companies that are likely providers.

"As to what you will need, to a great extent that depends on the situation in Bohemia and Silesia, and that's getting a bit far afield for my expertise. But, in general, the first issue is transport because good transport makes everything else easier and its lack makes everything else almost impossible. Whether that means Fresno scrapers for improving roads, small steam engines for barges, light rail, even wooden rail to get you through the next few years till you can replace it with steel, depends on your terrain and situation. There are also issues of where the roads should go, which depends on your relations with the neighboring landlords. It's not going to do you that much good to put in a road if the goods are going to be stopped at the border anyway."

"I've been corresponding with King Albrecht and he is supportive of the idea of improvements and so are the Roths," Karl said. "Silesia is a little more complicated. Well . . . difficult. I will have to convince Aunt Beth that I am not building roads to help my uncle invade."

"Is your uncle really likely to invade?"

"Not really, but it was a political marriage and was never a happy one," Karl admitted. He suspected—but didn't say—that the Wendell women would see what had happened back then as church-sanctioned rape. He was starting to look at it that way himself. In any case, it had left Aunt Beth with a distrust of the church and of men. At this point, after her duchy had been overrun by Protestant Danes, Aunt Beth had little faith in any confession and still less faith in men. But that wasn't something he wanted to get into with the Wendell women. Instead he continued. "The goal of both families was to unite the lands in Silesia, or at least most of them, under one rule." Actually, at this point Karl was pretty sure that the whole thing was a put-up job and an attempted land grab on the part of his family. But he wasn't going to say that either. "But my Uncle Gundaker is very dedicated to the Catholic faith, and interpreted the marriage to mean that Aunt Beth's lands were now his."

"What about you?" Sarah asked. "About the church, I mean."

"I was much as my uncle," Karl admitted. "And in a way I still am. But the Ring of Fire is its own holy writ. God—" Karl looked at Judy the Younger and grinned. "—or little green men if you insist, brought a town from the future and didn't choose a Catholic town. Anyway, Aunt Beth was always...ah...iffy... about her Catholicism and the enforcement. Besides, she figures she is the ruling duchess and Uncle Gundaker figures he is the man and therefore the head of the woman."

Sarah and both Judys snorted and made various comments about that.

Karl held up his hands and said, "I surrender, I surrender! Come, ladies, it's not my fault! But Elisabeth Lukretia von Teschen's lawsuits against Uncle Gundaker and the Holy Roman Empire were in the courts since her brother's death, until King Albrecht went ahead and confirmed her and her line as the proper heirs to the duchy. In response, though, the HRE found against her and is now claiming the duchy as part of the Habsburg lands. So Aunt Beth is not at all trusting of anything coming out of Vienna. Absent a railroad, she is in Silesia and any attempt to push her would have to go through King Albrecht's armies. Add in a railroad, and they can take a train right to her doorstep."

It turned into quite an interesting evening. Surveying equipment and surveyors came up, and Judy the Younger confirmed that Sonny Fortney had worked as a railroad surveyor, as well as a bunch of other things since the Ring of Fire. Micro-financing and micro-industry the way Boot's Bank in Magdeburg operated were discussed, where to put it and how to set it up. They talked about the things the up-timers had gotten right and the things they had gotten wrong. Local banking and investment could be better done by buying the equipment to set up micro industries, then reselling them to individuals and groups in his lands, either for a share of the business or on credit.

"Don't try introducing your own money, Karl," Judy the Younger said. "No one will take it."

"Judy!" Sarah complained. "There's no reason to be rude."

"You said it yourself," Judy said.

Karl had felt his face go a little stiff when Judy made that comment. Not because it was a surprise, but because it wasn't. "No, she's quite right," he forced himself to say. "I know that my family's reputation is not good when it comes to the issuing of money."

"It's not that we don't trust you, Prince Karl." Sarah flushed a little. "The fact is that full faith and credit isn't dependent on any one person, but on how most people will see the thing. I believe you about what happened in Kipper and Wipper, but my belief won't make your money good. Besides your territory is too small... well, I think it's too small... to be issuing its own currency."

"When taken altogether, it's actually about the size of Saxony. But it's not all in one place... or, at this point, even all in one country."

"That seems like enough territory," Sarah conceded, "but didn't you tell me something about it not qualifying as noble lands?"

"Imperial immediacy," Karl explained. "The princely title is a court title, so it doesn't involve rulership over any lands. We hold quite a bit of land and often enough we're the local government, collecting both rent and taxes. Both landlords and lords. However, those lands aren't held directly from the emperor. Instead some are in fief from the king of Bohemia, some from the king of Austria, and some from the king of Hungary."

"Isn't Ferdinand II the king of Austria and Hungary?" Sarah asked. "I mean, it's the same guy, right?"

"Actually, he's the king of Austria and the king of Hungary and the Holy Roman Emperor, plus other stuff. Yes, it's the same guy, but he's *legally* different people. And the only one who matters for a seat in the Council of Princes is the Holy Roman Emperor. Whereas all our lands are held in fief from someone who isn't the Holy Roman Emperor."

"Does that mean that Wallenstein is entitled to a seat in the Council of Princes?"

"Well, it would if he swore fealty to Ferdinand II. Of course, the first thing Ferdinand II would do is order him to execute himself for treason. I don't see him doing that anytime soon.

"But it doesn't matter. I would have to apply to both King Albrecht and King Ferdinand II for permission to issue currency. Besides, the point of this evening is to *remove* money from the accounts, not add it."

"In that case, as we said before, buy equipment and sell it on credit rather than simply giving loans," said Judy the Elder.

This would tie up his money quite well and had the added advantage of making corruption rather more difficult. If he just gave out the money, some people were going to take it and run. That had happened to the up-timers more than once as they tried to get the New U.S. industry going. If he gave them the equipment, they would at least have to find a buyer for it before running off with the money. Of course, it wouldn't prevent some thief in Silesia from taking his stuff and running into Poland hoping for a better deal. So shipping equipment rather than sending money was no replacement for due diligence.

Sarah and Judy had opinions about who he should buy from, which businesses were stable enough to provide the goods he would be ordering for delivery over the next year or so.

"Unfortunately," Karl said, "the Oder is the only major river into Silesia. It runs through Brandenburg."

"And that's a problem?" Judy the Younger asked.

Karl blinked. Judy was a very clever girl, but she had some blind spots. Anything farther than Magdeburg might as well be in China. "Brandenburg is ruled by Emperor Gustav's brother-in-law, George William. The one who, along with John George of Saxony, refused to come to Gustav Adolf's aid when he was attacked by France and the League of Ostend."

"We trade with France, for goodness sake," said Judy.

"True enough. But George William has decided that, since he is not part of the USE, he is under no obligation to allow free trade with the provinces of the USE. As usual, he is in need of money. This time to hire an army to hold his brother-in-law at bay. So, his tariffs on goods from the USE are quite high. And that's how things are going to remain, until Gustav gets around to dealing with his recalcitrant relative."

The Bohemian situation was a bit better. Bohemia had a border with the USE, but it was a long slog over bad roads. The main river corridors in Bohemia flowed through Saxony, which John George would no doubt find a major headache when Gustav got around to him. And Prince Karl Eusebius von Liechtenstein, having studied war under his father and uncles and having lived in Grantville, was quite confident that Gustav would sooner or later be free to deal with both of them. Which belief failed to fill Karl with joy. If he honestly thought there was anything he could do to restore the Holy Roman Empire, he'd do it. But he didn't think that. He didn't see a damned thing anyone could do to stop the Swede—or Wallenstein, for that matter. And if some of the things that the

Vatican II conference had said about freedom of conscience and the importance of respecting other faiths were true, then God didn't want the HRE restored. If the Good Lord didn't want conversion by the sword, the HRE had been doing it wrong. But that wasn't all the Holy Roman Empire did. It also protected Europe from being forced away from Christianity itself . . . to Islam.

Anyway . . . Karl pulled his thoughts away from that over-trodden path, back to the matter at hand. For right now it was going to be almost impossible to ship large stocks of goods to Silesia or even Bohemia. Small things were not that much of an issue, but caravans of goods would never get to their destination, or would get there with half their goods gone as tolls.

"Instruction sets," Sarah Wendell said out of the blue. "There are a lot of things that you can build with nothing but instruction sets, even simple steam engines. And even more that you can build using a few components and forms. It will be slower and more expensive, but it will get you started."

"Yes. I've already done some of that," Karl acknowledged. "I'd like to do more but I'm not sure what needs to be done."

"So set up the Bohemia and Silesia Advancement Corporation," Sarah said. "Hire some researchers—all sorts of researchers—and put together a prototyping and testing shop. Then have them come up with cheat sheets specific to your family's lands in Bohemia and Silesia. What sort of natural resources are there?"

"Quite a bit of coal and copper. According to the encyclopedias, and from our experience as well."

"So, coking plants to get you coke, coal tar and all sorts of stuff. You have the foamed rosin process for making copper and bronze parts. Copper wire for electricity, coal for steam to generate the electricity. Which gives you electrolytic refining."

"That's very good, but it will take time to set up."

"Yes. But not necessarily to pay for. If you pay in advance by funding the company and moving the money out of your accounts to the company's, you give the company a sound financial footing and it will be better able to hire people," Sarah said. "And skilled people are harder and harder to find. The pros can mostly write their own ticket."

"Which gives you an excellent reason for not pulling the money out, because to pull the money out so soon would destroy confidence in the company," Judy the Younger said. "You want an up-timer on the board, for confidence," she added in a thoughtful voice. "It can't be Mom or Dad. They work for the government. And it can't be Sarah, because she's going to work for the Fed as soon as she graduates. That just leaves me." Judy smiled brightly.

"Better would be David Bartley or the Partow twins," Sarah said repressively. "Even better than that would be Mr. Marcantonio or one of the up-time teachers at the high school. I doubt you can get Mr. Reardon or anyone like that. Aside from the public relations aspect, having an up-timer, especially one with a somewhat technical background, will be a help in terms of telling what can and can't be done."

"Only if they're balanced by down-timers with technical know how," Judy the Elder said. "One thing we have consistently underestimated is what down-time craftsmen can do."

"And don't think we aren't aware of that." Karl smiled. "Aside from farming and mining, what would you suggest as the best options?"

"Upgrades in the manufacture of things you're already producing should come first. Basically, labor-saving devices for small shops. Stamp presses and steam hammers for blacksmiths. Sewing machines for tailors. One of the most important things that does is free up labor for new types of work while increasing your productivity. Freeze dryers, and canning plants for the preservation of foods, so that you lose less of your farming output to spoilage. Both of which will help you avoid inflation."

"Don't forget consumer goods," Judy the Younger added. "Like grooming kits."

"Grooming kits?" Karl asked. "And why consumer goods?"

"Little pouches or folders that have stuff like fingernail and toenail clippers, nail files, combs, or brushes and maybe a little mirror. Grooming stuff. Why, is because you need to build a consumer base. You need things that are small enough for people to buy, and stuff they will use. Grooming kits in particular, because good grooming is important to how others see you and how you feel about yourself."

"And because the Barbies have an interest in a company that makes grooming kits," Sarah added with a look at her sister. Judy the Younger just grinned like an imp. And Karl laughed out loud.

Over the next week the Liechtenstein Industrialization Corporation was formed. The LIC charter had lots of high-sounding rhetoric in it and was officially a nonprofit, which had some tax advantages. It really was a nonprofit. Karl and the family would get their profits on the other end, in increased pieces of the action from the new companies it would help to form and finance. The slogan *"with a lic and a promise"* was considered for the company but rejected as soon as Karl found out what it meant. It struck just too close to home.

Karl talked to the local Abrabanel representatives about what the LIC was designed to do and how it might be expected to increase revenues in Liechtenstein lands over the next few years by fostering industrial development using up-timer knowledge. He specifically asked that the information be forwarded to the Abrabanel representatives in Vienna.

Then he wrote back to his Uncle Gundaker.

I'm sorry, Uncle, but you're catching me at an inopportune time. I have learned from my stay here that if our properties are not upgraded, the incomes they generate over the next several years will be diminished as they are forced to compete with up-timer influenced lands that produce more for less.

In order to avoid that, I have created the Liechtenstein Industrialization Corporation to introduce up-timer techniques into our lands. While the initial costs of such a program are quite high, in the long run they will much more than pay for themselves. For the moment, however, we are in the expensive part of the proposition and it will be a few years before returns outpace investment.

I have talked to the local Abrabanel representative and he concurs that should the investments I have been making continue, the income derived from our lands should double, at the least, over the next decade or so. However, should I pull the funds already allocated to that endeavor, confidence in that increase would be drastically diminished. Based on that assessment, I am authorizing you to borrow funds up to two hundred thousand Holy Roman guilder at a rate of interest not to exceed six percent annually, secured by the income from our lands in Bohemia and Silesia. I'm sorry it's not all you asked for and that I must limit the interest to six percent to secure the family's ability to repay the loans.

There is considerable coal under our lands, Uncle, enough to support a strong and profitable industrial development. To facilitate that development, one of the most important of the general improvements is a wooden rail railroad from Opole to Vienna. This will connect Vienna to the Oder by rail and hence to the Baltic by a combination of rail and river. It will also provide our lands ready access to markets from the Baltic to the Black Sea, politics allowing.

I don't expect the wooden rails to last long, five to ten years I am told, depending on many factors. However, I consider them an important stopgap measure to facilitate trade until we can develop iron and steel industries and replace the wooden rails with steel. I have written your good wife to ask her authority to facilitate the road in Silesia and hope that you and Uncle Maximilian will use your influence with His Imperial Majesty to facilitate its approval between the border of Silesia and Vienna.

Karl knew that his Uncle Gundaker wasn't going to be thrilled with his letter. Especially the part where he mentioned that he was appealing directly to Aunt Beth. Also, Gundaker wasn't going to be all that thrilled with the limits of two hundred thousand guilder and a maximum interest of six percent. Inflation was rearing its ugly head in the USE, but for the most part it had been put off on other currencies, including HRE guilders which were still circulating in the USE. The silver ones, anyway. People were anxious to get American dollars because they were anxious to have what American dollars could buy—or at least that was how it had started. By now, almost everyone in the USE just trusted American dollars. However, the HRE didn't have that advantage. There were things that you could buy with the HRE guilder more readily than with other currencies, but not nearly as many of them. Besides, HRE guilders based their value on the silver content, and silver had been dropping against the American dollar since the dollar's introduction. The HRE was suffering stagflation, because imports from the USE were expensive, but sought after. Karl was right about his Uncle Gundaker's reaction to his letter. In fact, he underestimated the case by a considerable margin.

CHAPTER 3

Plans and Proposals

June 1634

Fortney Home, Grantville

"Howdy, Prince Karl." Sonny Fortney held out his hand like the prince was just anyone. It was easy because, to Sonny, the prince *was* just anyone. He knew that a lot of down-timers and more than a few up-timers didn't feel that way, but he did. He felt that way before the Ring of Fire, when titles like doctor and professor were bandied about, and he felt it even more now. "I hope you'll excuse the mess. We've sold the house and there's a lot of packing being done right now."

"*Guten Tag,* Herr Fortney." Prince Karl held out his own hand, which was a good sign. "Think nothing of it. I trust you got a good price?" After they shook hands, Prince Karl continued, "I would like to watch you test Prince Ferdinand that way."

"Really? How'd you think he'd do?"

"Fairly well. He'd be surprised, but I think after he got over the shock, he'd be amused rather than offended. However, if my uncles were in the room, they would probably call for the headsman. So while I'd love to watch, I can't really recommend that you do it."

"I'll keep that in mind," Sonny said. He would keep both the opinion of Ferdinand and the opinion of the boy's uncles in mind.

"Well, *Uncle Gundaker* would call the headsman," Karl clarified. "I'm not sure about Uncle Maximilian. Still, most of the court

19

would act more like Uncle Gundaker, so if you do try it, don't do it in public. I would hate to have you beheaded before you managed to survey my railroad for me. Besides, Hayley is a nice girl and doesn't deserve to lose her father."

"Who is important at court, Your Serene Highness?" Sonny Fortney asked more seriously. "Who is likely to be a problem about the railroad?"

"That's hard to say. I have been out of touch. His closest adviser and perhaps his closest friend is the Hungarian nobleman Janos Drugeth. But Drugeth's expertise lies primarily in military and diplomatic affairs. He might not get involved in these issues at all. Reichsgraf Maximilian von Trauttmansdorff is another of Ferdinand II's close counselors. I'm honestly not sure whether he would support the railroad or not. Pal Nadasdy is fairly conservative as well. Peter von Eisenberg isn't on the privy council, but is a bright guy. You might be able to get him on your side, though he is a bit rank conscious. His grandparents weren't noble. Not even as noble as mine."

"I'll keep that in mind, too," Sonny told Karl in a more somber tone. "So, tell me about this railroad?"

"Possible railroad," Karl corrected. "I have written letters suggesting it to my Aunt Beth and to the family back in Vienna. I hope to get their approval, because it would connect the Danube at Vienna to the Oder at Opole. The Oder is mostly navigable up to Opole, with some breaks, so a railroad between the Danube and the Oder would link a route from the Baltic to the Black Sea by two rivers and a railroad. Which, according to Mrs. Wendell, would produce a lot of trade and a lot of wealth."

"Sounds reasonable to me," Sonny agreed. "You understand I am going to be working for Prince Ferdinand, so if you want me to try surveying the route for your railroad, you'd better write him a letter, too."

"I shall. Never doubt it," Prince Karl said. "Meanwhile, I took the liberty of having some maps copied from some of the up-time maps in the national library." He opened up the map and pointed. "Here is what I was thinking would make a good route."

Sonny looked over the route that the prince had in mind and made some suggestions that looked like they might make it easier. Karl agreed to some and disagreed with others for political reasons. Some of the landholders along the route were more likely to be reasonable about a railroad through their lands than others. Some liked his family, some disliked them, after harking back to actions taken by Prince Karl's father, who Sonny already knew had been something of a hard case.

"I'll do what I can, assuming that it doesn't conflict with anything Prince Ferdinand wants. But two things . . . one is I will have to look at the ground itself before any of this can be anything but tentative. Second thing is, this is going to be a lot of work. And I don't work for free."

Prince Karl smiled at Sonny and Sonny felt himself smiling back. "Do you want cash or shares?" the prince asked.

"I'm not sure," Sonny said. "I probably need to ask my fourteen-year-old daughter."

"Why not?" Prince Karl said. "That's who I consult . . . well, the Barbies in general, more than Hayley in particular."

Sonny did ask Hayley, and Hayley asked the Barbies and Mrs. Wendell. The answer that came back was, "It depends on how much stock and how much cash, but the odds are that Sonny could get a better deal for stock."

"Get a lot of stock, Dad," Hayley told him, "or get the prince to pay you in cash. Railroads are great for the territory they go through, but not so much for the companies that build them."

"So why not just insist on cash?" Sonny asked his daughter.

"Because you could end up with a lot of stock," Hayley said. "A *whole* bunch."

Duchess' Palace, Cieszyn

Duchess Elisabeth Lukretia von Teschen laughed as she read the letter from little Karl. Not so little anymore, and always more reasonable than his uncles. He had apparently been impressed, and improved, by the Ring of Fire. "Pawel, bring writing instruments." A railroad was probably a good idea, but she would write to King Albrecht about it first.

Liechtenstein House, Vienna

Gundaker von Liechtenstein didn't laugh. Instead he threw the letter across the room, then picked it up and went to complain to his brother, Maximilian.

Maximilian was in the office section of the house, dealing with Johannes Koell, the family's chief bookkeeper. The fussy little man took a few minutes to make his points, then Gundaker could get Maximilian into a private room to show him the crumpled letter.

"Actually, it's a fairly reasonable position," Maximilian said after looking over the letter. "Both for us and for the lenders. Should the emperor win and the lands be restored to us, the debt is good. Should Wallenstein win, Karl can be sued to make good the loan. It gets the emperor the money he wants from us—at least part of it. And keeps Karl in the good graces of Wallenstein because he isn't giving the money to the emperor, just authorizing us to borrow money on his lands to support the family. It's not his fault what we do with it."

"And the faith, brother? What of the faith?"

"Gundaker, Karl is living in a miracle," Maximilian said.

"Possibly a miracle," Gundaker corrected. "It could well be something less benign."

"Agreed. I don't know what it means and apparently Holy Mother Church hasn't decided yet. Though, considering that the pope has made the up-timer priest a cardinal, it is leaning toward approval. In any case, as to God's will, Karl is, quite possibly, sitting right next to it. We must trust him, for now at least."

In the years after the Ring of Fire, the nobility of the Holy Roman Empire had a great deal to adjust to. First, of course, was the Ring of Fire and the up-timers and their support of Gustav II Adolf. Then there was King Albrecht Wallenstein—who was assassinated in the original timeline. In the new timeline, he avoided assassination and carved a great big chunk out of the Holy Roman Empire to make his own kingdom. Specifically, he took Bohemia, Moravia and Silesia. Before King Albrecht, the Bohemian crown was held by Ferdinand II, who still claimed that crown. This put a whole lot of nobles in a somewhat touchy political position. A position made even touchier by the fact that a number of those nobles were residing in Vienna under the eyes of one claimant, while their lands were under the guns of the other claimant.

Royal Chambers, Prague, Bohemia

"It seems a perfectly reasonable proposal to me," Morris Roth said, looking up from the letter. He handed the letter back to the clerk.

"It seems an excellent way to move massive numbers of Austrian troops and their supplies into Silesia to attack us from the east," said Pappenheim.

King Albrecht, propped up with pillows, wasn't so sure. He knew that the railroads had been used in future wars to move men and materials at incredible speeds, but he also realized that they were a weak point in any transport system. Something about Sherman's Bowties. "What were 'Sherman's Bowties'?" he asked.

Morris Roth looked blank for a minute. "Oh, yes. It was the American Civil War. Sherman, a Union general, would heat rails on a bonfire till they were red hot, then wrap them around a tree like a bow tie." He paused for a moment. "I don't want to get sidetracked into a discussion of up-time fashions, especially since I think the bow tie is perhaps the silliest piece of male attire ever invented."

"Worse than the cod piece?" King Albrecht felt a smile crease his face as he recalled some of the French codpieces he had seen.

"Well, maybe the cod piece has them beat, but then again, maybe not. But, never mind that. Heating and bending the rails around a tree made them useless."

"But these proposed rails are to be wooden?" Pappenheim asked.

"So you use them in the bonfire," Morris said. "They can't run a train on ash any more than on Sherman's Bowties."

"If you realize what's happening in time," Pappenheim said. "I don't doubt that railroads can be disabled, but at the same time I can readily see them making the initial blow in a war decisive."

King Albrecht looked over to Morris, who shrugged. "I am not a military expert, Your Majesty. But, financially, such a rail system would be of great benefit to Bohemia."

"All of Bohemia or just Silesia?"

"There would be some benefit to the rest of the kingdom, but mostly to Silesia," Morris acknowledged. "But if the railroads follow a consistent gauge, then a rail line from Prague to Opole would let us trade with the Danube and the Baltic with much of the expense being borne by Liechtenstein."

"And us paying Liechtenstein fares on every pound," Pappenheim said. "That family is famous for the advantage they take."

King Albrecht considered. He had been both friends and enemies with the Liechtenstein family over the years. And what Pappenheim said was as true of him as it was of them, even more so. He had, after all, gained a kingdom. But perhaps it was time to be friends with them again, or at least with young Karl.

For now. But not for free.

"I think I'll insist that young Karl come to talk over the project personally," King Albrecht said. "And while he is here, he can swear fealty to me. I think we have let the boy sit on the fence long enough."

The Hofburg Palace, Vienna, Austria

Prince Ferdinand was even less sure than King Albrecht. Having a couple of up-timers to take care of his car and consult on matters of up-time techniques was one thing. Having one wandering around the kingdom making maps was something else. But he figured there were enough down-time spies running around that one or two up-time ones wouldn't matter. More importantly, he was unsure how the railroad would pan out in terms of generating wealth. Would it make Austria richer or Wallenstein richer? Both, he was advised, was the most likely answer, but he didn't find that overly helpful.

He managed to keep Karl's letter from coming to the attention of his dying father. He had no desire to explain to his emperor that he was recruiting up-timers. And he really didn't want to discuss with his father how the Sanderlins and Fortneys had been recruited by his agents in the first place, with Karl Liechtenstein grafting his job onto the group. The emperor, his father, didn't need his thoughts troubled and Prince Ferdinand didn't need the argument.

But it took a few weeks for all the mail to make its way across Europe. And in the meantime, Judy the Younger Wendell had moved into the Higgins Hotel and her parents and sister were getting ready to move to Magdeburg.

CHAPTER 4

𝔒𝔭𝔢𝔫 𝔖𝔢𝔞𝔰𝔬𝔫

June 1634

Higgins Hotel, Ring of Fire

Judy the Younger stretched on her bed in her suite at the Higgins Hotel. Mom and Sarah hadn't moved to Magdeburg yet, but Judy wanted to get settled before they left. Getting to stay in Grantville had been a massive struggle, but worth it. She wasn't staying on her own. Her parents wouldn't go for that. But Delia Higgins was considered a good influence. Mostly, Judy admitted with some chagrin, because Delia wasn't buying Judy's *schtick*. Most adults, Judy could get around, one way or the other. Not Delia. "Some people just aren't charmable," Judy muttered resentfully, stood up, and padded across to her desk. Not that she was really all that resentful. She just felt that she was supposed to be.

Judy's desk was oak, built since the Ring of Fire with a combination of up-time equipment and down-time craftsmanship and was a masterpiece. Literally. Judy knew the master. The whole top two floors of the Higgins was like that. Furniture, art, all made in a fusion of seventeenth-century craftsmanship and twentieth-century tools and techniques. Vernon Bruce, Delia's Scottish interior decorator, would have nothing less in the penthouse, even if Delia didn't care. Delia had given him his shot by hiring him to decorate the Grantville Higgins and now he was in high demand. She was his patron. Delia Higgins and David Bartley

25

tended to do that...collect retainers almost against their will. So did Mike Stearns, come to think of it. They couldn't all be natural leaders, could they? Well, Mike Stearns was. With Delia and David, though, it was something else. People saw opportunity in them and down-timers, especially, responded with personal loyalty. That happened to almost any up-timer who didn't screw it up. Not all the time, but a lot.

It had happened to the Barbies, that was for sure. In a way, the American Equipment Company disaster had been a godsend, and not just because it had got them together with the Ken Doll. It had also done really good things for their reputation. Everyone knew that they bought that company after it was already a failure in a big way. The fact that they had gotten most of the investors out with their skin intact had done wonders for their reputation, both for fair dealing and for sharpness. Judy decided that she really did need to do something nice for the Ken Doll for coming to their rescue like that. Which brought Sarah to mind. For some reason Judy couldn't see, Prince Karl was totally bonkers over her sister. The trick would be to get Sarah to notice.

In retrospect, Judy was amazed that Sarah had ever gotten together with David, because she didn't think Sarah would notice even someone as blatant as David was. Karl was a lot more subtle. A lot more careful. So careful that there was no way Sarah would see what was going on. He understood the up-timer rules pretty well, but love and sex were delicate areas any time. So Karl was doing his friendly flirtatious bit as a sort of a shield. But it was a shield that would keep Sarah from realizing he was really interested in her.

Judy picked up the phone. There was no dial tone. Instead, after a slight pause—no more than a couple of seconds—a voice came on the line. "Higgins Hotel switchboard. How may I direct your call?"

"Hi, Elsbeth. It's Judy. Would you set up a call to Prince Karl Eusebius von Liechtenstein for me and call me back when it's through, please?"

"Sure, Judy. Anything I should invest in?" Judy could hear the laughter in Elsbeth's voice. Elsbeth worked the switchboard and was training to be a concierge, but she didn't invest in the stock market. It was a running joke between them with Judy touting the most ridiculous nonexistent stocks she could think of.

"Sure! Casein dildos are expected to rise, due to reports of a splintering problem with their nearest competitor." Elsbeth would never tell a dirty joke, but loved to hear them. Judy could almost see her blushing and could hear the suppressed giggling.

"You are so bad. I'll get your call." Then the phone went dead.

It was only a few moments later that it rang. "What can I do for you, Judy?" Prince Karl sounded a bit distracted.

"How's your phone security, Karl?" Judy asked "Elsbeth won't listen and wouldn't talk even if she did. How is it on your end?"

"I suspect Frederic listens, but he won't talk."

It was an important question. Places like the Higgins and large properties like Karl's Grantville estate, or Prince Vladimir's estate, had live operators while the larger exchanges had electromechanical routers.

"Oh. I don't think that's good enough." Judy checked her schedule. "How about dinner at the penthouse, say, Thursday night?"

"Is it important?"

"Maybe. I'm being a busybody, Karl."

"Hm, I wouldn't want to miss that. But I have a dinner with Stavros Thursday. Something about steam engines for Greek fishing boats. Could we make it Friday?"

On Friday Judy had a date, as usual. This one to a play at the Grantville High Theater. *The Desk Set*, reset for the new timeline in Magdeburg with the Spencer Tracy role recast as an Up-timer Girl and the Katharine Hepburn role as Down-timer Guy. It was the opening and Judy's sources said it was a hoot. "Sorry. Booked up Friday and Saturday. What about Monday dinner?"

"That should work."

Higgins Hotel, Ring of Fire

The elevator operator took Karl up to the penthouse of the Higgins, where he was met by a maid who took his cloak and showed him to the small dining room. Delia was there, overseeing the staff as they put out the first course.

"Welcome, Prince Karl. David's in his office and Judy is on the phone, but they should be in anytime now."

"Just Karl, please, Frau Higgins," Karl said. "In Grantville 'prince' doesn't seem appropriate somehow."

"Then call me Delia, Karl," Delia said as her grandson David Bartley came in.

"Good evening, Karl," David said in Amideutch. "What's Judy the Barracudy up to now?"

"I don't have any idea, but it will probably be profitable."

"Just networking," Judy said, coming in behind David. "Nothing sinister."

David snorted in disbelief and Judy stuck out her tongue.

They took their seats and talk turned to business. The Higgins Hotel was doing well and getting a reputation as the swankiest hotel in the Ring of Fire area, though the new hotel that was to be built on the bluffs overlooking the south side of the Ring would probably beat them out for view. A new Higgins was under construction in Magdeburg and Karl spent some time lobbying to get one in Silesia. In return, Delia lobbied him to write King Fernando in the Netherlands about putting one in Amsterdam. They talked about the American Equipment Corporation debacle, and Judy the Younger brought up Sarah's objection to the whole deal, with Judy bashing Sarah, and Karl jumping to her defense. David spent his time being evenhanded, and Delia watched over the whole thing.

"I'm afraid that Judy is right about Sarah being better off in the public sector." David buttered a roll, as he explained. "It's not that she lacks the skills of business. At least no more than most of us up-timers. But she doesn't like it and, frankly, she finds it difficult to understand those who do."

"That may well be true, David, but that simply speaks well of her honesty and fairness." Karl took a sip of the hot cocoa.

Judy waited a moment to see what David would say, but when he didn't speak, she did. "Sarah isn't some plaster saint, Karl. She gets all self-righteous about it and forgets that all us greedy capitalist types are necessary. Also that we aren't bad people, we're just trying to get things done." Well, Karl did need to know what he was getting into.

"And the money's nice, too." Karl laughed.

"Don't go all noble on us, Judy!" David said. "We wouldn't know how to deal with a noble Judy the Barracudy."

Delia joined in the laughter. It was clear to Judy that Delia was aware of the various levels of the conversation. What was less clear was what she thought about it, though Judy had a sneaking suspicion that Delia was laughing at the children. Sarah and David's breakup had been about as amicable as such things ever are, but then David and Sarah weren't very open about what they were feeling. Judy was quite sure that both were hurting over the breakup. In their pride, if nothing else. She was also quite sure that they would both work hard to do the right thing as they saw it. So David and Karl were dancing around the issue of Sarah by talking about her financial skills and lack of business orientation. Delia would be aware of all that, and while she was fond of Sarah, David was her grandson.

"But won't it make your relationship more difficult to maintain with Sarah in Magdeburg?" Karl asked.

"We broke up, Karl. It was pretty friendly as breakups go, but there it is."

"Oh." Karl was clearly at a loss as to what to say to that.

Judy could almost hear him thinking. *Yes, Karl,* she thought. *"Yippee" is the wrong thing to say.*

The next day Judy got a call from Karl. "So what was last night about?" Karl asked as soon as she came on the line.

"Sarah is on the market, Ken Doll. Last night was giving you the heads up."

"What made you think I'd be interested?"

"Please, Karl. I'm not blind."

"Sarah . . . ?"

"She *is* blind, Karl. Even bringing her roses won't do it. You're going to have to tell her you're courting her or she won't realize it. Mom, by the way, isn't blind. She's known for months."

They talked for a while about the best techniques and what Sarah liked.

Wendell House, Grantville

"What's this?" Sarah Wendell took the card from Agnes, the maid. The card was white and embossed with the Liechtenstein coat of arms, printed in three colors on top quality white card stock. Aside from the coat of arms, it had Karl's full name and phone number. Along with an extension scrawled on the back. The phone number was for Liechtenstein House, a rather palatial residence located less than a mile from the Ring of Fire and equipped with all the up-time conveniences. The extension would have the caller put through to the prince's private office, or wherever he happened to be in Liechtenstein House, with the minimum delay. However, Sarah already had both the number and the extension. So she didn't see the point in Karl sending her his card.

Agnes rolled her eyes, but Sarah didn't notice. She shrugged and picked up the phone.

Liechtenstein House, outside the Ring of Fire

"I assume this is about the LIC," Sarah said as she entered Liechtenstein house, speaking to Karl even as she gave her coat to one of his footmen. "So, why all the intrigue? Are your uncles after more money?"

"Always," Karl said. "However, this is not about the LIC or the family lands. It's an entirely different matter."

"What has Judy done now?" Sarah asked. "Has she gotten you into that commodities trading company? You should have learned from the American Equipment Corporation."

Karl realized that Sarah was nervous. She didn't normally jump to conclusions so quickly. What he couldn't tell was why she was nervous. Was she afraid that he was going to tell her that he wanted to court her or afraid that he wasn't? Karl found it surprisingly hard to bring himself to broach the subject. He ushered her into the small dining room and seated her himself.

Finally, she asked, "All right, Prince Karl. Just what is this all about?"

"I would like to court you, Sarah. Date you. Whatever the up-time phrasing."

Sarah didn't say anything, just looked at him like a deer caught in a bright light. Karl waited as long as he could, which wasn't very long at all, then backpedaled a little. "I'm not asking you to marry me right now. I just want you to shift me from acquaintance to suitor in your mind. Get used to the idea. Get comfortable with it."

"But I'm moving to Magdeburg in two days."

"Magdeburg isn't that far. There are letters and telegrams, the trains and even airplanes."

"Not many, and they aren't safe."

"Not yet. But people are building them now. They will be."

"I don't know, Karl. Maybe you should wait a few years before you decide to become a jet setter."

Karl looked blank, and Sarah said, "Never mind." Then she looked at him. "Okay, Karl. I'll move you to possible suitor." Her lips quirked a little... "But suitors are supposed to sweep girls off their feet. Do you think you're up to it?"

Karl took her hand gently and lifted it to his lips, touched it with a butterfly kiss.

"I'll work on it," he said.

CHAPTER 5

𝔚𝔞𝔤𝔬𝔫𝔰 𝔥𝔬!

Late July 1634

On the Street outside the Fortney Property

"Do you have everything?" Judy Wendell heard at the Sanderlin lot where everyone was gathering to leave. The Sanderlins had a lot with two mobile homes on it, a single-wide for Ron, Gayleen and the kids, and a small trailer for Uncle Bob Sanderlin. One of the reasons they had taken the job was that it was getting harder and harder for them to make the rent on the lot. Besides, with one toddler and an infant, life was really hard on Gayleen, with the gradual loss of up-time labor-savers. Repairing things like washing machines and buying baby clothes... well, Judy could understand how it could get hard.

That wasn't why Hayley's dad had taken the job, though, and Judy couldn't figure out why he would. Sonny Fortney made pretty good money, even if he did bounce from job to job like a ping-pong ball. Hayley wouldn't talk about it, except to say that her dad had his reasons. Judy didn't think she approved of this move, but there wasn't anything she could do about it. Except to make sure that Hayley had someplace to call if she got in trouble and enough money to make sure she could afford to run. In support of that, Judy and the rest of the Barbies had put together a packet of mad money for Hayley, twenty thousand American dollars in cash, hidden in a false bottom of Hayley's steamer trunk. Steamer trunks came back into fashion again, after the Ring of Fire. The Barbies owned one of the companies that made them.

"I think so," Sonny Fortney was saying to the Ken Doll. "We have the maps and the extra surveying gear in the trailer. Plus a load of trade goods so that we will have the glass beads to buy Manhattan."

"Ahh," sighed Prince Karl. "I have exposed my poor countrymen to the shifty up-timers. Good Lord, forgive me for my sins."

"Why, Prince Karl," Judy interrupted. Then she batted her eyes twice, tilted her head, and said, "You think we have taken advantage of you?"

"I'm going to go get Sarah to protect me."

"Good idea," said Judy the Elder Wendell. "Judy, behave yourself. You have our address, Gayleen. If you need anything, write us and we'll send it off by mule train."

"Thank you, though the idea of getting stuff by mule train still freaks me out a bit," Gayleen said.

"Me too," Dana Fortney said. "Especially diapers. Praise be for the tubal!"

"I don't know about that. It's a lot of trouble but the truth is I like having babies," Gayleen said. "On the other hand, I'm getting close to forty, so maybe just one more."

Which, Judy the Younger thought, bordered on clinical insanity. Judy looked around. It was quite a procession. There was the pickup truck owned by Bob Sanderlin, pulling a trailer that had the 240Z on it. It was followed by the Fortney's 1994 Subaru Outback, also pulling a trailer, this time with their household goods. They would travel south toward Bamberg, then on past it to the Danube, where they would load the cars on barges for the trip down the river to Vienna. There were also several wagons, filled with both personal possessions, items Prince Karl was sending to his family, and almost anything else the travelers could think of. As well, their escort had a couple of wagons.

Istvan said, "We're burning daylight, people."

Everyone turned to look at him.

"Well," he defended himself, "it's a good line. Very descriptive of the situation."

"Maybe," Judy muttered, "but you don't look a thing like John Wayne." By virtue of the fact that only a limited number of movies had been brought back in the Ring of Fire, all of them had been seen on TV—most of them several times.

People started loading into the cars and wagons, and climbing onto horseback. It took another half hour before they actually got on the road...and between the horses and the wagons, they were moving at less than four miles an hour.

Wendell Household, Magdeburg

> *Dear Sarah,*
> *It was nice to see you when you came to see the Fortneys off last week. I thought you looked lovely in the blue paisley you were wearing. It brings out the color of your eyes, which looked as blue as the sky that day. But then, they always remind me of the sky.*

Sarah read the letter with a great degree of disbelief. She was, since her last growth spurt, almost as tall as her mother. But if Judy the Elder was statuesque, and Judy the Younger looked like a ballerina, Sarah was just a gawky scarecrow. Still, it sure would be nice if she actually looked like Karl seemed to see her. David had certainly never said anything like this.

> *I have an appointment with Adolph Schmidt in Magdeburg and am hoping that we might get together. I am trying to get him to sell me some steam engines for the LIC, but don't have a great deal of hope. Do you have any influence with Heidi Partow? In any case, it makes an excellent excuse to go to Magdeburg to see you. One that even Josef can't object to.*
> *I'll be taking the train up on Tuesday and meeting with Herr Schmidt on Wednesday. So, could we meet Tuesday evening? Or Wednesday, or wonder of wonders, both?*

Sarah found herself wondering if Prince Karl was interested in her or just her connections. And that was weird. Prince Karl was a prince of the Holy Roman Empire. About as noble as it got in Europe. At least, that's how it seemed to Sarah. He already *had* connections. It was weird, but it was, by now in Sarah's world, a fairly commonplace weirdness. In her job, she regularly dealt with *Graf* this and Prince that. In spite of which, she wasn't at all sure that she would ever get used to it.

> *That would make the trip wholly worthwhile, whether*
> *Herr Schmidt sees me or not.*

Sarah considered. She still wasn't sure but the only way to find out was to see him. On the other hand, she had no intention of pressuring Adolph Schmidt to sell the LIC any engines.

Wendell Household, Magdeburg

On Tuesday, Karl's riverboat was delayed so he didn't reach Magdeburg until late. Rather than make Sarah wait for him, he presented himself at the Wendell house, which was a nice town-house in the richer part of Altstadt. Magdeburg was no longer the burned out wreck that it had been after the sack. It was a boom town and a town of heavy industry.

He was met by a maid and shown into a sitting room, where Fletcher Wendell was waiting for him. "Have a seat, Karl. Sarah will be down in a few minutes. We heard that the boat was late again, and assumed that you would be delayed."

"I came directly from the docks, Mr. Secretary," Karl said, taking the seat Fletcher indicated.

There was an awkward pause. Then Herr Wendell said, "I understand you are courting my daughter. Do you really think that's a good idea?"

"Honestly? No, probably not. Certainly, my uncles would be unlikely to approve. A point that Josef has made several times. However, the world has changed due to the Ring of Fire. There is a song by Cole Porter . . . 'wrong's right today, black's white today, up's down today . . .'"

"'Anything goes.' But so far as my daughter is concerned, be aware, Prince Liechtenstein, that anything most definitely does *not* go."

"That's not what I meant, sir."

It was, of course, just then that Sarah walked in. "Dad, I'm eighteen."

Karl stood up and turned to Sarah.

"Eighteen or eighty, you're still my daughter," said Fletcher Wendell. "Know this, Karl, prince or not, if you hurt her, you're going to regret it."

Karl turned back to Fletcher. "That wasn't what I meant, Herr Wendell," he said a little stiffly. "It wasn't the 'anything goes' part. It was the 'wrong's right' part that stuck with me. Religious toleration, for instance. Very much wrong according to the Edict of Restitution and the Counter Reformation. But very much right according to the Constitution of the up-time U.S., the New U.S., the State of Thuringia-Franconia, and even the USE. We are having to unlearn a lot, all of us down-timers. My grandfather was a Lutheran, did you know that? My father and uncles converted to the Catholic faith. My father told me that his conversion was political, his ticket into the upper nobility. But Uncle Gundaker wrote an article about his reasons for converting to Catholicism and those reasons weren't political."

"So your father was Lutheran in his heart?" Sarah asked.

"No. He was a doubter," Karl told her. "He believed in something that had created the universe, but he said to me 'I don't believe any of them, priest, pastor or rabbi when they claim to speak for him.' And I suspect that Uncle Maximilian is more like my father was than like Uncle Gundaker. But Uncle Gundaker has the zeal of a convert."

"You think that your uncle will object?"

"Yes. In fact, I am virtually certain of it. Which wouldn't matter at all, except that the treaty of 1606 requires that the head of House Liechtenstein be Catholic, and Uncle Gundaker might be able to make something of that. Yet now we have the Ring of Fire. The pope has named Father Mazzare a cardinal. A Protestant saved the pope from an assassination attempt. And the world of faith is turning backwards somersaults in attempts to make it fit into our various doctrines. I don't know how it's all going to work out. I don't think anyone does. But I will follow my heart, and my heart leads to Sarah."

"Why do I suddenly feel like Spencer Tracy in *Guess Who's Coming to Dinner*?" Fletcher complained.

"I don't know," said Judy the Elder, who had walked in during Karl's speech, "because you're acting more like Sidney Poitier's father. Or at least the situation is a lot more along the lines of Sarah being in the Sidney Poitier role." She turned to look at Sarah. "Not that your dad is totally off the mark, dear. If you and Karl should marry, there are going to be a whole lot of people who are deeply offended, no matter how successful and competent you are. Either because you're not Catholic or because you're not a noble."

"First of all, you're all way ahead of yourselves. We're barely dating yet. Second..." Sarah planted her feet and crossed her arms. "...screw them if they don't like it. I am not prepared to kiss any royal backsides. No one is better than me because of who their parents were."

Karl smiled and walked over to Sarah. "I quite agree," he said, "Especially to the part about no one being better than you.

"You know the town better than I do these days, Sarah. So where are we going tonight?"

Schmidt Steamworks, Magdeburg

The next day's meeting with Adolph Schmidt didn't go well. Schmidt was apologetic, but firm. He simply didn't have any more capacity to pull out of his factory, not for any price, and all his present capacity was committed.

"What about adding capacity?" Prince Karl asked.

"New machines from Grantville? I've already ordered them. I'm on Dave Marcantonio's waiting list, and even the fact that he owns something like five percent of Schmidt Steam isn't moving us up on the list."

"I'm starting to think that between them, Dave Marcantonio and Ollie Reardon own five percent of the whole world," Prince Karl complained.

"No. Only the USE." Adolph Schmidt laughed.

Prince Karl joined in the laughter, then said, "Well, at least it gives me an excuse to come back to Magdeburg to try to persuade you."

"Why would you want to come back to Magdeburg?"

There was a very unladylike snort from the other end if the room. Both men looked over and Heidi Partow said, "He's got a thing for Sarah Wendell."

Adolph Schmidt glanced back at Prince Karl, who was turning a not overly becoming shade of red and said, "I sympathize, Your Serene Highness." Then, looking right at Heidi, added, "Up-timer girls can drive you crazy."

Fleischer's Steak House, Magdeburg

"Well, Sarah, you have a prince on your string for sure," Heidi Partow told Sarah a few days later. "He's actually in a hurry to come back to smoky, dirty, Magdeburg just to see you."

"I don't know, Heidi." Sarah jabbed a cherry tomato from her salad. She had been surprised when the Partow's older sister had arranged to have lunch with her. Now the reason was coming clear. "I think he may be trying to get a connection into the Grantville power structure."

"Naw. If that were it, he'd be going after one of the Catholic girls in town. Well, maybe a little bit. Your dad's pretty high in the Stearns administration. So, I guess rank could trump religion, but he was blushing enough when I teased him about it. I figure that means that it's mostly you, not your position." Heidi blinked. "Hey, that might make you the top of the list. We have girls marrying grafs and dukes and stuff. But you might just be first to have an actual prince on your string."

"Brandy Bates is engaged to Prince Vladimir of Russia," Sarah said. "And I don't have Karl on my string. We've had a couple of dates, that's all."

Heidi sniffed. "Is Vladimir a prince, or just a grand duke? Besides he's from Russia." Heidi sliced off a bit of chicken as though it was all of eastern Europe in one tiny bite. She popped it into her mouth, chewed a couple of times, and it was gone, and all the Russian princes in the world gone with it. "And don't kid yourself, Sarah. You have him hooked and you can reel him in . . . if you don't blow it."

"Can we talk about something else? Anything else?"

"Okay . . . we'll talk about my love life. Which is abysmal. . . . At least you dumped David. Stay away from the dedicated ones. You can never get their noses out of the machines long enough to notice you."

Over the next hour, Sarah learned that Adolph Schmidt was a jerk, but Heidi was determined to catch him anyway. Also about the social relations of the upper middle class to lower upper class of Magdeburg which concentrated on the up-timer connected. And, surprisingly, she had a fairly good time.

By the next week, everyone in Magdeburg knew that Sarah Wendell and Prince Karl Eusebius von Liechtenstein were "an item."

New Jewish Quarter, outside Vienna

"What is a Sarah Wendell?" Gundaker von Liechtenstein asked.

Moses Abrabanel ignored the phrasing and thought for a moment. They were in the Abrabanel offices outside of Vienna proper. They were here rather than at the palace because Moses was under a political cloud. He had gone to Grantville in late 1631 and had failed to be nearly as adamantly opposed to the up-timers as he should have after they had upset the political and military apple carts of the Holy Roman Empire. Besides, he was Jewish and Ferdinand II might find Jews useful and even necessary, but he didn't like them. "You know, I think I met her. She is the eldest daughter of Fletcher and Judy Wendell."

Moses got up and went to a file cabinet. He had seen several in Grantville, and had some made as soon as he got back to Vienna. One whole file cabinet was dedicated to all things Grantville. He selected the third drawer from the left, which included up-timers with last names from U-Z He opened it and found the Wendells. "Yes, here she is. Sarah Wendell...Oh yes. The sewing machines. She was one of the children with the sewing machine factory."

Moses returned to his desk, examining the file. "Are you interested in sewing machines?" He flipped over a page "Oh. Someone should have pointed this out to me." He looked up from the file. "I'm sorry, Prince von Liechtenstein. Someone sent a note about what is going on and it got put in the files, but not brought to my attention."

Moses looked around the offices trying to find a polite way of phrasing information in the file. "I assume that your interest is due to the fact that Prince Karl and Sarah Wendell are seeing each other socially?"

"You have confirmation of the rumors then?" Gundaker asked. "Is Sarah Wendell anyone important? It wouldn't be too bad if he had a fling with an unimportant up-timer, though it still shows a disappointing lack of self control."

Moses looked around the office again. It was no more help than it had been before. "I don't think that's the case here. Her father was on the finance subcommittee of the Emergency Committee, the people who wrote the New U.S. Constitution. Just a moment." Moses went back to his desk and got another file. "Yes,

I thought so. Fletcher Wendell, Sarah's father, is the Secretary of the Treasury for the USE. Essentially the same post that you hold in the Empire."

"I thought that was someone called Coleman Walker?"

"No, he is the head of their Federal Reserve Bank." Moses shrugged. "There is no good analogy to the Federal Reserve Bank in the Empire." It wasn't the partly government, partly private nature of the Fed that would be hard to explain to Gundaker von Liechtenstein. It was things like the limits on the infinite checkbook. Those things were hard enough for Moses to follow and he had been to Grantville and met the people. Anyway, that was all beside the point so far as Gundaker von Liechtenstein was concerned. "You know that they do not draw the lines of nobility the same way we do. This is not as concrete as I would prefer, but I would have to place the whole family in the upper echelons of the up-timers. In the same category as Mike Stearns, Ed Piazza or Julie Sims."

"Well, Karl can't be thinking about marrying the girl. Is she one of those up-timer pseudo-Catholics like that Father Mazzare?"

Moses blinked. Cardinal Larry Mazzare had been approved by the pope, but it was hardly a Jew's place to be telling that to a staunch Counter-Reformationist like Gundaker von Liechtenstein. Besides which, Gundaker was a very smart man whose intelligence was only outdistanced by his stubbornness. Instead, Moses looked down at his folder. "No. They are Baptist."

"What's that?"

"Apparently it evolved from the Anabaptist, or is related to the Anabaptist. Honestly, Prince Gundaker, I am no expert on the Christian faith."

"The Anabaptists aren't Christians. They are heretics!" Gundaker looked at Moses and then, after a moment, waved it off. Moses knew Gundaker's views, and knew that Gundaker dealt with him as a sort of necessary evil, but was firmly convinced that absent conversion to the true faith of the Catholic church, Moses was going to hell. He also knew that in Gundaker's world view, Moses, by virtue of being a Jew, *deserved* to go to hell. Gundaker tolerated Jews because of their usefulness, not out of any love for them or respect for their views. But the prince was still speaking. "I will have to write my nephew and warn him away from the up-timer."

On the road to Regensburg

"I don't friggin' believe this," Ron Sanderlin said. "This is not a road. It's not even a path. This is a friggin' game trail. Deer would find this a hard route."

The problem was a section of what, in a fit of aggrandizement, was locally called a "road." It was about four feet wide and consisted of mud impregnated with rocks. And from the size of the rocks, it looked like it was ready to give birth. That wasn't the worst part, though. The worst part were the two trees that were growing closer together than two trees that size ought to be capable of.

"Did you happen to bring a chainsaw?" Sonny Fortney asked.

"No. You know how much they're worth now and most of them haven't been converted to use alternate fuels. So I sold it."

"Yep. Me too," Sonny agreed. "I guess it's time for axes."

"What about the stumps?"

"We'll have to burn the stumps after we take down the trees. But, unless we want to burn the whole grove, we need to take the trees down first."

"Who owns the trees?" Hayley Fortney asked.

Sonny hooked his thumb at the village they had passed through about five minutes back. "Probably them."

Even when the road was "good," they made only about three miles an hour, because of the wagons. And now that they were in the Upper Palatinate, the roads were rarely all that good for all that long. It was a case of "go a little, stop, fix the road, and then go a little more." For the last eleven miles, they had been doing fairly well and they had passed a village without stopping about two miles back.

Istvan was sitting his horse. "I'll ride back and ask them." He turned to one of the mercenaries that were acting as guards. "Conrad, you ride ahead and check at the next village on the road. One of them at least ought to know. Meanwhile, we rest the horses and have an early lunch."

The two trees, in fact the whole grove, were part of the village that they had passed. The villagers had the right to gather firewood from the grove, but not the right to chop down whole trees. On the other hand, the villagers were supposed to keep the road in good repair. And that would justify cutting down at least one of the trees, possibly both. The village council was not in any great hurry to settle things—because their party were up-timers and, to the locals, something between a circus and a zoo. In spite of the fact that they were getting into harvest time, the village was happy to have them stay as long as it took to make the best profit—er, deal—possible.

By the middle of the afternoon, as Herr Bauer was—for the fourth time—discussing the great, *very great*, risk that letting the wagon train cut down the trees would be, Sonny could see that Istvan was just about ready to pull his sword and demonstrate the risk they ran by more delays.

"What about Captain Jack?" Brandon Fortney, Hayley's little brother, piped up.

"What about him?" Sonny asked.

"They have chickens!" Brandon insisted. "But they're down-time chickens. Captain Jack can improve their stock. That ought to be worth cutting down a couple trees."

Herr Bauer looked doubtful when approached about the possible solution, then Brandon showed him Captain Jack in the wire mesh cage.

Hayley could see the light of avarice enter the farmer's eyes. And he immediately started trying to negotiate for the permanent sale of the rooster in exchange for the permission to cut down the trees.

"Forget it, Brandon. They aren't going to be reasonable," Hayley said in German. "We'll have to send a rider to Amsberg and file an official complaint against the village for failure to maintain the road. That's breach of their rental agreement, and I would imagine that the leaseholder is looking for an excuse to get rid of some of his farmers to replace them with fewer farmers and better plows."

"Now, now," Herr Bauer said. "There is no reason to take that attitude. I'm sure we can work something out."

They got to cut down the trees and Captain Jack got to party hearty with the local hens for the two days it took. Then the wagon train made fairly good time . . . till the next impediment.

CHAPTER 6

Your Presence Is Required

August 1634

Liechtenstein House, outside the Ring of Fire

"You have another letter, Prince Karl," Josef Gandelmo told him when Karl got back from his latest trip to Magdeburg.

"Is it from Gundaker again?" There had been several letters from Gundaker, each ordering Karl to stop seeing Sarah Wendell and reminding him of his obligations under the 1606 treaty between his father and uncles.

"No, it's from King Albrecht."

Karl paused at Josef's tone. "Seriously?"

"He wishes to see you and will not approve the railroad until he does."

"Oh." Karl had known this was coming, but had hoped it would wait a while. "I knew him, you know, when I was a boy. He and my father were friends then."

"Kipper and Wipper?" Joseph asked.

"Yes. The emperor needed money for the war. My father and the others tried to create it by mixing more copper into the silver coins. It didn't work, and a lot of people got stuck. After that, Wallenstein and my father had a falling out. I honestly don't think they disagreed about Kipper and Wipper, but about Wallenstein's ambition. The breach was more between Uncle Gundaker and Wallenstein, because an adherent of Wallenstein's pushed Uncle

43

Gundaker out of an important post in the Empire. But it brought in the whole family, and Father was one of the ones pushing for the execution of Wallenstein for treason a few years back."

"Well, you have to admit, Your Serene Highness, your father called that one pretty accurately."

"Maybe. Even probably. But there was more than a little self-fulfilling prophecy in it. Would Wallenstein have gone for the crown if Ferdinand II hadn't tried to have him killed?"

"We'll never know, Your Serene Highness. And it's rather beside the point. The question is, what are you going to do?"

"There isn't any choice. I am going to go see King Albrecht of Bohemia and bend my knee to him. Then try to convince him that a railroad will benefit him and not be a knifepoint at his kidneys, held by the Holy Roman Emperor. But can we put it off?" Karl asked.

"Yes, Your Serene Highness, but not forever. And it's a safe bet that approval for the railroad will not be forthcoming until you visit Prague."

"That's not all that urgent, Josef. I don't think Sanderlin-Fortney party has even reached the Danube yet."

Regensburg

Hayley Fortney looked at the Danube much as the Israelites must have looked at the River Jordan. Well, she guessed. She really wasn't all that up on what the River Jordan represented in Judaism. Or Christianity, for that matter. She didn't really pay that much attention, except for a couple of weeks right after the Ring of Fire. But the trip from Grantville to the town of Regensburg on the Danube had been long, hard, irritating and maddening. Floating on a river had to be better than that.

But there it was. At last. The Danube, and just across it, Regensburg. They could pick up some barges here.

"What do you think, Dad? Will you be able to set up a steam engine on one of the barges?"

"I don't know, hon. Let's see what they have. It's going to be hard enough to carry the cars."

"Maybe not, Dad. They ship a lot, but I am not sure how big the barges on the river are."

As it happened, that wasn't the trouble. The Ulm boxes—flat-bottomed boats capable of carrying large loads—were plying the river. Sonny Fortney had a steam engine. It was a small one that he had mostly built up-time. After the Ring of Fire, he had finished it and then not known what to do with it but couldn't being himself to sell it. So they had packed it and his boilers along. After a bit of negotiation, they worked out how to hook his engine up to a propeller and use that barge to pull the others. They wouldn't go fast, but they would go fast enough to have control. Not that the bargemen needed their help.

It took a week and more to get everything loaded on the Ulm boxes. Then they stopped and waited.

"We will be staying here for a while," Istvan Janoszi said quietly to Ron Sanderlin, as they sat in the inn yard looking out at the Danube.

"What for?"

"For word of the emperor. He is in failing health and the prince doesn't want his father taxed in these, his last days."

Sonny Fortney held his peace.

Liechtenstein House, outside the Ring of Fire

"I'll need to go to Magdeburg," Karl said, reading through the latest letter from King Albrecht von Wallenstein. It was still polite, but he was definitely pushing.

Josef winced. He knew that the reason Karl wanted to go to Magdeburg was to talk to Sarah Wendell. And he had received letters from Gundaker, and even one from Maximilian, all insisting that he keep Karl away from the up-time gold-digger. Not that they had used that expression. "A telegram perhaps?" he offered.

"No. This is not the sort of news that a telegram will handle. There will be questions and Sarah will, I do not doubt, have insights." Then he grinned at Josef. "It won't be so bad. I won't be gone long."

"Yes, Your Serene Highness," Josef said dutifully. And truthfully he wasn't concerned about the difficulties of the trip. Travel between here and Magdeburg was getting easier and cheaper all the time. What concerned Josef was the why, not the what.

Josef had nothing against Sarah Wendell. He liked her and her parents, even her younger sister. But up-timer or not, she wasn't Catholic and she wasn't of the upper nobility. Josef didn't think she would accept the role of concubine, no matter how well loved, and she was utterly unsuitable as wife.

He was tempted to say so again, but he had already had that conversation with the prince and it wasn't an experience he wanted to repeat. Instead he simply nodded and went off to get ready for the trip. There would be briefings and discussions of ongoing projects for both the prince's business interests here in the USE and the family's properties in Bohemia, Moravia, Silesia, Austria, and Hungary.

Magdeburg

This time Karl checked into his hotel and sent a note to Sarah asking when she could see him. Then he cooled his heels for a while and occupied himself with paper work.

It was the next day at noon when he met Sarah at the American Cafe. "So what's so important?" Sarah asked, before they had even ordered.

"Let's put in our orders first," Karl said. It wasn't like they were going to wait long for service. He was Prince Karl Eusebius von Liechtenstein and she was the daughter of the Secretary of the Treasury. Their waitress was there before they sat down. And they knew the menu.

"Burger and fries," Karl said. "What about Sprite?"

The waitress gave him a sad look and shook her head.

"Doctor Pepper then."

"I'll have the same, but make mine a wine cooler," Sarah said.

The waitress went off to inform the chef, a German who had spent two years in Grantville learning to make hamburgers and other "fast" foods.

"Well, we've ordered. What's so important?"

"The latest note from King Albrecht. I'm not going to be able to put it off much longer."

"This is so unfair," Sarah said. "Everyone gets to go off and have adventures in the world and I am stuck in an office, calculating the mean income distribution for the USE. And developing a standard market basket when the stuff that goes into it is changing faster than it did up-time."

Karl looked at her in surprise that turned rapidly into shock. Sarah meant it. She was really angry and he didn't have a clue why. Not knowing what to say, he opened his mouth and blurted the first thing that came to mind. "Come with me, then."

It was the right thing to say. Or, at the very least, it wasn't a totally wrong thing to say. Sarah had stopped her litany of complaint and her mouth was hanging open. Then it snapped shut. "I can't!"

Never one to lose an advantage, Karl shot back, "Why not? It's not like you actually need the job at the Fed." Then, seeing her expression, he backpedaled fast. "I'm sure we can come up with a good reason for you to go. Certainly good enough so they won't fire you for it. You can go to study economic trends in Bohemia. They have a market basket, too, and they probably have even less of a clue what goes in it than you do here."

Sarah's expression had gone thoughtful and Karl heaved a very well-hidden sigh of relief. A mine field had been crossed, and he hadn't even known it was there.

"I'll think about it," she said as their order arrived. "In the meantime, why does King Al want you to sign on the dotted line now?" Sarah asked, then dipped a cottage fry into something that claimed to be ketchup, but wasn't. They had discussed the very polite and vague letters that Karl and the king of Bohemia had exchanged before.

Karl's relations with King Al, as Judy the Younger had christened him, had been by mail. Before Wallenstein had become King Albrecht, Karl had made a whirlwind trip to take the oaths of his people. That gave Karl quite a lot of legitimacy and made it difficult for King Al to go all Capone on him unless Karl did something serious.

In spite of the fact that several people thought he had bent the knee, Karl hadn't quite done so. He paid his taxes on time, while his uncles were paying the same taxes to Ferdinand II. "I don't know. It may be that the railroad makes him nervous."

"Why?"

"Your American Civil War probably," Karl told her. "They were used quite extensively to move troops and supplies."

Sarah nodded. She wasn't, Karl knew, all that conversant in military history.

"Well, the railroad will help your lands a lot," Sarah said. "How bad is it going to be?"

"I don't know." Karl shook his head. "I know that the up-timers, and the USE in general, don't have any great affection for the Holy Roman Empire, but it's Christianity's shield against Islam and has been for centuries. It's my country. My father and my uncles fought and bled for it and I expected to do the same when my time came. Now it's disappearing before my eyes. There is no way that Prince Ferdinand will get the votes to become emperor, and less chance that someone else would get those votes."

"I know," Sarah said. "I wonder how I would feel if I had to watch the up-time United States slowly disintegrating before my eyes."

Karl looked at her, and felt himself starting to smile. As he'd said, Sarah Wendell wasn't overly fond of the HRE. Nor did she have a lot of reason to be. But it was very...encouraging...the way she was trying to see things from his point of view. Even if the situations weren't quite parallel.

His smile died as he thought about the reality of the situation. The HRE had indeed been the shield of Christianity for over eight hundred years. Protecting Christian ideals from Islam while Europe grew strong and wealthy...was that enough to justify the Edict of Restitution? Well, maybe, at least in that other time-line. But the shield was coming apart, whatever he thought about it, and there was nothing—nothing at all—that he could do to prevent it.

Besides, Karl wanted that railroad. It was necessary to the improvement of his lands. That had to be his first priority.

"So how long is it going to take?" Sarah asked.

"A small troop with good horses, but bad roads," Karl thought aloud. "Avoiding Saxony. I don't want to be John George's ransom to bring the HRE in on his side. Figure twenty-five miles a day on average. A week to Prague. And while I'm at it, I should visit Aunt Beth. So that's another week. Plus whatever time..." Karl paused not at all sure whether to say "I spend" or "we spend" and settled on "...it takes to negotiate with King Al and my aunt. So at least a month, probably a month and a half."

Now Sarah was looking distressed. "I'll have to talk to my boss. That's a long time to be gone."

Wendell House, Magdeburg

"Are you nuts!" Fletcher Wendell didn't quite bellow. Not quite. "Karl, you at least, ought to know better. Two hundred plus miles over rough country, with either one of you a bandit's dream come true. What's your ransom value, Karl? Half of Silesia? And you, Sarah? Half a million shares of OPM? You would have to take a flipping army with you just to fight off the bandits."

"I'm not insensitive to the situation, and the newspapers make it much harder to get where you're going before the bandits know about the trip," Karl agreed. "On the other hand, King Albrecht is insistent that I go."

"And my daughter? Is King Albrecht insisting that Sarah go with you?"

"No. But I'd rather tell King Albrecht no than tell Sarah that. If you don't want her to go, then you get to try to convince her she can't." Karl couldn't keep just a touch of smugness out of his voice as he said that and it clearly didn't please Herr Wendell.

CHAPTER 7

A Trip to Bohemia

September 1634

Prague

As it happened, Karl's wait for the king's pleasure wasn't long at all. In fact, the king's call came as soon as they arrived at the palace. Karl was escorted to a small throne room, not the big one, more of an office really. And before he could even finish his bow, Wallenstein asked him, "Was your father a thief?"

"I don't think so, Your Majesty," Karl answered carefully. "Though I am aware that others hold a different view. I prefer to think he was simply a practical man."

"Not exactly a ringing endorsement from a son." Wallenstein snorted. "I take it you don't think I'm a thief, either."

"No, Your Majesty."

"Then you would accept paper money issued by the crown of Bohemia. That is, by me!"

Karl had apparently landed in the middle of a rather heated debate. He noted the presence of Morris Roth, Uriel Abrabanel, and a few other people that he suspected were counselors to the king or money lenders. Bankers, as the up-timers would have it. He began to get an inkling of what was going on. King Albrecht was setting up his national bank. The timing seemed about right. And the king had just been told that there were problems.

Karl had a decision to make and he had to make it fast. Telling

50

truth to power wasn't a safe thing to do, but if what the family said about Wallenstein was true, lying about this could be incredibly costly. He hesitated, saw the expression on King Albrecht's face, and blurted out, "Not if I could safely avoid it, Your Majesty."

"You acknowledge that I'm not a thief, but wouldn't accept my money?" King Al gave Karl a hard look. "Which time were you lying?"

"Neither, Your Majesty. But just because *I* trust your money's value, doesn't mean I can spend it. That would require that the person I'm buying from trust it. Sarah Wendell is the person you should be talking to about this."

"Who is Sarah Wendell?" King Albrecht looked around the room as though she might be hiding in a corner.

"She's the daughter of the USE Treasury Secretary," Morris Roth explained.

"She's his girlfriend." Pappenheim jerked a thumb at Karl. "I read it in the *National Inquisitor*."

"She was the chief financial officer for OPM before she resigned to take a post with the USE Federal Reserve," explained Uriel Abrabanel.

"She's just outside," Karl said, all of them speaking pretty much simultaneously.

King Albrecht took it all in, or at least he seemed to. He motioned to the soldier waiting by the door, "Invite the young lady in."

Sarah entered the room to see the king in a chair only a little grander than the chairs of the others in the room. Except for Karl, they were all sitting. Pappenheim was on the king's right, Morris Roth and Uriel Abrabanel on his left. There were three other men she didn't recognize. She did an awkward curtsey and went to stand beside Karl.

She wanted to take his hand but doubted that would be appropriate. She wondered when taking his hand had become such a natural first response.

The king looked at her and at him, and waved them to chairs. "Miss Wendell, Prince Karl here says you're the person I should be talking to about introducing Bohemian paper money. That you can explain to me why my money will be no good in spite of the fact that Karl says he trusts me?"

Suddenly she didn't want to hold Karl's hand. She wanted to hit him in the head. Hard!

Karl saw her expression and, risking royal displeasure, hastened to explain. "His Majesty asked me if I trusted him, then if I would take his money. I remembered how you had explained the situation regarding me issuing money on my lands."

"Who gave you permission to issue money?" King Albrecht asked.

"No one, Your Majesty, and I hadn't brought up the subject. It was a preemptive lecture, lest I should fail to consult them before doing anything so foolish."

"So my issuing money is foolish?"

"No, Your Majesty. *My* issuing money would be foolish."

Sarah was not by nature a pushy person—at least, she didn't think she was. But she didn't like being bullied nor did she like those around her being bullied. "Actually, Your Majesty, your issuing money would be equally foolish. No, it would be *more* foolish! Karl wasn't personally involved in Kipper and Wipper, only his family was. You, on the other hand, were one of the major beneficiaries.

"Holy Roman Empire money is the next best thing to waste paper in the USE, in large part because Karl's Uncle Gundaker is Emperor Ferdinand's finance minister and he, like Karl, wasn't involved."

"Actually, Gundaker was instrumental in getting us the deal."

Sarah stopped and took a deep breath. "I didn't know that, Your Majesty, and it's really beside the point. If the name Gundaker von Liechtenstein was enough to ruin the credibility of HRE paper, what do you think Albrecht von Wallenstein is going to do to Bohemian paper?"

"She is right, Your Majesty," Morris said.

"Maybe so, but it doesn't make me like being called a thief."

"I didn't call you a thief, Your Majesty," Sarah said. "If you and the others had known in 1618 what we know now, it would have been different. You could have introduced silver-backed paper money, used a partial reserve system with a guarantee of silver on demand and added more money without ill effect. But you didn't have the knowledge. It was acquired bit by bit over centuries. No one knew. But, however noble your motives, today the names Liechtenstein and Wallenstein are not names to instill confidence in monetary policy."

"What name is then?"

"Up-timer," Karl said quickly. "Perhaps Abrabanel, but 'Someone von Up-time' would be best. Preferably someone who worked at the Grantville Bank or the Credit Union. In fact—" He waved at Sarah. "—Sarah would be among the best choices, if she were interested in the job."

"I'm too young," Sarah said.

"I disagree," said Uriel Abrabanel. "Sarah's paper on comparative economics and the effect of the American dollar is read all over Europe. As are several others."

"And I'm not looking for a job," Sarah added. "Besides, what you really need is the bank to be independent of the crown, even if you got me to head it. It wouldn't matter unless it was made clear that you couldn't order me to create money because you wanted a new palace."

"I'm not so sure of that," said Uriel Abrabanel. "'Up-timer' is a word to conjure with, especially in financial matters."

"Remember all the fights between Coleman Walker and the President, ah, Mike Stearns—" Sarah corrected herself. She thought of Mike Stearns as the President of the USE because he had been the leader of her nation in a couple of very formative years. But, in truth, his fights with Coleman Walker had been as much when he was the Chairman of the Emergency Committee as when he was the President of the New U.S. "Those fights were a lot of what gave the American dollar its credibility. It was clear that the government couldn't just create money, that the money had to represent something real. Even if almost no one knew what GDP meant, everyone was convinced it meant *something*."

Uriel nodded. "I agree. But that was then, and this is now. Now everyone knows that up-timers can create money and that money is good. I think as long as you didn't increase the money supply too much, just Sarah Wendell von Up-time would be enough to provide credibility."

"I hate that expression," Sarah said, referring to the "von Up-time." It was a tag that the *Daily News* had put on up-timers with an op-ed piece that claimed that they were the true nobility. And it was becoming fairly popular with some up-timers and a lot of down-timers. "And, like I said before, I am not looking for a job. Besides, even if the person you get to head your bank were an up-timer, even if it was Coleman Walker or my dad, it wouldn't make any difference if everyone thought the king could order them to print more money."

Uriel and Morris were both nodding. Uriel said, "It must be arranged so that the continued value of the money is given precedence over the short-term gain from just adding more."

"And it must be seen that that is the case," Sarah said. "Your Majesty, you need someone that people will trust and who will argue with you. Publicly."

By now King Albrecht was looking at Morris Roth. Don Morris shook his head. "I'm too closely associated with you, Your Majesty. I'm not sure people would accept my independence."

"What about Dame Judith?" Uriel Abrabanel was grinning like a Cheshire cat.

"Fine. But you tell her!" Morris Roth snorted in return.

"Actually, that's not a bad idea." Karl looked Morris Roth in the eye. "She is both an up-timer and Jewish. And prejudice works for us here. Everyone knows that the up-timer money is better than silver and everyone knows that Jews are tight with money. If none of the money goes to her, and if the Abrabanels support her, the rest of the Jewish community will, too. It could work quite well. Especially if Don Morris were to publicly complain about the appointment, because he doesn't want to be caught in the middle when Your Majesty and his stubborn wife butt heads."

"You're crazy. I don't know a thing about monetary policy and Judith knows even less. Well, not much more, anyway."

"What she doesn't know, she can learn," Uriel said. He wasn't laughing now. "And she will have excellent advisors. What we have learned about monetary theory from the up-timers' books is valuable, but the truth is that no true economists came back in the Ring of Fire, with all due respect to Sarah here. By now members of my extended family know as much or more about how money works as any up-timer does. What we need is the *belief* in money, and that your wife can provide simply because she is an up-timer. Prince Karl is quite correct, and it has other advantages as well. A Jewish woman with a position of great authority will be another assurance that Your Majesty means it when you say that Jews will be treated equally in your kingdom. Both for the Jews and for the Gentiles, and it will set a valuable precedent for women in the Jewish community."

Morris Roth was clearly looking for a good reason to squash

the idea, but it was equally clear that he wasn't finding one that would hold water. "Fine. You tell her," he said again.

"I'll tell her," King Albrecht said. "In the meantime, Prince, tell us about this Liechtenstein Industrialization Corporation of yours."

Over the next few days they talked about what railroads, even wooden railroads, and other bits of advanced tech would do for the Liechtenstein lands in Bohemia, Moravia and Silesia. As Karl had expected, Wallenstein didn't really have a problem with what Karl wanted to do. What he wanted was a public swearing of fealty that included Gundaker von Liechtenstein's domains of Kromau and Ostra. *Which is sure to thrill Uncle Gundaker*, Karl thought sardonically. "Why Ostra, Your Majesty?"

"If Ferdinand insists that he can grant Kromau in Moravia, I can grant Ostra in Hungary." King Albrecht gave Karl a cold little smile. "I imagine that when it's finally settled, your uncle will end up with Ostra and you'll keep Kromau." As it worked out, the part about Ostra was mumbled a bit in the swearing and buried in the fine print in the documents, but that was at King Albrecht's insistence. "I don't want to make a big thing of it. It's just a negotiating ploy to let Ferdinand save a bit of face when he finally acknowledges that I rule Bohemia and Moravia."

Roth House, Prague

"He wants me to do what?" Judith Roth looked stunned, and Sarah tried not to smile. They were in the Roth's huge salon. There were etchings on the walls and conversation nooks scattered around the walls.

"It wasn't my idea." Morris walked over to a down-time-made recliner. "On the other hand, their reasoning was fairly sound."

"I don't know anything about running a federal reserve."

"You probably don't want a federal reserve system." Sarah looked around, trying to figure out where to sit. "We have a modified one in the USE, because we got it from the SoTF, which got it from the New U.S., which got it from the USA up-time. And the up-time Fed was a disorganized mess that was developed out of a compromise between a whole bunch of people with very strong opinions about monetary policy and not a lot of understanding of it. It's a mare's nest of conflicting regulations. You probably want something closer to a Bank of England system, with the government owning a lot of nonvoting interest in the bank. Interest that can't be sold or borrowed against, but just pays dividends when the bank makes a profit."

"So why aren't you . . . ?" Mrs. Roth waved Sarah to a couch.

"I don't live here, Mrs. Roth," Sarah said. "I can help you set it up while I'm here, but not do it for you."

"I don't even know what we should call our money."

"Dollars or thalers is probably simplest. I wouldn't call them Albrechts or Wallensteins," Sarah said, then she grinned. "You could go all science fictiony and call them credits."

Judith shuddered. "Not the way the Catholic church feels about usury. I think just 'Bohemian dollars' will be best."

"So how many dollars to a HRE thaler?" Sarah asked.

"Shouldn't we just let it float?" Judith Roth asked.

"Yes, certainly. But a big part of your job will be to help set the value by controlling how many Bohem—" Sarah grinned. "—'boys' are in circulation."

Judith Roth wasn't pleased to be appointed to head the Bohemian National Bank, but Bohemia did need money that people would have faith in.

As it turned out, Sarah had plenty of time to work with Judith Roth and Uriel Abrabanel on designing the structure of the new national bank of Bohemia. Enough time for King Albrecht von Wallenstein to yield his right to create money to the bank, in the interest of a stable and prosperous nation. She had the time, because it took a while for Karl to arrange the visit to his aunt in Cieszyn.

CHAPTER 8

Family Reunion

September 1634

Prague

"Ferdinand II is dead," King Albrecht said. "In this universe, at least, the fanatic didn't manage to outlive me." There was considerable satisfaction in his tone.

And, in spite of himself, Karl realized that it was more than a little justified. Wallenstein was opposed to the Edict of Restitution, and a large part of the motive for the revolution that he may or may not have planned would have been to repeal it. Five years ago, Karl would have agreed with Ferdinand II, but then the Ring of Fire happened and they had all been able to see how the world had unfolded in that other timeline. Now he found himself agreeing with Wallenstein.

"Will Ferdinand III try for the crown of the Holy Roman empire?" Karl asked.

"It doesn't seem like it. He is styling himself 'Emperor of Austria-Hungary.' And he managed to do what I never could, and get his father to repeal the Edict of Restitution on his death bed. If Ferdinand II had done that two years ago, I would never have taken Bohemia," King Albrecht said, sounding sincere. Then he added, "Well, assuming that he didn't try to have me assassinated."

Karl wasn't sure he believed Albrecht von Wallenstein about that. The man was ambitious and ambition can always find an excuse. On the other hand, Karl wasn't entirely sure that he didn't believe it, either.

"Might there be peace between your realm and Ferdinand III's?"

"I'm willing if he is," King Albrecht said. "But I don't think he is. He's still making noises like I'm a traitor and he's the king of Bohemia."

"Might you come to some sort of accommodation?" Karl asked cautiously. "Might Bohemia rejoin the HRE?"

"No. Two assassination attempts in two universes are all they get. I'll not bend a knee to the Habsburg family again."

After that, the discussion turned to the rest of the news. A bit later, King Albrecht said, "You're still going to have to publicly swear fealty to me in regard to all your family's lands in Bohemia, Moravia and Silesia. But, in exchange, I am willing to endorse the railroad and even add a line to Cieszyn out of the crown purse. And I'll support your LIC as well. There are several projects that Morris wants to do that can be done in cooperation between us."

Karl nodded. He hadn't been expecting any other result, after all.

"I'll see you when you get back," Sarah said. Her strawberry blond hair was in a bun and escaping the confines of her scrunchy. She had a charcoal smudge on her nose and was utterly focused on a book of ledgers that had been gathered from a market here in Prague. She looked adorable. Unfortunately, she had no attention at all to pay to Karl. She hadn't even looked up.

Cieszyn

"Hello, Aunt Beth." Karl looked around the palace hall. It had a more worn look than he remembered. Aunt Beth was maintaining her palace, but apparently not spending any more on it than absolutely necessary.

Elisabeth Lukretia von Teschen looked Karl up and down and he felt himself straightening under her gaze. "Good afternoon, Karl Eusebius! How was the trip from Prague?"

"Uneventful, always a blessing when it comes to travel. I have more letters from King Albrecht and Morris Roth. Also, Judith Roth is going to be the head of the National Bank of Bohemia."

"Do you think I should print my own money? It would certainly solve my financial problems."

"Please don't, Aunt. You will be much better off getting improvement loans from the National Bank—or from me, for that matter. Through the Liechtenstein Improvement Corporation."

So it went. They spent two days talking about what he had set up in Grantville and what King Albrecht had thought about it. About the Fortneys, who were at this very moment somewhere on the road to Vienna. About the Barbie Consortium and—very much in spite of himself—talking about Sarah Wendell, how smart she was, how beautiful, how clever and kind.

"So tell me about this Sarah of yours," Aunt Beth said. "Are the Wendells of a noble house?"

"She's not mine," Karl said. "At least not yet. And the up-timers are different. If anything, my title probably hurts my suit."

Aunt Beth gave Karl a look that conveyed her displeasure at his obfuscations.

Karl continued. "By the up-timer standards, yes. The Wendell family are near the upper echelons of those who came back in the Ring of Fire. Her father, Fletcher Wendell, is the USE Treasury Secretary, who knows and is known by Gustav Adolf and Fernando, as well as Mike Stearns and Ed Piazza. And her mother, Judy Wendell the elder is, if less well known, even more astute in financial matters. Sarah takes after her mother in that. Right now she is working out the design of the Bohemian National Bank with Judith Roth and Uriel Abrabanel."

"Aside from smart, what's she like?"

"Well..." Karl paused. "She's taller than I am by a couple of inches and she's still growing. She has light blond hair with just a touch of red, what the up-timers call a strawberry blond. She is thin and I must admit she's no horsewoman, but she loves flying and books and plays and solving problems."

"Is she pretty?"

Karl laughed. "I think so, but she doesn't. That's probably because her younger sister is perhaps the greatest beauty in Grantville. Up-timers tend to be comely people by our standards, so even what we would consider pretty or handsome doesn't stand out among them." He smiled and Elizabeth noticed that his teeth were both straighter and whiter than she remembered. Not that they had been particularly bad before, but the evenness of his teeth now was remarkable. "Sarah considers herself gawky..."

"Gawky?"

"Sorry, I slipped in an up-timer English word. It means tall and awkward. And it's true she is more at home with books than sports or dances. But there's a vibrancy to her that is hard to see till you get to know her."

"Is she Catholic?"

"No. Her family belongs to a Protestant sect that is vaguely similar to the Anabaptist. They are called Baptist. However, she is not devout. It's not that she lacks faith. She once told me that you couldn't go through the Ring of Fire and not believe in something. But she is doubtful of the certainty—" Karl paused a moment. "—professed by so many of what it means. She tends toward Pastor Steffan Schultheiss' sect."

"Who?"

"A Lutheran pastor from Badenburg. He didn't see the Ring of Fire itself, but you can see the Ring from the walls of Badenburg. He has come to some disturbing conclusions about what God was saying when he delivered the town of Grantville to our time."

Clearly, Aunt Beth wasn't going to be distracted, even though her conversion to Catholicism was almost as unwilling as her marriage to Gundaker. "What about you, Karl? When last we spoke in person, you were almost as Catholic as your uncle, if less vicious about it. Can you live with a Protestant and not try to force her to become Catholic?"

"For myself, yes certainly. The Ring of Fire provides faith, but for me at least, it also instilled doubts. Politically, it would be better if she were Catholic and we will discuss the possibility of a conversion if we get that far. I won't attempt to force her, but you should know, Aunt Beth, that the Catholic church of Grantville is not the Catholic church of Ferdinand II's court. Oh, have you gotten the news yet that the emperor is dead?"

"It was in the letters. I didn't know either the father or the son well, so I hesitate to guess what it might mean to us here."

Elisabeth Lukretia von Teschen watched her nephew ride away, smiling. The news, from her point of view, was almost universally good. She had several letters from King Albrecht, and from what Karl had said there were good opportunities to get loans to repair the damage done by the Danes a few years before the Ring of Fire.

And Karl was falling for a girl who was not even Catholic. Gundaker would have a fit. With a bit of luck, he might even expire from it.

The railroad going from her capital of Teschen to Vienna would happen. At least on the Teschen side of the border. Better, there would also be a rail line, wooden rails, from Prague to her capital. Between the two, they would make her capital a transhipment location for goods going to half of Europe. Aside from the trade advantages, it would turn long, uncomfortable trips into relatively short, comfortable ones. At least, that's what Karl said.

In a way, her little Cieszyn had weathered the war so far fairly well. Most of her tax base was intact. She had told little Karl, not so little anymore, that he would have support for the part of the railroads that went through her lands. Beth wanted to visit Grantville.

Meanwhile, she heard from friends, Grantville was having an influence on Vienna. Someone in Grantville had had a tourist guide book on Vienna. An enterprising merchant had brought it to Vienna, and somehow it had become fashionable to copy from the book. Perhaps because it was both modern and, in a way, traditional. Grantville's windup record players had made their way to Vienna and along with them quite a bit of the up-timer music. It was all the rage among the younger set. Fashions were another issue. People were picking from four hundred years of fashion, and different years, decades, or even centuries, appealed to different people. Some people—she shuddered—mixed and matched with little regard to what went with what.

Liechtenstein House, Vienna

Karl was still visiting his aunt when his letters reached Vienna. Gundaker von Liechtenstein threw the letter across the room. "How dare he! The arrogant little pup. We need that money to be able to make the loan to the crown."

"And we'll get it, most of it anyway," Maximilian told his brother. "From what we have heard, he did quite well in Amsterdam. Those investments in our lands will pay handsomely."

"He should be removed as head of the family."

"On what grounds?" Maximilian asked.

"Treason against the empire," Gundaker said. "He swore fealty to Wallenstein."

Maximilian said, "Drop the whole matter. We have very little leverage over our nephew, Gundaker. If you force a breach, there will be no funds at all forthcoming and you would give Wallenstein a *casus belli* against the emperor of Austria-Hungary. Not all the family lands are in Bohemia, you know. Karl Eusebius owns this house, according to the family charter. Which would allow Wallenstein to invade Austria in defense of his new vassal's property rights. More likely, Wallenstein would simply seize the property in Bohemia if we challenged Karl Eusebius, and probably give it to one of his henchmen. We were lucky, or Karl Eusebius talked really fast, to avoid having Wallenstein do that in the first place."

"Bah. Now that he is claiming to be a king, Wallenstein is trying to reform his image."

"Certainly in part. It might also have helped that Karl Eusebius was on good terms with the up-timers. But if we repudiate Karl, or the new emperor repudiates Karl, most of our lands and most of our wealth disappears at a stroke...as does all of our influence at court and any hope we have of helping the empire."

"I am not thrilled with Ferdinand III, Maximilian. Did you know that Father Lamormaini was denied access to the old emperor while the boy forced him to revoke the Edict of Restitution? What happened to faith and the will of God?"

CHAPTER 9

Rollin' on the River

September 1634

Regensburg

"Emperor Ferdinand II has died and Vienna mourns, but it is time for us to move," Istvan Janoszi said.

"It's weird," Hayley whispered to her father as Janoszi turned away. "He was...I don't know...the bad guy. Ferdinand II signed the Edict of Restitution that has been the justification for so much war and out-and-out banditry that it had halfway trashed central Germany before the Ring of Fire."

"I know what you mean, Hayley, but go light on the bad guy part of that thought once we get to Vienna. For that matter, go light on it here. Because he was their emperor, and whatever their politics, there will be a hole in the heart of most of Austria for a while."

Hayley nodded. After that, everything went smoothly for the rest of the trip to Vienna. Sonny's little steam engine barely produced enough way for steering. On the other hand, they were going downriver, so the current was with them.

On the Danube

"Honestly, Hayley, I don't understand how you girls managed to get rich," Mrs. Sanderlin said as they were steaming down the

Danube the first evening out of Regensburg. Hayley looked at the shore going by, muddy banks and green grass with a small herd of cattle coming down to the river's edge to drink. The *chug-chug* of the steam engine made a background to the conversation. The question had come up before and there were standard answers that Hayley and the rest of the Barbies had put together.

"We didn't have anything else to do," was the one that Hayley used this time, but Mrs. Sanderlin's look suggested that she wasn't going to let it go at that.

"Well, it's true," Hayley insisted. "Right after the Ring of Fire, everyone was busy and no one had much money. Then Judy found out about Mrs. Higgins' doll collection selling for so much. We didn't have anything like that many dolls, but we had some. And . . . well, everyone—and I do mean everyone—in Grantville was really busy. There was a lot of 'just take care of yourself, kids' right around then. As long as we weren't getting in trouble, our parents had other stuff on their minds. Some of the kids in Grantville got in trouble just for the attention, but most were trying to pitch in in some way. Our way was to take our doll money and invest it. We didn't know all that much about investing, but we got some good advice from Mrs. Gundelfinger and from Judy's parents and sister."

"So you had the advice of Helene Gundelfinger, the Secretary of the Treasury for the USE, and a renowned scholar of economics who works for the USE Federal Reserve Bank? No wonder you got rich."

"Not to mention Karl Schmidt, David Bartley, Franz Kunze, and half a dozen other members of what has become the financial elite of the State of Thuringia-Franconia and the USE," Hayley admitted with a grin. "The real question is: with all that good advice why aren't we richer?"

Mrs. Sanderlin looked at Hayley for a minute, then shook her head. "No, it's not, Hayley. The real question is: how did a small West Virginia coal-mining town have Mike Stearns and Ed Piazza. How did it have Fletcher Wendell and Tony Adducci, not to mention David Bartley, the Stone family, Dr. Nichols and all the rest? One or two, sure. But dozens, even hundreds?"

"I've asked myself that question every day for the last year and a half or more." Sonny Fortney interrupted their conversation.

"Any answers, Dad?" Hayley asked.

"The best I can come up with is 'people rise to the occasion.' Or, put another way, 'talent is a lot more common and opportunity to express it a lot less common than we tend to think.'"

"I'm not sure it's just opportunity," Hayley said. "I think it's need, too."

"Maybe, darlin', but you and your young friends argue for it just being opportunity. You didn't need to become investors. You could have just sold your dolls and bought dresses. A lot of kids did. Which, I guess, argues against my point."

"It doesn't matter, Sonny." Mrs. Sanderlin bit her lip in concentration. "Even if only ten percent took advantage of the opportunity when it happened, that's still a lot more talent than we expect. Or at least than we expected, up-time. How many inventors, statesmen, businessmen and entrepreneurs were washing dishes and sweeping floors up-time? Because there wasn't an opportunity for them to shine."

"Down-time was no different. Even worse, probably," Hayley said. "Look at Karl Schmidt. Without the Ring of Fire he would never have been anything but the owner of a minor foundry in a small town. Anna Baum would still be spinning thread at starvation wages if she hadn't actually starved by now. Or Mrs. Gundelfinger. Well, she might have owned her shop, but never much more than that, I think."

"So how did the Ring of Fire change things?" Mrs Sanderlin asked. When Hayley and Sonny Fortney looked at her in confusion, she tried to explain. "Look, up-time America and Europe had all this stuff and Africa and South America didn't. So it can't be just the know-how, otherwise Peru would be building super jets and Zambia or wherever would be building rocket ships and computers. I mean, they could even order the parts that they couldn't make themselves."

"I think that may be the key," Sonny said after a little thought, looking out over the Danube as the sun slowly set. "They could buy it. They didn't need to build it."

"But they couldn't buy it," Mrs. Sanderlin said. "They didn't have the money."

"But they could buy shirts easier than they could buy shirt factories. They could buy cars easier than they could buy car factories."

Hayley's memories of up-time were starting to get more than a little vague. Three and a half years is a much higher percentage of a teenager's life than the life of her parents. But here, experience in down-time business was fresh. "Competition?" she asked doubtfully. "Competition isn't that much of a problem, Dad. There is always more market than product to fill it."

"Selling up-time products down-time, sure," Sonny told her. "But up-time the competition of established industries was a real problem for start-ups."

They continued to talk about the meaning of opportunity and the effect of the Ring of Fire.

"Here you go, Mrs. Simpson," Brandon Fortney said as he poured some grain into the bird's food dish. Mrs. Simpson was his favorite Rhode Island Red and was normally a good layer, but she was upset by the move. Brandon had four dozen fertilized eggs in a rosin foam incubator, a Rhode Island Red rooster, Captain Jack, and another hen, Eliza, also a Rhodie. He hoped that would be enough to establish a good up-time laying flock in Vienna. Meanwhile, the hens weren't laying, and though he knew it was probably just the trip, it still worried him.

Well, that, and the whole business of heating water for the hot water bottles that had to be in the incubator. That was really a hassle on the road, but he had managed.

Once he was done with the chickens, he moved to the rabbit hutches. He had a pair of Satins, which had a good growth rate and a good meat-to-bone ratio. Some girls might make those silly Angora rabbits into pets, but in Brandon's mind, you took care of the animals you intended to eat, only it didn't pay to get sentimental about them. Besides, his big sister Hayley was rich and it was embarrassing not to have a business of his own. Animal husbandry was all he had been able to come up with, since there didn't appear to be a lot of money in entomology.

Brandon sighed over that. He had a great bug collection and it was utterly unfair that Hayley's Barbies had been worth so much more than his bugs. He'd been afraid that Mom and Dad might make him leave it in Grantville, since they were so concerned over weight. And honestly, on the overland trip before they got to the Danube, he had almost regretted bringing the bugs. They had a whole wagon train just of their stuff, not including the cars for the Austrian prince guy. But now that they were on the river, it was a lot easier. He had more time to take care of the chickens and rabbits, which was a good thing because it was getting real close to time for the eggs to hatch. It had taken them longer to get to the river than they expected, and then they had sat in Regensburg for a week, waiting for word that it was all right to come ahead. He was pretty sure the eggs were going to hatch before they got to Vienna. They were moving a lot faster now that they were on the river, but it was still only about nine miles an hour. They would still be on the river when they hatched, not situated in Vienna, according to plan. That was going to be another problem. The chicks would have to be kept warm, fed, and watered.

The next day Brandon's concern became fact as the eggs started hatching. Before they reached Vienna, he had thirty-eight chicks. There were chicken sexers in Grantville now, but Brandon wasn't one of them. The chicks would have to wait till they got older before he would know how many of each sort he had. He hoped for more hens than roosters, but it would probably be about even. Meanwhile he had all those chicks to take care of in circumstances that were hardly ideal.

"Brandon! When is that chicken pen going to be ready?" Dana Fortney was trying to sound severe, but it was hard. First, the chicks were cute as buttons. Chicks usually are. Second, it was hardly Brandon's fault that the trip had taken longer than expected. He had expected to be in Vienna when they hatched. Meanwhile, he had hired one of the boatmen to help him weave a fence out of tree branches and currently had boxes containing the chicks. Well, almost containing the chicks.

Docks, Vienna, Austria

The barges pulled up to Vienna carrying two cars and several tons of up-time or up-time-designed goods. They were met at the docks by a royal factotum, who set about organizing the transport of the cars through Vienna and out to what would become the race track. Oh, and the rest of them, too.

"Chicks?" the official said, in slightly offended tones. "Why on Earth did you people bring chickens? We have chickens. What do we need with up-time chickens?"

"Not like my chickens, you don't," Brandon said stoutly. "My chickens lay bigger eggs and more of them. They are also bigger than your chickens, more meat. And they are my chickens, not yours. We just need a coop to hold them."

"We have the cars, the prince's 240Z," Bob Sanderlin said. "And ours as well, but there isn't a lot of room for them here in the city. I doubt the 240Z could get through a lot of your streets. They ain't wide enough."

"The emperor!" the royal flunky said haughtily, and Hayley suppressed a grin.

"Where does His Imperial Majesty want us to set up?" her dad asked.

What followed was confusion and irritation for all concerned, till His Majesty, Emperor Ferdinand III, turned up and put matters right. The new emperor was there to meet them. Well, he was there to meet his new car. It was pretty clear that in his mind the mechanics were secondary. He swept in, asked lots of questions and swept out, leaving them in the care of the same official who now had a different attitude and clear directions.

Cars and wagons were unloaded and made a parade through Vienna.

Father Wilhelm Germain Lamormaini watched the parade through Vienna and knew that Prince Ferdinand had betrayed both his father and church by hiding his pet up-timers till his father died. Even the father's death was the fault of the Ring of Fire. It had to be. The histories in the Ring of Fire had Ferdinand II living to 1637.

The Ring of Fire must be an act of great evil, not of the Good Lord, because if God had been a party to it the church would have been warned. No, the very fact that it was a surprise to faith was evidence of its evil nature. The Ring of Fire was an act of the great deceiver: poison coated in honey to distract the poor and weak-willed from eternal salvation. Satan walked the world as he always had, but his agents—knowing or unknowing—were the up-timers.

Yet everyone was being drawn in by Satan's trap. Even Pope Urban had elevated the up-time priest Mazzare, making him a prince of the church.

Lamormaini turned back to the Hofburg. He still had his rooms there, but who knew how long that would last? He was no longer the emperor's confessor and his influence at court was greatly diminished. What was the pope thinking to elevate that up-timer who was no true Catholic? Not if he followed the unholy strictures of Vatican II. There must be something he could do. There *must* be.

Liechtenstein House, Vienna

"Prince Gundaker, it is good of you to see me." Father Lamormaini bowed as was the due to a person of Gundaker von Liechtenstein's status, and perhaps a little more.

"You always gave the old emperor good counsel, Father. And I, for one, miss it." The prince gestured Father Lamormaini to a chair with fine condescension.

"Thank you, Your Serene Highness. It is always good to hear that one's counsel is appreciated and it's something I have heard little of, of late. All I wish is that I didn't feel that the restoration of Europe to the true faith hadn't suffered a severe blow when the Ring of Fire happened. It has cast doubt on all our goals as I am increasingly convinced was its intent."

"You do not believe that it was an act of God?"

"No. I can't convince myself that God would force us into such a state of doubt. The effect of that event was to separate the wheat from the chaff. There will be an answer in Jerusalem. I think that the six mile circle is the beast itself. Six miles across in height, six miles across in width, and six miles across in length. A perfect sphere of evil to counter the celestial spheres of which it denies the existence."

Father Lamormaini stopped in sudden realization. He had not thought of that before. He had had a feeling of evil from the place and what it stood for from the moment that he had heard of it. The notion of Catholic and heretic living together in peace was a betrayal of faith so basic as to demand abhorrence from any person who truly sought God's grace. But until just now, he had never realized that the Bible actually spoke of the place, recorded its evil for those with eyes to see. But there it was.

Prince Gundaker was staring at him in horror. "How could you fail to to report this to the Holy See? How could you fail to report it to the old emperor?"

"I failed to see it, Your Serene Highness. I failed to see it till just this moment. The words came out of my mouth before their meaning reached me. They came out of my knowledge of mathematics and they were so simple, so straightforward, that I am shocked that we didn't see it from the beginning. All of us should have seen it from the very first. The radius of the sphere was three miles, the diameter six. But it was called the *Ring* of Fire, not the Sphere of Fire. So the terms were wrong. A ring with a radius of three miles. What of six six six is in that? The devil was subtle, but God was more subtle still, and gave us a warning...if we had the native wit to see it.

"The American dollar. It rapidly comes to pass that you cannot buy or sell without possession of American dollars. Yet what are they? They are not gold or silver, not even copper or iron. No. They are just marks on paper. As Revelations warned us, it has come to pass that to buy or sell you must be possessed of those marks on paper."

Gundaker wasn't convinced that Father Lamormaini was correct...but it was a worrying thought. He decided that he would put a watch on the up-timers.

CHAPTER 10

Outside Vienna

September 1634

Village of Simmering, Austria

"You know anything about oil wells, Sonny?" Ron Sanderlin passed the well-worn book over and took a seat in the sitting room of the large house that they had been situated in. The house was in the village of Simmering, about three miles from the walls of Vienna, and it was where Prince Ferdinand had decided to set up his race track. It was near an imperial hunting lodge established by Maximilian II and there were extensive gardens nearby.

"I know I wish I'd owned one up-time," Sonny Fortney told him. "But other than that, *nada*." One single sentence in the book mentioned that the Matzen oil field was about twelve miles northeast of Vienna and was the largest in Austria. But it didn't say another thing about it. It was a book on sights to see in and around Vienna and that line was in the vital statistics portion of the book. It didn't even say whether "largest" referred to land area or barrels of oil.

Ron's Uncle Bob was shaking his head, indicating he didn't know either. They had just gotten to Vienna and hadn't even started Ron's 240Z. Well, Emperor Ferdinand's 240Z now. And Janos Drugeth's uncle, Pal Nadasdy, wanted them to tell him how to get the oil in the Matzen field out of the ground.

"Look, oil drilling is a pretty specialized business," Sonny said. "And there hasn't been much along those lines in Grantville since the twenties. Uh…the nineteen twenties, I mean. There are a couple of older folks that were kids way back then and a few old books tucked away. But I'm pretty sure there is not a single petroleum geologist in Grantville and that means in the world. The wildcatters, ah, the people who are doing the drilling, are mostly up at the oil fields near Wietze.

"Ron here can get the car up and running, and I can build you a track for it. For that matter, with the help of your local smiths and Bob, I can build you a steam boiler and between us we can build you some steam engines and locomotives. I can survey rail lines for you. But none of us know much of anything about drilling an oil well. And you're probably going to need to drill a bunch of them. We'll ask our families if they know anything about it, but I doubt they do. Failing that, we can probably get a geology cheat sheet to at least give you guys a notion of what to look for."

Count Nadasdy nodded almost as if he had expected the answer. "Please send your letters to get the…geology cheat sheet, was it? In the meantime, it has been proposed that a wooden rail railroad could be built between here and Teschen. Would that be a good idea?"

"Yep. Prince Karl mentioned something about that before we left. Well, more than mentioned. He sent along a bunch of maps. So he got permission, did he? But I don't remember anything about Teschen. Where is Teschen?"

"It's in Silesia on the Oder River. The Poles call it Cieszyn. The notion, as it has been proposed, was to form a rail link between the Danube and the Oder and hence between the Baltic and the Black Sea."

"Yep. That's the place. I think he called it Cieszyn. Prague would be closer, though," Sonny said. Not that he really expected Nadasdy to support a railroad from Emperor Ferdinand's capital to King Al's. But just to get the reaction.

Count Nadasdy looked like he had just gotten a good whiff of skunk. "Perhaps at some time in the future. For the moment, however, it would not be feasible."

Sonny nodded. "But Teschen is?"

"Yes. It turns out that Prince Karl Eusebius von Liechtenstein, despite his other faults, is prepared to invest a considerable amount in its construction."

"Well, he'd have the money for it."

✧　　✧　　✧

The next day, while Ron was getting ready to start the 240Z, Hayley Fortney went with her mother and little brother to the University of Vienna. They were looking for a tutor, mostly for Brandon, but partly for Hayley. It was a warm summer day with white puffy clouds dotting a blue sky and none of it made any impression on Hayley. She still wasn't happy about ending up in Vienna. She had friends in Grantville and work that interested her. She was the closest thing to a real techie that the Barbies had. She was a steam head and was becoming a tube geek. In Grantville, the new down-time in Grantville, that was perfectly acceptable for a young lady.

In Vienna... She had a dark suspicion that wouldn't be true. The fact that the city had the oldest university in the German-speaking world, established in 1365, didn't impress her at all. There was no engineering school anywhere in Vienna, including at the university. The closest thing to it was the college of natural philosophy at the University of Vienna.

She was going to miss her last year at Grantville High and have to make do with correspondence courses and a down-time tutor. It was worse for Brandon. He was doomed to the tutor and correspondence courses for as long as their parents decided to stay here.

Hayley's mother was interviewing tutors. Her mother, not her, in spite of the fact that Hayley was paying, because Hayley was more than a little tired of being the rich up-timer member of the Barbie Consortium. She was ready to be a teenager again. Sure, the teenage daughter of wealthy parents, but not the wheeler-dealer that she had been seen as in Grantville. At the same time, she was finding authority a hard habit to break. She kept wanting to interrupt her mother.

She was following along, listening to her mom talk about the history and beauty of Vienna when Ron Sanderlin started the 240Z. There were three young men and a gaggle of little boys hanging around the track. And Hayley couldn't help but overhear what they were saying.

"It's evil spirits that are making the noise."

"Nay. It's the herd of horses is doing it."

"Horses? It can't be. You can't see no horses."

"They have a whole bunch of them, though. Hidden under a magical hood. Makes them invisible, it does."

"So it's evil spirits, after all. But they use them to hide the horses."

Hayley didn't know what to say. Vienna was supposed to be civilized, at least by down-time standards. People ought to know better than that. It made her wish she had convinced her parents she should stay in Grantville like Nat. It made her want to correct the boys, explain that horsepower was just a measurement. That there was no magic involved.

Then she heard the giggle. Then all the boys were laughing and Hayley felt like an idiot when she noticed the smaller boys, maybe Brandon's age. It wasn't down-timer ignorance but down-timers playing at ignorance in order to entertain little boys. Hayley hadn't been in Vienna long enough to recognize that the three young men she saw were all wearing the seventeenth-century Vienna equivalent of "college casual." As it turned out, there were three students from the college of natural philosophy, teasing younger brothers and cousins, while watching the car being put through its paces.

University of Vienna

At the university, Hayley and her mother met with Professor Lorenz, who became very cooperative as soon as he saw the letter from Emperor Ferdinand. Not surprising. He was the king, after all.

Not that Professor Lorenz was particularly uncooperative before that. It was just that before the note he was more interested in picking their brains than helping them find a tutor. The little note from Emperor Ferdinand had given them a good example of their status, both good and bad. Emperor Ferdinand had talked past them the way a German noble would talk past a merchant or a servant. It wasn't, Hayley thought, intentional cruelty or arrogance. Emperor Ferdinand had simply never learned to talk to people of their rank as people. He asked questions of the air and was interested in the cars and how they worked, and clearly intended that his auto mechanics would have everything they needed to do their jobs well and be happy in their work. But it was almost as though they were extra equipment, accessories to the cars. When Hayley's father had pointed out that he was going to need a tutor for his daughter and son to continue their education, the king simply had one of the clerks that followed him around make a note of it, as though it were five thousand pounds of gravel for the track or ventilation ducts for the shop. That was the bad, and in all honesty, Hayley wasn't at all sure how much of that was simply because he was new at the job of king. The good was that by that afternoon they had a note over his seal, instructing the university to see to their needs, i.e. give them whatever they wanted. Emperor Ferdinand wasn't uncaring, just busy and dealing with the changes since his father's death.

"Hm," Dr. Lorenz mused, "Professor Himmler is available but unlikely to be willing to instruct young ladies. Besides he is convinced that Copernicus was a dangerous radical."

"I watched Neil Armstrong step onto the moon when I was a child and we've all seen the images from probes to the outer planets and, of course, the Hubble space telescope," Dana Fortney said. "Might he be persuaded by eyewitness accounts?"

"Not even if he was the eyewitness." Dr. Lorenz smiled. "He's not stupid, you understand. Just incredibly stubborn. He would find a way to explain it all away. Aristotle said there were crystal spheres, so there are crystal spheres." Dr. Lorenz looked at Hayley and Brandon. "But if what you're after is a stern disciplinarian, he might just be prevailed upon."

Brandon started to speak, but Hayley stepped on his foot. *Let Mom handle it* was the clear message.

"Tempting as that thought sometimes is," Dana said with a grin at her kids, "I think we would all be happier with someone more open to new concepts. After all, Brandon and Hayley will both be working from correspondence courses from Grantville." Dana Fortney left unsaid the fact that much of what the tutor would be expected to teach was going to be concepts utterly new to the seventeenth century, so he was likely as not going to be struggling along only a day or so ahead of his students.

"In that case, I think your best option would be a recent doctor of natural philosophy. He is quite good with boys and interested in the knowledge brought by the Ring of Fire." Dr. Lorenz hesitated a moment, looking at Hayley. "He is rather young, only twenty-four. He was going to have to leave Vienna to look for work, which would have been a shame because he is working on several experiments with magnets and coils of copper wire. Continuing those experiments would have been more difficult without the facilities of the university."

For the first time since they'd been introduced, Hayley spoke up. "Are a lot of people leaving Vienna to look for work?"

"Those who can," Dr. Lorenz said. "Those who have someplace to go."

Village of Simmering, Austria

Count Amadeus von Eisenberg, Baron Julian von Meklau and several of their friends rode up to the village two days after the cars had made their procession through Vienna. They found a muddy field and a barn that had been roughly converted into housing for the emperor's car. There was a canvas tent tied to the side of the converted barn that presumably held the other up-time vehicles, the ones owned by the mechanics.

"Show us the 240," Julian commanded.

"Can't do it, boys," said one of the mechanics.

"What? I am Baron Julian von Meklau."

"*Howdy.*" The first word was new to Julian, who had some English, but not a great deal. Then the man continued in badly accented German. "I'm Bob Sanderlin. And the 240Z belongs to Emperor Ferdinand III, so you need his permission to drive it, or fiddle with it or even look at it. Shouldn't be a problem, though. All you gotta do is go back to Vienna and tell the emperor to let you see it, just the way you told me. I'm sure he'll be in a right hurry to do what you tell him to, you being a baron and all."

Julian was suddenly quite uncomfortable. He couldn't back down in front of his friends. At the same time, if he whipped the dog the way he deserved, Julian would certainly incur the emperor's displeasure.

"Julian," said Amadeus von Eisenberg, "leave off."

Julian looked over at Amadeus, but the count wasn't looking at him or Ron Sanderlin. Instead he was looking at a small window in the barn and at the gun barrel that protruded from it. It was an interesting gun barrel, very well made and colored a sort of dark blue gray. It was a small bore, which was easy to tell because it was pointed right at him.

Vienna, Austria

"They pointed a gun at Julian, Father," Amadeus von Eisenberg said.

"I don't need this, Amadeus," Peter von Eisenberg said. "Karl Eusebius wants to put a railroad up to Teschen. And Sonny Fortney is a qualified surveyor. You and that drunken rabble you run with getting yourselves shot by the emperor's pet up-timers is not going to make things easier. I will discuss it with the emperor, but in the meantime you and your friends stay away from the up-timers. I don't need you in drunken brawls with peasants. Especially useful peasants. Leave them to the local peasants."

"Yes, Father," Amadeus said resentfully. He wasn't happy about it but he would do it.

Village of Simmering, Austria

Hertel Faust, the new tutor, smiled as he looked at the carefully preserved insects in the four glass cases. "These are marvelous. You have examples from up-time America?"

"Uh huh," Brandon agreed. "That's this one and that one." He pointed at two of the cases. "The others are from down-time Germany. Well, around the Ring of Fire anyway. Some of 'em are American insects that I caught after the Ring of Fire but—" he pointed "—that one and that one are maybe crosses between up-time and down-time insects."

"That would seem unlikely on the face of it," Dr. Faust said cautiously. "On the other hand, I have never seen ones quite like these."

Hayley kept her peace. Herr Doctor Hertel Faust was a reasonably handsome young man, well-read and open-minded. If he had the normal male interest in icky, squishy bugs, well, it was unlikely that they were going to find a tutor who didn't.

After he and Brandon finished ooh-ing and aah-ing over the skeletons of dead bugs, Hayley managed to get Faust back onto something interesting. She showed him an electromagnet and demonstrated the effect of moving a permanent magnet across it.

Dr. Faust looked at the needle on the voltmeter moving and asked, "Please explain to me again why moving a magnet across a coiled wire produces electricity and moving it across a straight wire doesn't. Does the curve cause the effect?"

"A straight wire does produce electricity when a magnet is moved across it. But it's just one wire. A coil has lots of strands of wire being affected. You coil them to make the magnetic field produce more electricity."

"Why not use one big wire? They carry more current, don't they?"

Hayley wasn't sure how to explain. "Yes, but the movement of the magnetic field would only produce a little energy no matter how big the wire is. With the coil the magnetic field is acting on lots of separate wires."

"Then what would happen if you had hundreds of parallel wires, rather than hundreds of coils?"

Hayley started to say something but was stopped by the fact that she didn't have a clue what would happen. "I don't know. Maybe you'd get lots of very weak currents of electricity?"

"Perhaps. But assume that all the wires split off from one wire on one side of the magnet's path and recombined on the other?"

"I don't know . . . ?"

"Sounds like a neat experiment, though," Brandon said.

Dr. Faust was going to fit in just fine, Hayley thought.

Hertel Faust gave a little half bow to one of the gawkers they passed and Hayley wondered why. She didn't interrupt, though. She, Brandon, and Dr. Faust continued their walk, identifying tree and birds. Once they were out of earshot of the person Dr. Faust had bowed to she asked, "Who was that you bowed to back there?"

"Herr Weber, you mean? He is of the *They of Vienna*."

"What's that?" Brendan asked. He had clearly heard the emphasis as well as Hayley had.

"The they or the them of Vienna are . . ." He paused searching for a word. "Elite. Yes, I think that is the word. The elite of Vienna. Not exactly the nobility, more the patrician class of Vienna. It is important that you know the social rules. The They of Vienna run the city. They hold the important posts and are the most important of the merchants and master craftsmen in the city They are often titled in some way, but not always. Herr Weber, for instance, is simply a very wealthy merchant, but he and members of his family have been involved in the politics of Vienna for the last half century at least. He has influence over which laws and regulations are passed and what exceptions are available."

"So why the bow?" Hayley asked.

"A lack of respect might cause you trouble."

"They better not try," Brandon said belligerently. And Hayley felt tempted to agree with him. But Dr. Faust was shaking his head. "It could cause your parents trouble to show them a lack of respect. It's better to give them the bow and avoid the trouble."

Bernhard Moser was one of the better qualified applicants to the race track work force. He was a journeyman blacksmith who had been let go when his master had gotten a steam hammer. The master had three journeymen working for him, including his two sons. So Bernhard was the one who got cut when the steam hammer had arranged for them to need one less worker. He was a friendly sort and had the solid muscles expected of a blacksmith. Better yet, he was at least a little familiar with steam hammers. Ron Sanderlin hired him on the spot to work in the shop. Bernhard started out on Fresno scrapers.

Vienna, Austria

"So far, sir," Bernhard told his contact, "it's just what you would expect. They are making Fresno scrapers, picks, shovels, all the sorts of things that you would expect to build a road. The up-timers themselves seem friendly and down-to-earth, but they have a truly horrible accent." Bernhard shook his head. "It's like nothing I've ever heard before.

"This is not about the up-timers themselves, but one thing. The housekeeper that the Fortneys hired is Annemarie Eberle, and I am fairly sure she works for Janos Drugeth."

"Did she recognize you?"

"I don't think so. It wasn't that we had ever worked together, but someone pointed her out to me once when she was acting as an under maid in the palace."

The contact nodded. "Come and see me once a week for now. If anything urgent comes up, you know the signals."

"Yes, sir."

Race Track at Simmering, Austria

The unemployment situation in Vienna became increasingly clear over the next few days, demonstrated not by numbers reported on TV, since they didn't get any TV in Austria, but by the numbers of people showing up looking for work on the new race track. Ron Sanderlin couldn't hire them all; he couldn't even hire an appreciable fraction of them. At the same time, he hated turning away hungry people.

"Sonny, can you hire some of these guys to do something, anything?" Ron asked their third day in Simmering.

"What? Why me?"

"Well, you know." Ron shrugged. He didn't want to come right out and say *can you get your teenage daughter to hire a bunch of these people*? The up-timers had only been dealing with newly rich relatives since the Ring of Fire and asking those newly rich relatives for money was handled in different ways by different people. Everything from the assumption that what they had was yours to *I'll starve before I drag them down with me*. It became especially difficult if those newly rich relatives were sons and daughters, because of the embarrassment factor. "Why am I still a working stiff when little Billy—or, in this case, little Hayley—has managed to turn herself into a millionaire?"

The elder Fortneys took a not-fanatical hands-off approach. They didn't ask Hayley for money or stock tips but if she volunteered they would mostly let her help if it wasn't going to endanger her future prospects. Ron knew, for instance, that Hayley had offered to pay for the tutor. Which Sonny and Dana had agreed to, but the maid was paid by Dana.

"I know how you feel, Ron, but..."

Just then another person showed up. He wasn't a prepossessing fellow. He was balding, with bad teeth and a wart over his right eye. But it was also clear that he was desperate for work.

Ron looked at Sonny then back at the man. "Check back in a couple of days. I can't promise anything, but maybe we'll have something."

After the guy had left, Ron just looked at Sonny.

"I'll talk to Dana. That's the best I can do," Sonny said.

Fortney House, Simmering, Austria

Sonny talked to Dana and Dana talked to Hayley.

"The thing is, Mom, I'm not really all that good at business." Hayley looked around the sitting room in their new home as though she could find the explanation in the whitewashed walls. "That's mostly Susan, Millicent and Vicky. I'm the tech geek. In most of the businesses we've taken over, it wasn't that the tech didn't work. It was that the business didn't work."

"I understand, Hayley, and neither your father nor I want you to endanger your future over this. It's just really hard to say no to hungry people looking for work."

"I'm not saying no. At least not yet. Let me think about it. Okay?" Hayley looked around the sitting room again. There were windows with glass in the standard down-time diamond pattern, a big fireplace with no fire at the moment. A polished wood floor with a rug. It was a nice room in a nice country house, that was easily three times the size of their place back in Grantville. No indoor plumbing. Instead they had people lining up to empty their chamber pots. No microwave, electric toaster or natural gas oven. In this day and age, cooks worked from before dawn to after nightfall to make bread and stew. It was, to Hayley, as if the Ring of Fire had just happened.

"Dr. Faust?" Hayley knocked on the third door of the third floor room.

"Just a moment."

Hayley waited as Dr. Faust got himself together. Then he opened the door to a room that was a bit bigger than a closet but not much. There was a bed about the size of a camp cot, but probably not as comfortable and a stack of books on the floor.

"What can I do for you, Miss Hayley?"

"Do you know anything about business law as it is practiced in Austria?"

"No, I'm sorry. I studied natural philosophy and for a while medicine, but the law never held any interest for me. Why?"

"Well, do you know anyone who does?" Hayley asked.

Dr. Faust looked at her a moment. "Jakusch Pfeifer was studying law to work with his family in shipping, but they lost several craft, ah, upriver. They had to stop going that far and he's short of tuition money. But again, why?"

"Just a plan Mom and Dad are thinking about."

As it happened, Dana Fortney was the keeper of the family accounts, as was Gayleen Sanderlin for the Sanderlin family. Between them they had a pretty complete listing of what the families had brought to Vienna. It was quite a lot. It included a Higgins Sewing Machine, a typewriter—also down-time made—an adding machine, but not, unfortunately, a computer. The Sanderlins had had a computer, but they sold it to the Higgins Hotel when they moved to Vienna. They had Brandon's rabbits, his roosters and hens and thirty-eight chicks that were starting to turn into cockerels and pullets, and a rosin foam incubator ready for the next batch. There was a lot more stuff on the list.

"I can't run the business on my own, Mom," Hayley said. "If you and Dad want me to hire people, you and Mrs. Sanderlin get to keep the books. And keeping those books is liable to end up as a full-time job for the both of you. We're going to need extra household servants, because between the lack of things like vacuum cleaners..."

"We knew we were going to need servants when we came, Hayley," Dana said. "We already have two maids and a cook. Not to mention Dr. Faust and—"

"But not how many, Mom," Hayley said. "We're not going to have a couple of maids to help out; we're going to have staff. A cook and probably two undercooks, four or five maids and an overmaid to run them. Also a couple of groundskeepers. And the Sanderlins are going to need the same because you and Mrs. Sanderlin won't have time for housework, not even for much in the way of supervising. Neither I or Brandon is going to have time for chores, because Brandon—the little creep—is going to be managing the groundskeepers. Teaching them about those silly rabbits and chickens of his and modern corn, tomatoes, watermelons and stuff. And I'm going to be looking for stuff to build using what we have. Not to mention instructing master craftsmen in the crafts they have spent the last forty years learning. Between that and our school work, we won't have time to turn around."

"Do we really need all that?" Gayleen Sanderlin asked.

"No, of course not, Mrs. Sanderlin. But the people out there waiting around hoping to be hired... *they* need it. If we are going to do more than set up a soup kitchen for the poor of Vienna, we need to get things organized so that the business pays for itself after the initial investment. Even if we were just setting up a soup kitchen, we would need staff to run it and it would take up a fair amount of time."

"Why not hire people to manage the business instead of to do the cooking?" Hayley's mom asked. "I'd rather cook than do accounts."

"Because we don't know them, Mom. Sure, I figure most people are basically honest, but if they start looking at us as rich idiots with more money than sense, at least some of them are going to decide that it's not really wrong to rip us off."

At that point both women nodded. A lot of up-timers, including the Sanderlins, had gotten suckered in the first few months after the Ring of Fire. Often by people who wouldn't even think of such a thing when dealing with a fellow down-timer. Up-timers were often seen as rich sheep to be sheared, who had arrived with too much wealth and too little sense, easy marks who deserved to be taken, because of their naivety, wealth and arrogance.

Hayley continued, "We have to be seen to know what we're doing."

"So you'll be in charge of the business?" Mrs. Sanderlin asked.

"No. I'll put up the money, or most of it, and I'll advise about which products are buildable. If you guys want to do this, it's going to have to be you, Dad and Mr. Sanderlin, maybe both Mr. Sanderlins... but with them busy working on the emperor's projects, you two will be the ones actually running the business. I shouldn't be in charge for a couple of reasons. One is that it's going to be really hard for them to take me seriously as the boss. The other is... well, you've had people coming to you for two weeks looking for work. I've had it for two years. Since Karl and Ramona's wedding. 'Invest in this, give me a loan for that.' It was bad enough just being part of the Barbies. I don't want it to be all on me.

"And that's another thing... we want to keep the business under the radar as much as we can. Because if you think people looking for work is bad, wait till you get hit by people looking for investors. You don't want to turn them down because it's their dream you're killing. But suppose it's a really crappy idea? Or it's a good idea, but they aren't the people to run it? Another reason to keep quiet is because even if it's not a zero sum game, there are winners and losers. Just the fact that some people get jobs from us is going to pis...ah, upset people, the people who wanted to hire them for starvation wages. And if the business gets too big, they will try to shut us down. We don't have Mike Stearns and the army to protect us this time. All we've got is Emperor Ferdinand's interest in cars. If we get to be too much trouble, he'll stick the cars in the garage and send us packing or lock us in a dungeon somewhere."

"I'm starting to think maybe this wasn't such a good idea," Dana said.

"It's not, Mom. But you and Dad are right about one thing. Creating jobs for people is the right thing to do, even if it's not the smart thing. If we're careful, we can help a lot of people before they shut the business down. If we're careful enough, they might *not* shut it down."

Fortney House, Simmering, Austria

Annemarie Eberle showed Herr Pfeifer into the sitting room and then went out to fetch coffee.

Jakusch Pfeifer smiled at the three women. Two were older than he was and the third was younger. He wondered why she was here but didn't let it show on his face.

"Have a seat, Herr Pfeifer," said one of the older women. "I'm Gayleen Sanderlin. This is Dana Fortney and her daughter, Hayley."

Once Jakusch was seated, it was Dana Fortney who got down to business. "What can you tell us about business law and the management of trade in Vienna?"

"Not as much as I would like, if you're talking about the guild restrictions on manufacturing in Vienna itself. On the other hand, you aren't in Vienna. You are three miles outside it, and I am familiar with the laws governing trade into and out of the city. Vienna's rules don't apply here."

"Yes..." Hayley paused a moment. "I guess it's a pretty long walk from Vienna to the race track."

"It's not so bad," Herr Pfeifer said. "Only four miles and I caught a ride with Cousin Paul. The race track is only a mile or so from the Danube. Though, it is a bit muddy right at the shore."

The maid laid down the coffee service and Mrs. Sanderlin thanked her.

Dana Fortney smiled. "You know all those stories grandparents tell, Hayley? The ones about walking two miles in the snow to get to school."

"Yes," Hayley muttered, not really paying attention, "uphill in both directions."

"I'm starting to think that at some point, maybe in my grandparent's day, there was some truth to them."

"Um." Hayley still wasn't paying that much attention, Herr Pfeifer noticed. He looked at Frau Fortney, then at Hayley. Frau Fortney grinned a bit and touched a finger to her lips. Hayley was oblivious to it all.

"The workers, to come from Vienna to the track each day and go back each night, have to walk four miles, sometimes more. It's shorter from the banks of the Danube and if we were to use the Fresno scrapers to dig a canal and put in a dock next to the track, it would change a two-hour walk each way to a comfortable half-hour boat ride. That would be worth paying for."

"It would also make it easy for people to come see the cars race around the track," Dana agreed. "Maybe it's something that Ron ought to talk to Emperor Ferdinand about."

"Yes," Hayley said. "As soon as he can get an appointment."

"It's too expensive," Herr Pfeifer said. "How many people working on the track can afford even a pfennig a day for just a ride to work, much less two?"

"More than you might think, but we'll give them a bargain anyway," Hayley said. "Sell boat passes that are good for a month for twenty-five pfennig each, or even twenty."

"Or you could do it like some of the bus companies did uptime," Frau Fortney said. "Sell tickets and give your boatman a paper punch. The ticket has however many circles or boxes printed on it. Each time they ride, the captain or someone punches out a circle or box on the pass. When they're all used up, they have to buy a new ticket."

Herr Pfeifer wasn't sure what they were talking about, but decided to let it ride for now. "However they pay, it costs money to run a barge on the river."

"Sure, but not that much," said the young girl. "Put in seats and maybe an awning to keep people dry when it rains. There are around a hundred people who come out here every day, working on the track. Fifty people per trip and four trips a day—two here, two back. That's two hundred tickets at a half pfennig per head...a hundred pfennig a day, every day. A bit over a reichsthaler every three days, gross. Your boatman will get a couple of groschen a day and there will be docking fees...but even with the cost of the boat and steam engine amortized in, you should make a decent regular profit. Not a great big profit, but a steady one." Two groschen a day was fair pay for a worker. It was what the day laborers at the race track were getting. But the surprising thing for Hayley—all of the girls, for that matter—was what a groschen would buy. There were twelve pfennig to a groschen. In Grantville or Magdeburg a pfennig was about equal to a quarter, but you could buy a small loaf of bread, about half a pound, for a pfennig in Vienna. Gayleen Sanderlin had said several times that it was like the prices in Mexico, back up-time.

By the end of their conversation, several things had happened. One was that Jakusch Pfeifer got his name shortened to Jack. He also figured out that Hayley Fortney was actually running things, not Frau Fortney acting for her husband. Perhaps more importantly, he was smart enough to guess some of the reasons for the subterfuge and to keep the secret. Jack became the lawyer for the Sanderlin-Fortney Investment Company and Jack's family got in on the ground floor of the Vienna ferry business.

Annemarie reported two days later, when she had her contact, that the Sanderlins were going to try to build a canal to the race track. She didn't report that it was the women arranging it. She just assumed that they were acting on instructions from their husbands.

It took Bernhard Moser an extra couple of days to report the development. Not because of any incompetence on his part, but simply because he was working out at the shop and it had taken a couple of days for the news to come up in conversation.

Vienna, Austria

"They seem harmless enough," Bernhard told his contact. "Even the canal they want to build seems to mostly be about giving people work."

"And who's going to pay for the work?" his contact asked. "That money's got to come from somewhere and I don't see where."

"Neither do I," Bernhard acknowledged. "Then again, I'm not an up-timer."

It wasn't a really satisfying meeting. Not because Bernhard had been unable to get the information. About the only thing he had missed was that Hayley Fortney was the one in charge. He'd even figured out that it was the women running things. Mostly that was by the process of elimination, because he couldn't see Ron Sanderlin—or either of the other two men—running a business. But Hayley Fortney was just a teenaged girl. The idea that such a person could be able, much less trusted, to manage large sums of money and major projects was so ridiculous that it never even occurred to him. As well to think it was all being run by Brandon's chickens.

Magdeburg, United States of Europe

Francisco Nasi brought up the next report. He'd already read it, of course, so all he needed to do was give the contents a quick scan to refresh his memory.

"This is from our correspondent in Austria."

Mike Stearns got a crooked little smile on his face. "'Correspondent.' Sounds so much nicer than 'spy.' I assume we're talking about Sonny Fortney, right? Or is that 'need to know' and I don't?"

Nasi pursed his lips. "Interesting protocol issue, actually. Since you're the head of government, I suppose you technically need to know everything. In any event, you're my employer, so if you tell me you need to know I'll take your word for it."

Mike shook his head. "I'm not sure how that worked back up-time. At a guess, judging from the screw-ups, the CIA and the other spook outfits didn't tell the U.S. president more than half of what they should have. In our case..."

He pondered the problem, for a moment. "I'll take your word for it, whether I need to know something or not. Just make sure you let me know there's something I might or might not need to know in the first place. If the grammar of that sentence doesn't have you writhing in agony."

Nasi smiled. "In this case, as it happens, Sonny really is more in the way of a correspondent than a spy. He does report to me—as I'm sure the Austrians have already figured out—but I don't have him creeping around listening at keyholes or peeping into windows."

"For that, I assume you have other people. Call them 'real spies.'"

"I don't believe you need to know that, Prime Minister."

"Spoilsport. So what's happening in Austria?"

"To summarize... The Austrians are adjusting to the American presence. More slowly and with greater difficulty than they should, of course, but they're doing better than I expected."

He set down the report. "But it's very early days—and now we have a new emperor. Ferdinand III will be one mainly setting the tone and the pace."

CHAPTER 11

Dealing with the New Emperor

September and October 1634

Race Track at Simmering, Austria

"Did you point a gun at Baron Julian von Meklau?" Emperor Ferdinand III asked Ron Sanderlin as he entered the garage. It had taken a while for word to reach the emperor and Ron wondered if the youngsters had talked or just someone that had seen the confrontation.

"Uncle Bob did, Your Majesty. But only because it looked like the boy was going to try and take a horsewhip to me." Ron looked at the retinue that followed the emperor around everywhere. "Mostly it was to warn the kids off so things didn't get out of hand." Ron considered, then added, "Actually, I'm a little surprised that there hasn't been more trouble. We've had a lot of gawkers, but no one trying to take anything. And aside from von Meklau and his friends, no one trying to throw their weight around."

"Now that I think about it, Herr Sanderlin, I'm a little surprised myself." Ferdinand motioned and Ron followed him out of the garage to the muddy field. The gaggle of hangers-on surrounded them both. Ferdinand III continued, "This is to be the road for the 240Z?"

"The track, yes," Ron told him and went on to explain what he, Bob, and Sonny had worked out. There were several side trips into up-time terminology, what an automobile race track was and how it differed from a horseracing track.

About halfway through the explanation, Ferdinand interrupted. "Take me for a ride."

"Your Majesty..." Ron started to object, then seeing the excited expression on the emperor's face, gave in. It was his car, after all. They got Ferdinand in the passenger seat with the seat belt fastened. Then Ron put the key in the ignition and Ferdinand stopped him.

"What's that?"

"The key."

"Like a key to a lock?"

"Yes, Your Majesty. You can't start the car without it." Ron chose not to get into the whole issue of hot wiring.

"That's clever. But what if the key is lost?"

"We have three sets, Your Majesty. I had one and Gayleen had one before the Ring of Fire and we had a metal smith make up another one when we sold you the car." More time was spent while Ron showed the emperor the key and that it was a perfectly ordinary piece of metal, nothing particularly high tech.

Finally Ron got to start the car, describing what he was doing as he did it. He pulled the car out of the converted barn and drove it around the muddy field. It had rained last night, sleeted actually, and then thawed this morning, soaking the ground. Ron was careful and the field was still covered in grass, so they managed a loop, with only a little sliding. It was a slow loop. Ron didn't think they had topped fifteen miles an hour.

"I want to drive!" the emperor said. Ron tried, without much hope, to talk him out of it, then traded seats.

By this time, Sonny and Bob were watching, as well as a couple of crowds of down-timers. There were the villagers and the courtiers—not mixing—and the workers that Ron and Sonny had hired—not really mixing with either group, but closer to the villagers.

Ferdinand III did fairly well. He had the standard gas-brakes-gas issues of new drivers, but not bad. And he had good control for the first loop. He started speeding up on the second loop. When he hit the back end of the second loop, he pushed it and they were doing thirty-five into the next turn. Two previous trips over the same ground had ripped up the grass that was holding the mud together. When they started to turn, the rear wheels decided that Newton's first law of motion should guide their actions, since friction was on a vacation. The emperor slammed down on both the gas and the brake pedal, and the 240Z did a 540 degree turn. They stopped, facing the way they'd come, rear wheels buried in mud up to their axles and the front wheels not much better off. The combination of brakes and gas had killed the engine and—Ron sincerely hoped—flooded it.

Ferdinand III sat still for several seconds, his white-knuckled hands gripping the plastic steering wheel hard enough that Ron was afraid he might break it. Then he took several deep breaths and smiled. "My, that was exciting."

Ron took a couple of deep breaths of his own. "Yes, Your Majesty."

Ferdinand III reached for the keys again.

"You may have flooded the engine, Your Majesty."

"Flooded it?"

Ron explained. The emperor listened. Then, with his foot carefully off the gas pedal and the car in park, turned the key. It started right up. The emperor grinned and Ron suppressed a groan.

The emperor put it in drive, and hit the gas. The wheels spun and mud flew.

All this had taken a few minutes and about the time the emperor hit the gas, there were half a dozen people of high estate in range of the flying mud. They retreated faster than they'd come, but the car didn't move more than an inch. And as soon as Ferdinand let of the gas, the car settled back into the mud.

"We're stuck, Your Majesty. You might as well turn it off and save the gas. We'll have to pull it out."

Ferdinand looked rebellious, but after a moment he turned off the car and unbuckled his seat belt. He opened the driver side door, and swung his legs out of the car. The imperial boots sank half way up the calves, in peasant mud. It was a good thing he had hands to help him or the emperor of Austria-Hungary would have landed face first in the mud.

Ron was expecting royal distaste, at least. He didn't get it. Ferdinand had ridden horses all his life, and even if there was usually a groom to handle the beast when he was done, Ferdinand was familiar with the effects of hooves on muddy ground and was unsurprised to find out that spinning wheels had a similar effect.

It was a few minutes later, back in the barn-cum-garage, that the emperor expressed his will. "Yes, I want a race track and a good one. In the meantime, just to avoid any trouble, I'm going to assign a small troop of soldiers to you out here."

"Where are these troops going to sleep?" Dana Fortney asked.

"That's a good question," Ron Sanderlin agreed. "Your Majesty, we're already pretty crowded."

It worked out that they were authorized to use the workers they were hiring to build the track to construct housing for the troops and to expand the garage and houses they had, but the Sanderlins and Fortneys would have to pay for the materials out of their own pocket. Over the next weeks, they bought bricks, stone, and wood, shipped in on the Danube. Using those materials along with the goods they had brought with them and locally done metal work, they expanded their homes and added housing for the squad of soldiers assigned to them. Fifteen men with their wives and children. Also their horses, because it was a cavalry troop commanded by Erwin von Friesen, an imperial knight. The garage gained room for the Sanderlin's truck and the Fortney's Range Rover. All of the construction had to be overseen by someone.

Docks, Vienna, Austria

"What does it look like, Dad?" Hayley asked. The Pfeifer family had a steam barge that they had built from up-time instruction sheets, which were fairly vague and incomplete. That information was filtered through the knowledge and preconceptions of the local smiths and scholars.

"Well, it's a steam engine," Sonny Fortney said, wiping his hands on a greasy rag. "Two pistons and it does have rods, but there is a gap of almost a sixteenth of an inch between the cylinders and the cylinder heads. And that is a very good thing, because if that sucker ever built up a good head of steam, it would blow up. The gap was inconsistent—only that wide in a couple of places."

"What about the boiler?"

Sonny shrugged. "It's a pot boiler, not a tube boiler."

"Can you fix it?"

"If I had time. But I don't. I have the grading of the race track and the digging of the basement for the barracks for Erwin von Friesen and his boys. The expansion of the garage. I can advise your people and they can fix it."

"Can't Ron and Bob do that?"

"Part of it, but I'm going to have to do the surveying. I don't trust the wells. We're too close to the Danube and the water table is too high. So Dana is going to be busy testing the water. Bob is working out what goes where with the brewery." One of their neighbors was a brewery in Simmering. "And Gayleen is running the kitchen to feed the workers..."

As it happened, Hayley got the job of delivering the instructions on rebuilding the steam engine on the Pfeifer barge.

Peter Krause's Smithy, Vienna, near the docks

"No. You see that piece of heavy paper there?" Hayley Fortney pointed at the gasket. It was twenty sheets of thick down-time-made rag paper, glued together, rolled through a wringer to eliminate any air pockets, and then waxed. It had taken Hayley almost a week to get it made. That was all right, though. It was taking just as long to get the cylinders and the pistons remade. And like Dad had said, it was probably a good thing that they had not had proper gaskets, because the boiler was the real issue. It was a steel pot with the lid welded on, and a hole cut into that, with a copper pipe coming out and going to the engine. It took the thing upwards of thirty minutes to build up a head of steam and there was very little in the way of controlling the steam.

Meanwhile, Peter Krause was looking like he would really like to kill her and she almost didn't blame him. He was forty-five years old, a master smith and it was understandable that he wasn't thrilled to be told how to do his job by a teenage girl. Unlike most of the people she had dealt with since the Ring of Fire, Peter Krause had never seen the Ring Wall and wasn't sure he believed in it. Hayley sighed. "Look, no matter how good you are, no two metal pieces fit so perfectly that gas can't pass between them. You know that. You know that the steam engine you built leaks. You've suffered burns from the escaping steam."

Herr Krause nodded grudgingly.

"Well, it's not because you aren't a good smith. It's because the tolerances are simply too fine for any smith. That's why the gasket and flange arrangement. The gasket deforms to fit the minor irregularities that are going to be there. The only thing I have ever seen that didn't have those irregularities was the Ring Wall itself, and that only right after it happened. The only hand that can cut that smooth is the hand of God. So the rest of us have to accept imperfection and figure out ways around it."

Herr Krause wasn't smiling, but the left side of his mouth was twitching up just a little. "Well enough," he said. "The gasket is because no mortal hand is perfect, but it's paper. How do you expect paper to withstand the pressure that you claim the good steel of my cylinder won't withstand? It's paper!"

"Right, it's paper. But it is compressed by the bolts. There is a rule about the gaskets. The harder they are pressed, the stronger they are. That is why my dad insisted on so many bolts holding the parts together."

Hayley hid a sigh. This was taking a long time.

Sanderlin Home, Simmering, Austria

"No, Mrs. Sanderlin, nothing too big or grand. I'd like to hire hundreds of people, too. But it would make too much noise."

"But we can order a hundred sewing machines from Grantville and you know you could get them."

"No. If I order a hundred I'll get ten and a polite note from Karl Schmidt telling me that he will get us the rest as soon as he catches up with his back orders. Which ought to be sometime around the year 1700."

"Well, then, why don't we start our own sewing machine factory? You can get the machines, can't you?"

"Maybe. But it would be a major investment and, for all I know, we would be burned out by irate tailors. Look, we'll hire your friend Maria Bauer's husband and set up a tailor shop out by the race track the emperor is building. But we can't hire everyone."

Gayleen Sanderlin went away disappointed, and truthfully Hayley was disappointed herself.

Fortney House, Simmering, Austria

"It's called casein and it's made from milk and vinegar," Dana Fortney said to the delegation of widows and orphans that she had gathered for the casein case venture. They were in the outdoor kitchen just behind the house and the women were standing around a long trestle table. It was a sunny fall afternoon, and the smell of vinegar was having to fight against the scent of flowers and mown hay on the breeze. "We use stamps and hot milk and vinegar. We stamp it into shapes and let the shapes sit for a few days. Then we varnish it. Now, I have never done this myself, but I have instructions on how to do it. We will be providing the raw materials and working with you on making stuff. Let me walk you through a sample batch."

Carefully following the instructions from the cheat sheet, Dana made a small batch of casein. Once it was rinsed in cool water, she put the blob in the mold they had had made and pressed it in. It came out in pieces. Well, it was her first try.

Within a few days, the ladies of the casein factories were producing casein items. They had been moved to a empty room in the brewery. It took a few hundred dollars of wasted milk for them to get the hang of it, but after that they could make casein buttons and clasps, knitting needles and crochet hooks, boxes and bottles and lids.

Simmering, becoming Race Track City

There were buildings going up around the race track and new shops in each building. The casein shop had shelves full of items made out of casein plastics, but that wasn't the only place that casein was used. There were casein buckles on the boots made by the boot maker, and casein buttons on the pants and shirts. Also casein eyeglasses frames were made by a craftsman from the University of Vienna. The man had been making eyeglasses since long before the Ring of Fire. The little industries in the area around Ferdinand III's race track were starting to feed off each other.

Better yet, the steam barge was finally up and running. And they were selling tickets to more than just the workers on the track. More people were walking out to see the track than were taking the shuttle barge, but enough were taking the barge so that they were making an extra trip every day for tourists.

✧　　✧　　✧

Ron Sanderlin watched with considerable amusement as the 240Z made its way around the track. He didn't know Janos Drugeth, but he had seen the man's uncle. Pal Nadasdy had been the next best thing to incoherent after his ride a few days before. The 240Z slid a bit going around the far curve but the emperor got it back under control well enough. Ron was wondering how the cavalry officer and spy master was going to manage. Ron glanced at his uncle. "Think he'll barf like the banker did?" The elder Abrabanel had gotten a ride, and thrown up in the car seat. Which they had had to clean.

"Could be." Bob Sanderlin gave a twitch of his shoulders that was not quite a shrug.

"Doubt it," said Sonny as they moved out from the garage as the car came in. "He's a cavalry officer."

"So?" asked Bob.

"He's got stuff to prove."

Bob's shoulders gave that half-twitch again, and he and Ron headed out to open the doors.

"Nice recovery on that last turn, Your Majesty," Ron offered as he opened the door for the emperor. Bob didn't say anything as he opened the door for Drugeth. Bob now had dentures, but for most of his life he had had bad teeth and he had a tendency to keep his mouth closed out of old embarrassment. Especially around people he didn't know well.

"It worked splendidly! Just as you said!" The emperor was grinning like a kid.

A moment later Drugeth lurched out of the car and stood stiff-legged beside it.

The emperor put his hands on his hips and looked around the race track. At this point it was just dirt, shaped by Fresno scrapers. But the emperor seemed pleased. "You were right, Ron," he announced. "We need to build up the banks of the track on the curves."

"Yup. Even at only sixty miles an hour, which is nothing for a 240Z, you almost spun out. Of course, it'll help a lot once we can replace that packed dirt with a solid surface. Tarmac, at least, although concrete would be better."

Ferdinand nodded. "We can manage that, I think, given a bit of time. We'll need to build spectator stands also."

He turned to Janos, smiling widely. "We'll call it the Vienna 500, I'm thinking. You watch! One of these days, it'll draw enough tourists to flood the city's coffers."

The expression on Janos Drugeth's face was a study. Clearly, he had no idea what the emperor was talking about. But Ron knew. It was Ron who had suggested the idea.

The Hofburg Palace, Vienna, Austria

"Well, Your Majesty," Ron Sanderlin said, "if there were a canal to the race track there would be a lot more people coming out to watch you going round the track."

The emperor of Austria Hungary, who had renounced the title of Holy Roman Emperor, raised an eyebrow at Ron Sanderlin. "It's only three miles. Hardly too far to walk. A canal, even a short canal, is very expensive. Why don't you have your friends the Pfeifers simply build a dock on the Danube at that point? It would only be a mile walk."

It was a good question and Ron didn't have a particularly good answer. He fell back on honesty. "Because people need work, Your Majesty. When we got here and the race track project got started, we were deluged with people who were desperate for work. And we've done what we can but it's not nearly enough. A project like the canal would employ hundreds of people, and at the same time it would make for an easy, quick transport from Vienna proper to Race Track City..."

People had started calling the area around the race track Race Track City a month or so ago, but just after he said it Ron realized that he didn't know if the emperor had heard the term. It also occurred to him that he didn't know what legalities were involved in being a city. He knew only vaguely that there were imperial cities that had imperial charters, and that Race Track City didn't have much of anything along those lines.

Fortunately, the emperor didn't seem to notice his gaffe. He just nodded and excused himself for a moment. When he came back, he had Reichsgraf Maximilian von Trauttmansdorff with him. After that, the emperor of Austria-Hungary sat back and watched as his chief negotiator skinned Ron Sanderlin and tanned his pelt for hanging on the wall.

"I sympathize with your intentions, Herr Sanderlin, but the royal purse isn't bottomless," Reichsgraf Maximilian von Trauttmansdorff said.

"Yes, Your Grace." Ron Sanderlin wished he had gotten a bit more advice from the Fortney girl about how to set up a partnership with the emperor. Except she had never done that either. "Well, we were thinking maybe a partnership of some sort, if we can come up with the money or rather part of the money to build the canal...?" He let the question trail off, not wanting to ask, "What do we get out of it?"

"How much of the funding would you be putting up?" Trauttmansdorff asked.

"That depends, sir." Well, there was no getting around it. Ron plunged in. "What are we going to get out of it? I mean if we put up, say, half the money to dig the canal, what do we get?"

"What do you want?"

"Clear title to some of the land around the race track and a farm for the seeds and stuff we brought."

"How much land?"

Ron pulled out a map. The area had been surveyed by Sonny Fortney and he had clearly delineated the area between the race track and the Danube. Up to now that area had belonged to the emperor. The Sanderlins and Fortneys had simply had the use of it as part of their employment agreement. They had stretched that pretty far in setting up businesses, but they had gotten permission for each business. Now Ron showed Ferdinand III and Reichsgraf Trauttmansdorff a map of a good-sized town, almost half a mile across in either direction, but that included the race track and canal, centered just northeast of the race track. It was small compared to Vienna and tiny compared to an up-time city, but it was clearly a town. It included the race track and room for up to fifty separate businesses. There was already an agreement between Brandon and the chief gardener at the emperor's hunting lodge to have Brandon and some of the gardeners plant the up-time plants come spring. But the plan expanded that into a village between the hunting lodge and Race Track City.

Again, it was stuff that they had sort of started on already, but on a semi-official basis.

Ron pointed at the map. "The parts that are crosshatched would be ours and the rest would be the crown's to do with as you like, but you might want to put some businesses in from here to here. That will be prime real estate as the town grows up." At least that was what Hayley had said, and it made sense.

Trauttmansdorff was not one to take the first offer though. "For that you ought to pay for the whole canal." But he was smiling when he said it.

They spent half an hour bargaining back and forth, and by the end of it Ron Sanderlin knew he had been skinned good and proper. A fact Hayley Fortney confirmed with loud lamentation as soon as she heard the results.

Fortney House, Race Track City

"We're going to be overrun with *Hofbefreiten* and we get to pay most of the cost of building the canal for the privilege," Hayley pointed out.

"What are holfbitten?" Dana wanted to know.

"People. People who have a special status. *Hofbefreiten* means court-freed or court-exempted. The way it works is that they pay the court for the privilege of providing stuff to the court. Anything from socks to carriages to coffeecake, and they get to sell stuff to the general public without paying the local taxes, the *onera*. Which can be quite onerous."

Gayleen groaned and Dana made to whack her daughter.

Hayley ducked and continued. "He must have figured it out before you even finished talking about the effect of the canal."

"Figured what out?" Bob Sanderlin asked, moved to rare speech by his confusion.

"That the steam ferry and the canal make Race Track City *effectively* part of Vienna, but not *legally* part of Vienna. Which gives all of Race Track City effective *Hofbefreiten* status without him having to officially do it, so the burghers who do have to pay *onera* won't start screaming till it's too late. Remember, they pay for the privilege of being *Hofbefreiten* and that's money in Ferdinand's pocket. I figured he'd insist on us paying for more of the canal and give us more of the property to dispose of, but he saw the potential. He can move *Hofbefreiten* out here to Race Track City and it will seem like a big concession to the burghers. And he can sell *Hofbefreiten* status to new craftsmen too. Make his tenants out here official *Hofbefreiten*. He'll recover his whole share of the cost of the canal in the first year's rents."

"Well then, you should have done it yourself," Ron groused. "I never claimed to be David Bartley."

CHAPTER 12

The Nebulous Beginnings

November 1634

Liechtenstein House, Vienna

Gundaker von Liechtenstein was not overly distressed by the emperor's interest in the cars. Quite the contrary. The more time Ferdinand III spent playing with his new toy, the less time he would spend on interfering with older, wiser heads in the managing of the government. With the Edict of Restitution revoked, a whole new round of lawsuits had been issued. Protestant churches were demanding their buildings back. Protestant nobles and burghers were demanding their property back. As often as not, those properties had changed hands again after being returned to the Catholic church. Sometimes the same day. As it happened, Gundaker von Liechtenstein owned a number of them.

"It's vitally important that the revocation of the Edict not be interpreted to mean that those properties already returned to the church must be given back to heretics," Gundaker told one of the family's lawyers.

"Unfortunately, that seems to be the way Ferdinand III is leaning."

"Then the cases need to be decided below the imperial level, and appeals to the crown need to be delayed in the courts long enough so that there is time to persuade the headstrong boy that such a policy would be an unholy and impious act."

After the lawyer had left, Maximilian cautioned his brother. "Be careful how you refer to His Majesty, even with our own people. I'm not overly thrilled with the effect the revocation of the Edict will have on our family's property either, but he is the emperor."

In the cathedral of St. Stephens, Father Lamormaini was discussing the Sphere of Fire with his fellow Jesuits, and not getting very far.

"First of all, it's not exactly six miles across," said Father Fuhrmann. "It's a little over six miles across, or maybe a little less depending on whose miles you're using. I think that from Ring Wall to Ring Wall, it's six miles, two hundred seventeen feet, six and a half inches."

"It's six miles within any reasonable measure," Lamormaini insisted. "You said yourself 'depending on whose miles you're using.' It might be more or less than six miles."

"Second, it's not a sphere. Even if there was a sphere in the moment it occurred—and not all the accounts agree on that point—it's not one now. A half-sphere at best. That would make it six broad, six long, and only three high. Not the number of the beast. I grant it's a clever conceit, Father, but not evidence of a message from God."

Lamormaini stood, his face red. He had seen the truth as God had revealed it, and now Fuhrmann was splitting hairs to avoid the truth. "Father Fuhrmann..."

"No, Father. While His Holiness has not ruled on the matter, it would be worse than premature to attempt to preempt his decision. I will make note of your observations and send them to the Father General, but don't expect any action till His Holiness has had a chance to consider all the ramifications of his decision."

Lamormaini sat back down. He would write the Father General as well but—much as he hated to admit it—Fuhrmann was right, at least about the likely response of the Holy See. Still, he couldn't sit around and do nothing till His Holiness got around to noticing that Satan had arrived and the end days were upon them.

Inn in Vienna

"I need you to go to Grantville," Father Lamormaini said once they were seated and the tavern girl had left them their beers.

Friedrich Babbel didn't blink or let his surprise show in any way. "It will be expensive, Father." He wondered how much Lamormaini was willing to pay. The change in administration hadn't done Friedrich's prospects any good at all. Janos Drugeth was a sanctimonious prick who didn't want the reports adjusted to suit the listener, and that wasn't a practical attitude. Friedrich took another drink of beer while Father Lamormaini pondered his purse.

"Don't try to hold me up." Lamormaini's voice was laced with distrust, but there was a hint of desperation there, too.

"I'm not, Father. The simple truth is that the area around the Ring of Fire, and especially inside it, is the most expensive place to live and work in Europe. Rents are outrageous, food expensive, and the cost of labor is insane. A housemaid in Grantville earns what a master smith makes in the Viennese countryside."

"Their famous library is free."

"Yes and no, Father." Friedrich would have continued but Lamormaini waved him to silence. The old crook had enough money that he shouldn't have been arguing in the first place. Not that Lamormaini would ever admit that any of the money was for him. It was all for the church.

Lamormaini had used his position as confessor to Ferdinand II to acquire quite a bit of wealth. All for the church. Friedrich suppressed a laugh. Lamormaini hadn't taken bribes; he had accepted donations. "What is it you want me to find, Father?"

"It will be in their records somewhere. Probably hidden in plain sight. Find references to the devil!"

Friedrich felt his face twitch. But he didn't say anything as Lamormaini explained his theory about the true origin of the Ring of Fire.

Babbel left a few days later. He would find or create what the priest wanted.

Sanderlin House, Race Track City

"I would be happy to provide you with concrete for the race track, Herr Sanderlin," Baron Johannes Hass said. "Unfortunately, we are lacking in the equipment. When the crown granted me the patent on concrete, it wasn't yet known how difficult it would be to produce the stuff. I have had experts go to your libraries and it turns out that they need massive rotating kilns to make the Portland cement efficiently."

Ron was confused. Even after the Ring of Fire he hadn't been much interested in how concrete was made. Well, how Portland cement was made. He had poured a patio back in 1998 before the Ring of Fire, and he knew how to mix quicklime and aggregate in a wheelbarrow. The way you got the Portland cement was by going to Clarksburg and buying it at the Home Depot. He knew that after the Ring of Fire there had been a program to make concrete. It had worked, too. Portland cement was available in Grantville and Magdeburg. Expensive compared to up-time, but available. He hadn't learned how it was done but he knew they could do it. "Well, they make it in the USE. What about shipping in the Portland cement from there?"

"That would be very expensive. Also illegal, because the old emperor granted me the sole patent."

They talked some more but didn't get anywhere. Even though they were both speaking German, it seemed like they were talking a different language.

After his unsuccessful attempt to get concrete from Baron Hass, Ron looked into the possibility of blacktop. Asphalt, it turned out, was a petroleum byproduct. But Ron knew that they could use coal tar and there had to be coal around here somewhere. Didn't there?

Yes, there was coal, Ron discovered. But it was as yet mostly not found. The one bit of good news was the Danube. Shipping cost would be much less over a pretty long stretch, because of the Danube. The bad news was the patents that Ferdinand II had been issuing to anyone with the money to purchase one. Patents had been sold on most inventions and industrial processes brought back by the Ring of Fire. At least, on the ones that Austrians had found out about.

The Liechtenstein family owned a bunch of them, and so did lots of other wealthy nobles. Including the Abrabanels. Often enough, it wasn't even because they wanted them. More a case of the emperor saying, "Yes, I know that I owe you a fortune, but take this patent on helicopters and we'll call it even."

It was apparently pretty hard to say no to an emperor.

"It's almost tempting to buy some of these patents." Hayley nibbled on one of Frau Mayr's honey nut rolls. The woman was doing her best to make Hayley fat. "A bunch of people are offering to sell patents at a loss, and no one knows what they are worth."

"Are they worth anything?" Ron Sanderlin asked.

"Not in Grantville or the USE. But here? Maybe." Then Hayley shook her head. "No. At some point they are going to have to make peace and regularize the patent laws, and then almost all of these patents are going to be worthless. In the meantime, though, there are a bunch of relatively powerful people trying to get their money back on patents that they were forced to buy. It's going to make it hard to do much."

"What concerns me," Dana Fortney said, "is that any business we start is going to run into one of these patents. I wonder who owns the patent on casein and when we are going to get sued."

"That's a good point, Mom," Hayley said. "I think we need to have a talk with Jack. And maybe a talk with the emperor about his race track. Meanwhile, Mom, can you get an appointment with Moses Abrabanel? I am probably going to have to get some sort of money transfer from Grantville."

Abrabanel House, outside Vienna

Dana Fortney managed to get an appointment with Moses Abrabanel, but it took a week. She was simply the wife of the second assistant mechanic of the emperor's car. Sonny was out of town at the moment, working with a team of down-time surveyors to get started on the route for the railroad.

"Have a seat, Frau Fortney. What can I do for you?" Moses was a young man. About thirty, Dana guessed. Down-time thirty, which looked older to up-time eyes. He looked about her age. He wasn't balding, but his hairline was definitely in retreat. He wasn't fat, but was developing a bit of a paunch. He was well-dressed and bearded. The dress included the special feature that Jews were required to wear, but was of very good quality. The room was small like most down-time offices but there were file cabinets along one wall. They were wood, probably oak, she thought, and inlayed with a lighter wood, but definitely file cabinets. He also had an up-time style desk and chairs.

"Well, we're going to have to send home for some money," Dana said. "I understand that you have contacts with the Grantville national bank."

"Yes, I do. But I must admit to some surprise," Moses told her. "I am involved in the court payroll, and as per contract your family has been paid every month, as have the Sanderlins?"

Dana could hear the implied question. Not that it was any of his business. On the other hand, she knew perfectly well that a lot of people in Vienna resented the fact that the Sanderlins and Sonny were getting paid every month. She had learned after they got here that actually being paid by the crown was unusual. Also he might be able to help. "It's the patents. We have been putting people to work and a few days ago, on the emperor's instructions, Ron Sanderlin started looking into the possibility of getting concrete to pave the race track. It was then that we learned that the Holy Roman Empire had issued patents on the devices and techniques brought back in the Ring of Fire." Dana could hear her own resentment and tried to modify her tone. "There are no such restrictions in the USE and we were, until then, unaware of the restrictions here."

The youngish man winced a little. "It was necessary," he explained. "The tax base of the empire has been badly stressed by the military reverses we have suffered in the last few years, and yet the demands on the royal purse have only increased."

"In any case, it is an unexpected expense and we don't know how much it's going to cost."

"Perhaps I can help with that. I know a clerk in the office of patents who can probably tell who, if anyone, holds the patent on a specific product or process. And then I should be able to point you in the direction of the patent holder."

They talked some more and Moses agreed to make the necessary inquiries to establish a credit line from Grantville. A few days later, Dana sent him a list of products and processes that they were interested in. It turned out that no one owned the process of making casein. Someone did own the patent on sewing machines, but it was on making them, not using them.

They managed to buy the patent on the manufacture of plastic for the area around Vienna. The assumption had been that plastic was beyond the present ability of the up-timers, and the realization that casein was plastic hadn't penetrated the court. So the patent on plastic was not considered of any great value, at least not yet.

Sanderlin House, Race Track City

"This includes a lot of guesswork," Dana Fortney told Gayleen and Hayley. Then she took a sip of coffee and didn't grimace. She liked sugar in her coffee, but sugar was much more expensive than coffee here in Vienna. "What seems to have happened is some of the old emperor's agents sent back long lists of products and processes. Some of them very general, like plastics, and some very specific, like injection molding of toy soldiers. What they didn't send was much information about how any of it worked. That was left up to the people who bought the patents."

"They must have sold them to the very rich," Gayleen said. "Most people can't afford to send an agent to Grantville to figure out how to make..."

Dana was shaking her head. "You're right about most of the people not being able to send agents to Grantville. But that's not how they did it. Instead, people were encouraged to attend auctions and bid on something. The old emperor apparently didn't didn't care much what they bid on or how many patents they got as long as they spent enough money in total to fit their status at court. Some people bid the required amount on whatever came up and wasn't being bid up by other people."

"Why didn't anyone get plastic?" Hayley asked.

"Because it wasn't all that long after Delia Higgins' dolls hit Vienna and among the notes on the dolls was that they were made of plastic, a material that could be made up-time but not down-time. So everyone knew that plastic couldn't be made down-time."

"So it was all about the rumors of what could be done coming out of Grantville back in 1631?" Hayley more said than asked.

"Early 1632, but basically yes. The patent on the Bessemer steel process went for a pretty penny and the patent on the integrated circuit is still sitting there waiting for a buyer. So is the electric motor, by the way."

That added another job once the word got around. Patent consultant. Actually working on the car didn't take much time at all. Mostly it was keeping it clean—well, supervising the down-timers who kept it clean. It would be four more months at the earliest before it needed another oil change. And there was only so much time that they could spend on it. When the emperor came out, Ron and Bob had to be on hand just to show that they were doing something. But a car is not a horse. It doesn't need to be fed every day and its stall doesn't need to be mucked out. Nor does it need rubdowns every day. Every week is more than sufficient, and up-time the 240Z would have gotten a wax job every six months or so.

Sonny was busy enough working on surveying a railroad and designing steam engines to pull trains along it. But Ron and Bob found that good pay for little work was frustrating. Now they were constantly being called in to look over patents and try to tell the patent holder how to build whatever the patent was for.

Not the big ones like concrete or steam engines, but the little things that the lower-level courtier and the mid-level Them of Vienna had gotten stuck with. Clothespins and clipboards, eggbeaters and egg separators, safety pins and spatulas, that sort of thing.

Meanwhile, the owner of the coking patent wanted Ron to go over the notes on how coking worked to help get him into production.

Sanderlin's bedroom, Race Track City

"I hate this," Ron complained to Gayleen in late November. "I was never into books and you know the trouble I had in my senior year of high school." He waved the papers at her.

Gayleen did know. Ron was good with his hands, but he wasn't much for book learning. He never had been, which was why she was the one who handled the family finances. Ron had to sell the car to get the money to get his mom a place in one of the villages outside the Ring of Fire. And to sell the car, he had to provide a mechanic. That worked for Ron because he was a mechanic, and was one of the main reasons that they had beat out the other people who were interested in selling their cars.

Uncle Bob had never gotten along with Vera May, Ron's mom. In fact, Bob didn't want to stay in the same state as Ron's mom—an attitude Gayleen couldn't help but agree with. Nothing really wrong with Ron's mom, except she ruled whatever house she was in. In Gayleen's case, there was also the issue that Mother Teresa and Miss America combined wouldn't be good enough for her little Ronny. She looked over at her husband and tried not to grin. "Sorry, dear, but they are paying pretty good."

"They're paying damn good. I just wish Sonny was here to look at this stuff."

Ron had never told Gayleen outright, but she was pretty sure that Sonny Fortney was some sort of spy the government wanted to put in Vienna. It made her a bit nervous sometimes. "Why?"

"Because he was involved in the coking works that they set up in Saalfeld after the Ring of Fire."

"It seems like he was involved in everything after the Ring of Fire."

"He was. He was the go-to guy for the Mechanical Support division after the Ring of Fire. He worked on the natural gas conversion and the coking ovens. Then they moved him over to the surveying corp, and I don't know what all else. But he knew Treasury Secretary Wendell, Quentin Underwood and Chad Jenkins, that whole banking bunch, before the Ring of Fire. He could have been one of the financial movers and shakers."

"So why wasn't he?" Gayleen asked. Ron rarely talked about Sonny Fortney.

"He went to work for Mike Stearns and Frank Jackson," Ron told her. "There were some rumors when he got put in the mechanical support division. And it turns out, they were true."

"He's a spy," Gayleen said.

"Not exactly. He's more of a general fixer, I think." Ron looked over at her and Gayleen was surprised at how serious his expression was. "You remember what Mike said at the town meeting three days after the Ring? The part about starting the American Revolution early?"

Gayleen nodded.

"I think Sonny's been doing that ever since the Ring of Fire. That's why I agreed to let him come. 'Cause I believe in America. Up-time or down-time, it's still America. It's still the same truths that Jefferson talked about. And it's still the same stakes."

Gayleen nodded again. Though, if she was entirely honest, she really wished that it wasn't her and her babies risking their lives, fortunes, and sacred honor. She had no desire at all to see the inside of an Inquisition torture chamber.

The New Church at Race Track City

"They should be brought before the Inquisition," Father Lamormaini said, though not, Father Degrassi thought, with any great heat. "They are heretics, after all. And from what I understand, that woman Dana Fortney is something called a New Age spiritualist. They say she practices yoga...whatever that is."

That much was true, Father Degrassi knew. They were sitting in his apartments in the new church that had been built along with the other new buildings at Race Track City. He was in a delicate situation. He was a parish priest as well as a Jesuit, and in his parish the only people who weren't Catholic were the patricians of Race Track City. "I talked to Dana Fortney and she showed me her books on yoga. It's an interesting exercise, but hardly the work of the devil. Besides, they are under the protection of the emperor, and he knew that they were not Catholics before they were hired. And I think there is a real possibility of converting some of them."

"Secret up-timers." Lamormaini snorted.

"Cardinal Mazzare!" Father Degrassi shot back, even though he appreciated the wit of Lamormaini's play on "secret Jews."

"Politics. Mazzare is as much a political cardinal as is the cardinal-infante. Politics, not faith."

"We are Jesuits, Father, and Pope Urban has spoken."

"Not definitively."

Degrassi wasn't sure that Father Lamormaini was wrong, but he wasn't willing to push things. The truth was that the Ring of Fire had challenged his faith in way that he never would have expected, and he didn't know how to handle it. He was a cautious man by nature and his focus was on scholarship, so he was not going to be rushed into any position. As well, he rather liked Dana Fortney and was considering taking her yoga classes.

CHAPTER 13

𝕿𝖍𝖊 𝕯𝖊𝖋𝖊𝖈𝖙𝖔𝖗𝖘 𝕬𝖗𝖗𝖎𝖛𝖊

December 1634

Race Track City

"I heard that they killed someone in Grantville and that's why they ran," Gayleen Sanderlin said over coffee and pastries at the still-not-completed pastry shop. The shop was located about a hundred yards from the race track and mostly catered to the race track workers.

"I hadn't heard that," Dana Fortney said. "But we'll know when the next letter from Grantville arrives. Thurn and Taxis are really good. I was surprised at the speed they can deliver mail."

"Should we invite them over?" Hayley asked. "The up-timers, I mean, not Thurn and Taxis."

"Let's wait on that till we have a better handle on what happened," Ron Sanderlin said. "I don't know the Barclays, but Jay Barlow was one of that Club 250 bunch. For him to run off to live among down-timers, it would have to be something serious. I'm not sure that they are the sort of people we want to be involved with." Ron Sanderlin was a reasonably bright guy, however it was the "think with his hands" sort of bright, not the book learning sort of bright. He had made it through high school, but barely. He wasn't overly fond of the sort of self-important jerks who waved their credentials in everyone's face. That was one reason he still wasn't fond of Simpson, even if the guy had sort of reformed. This group, with Club 250 types and college grads who still couldn't make it in Grantville, didn't sound like anyone he wanted to meet.

University of Vienna

"No." Peter Barclay looked around the classroom, and saw the lectern that they called a desk. "I doubt the Fortneys and Sanderlins will be much help. They are no doubt decent enough people of their sort, but they lack the education to be of much help to us. As I understand it, they have but two high school diplomas between them, and no university training at all." Peter wasn't in any mood to deal with people from Grantville who would look at him and his companions as traitors in spite of the fact that they were here, too.

"That was my impression as well," Herr Doctor Himmler proclaimed from the lectern. "Craftsmen, useful at their craft, but lacking the understanding needed for higher callings."

Peter Barclay had no idea why Herr Doctor Himmler was so willing to agree with him. He didn't know that the doctor had heard about the Fortney family choosing Faust over himself to educate their children. Not, of course, that Herr Doctor Himmler would have taken the post had it been offered...but it should have been. All Peter Barclay knew was that Herr Doctor Himmler was clearly pleased to hear anything bad about the up-timers who were already residing in—or rather, near—Vienna. In fact, there were a number of the elite of Vienna who were pleased to hear anything bad about any up-timer. Especially members of the Fortney and Sanderlin clans.

Dr. Himmler asked a question about steam and Peter gave him the formula for the calories needed to turn water into steam. Then another professor asked him another question and he answered it. Peter knew a lot of this stuff of the top of his head as much because of the work he had been doing since the Ring of Fire as because of the engineering degree he had gotten years before. He explained that internal combustion was more efficient, working at higher temperatures, and that because of weight, aircraft engines would have to use internal combustion engines. He knew, but didn't point out, that up-time there had been at least one steam aircraft that had operated. However, he felt that with down-time tech the only way to make an engine that would work in a flying machine was internal combustion reciprocating engines. A project that he knew he was better qualified to lead than anyone else, even Hal Smith. Smith might be an *aeronautical* engineer, but Peter Barclay was a *mechanical* engineer, so knew more about the design of engines.

Fortney House, Race Track City

The mail arrived. There were letters from the Barbies to Hayley, from friends and family to the Sanderlins. Dana had one from her sister Holly, wanting reassurance that the evil Austrians weren't holding them prisoner, and Sonny had a rather long one from a down-time friend named Cavriani. It was quite a long letter, full of gossip including quite a bit about Istvan Janoszi who had recruited the Sanderlins and him, and apparently had also had a major hand in the recruitment of the defectors. Sonny was more than a little disappointed in Janos Drugeth. He had thought better of the man. Both as spy and as a man.

The first meeting with the defectors was stiffly formal and polite. The Barclays were brought to Race Track City to look over the race track and comment. Comment they did, but later. For now, they made notes.

Sonny showed them the race track and told them about his idea to bank the track on either end.

Ron showed them the 240Z and the garage. Peter and Marina Barclay made notes and asked questions.

The adults mostly ignored the children who were carefully doing the "seen and not heard" bit, partly because the kids on both sides were aware that there were politics involved and didn't want to be involved. And also because the kids—Hayley, Carla Ann, Brandon, and Thomas—knew each other from Grantville, having been in the same grades in the same schools.

"What are you guys doing about school?" Carla Ann asked. "I hate that we moved here before I graduated."

"There is a school here for young ladies," Hayley Fortney told her. "It's run by the Jesuitesses, the English Ladies. But I'm being tutored and taking correspondence courses."

"Why aren't you in the school?"

"I think I may not be high class enough." Hayley grinned. "After all, my dad's just the assistant auto mechanic for the emperor's car. Besides, I like having a tutor better."

Carla Ann nodded. *Of course Hayley Fortney of the Barbie Consortium has her own tutor. I'll be lucky to get tuition to the English Ladies' school.*

"How are your rabbits?" Thomas Barclay asked Brandon.

"Acting like rabbits." Brandon grinned. "Velma has another bunch in the oven and we should have more soon. With luck, satins will become a big seller. They have more meat than the local rabbits. I figure I'll be able to sell a bunch of breeding pairs."

"Why not sell the meat and keep the breeding pairs?"

"That would be stupid. It would make a lot of folks mad and we don't need the hassle." Brandon didn't say that his original plan had been to do just that and Hayley had jumped on him about it, then gone to Mom, who had made it clear that if he tried it, she would take the rabbits away from him.

"What angle of ramp are you planning on?" Peter Barclay asked.

"About thirty degrees, I think. That's what they had on NASCAR tracks up-time." Truthfully, Sonny wasn't sure. He had seen races up-time but he was hardly a NASCAR buff.

"I'll calculate the angle that will be needed, assuming you can tell me the average and top speeds that will be used," Peter Barclay declared.

Sonny shrugged. It wasn't an issue that he felt was all that important.

Ron said, "Sure. Figure an average of around sixty and a top speed around one twenty, but that could go up in a few years."

"I will look into it."

"Well, if you do look into it, we'll need it fairly quickly. His Majesty doesn't want the track closed for months while you do your calculations," Gayleen Sanderlin said. Gayleen wasn't overly impressed by the new additions to the Viennese up-timer community.

"The track is dangerous as it stands now, and will become even more dangerous if they try to build their bank without the proper calculations," Peter Barclay explained to Janos Drugeth and Gundaker von Liechtenstein that evening.

Janos wasn't greatly swayed by Peter Barclay's pronouncements, but Gundaker was. Gundaker wasn't all that impressed by the up-timer engineer, but at least he was a scholar of sorts.

Carla Ann Barclay listened to the self-satisfied way that her father and Prince Gundaker decided that whatever the Sanderlins and the Fortneys had done was meaningless and unimportant because they weren't the right sort of people. She had gotten that her whole life from her parents. Not the right color, not the right education, not the right "sort." It amazed her how people so unsuccessful could be so full of themselves. Especially after the Ring of Fire, when Mom and Dad had become two of the very few people on earth that had actual up-time college degrees and they had still managed not to get much of anything done. And it wasn't that they were stupid or incompetent, though her dad was certainly stupid when it came to people.

So was she, Carla knew, as much as she hated to admit it. But, damn, Hayley Fortney was part of the Barbie Consortium and they had gotten rich in less than two years after the Ring of Fire. And Mom and Dad didn't even notice she was here. Well, Carla sure as hell wasn't going to tell them.

English Ladies' School, Vienna

A few days later, Carla Ann Barclay sat and waited as her parents discussed her future with the Jesuitesses. She felt like a spoiled child's rag doll. The child would scream and throw a fit if it was taken away, but as soon as it was returned she would casually toss it into a corner. A dirty corner. The English Ladies' school was the corner she was being tossed into and she had no idea how Jesuitesses would take to up-time knowledge. Honestly, she was a little worried that she would be facing exorcisms or the Inquisition.

It's bad enough we got thrown back to this time, Carla Ann thought. *But then my idiot parents do this to me!*

The elite of Vienna came in two categories, townies and court, burghers of Vienna and the *Hofbefreiten* of the court. The *Hofbefreiten* included a lot more than Carla Ann had ever thought of as courtiers. Oh, the *Hofbefreiten* included the courtiers, but also the third assistant dressmaker to the Countess von Nowhere Important. *Hofbefreiten* were anyone who had some right to serve the court in some way and were therefore excused from the normal fees and rules that the burghers and craftsmen of Vienna had to deal with. Of course, most of Vienna wasn't in either group. But the daughters of both courtiers and burghers went to the school of the English Ladies. There they mixed, as did their parents. Together they made up the people who mattered and they were busy those first days after Carla Ann joined them, figuring out where she fit in the category. Her parents were hired by the court, which was almost a unique status. Most people who worked for the emperor paid for the privilege and got some set of rights or privileges in exchange. From people like Wallenstein, who raised his army out of his own pocket to the guy who polished the emperor's boots who paid for the right to do so then made his living selling boots. People who actually got paid by the emperor were few and far between. On the other hand, the Barclays weren't actually being paid that much in comparison to what a clerk of the court made in bribes.

On the third hand, there was the fact that Carla Ann had actually experienced the Ring of Fire. What it all came down to was that the other girls weren't at all sure what to do with her and she had the potential to take over the queen bee slot so far as the school hierarchy was concerned.

That status was as obvious to the English Ladies as to the students, and they, in all honesty, were as curious about the Ring of Fire as anyone else. With their leader, Mary Ward, in Grantville at last report, the English Ladies were still more curious.

Carla Ann caught the ferry out to Race Track City the first Saturday after they got to Vienna. She wasn't the only one; two of the girls from the English Ladies' school had gone out to see the emperor making laps, something that the emperor did most Saturdays. The other two girls were wearing seventeenth-century chic. Carla was wearing a mix. She had on a paisley blouse that would cost a fortune down-time, if less of a fortune now than just after the Ring of Fire. Jacquard looms had been appearing all over Europe for the last couple of years, and the price for down-time made paisley was just exorbitant, not armed robbery.

However, Carla's blouse was an actual up-time blouse. She didn't have much money, but she did have some clothes that her sister didn't want. She was also wearing a used navy peacoat, which wasn't fashionable but was darn sure necessary in Vienna in December during the Little Ice Age. A long split skirt hid the heavy wool socks that went up to her knees, and she'd sneaked a pair of her sister Suzi's combat boots to wear. They looked ridiculous, but the other girls thought they were the height of fashion.

The boat stopped at a dock on the river and the girls had to walk about a mile on a pretty smooth dirt road. They could see where the workers were digging a channel to the race track, but the last of the canal to be dug was the part that connected to the river, so there was a stretch of about thirty yards between river and mostly dry canal works.

The morning was cold, but they were used to it, even Carla Ann. It took them about a half an hour to stroll to the race track, and by the time they got there Carla was wishing one of the girls had been willing to spring for a cab ride from the river to the track. There were cabs that made the trip, but that cost four pfennig each way. Worse, a pfennig wasn't a penny; it was worth more than that. And Carla was on a pretty restricted allowance. Her parents had been provided with a place to stay, but they hadn't been paid. And as things had turned out, they weren't going to get paid. Instead, they were given *Hofbefreiten* status in exchange for consulting with the crown on demand. They had some money to start out, because they did get paid for the stuff they brought with them. But so far there wasn't any work besides the work for the government. That wasn't paid, so they were living off the money from the stuff they brought.

To Carla Ann, what all that meant was that she didn't have any money to speak of and that lack was likely to put her in a bad spot in the English Ladies' school. She needed a way to make some money of her own, and if any one in Vienna could tell her how it was Hayley Fortney.

There was no fee to watch the emperor race around the track, but for Carla Ann there wasn't much excitement in it either. She had seen real NASCAR on TV up-time. One guy in a 240Z traveling at maybe 60 miles an hour didn't get her blood pumping. The other girls were the next best thing to in awe, though, so Carla couldn't let herself seem too bored.

While the other girls were watching the emperor go around in circles, Carla Ann slipped away and found Mr. Sanderlin, the younger one—she didn't know his first name—and asked where Hayley was.

"Hey, Carla. What's up?" Hayley said. She was in a shop behind the garage, working on what looked like an engine block with a big down-timer. There was actual glass in the windows of the shop. It had ripples in it, but it was glass.

"Are you building an engine?"

"Steam four cylinder," Hayley said in English, then continued in German that was starting to take on an Austrian accent. "And Herr Groer here is the one building it. I'm just helping with the measuring. He's a master smith and this thing is expected to put out about six horsepower when he gets it finished in another month or so."

"Ah, isn't that a pretty slow way to go about it? Hand building the engines, I mean? Is it the price of iron?"

"No, though the cost of iron has gone up even here," Hayley said. "And it sure is a slow way to go about it. But building an engine factory would cost a fortune. And we can't do it anyway, because we can't afford the licensing fees."

"Licensing fees?"

"Never mind," Hayley said. "It's silly, but it's the rules. We could afford a few individual licenses, but the owner wants a fortune for the licences for mass production of engines."

"What about steel?" Carla knew that the price of iron had gone through the roof in the USE since they got started on the railroads.

"Yes, it's gone up even here, but they import up the Danube from Hungary and points south. They also have iron mines near Linz and just north of Judenburg. Plus, it's both hard and expensive to ship anything heavy from Vienna—or just about anywhere in Austria-Hungary—to the USE. You either have to go around Europe by way of the Black Sea and Mediterranean, up the Spanish and French coasts, past England and around to the Baltic. Or you go over really bad land routes, through lots of little lordling's territories. Either way, the price goes up a lot. So iron, copper, and a lot of stuff is cheaper here than in the USE."

Hayley blathered on about the price of this and the shipping cost of that, and Carla finally couldn't take it anymore. "Can I talk to you?" she blurted out.

Hayley didn't wince, but Carla could tell she had to work at it. And Carla, a bright and fairly well-educated girl, knew why. Last year in Grantville, Hayley was always being hit on by people who wanted the Barbies to invest in something, or wanted Hayley to tell them what the Barbies were doing, or just loan them—better, give them—money. In a way, that was what Carla was here for and she hoped that them being the only up-timers would help.

Hayley gestured Carla to a bench and came over to sit down next to her. Hayley's dark brown hair was held back with a scrunchy and there was a grease smudge on her forehead that Carla wanted to wipe away.

"What can I do here to make money?" Carla didn't mean to say it that way, but it just spilled out of her mouth as soon as she opened it. "I'm sorry. I didn't mean to blurt it out like that, but I don't know how things work here. And...well, Mom and Dad didn't exactly ask my opinion before they brought me here." Though she didn't know it, that was the right thing to say.

"I'll try to help," Hayley said. "What do you know about?"

"I've been thinking about that. I was in theater arts at Grantville High, stage setting, some acting. I've learned German, of course, and some French and Latin. From before the Ring of Fire, I know tap dancing, though I'm out of practice. Mom and Dad had me taking lessons since I was six, and I didn't like ballet as much as tap. And I can play the piano. Not real well, but I can play it. They made me take a gymnastics class on Saturdays. I've sort of kept that up since the Ring of Fire. Wednesdays were Japanese classes, 'cause Dad said the Japanese are really big in electronics."

"I doubt Japanese is going to be much use, but maybe the piano." Hayley paused a minute. "Do you know how a piano is made?"

"Sort of. I know the basics."

"See if you can find out if anyone owns the patent on pianos. And if someone does, they probably don't know how to build them. You can probably make some money working with whoever they have trying to build them. I don't know about the tap dancing or gymnastics. Would the English Ladies think it was a good idea? Maybe you could teach tap or gymnastics at the English Ladies' school."

Carla grimaced at that.

"What's wrong?"

"Well, it's the school. The students aren't the children of the washer woman. They're pretty status conscious and I'm not sure how comfortable they would be with going to school with someone who is being paid by their parents to teach them something."

"I'm glad we have the tutor," Hayley said. "Are you doing the correspondence course?"

"No. No one knew we were leaving. *I* didn't know we were leaving. We have some course work in the baggage we brought, but not enough. And it's been turned over to the English Ladies as my tuition to the school."

"Well, that's good," Hayley said. "At least some of it will get to the people here. What courses?"

"We have the textbooks I was using in Grantville, both a copy of the English version and new German version. Biology, comparative history and German lit, also stage dressing and blocking, and studio management. It's the senior year stuff for theater arts behind-the-scenes program. Before this happened I was going to be the down-time Frank Capra or Busby Berkeley.

"But it's just the textbooks, not the course notes and like I said, my parents gave them to the English Ladies, so I have to share them with the whole school. And it's not like I can write back to Grantville and get another copy. I think the books are hot."

Carla was trying very hard not to cry. None of this had been her idea, but she was going to be tarred with the same brush as her parents. It wasn't fair.

"Well, I'll talk to Herr Doctor Faust and see about getting your school copies of the course outlines."

Carla choked a laugh. "Your tutor is Dr. Faust? Has he sold his soul yet?"

"No, but he does get teased about his name a lot," Hayley said repressively. "The stories are over a hundred years old, even in this time. And his taking up natural philosophy rather than theology fit too well with the legends."

"Sorry," Carla said.

"It's okay. He's a nice guy, and I think he's sensitive about it, even though he tries to laugh it off. So I thought I should warn you." Hayley changed the subject. "I can write back to Grantville. Are there any messages you want me to send?"

"Yes, I had some friends who came to the school from Rudolstadt. Not that I have any idea what I'm going to say."

Carla looked at her watch. It was a down-time-made pocket watch. Those could be had in Grantville and Magdeburg now. "Oh, shoot. The girls from school are watching the emperor. Do you know how long he's going to be driving around the track?"

"Not long. He generally goes for about ten minutes at a stretch. You should probably get back to them."

"About that, Hayley. Some of them have made some comments about you being just the daughter of a mechanic. Which they figure is about the same as a groom in the imperial stables. Should I tell them you're part of the Barbie Consortium and could buy their parents out of pocket change? I don't know if you've been keeping quiet about it on purpose or if they were just being snooty."

"Well, they *are* just being snooty." Hayley smiled. "What's wrong with a groom, after all? But, no. Don't tell them, please. I really don't want them pressuring me, or their parents pressuring my family, about money."

"I won't say a thing." Carla assured her, thinking, *Well, that at least gives me an in.*

"Thanks," Hayley said. "And I'll be thinking about what you can do to earn a bit of extra cash."

Carla ended up too busy to do much in the way of starting businesses because the English Ladies put her to work teaching algebra to the young ladies of good family. Not on the basis of her owing it to them or anything. Just because she had had algebra and knew more about it than anyone else. About half Carla's school day was spent as the teacher of this or that up-time discipline, often as not with two or three of the English Ladies as students. It put an uncomfortable distance between her and her fellow students, but the English Ladies didn't seem to care.

CHAPTER 14

𝔅arbies' 𝔙ienna 𝔅ranch

January and early February 1635

Sanderlin House, Race Track City

"Frau Sanderlin, may I give credit to Ursula Kline?" Magdalena Hough asked timidly. "She is a good woman and if she can get some of the bottles for her herbs, she will be better able to sell them."

Gayleen Sanderlin was at a loss. "Well, I guess so. I mean, it's your shop. What do the other ladies who work there say?"

Magdalena hesitated. "Well, some agree. Others think we don't have the money to give credit."

Fortney House, Race Track City

"Frau Fortney, may I give credit to Renate Treffen?" asked Peter Zingler. The bootmaker was literally hat in hand, and Dana Fortney didn't have a clue what to say. She knew who would, but her daughter was in the shop working with Sonny on the boiler for the steam car they were trying to build. And Brandon, who might know what to do, was out at his experimental farm, mulching God-knew-what with chicken poop to make compost.

"Let me think about it, Herr Zingler. Do you have to have an answer right now?"

240Z Shop, Race Track City

"Herr Sanderlin, can you get me credit at the Up-time Diner? Things have been tight and..."

Ron Sanderlin looked over at Pete Greisser. He was a good guy, if not the brightest Ron had ever met. Hard worker and willing, but not great with money.

"Just till next payday. Maria, my sister, is in from the country and, well, money is tight and..."

Again Pete trailed off and this time Ron had to fight back a curse. The pay was late again. He knew that the empire was having financial troubles but, damn it, when you hire people you're supposed to pay them.

It was on the tip of his tongue to tell Pete that of course he could have credit at the Up-time Diner, but then he remembered he didn't own the diner. "I'll see what I can do, Pete."

Dana's Office, Fortney House, Race Track City

"We're getting a lot of people asking for credit," Dana Fortney told Gayleen Sanderlin. The office now had its own set of filing cabinets. Dana had gone to the cabinet-maker Moses Abrabanel recommended. She also had a nice roll-top desk she had had made right here in Vienna. It had cost a fortune, but was worth it.

"I know, but what are we going to do? Most of those people have jobs. A lot of them have jobs with the government. They aren't getting paid. And even the bribes are barely enough to keep body and soul together. If they aren't government employees, they aren't even quartered."

"Sure. But that doesn't pay for the raw materials we need."

"Talk to Hayley," Gayleen said. Then she shook her head. "It's really weird asking a fourteen-year-old for financial advice."

"Fifteen now," Dana said automatically. Then, "And how do you think I feel? She's my daughter. She's supposed to be coming to me for a raise in her allowance while I tell her to be more frugal. Not the other way around."

Gayleen laughed. "Oh, stop bragging."

✧   ✧   ✧

"This isn't working," Hayley said. "And I don't know why."

It was pretty clear that the sudden increase in the credit requests was because the emperor was late again with the wages, and not just for the race track workers but for everyone in Vienna. And a lot of those people were owed a lot more than a couple of weeks' wages.

"Well, it's not their fault that the pay is late," Gayleen Sanderlin insisted. "What the heck is wrong with Ferdinand III?"

That was true, Hayley knew, but that wasn't what she was thinking about. "He's probably broke, too. Meanwhile, we have to figure something out." *Damn it, this should be working better.* They were selling good products, really good products, at bargain prices. Stuff people needed, stuff that would make their lives better. They ought to be selling more. Hayley wished Susan Logsden was here, but she didn't know what Susan could do that she wasn't. Then she realized that who she really wished was here was Sarah Wendell. "It's an economic problem," she blurted out.

"Okay?" Gayleen said doubtfully. "It's an economic problem. What is the problem? And more importantly, what's the solution?"

"I have no idea!" Which was true in general, but in this particular situation, the answer was that they would have to give credit.

Hayley consulted with Jack Pfeifer, their lawyer. "The problem is that we want Sanderlin-Fortney Investment Company to give credit, but discourage using it."

"What do you mean?"

"We're actually in a pretty good situation here, right on the Danube with a couple of north/south trade routes so there are plenty of raw materials available and not all that expensive. But that doesn't mean they are free. When we sell something on credit, a pair of pants, a box of aspirin, or whatever, we have to pay cash for the materials to replace it."

Jack was nodding.

"Right. Cash would be better. But if we don't give credit, we run out of customers, or close to it. If we make it too easy to get credit, then people who should be paying cash will be buying stuff on credit."

"Charge interest?"

"Sure. But most of our sales are small. Keeping track of who owes how much interest would be a nightmare. For us and them.

And some of our sales, well, they aren't quite charity, but close to it. We really don't want to send a bunch of people to debtor's prison."

"You can always forgive a debt," Jack said. "And you can do it selectively. You can forgive or not, as you see fit. You can forgive some, but not all. You can forgive the interest. You can decide not to call it in this month and maintain your right to call it in next month. Once you own the debt, it's pretty much up to you what to do with it."

"What we need is a form that we can have printed up that makes it clear, so that we have a legal record. They fill in the amount and sign it. Then it goes in the money box. And we keep a ledger of who owes what. We'll leave it up to the shopkeepers who to offer credit to, but everyone who gets credit signs one every time they use it."

"That should work and is not that different from what merchants are already doing. How much interest and how do you want to work that part?"

"Let's set it up so that each year after harvest, we apply five percent to the total owed."

"That's not very much. And if they manage to pay off their debt or even pay it down just before harvest, they will pay even less interest."

"I know, but I don't want to drown people in debt. I just want to make them think about paying cash."

"I'm not at all sure this will make them think *hard enough* about paying cash."

February, 1635

Carla was back in Race Track City with her girlfriends. They were in the little shop that sold casein buttons and other knick-knacks. It was a pretty place, with lots of glass windows in little diamonds along one wall so that there was plenty of sunlight. Carla's paisley shirt had lost a button, and they were white plastic buttons. Utterly irreplaceable. But if she took off all the buttons that were left and replaced them with the casein buttons...that would work. Besides, the casein buttons were actually prettier. There was a set that had little 240Z embossed on the buttons and another set that had little crosses. She picked a set of cream-colored buttons with pale blue crosses to go with her shirt. They weren't expensive, but she was broke.

Her girlfriends weren't exactly flush either, so there was quite a bit more wanting than buying going on. Then a dumpy middle-aged woman came in and picked up three casein canisters with lids. She went up to the counter and said, "*Guten Tag*, Maria."

"*Guten Tag*, Katharina. Do you have cash today?" the woman at the counter asked.

"No, not till I fill these and sell them. Things have been tight."

"All right then." The woman behind the counter pulled a sheet out of a drawer and wrote something on it, then the woman buying the canisters signed it, took her canisters and left.

Sofia Anna, seeing this, grabbed a set of casein thimbles she had been eyeing and marched up to the counter.

"That will be eight pfennig," said Maria.

"I will charge them," Sofia Anna proclaimed. "I am Sofia Anna von Wimmer."

Maria looked at Sofia, then at the other girls. Then she carefully said, "I am most sorry, ma'am, but I must have your parents' approval before I can even start the process of setting up a credit account."

The others sighed and Carla had an idea. She recognized Hayley Fortney in this. She didn't know how Hayley was involved, but she was pretty sure that the Barbie Consortium's mechanical genius was involved somewhere. "Well, I guess I'll just have to get my parents to agree," she said to the other girls. "They'll probably have to come out here to set up the account, too. So the buttons will have to wait till that's done."

Maria looked cautiously grateful as she nodded to Carla.

While the girls were eating apple strudels, Carla excused herself and went to see Hayley. She wasn't at all sure what she was going to say. *Hayley, can you get me a line of credit at the casein shop?* didn't seem quite the right thing to say.

"Hayley," she said when she found Hayley—as usual—in the steam shop. "Can you explain how credit works out here?"

"I'll try, Carla," Hayley said, looking around the shop.

Carla looked around the shop and saw the people looking at her and Hayley. "Well, I would have gone to your mom, but

I figured she'd be busy." Then she switched to English. "Sorry, Hayley. I didn't mean to out you."

"It's okay. But I *am* trying to stay in the closet on this."

Carla grinned. Who down-time was going to get what "staying in the closet" meant, even if they spoke English?

"Come on," Hayley said, still in English. "I'll take you to Mom and she can help you out."

Once Hayley had bundled up and they were out of the shop, Carla continued. "Thanks, Hayley. I haven't had time to make much money. The English Ladies have me teaching math and science. Meanwhile, I lost a button off my favorite shirt.

"Also, you need to know that the girls at the school are probably going to be trying to get their parents to set them up with lines of credit. I don't know how you're going to deal with that. Some of them are people you don't want to say no to."

"Well, the English Ladies ought to be paying you for teaching."

"I know that, and you know that, but I don't think you're going to convince them or my parents of that. Come on, Hayley. We're kids and putting kids to work for the grownups' benefit is standard practice. More here than up-time."

"Sure. But if they sent you off to be a maid, you'd get paid. Maybe not much, but something. And if you were apprenticed, you would be learning a trade."

"Right. But money is supposed to be beneath our notice."

"It's not beneath Prince Liechtenstein's notice," Hayley said.

"Sure, it is," Carla shot back. "That's what he's got the Barbies for."

"Naw. That's just because he's not real good at it," Hayley said. "Anyway...look, I'll get you some credit. But you need to get your folks to come out and talk to Ron Sanderlin and my dad."

"Why? About the credit account?"

"No. Because about five months ago the Bessemer steel mill at Linz blew up. They were going from cheat sheets, and we hadn't arrived yet. They started rebuilding it and a couple of weeks before you guys got here Dad and Ron Sanderlin took a trip up the Danube to see it.

"They saw some stuff and made some suggestions, but Dad's not an engineer and Ron is a mechanic, and those guys need your dad's expertise."

"Things are tight right now, Hayley," Carla said. "My parents got promised a bunch of stuff. None of those promises has been broken, but they have been reinterpreted quite a bit since we had to run from Grantville. The government isn't going to be paying my dad. Instead, he's been made *Hofbefreiten*. He has a fancy new title, Royal Adviser on Up-timer Engineering, but no one knows what to do with him."

"We heard," Hayley said. "But this should be a paying gig. Count von Dietrichstein got the patent for the Bessemer by promising to provide the crown with lots of good steel, as well as the silver he paid for it. The guy has to get that thing running *now*. I'm not saying your dad can write his own ticket, but the job should pay well."

"I'll tell him," Carla promised.

Sonny and Ron spent a couple of hours going over the state of affairs in the Bessemer mill at Linz with Peter Barclay. It was in the process of being rebuilt. And they put him in touch with Count von Dietrichstein.

After he had left, Ron muttered, "Maybe we'll get lucky and the count will have him executed." Peter Barclay had been both condescending and critical. And, Ron admitted to himself, at least half right. Even from only the discussion they had, Barclay had spotted things that Ron and Sonny hadn't. Which shouldn't have been surprising. Peter Barclay was an engineer and had consulted on the first Bessemer plant located just outside of Saalfeld.

Meanwhile, Hayley set up a line of credit for Carla and bought some stuff from her to get a little cash in the girl's hands. Hayley had also set up a policy for the parents of the girls at the English Ladies' school. If they wanted credit, their parents had to agree to put up the money. In exchange, the parents would get a copy of the bills and would know what the girls bought. So the "Them of Vienna" were effectively required to pay in advance, but didn't have to look like they were.

Some people didn't want to sign the credit slips and went elsewhere, but all the new businesses that the Sanderlins and Fortneys backed had some up-time or new-time tech that made their production cost less so they were mostly inexpensive. They didn't lose that many customers. Others decided that it was better to pay cash if they had it. So the new businesses were getting more cash in, but SFIC was still losing money—if you didn't include the money owed to them. Most of the businesses in Vienna were facing the same problem.

One side effect showed itself a month or so after they started giving credit. There were a number of government employees who got paid either spottily or not at all. And quite a few of them had bought clothing, packaged foods, or other products from one or more of the shops that had sprung up near the race track. When Albertus Kappel, one of the "Them of Vienna," decided to shake down SFIC for a large bribe, he ran right into a brick wall. That wall wasn't the emperor, it was the clerks.

"How did he find out about us?" Gayleen Sanderlin asked.

Barbara Klein grimaced. "It was the IOUs. They all say Sanderlin-Fortney Investment Company."

"So this guy, one of your customers, came in and told you this...just out of the blue?"

"Young Benedictus owes us quite a bit," Barbara said. "He's very in love with his own looks." She grinned. "Very much in love with himself. But he's not a bad boy and he knows we've been treating him fairly. Besides, if we get closed down, where would he get his clothes?"

In the various offices of the city and national government, clerks who owed SFIC money provided warning and back-dated forms documenting that everything had been done by the book. Well, most of it had, but it was impossible to follow all the regulations. Having clerks who owed you money helped when it came to paperwork.

"Yes, I know they have an agreement with the emperor," Albertus Kappel snapped. "But that doesn't make Race Track *Village* an imperial city. And it *is* within the traditional purview of Vienna. Legally, it is no more than a village owned by the emperor and his partners. Not even crown lands, but part of the emperor's personal holdings. Besides, we have more of the up-timers now."

"Fine. But the emperor is a part-owner of Race Tra—the village," Peter Grochen said.

"We will not be asking the emperor for anything. But this Sanderlin-Fortney Investment Company is abusing the emperor's trust and getting above itself." Visibly, Albertus got himself under control. "The new emperor is young and perhaps overly enthusiastic about up-time innovations. But he has advisers...older, wiser heads...that he will listen to. This flaunting of the traditional privileges of 'Them of Vienna' has to stop."

Peter Grochen, who was no more pleased with Race Track City than Albertus—but was rather more leery of imperial whim—left Albertus to it.

"The tradition and law has always been that the *Hofbefreiten*, court merchants, do not pay municipal taxes," Albertus Kappel granted portentously. "But these are not *Hofbefreiten*. They haven't paid the fees the royal court charges for that privilege. Yet they don't pay the *onera* that guild artisans and merchants pay, either. Nor have their techniques been approved under the rules of the guilds of Vienna."

"Perhaps," Ferdinand III said calmly, "that is because they are not in Vienna." Ferdinand III was pretty good at saying things calmly when he would prefer to rip someone's head off. It was part of the job and he had been raised to the work. "Race Track City is located on imperial lands, almost four miles from the city wall."

It was clear to Ferdinand III that Kappel wasn't thrilled with how the interview was going, but the jackass went gamely on. "They are within the cities environs, Your Majesty."

"No, they are not!" Ferdinand III said.

"Your Majesty, while the land is owned by Your Majesty, it is not, in fact, crown lands."

Ferdinand held out a hand, and into it was placed a document that bore several seals. One of them, in fact, was Albertus Kappel's own seal. The document acknowledged that the land in question was not legally part of Vienna or its environs. Ferdinand was a little curious about where it had come from, but not very. As it happened, Albertus' clerk, Benedictus, had handed that document to Albertus Kappel a week before, in a stack of similar documents that Kappel had signed and sealed as a matter of course, without ever looking at the contents of any of them. Ferdinand showed Kappel the document and the seal.

For Albertus Kappel, the interview went downhill from there. Albertus was one of those who held both imperial and city rank, which wasn't supposed to happen, but did constantly. By the end of the interview, he held neither.

✧   ✧   ✧

Albertus' secretary, Benedictus, was the dapper young man with a taste for clothes that really shouldn't have been beyond his means—if he had been being paid what he was supposed to be paid. Benedictus and several other young men found that their debts to several shops in Race Track City had been forgiven. After that, the SFIC-backed businesses had very little trouble from the burghers of Vienna, as long as they didn't try to do business in Vienna proper.

The race track, with the support of Ferdinand III, developed its own small town with barbershops, beauty shops, restaurants, a tailor shop. A toy store that sold little casein plastic models of the 240Z, and other cars and trucks. Casein dolls, which if not up to the standards of a Barbie, weren't all that bad. Also soccer balls, baseballs, softballs, and bats, toy soldiers, lego-style blocks, and a variety of other items. There was a grocery and dry goods store which sold packaged foods, makeup, toiletries, casein containers for holding things like dried beans and flour.

Through it all, almost no one knew that Hayley was financing most of it.

SFIC wasn't the only investor in new tech. Even before Emperor Ferdinand II had died, up-time tech had been creeping in. The cheat sheets that were produced for the USE worked just as well in what was left of the HRE. The burghers and *Hofbefreiten* of Vienna adopted them and many of them had to do with how to get more product out of less labor. As the new tech was put in place, the amount of product increased as the need for labor decreased. When the old emperor died, the new emperor tried to get as much of the new tech as he could.

What none of them realized, not Hayley, not the emperor, not the emperor's advisers, and not the burghers and *Hofbefreiten* of Vienna, was that they were all making the economy worse. It's what Hayley hadn't known, save that something was wrong with the economy, and she needed Sarah Wendell to tell them what.

CHAPTER 15

Karl's Ring

February 1635

Grantville, United States of Europe

"I have a letter from Hayley," Judy the Younger Wendell told the girls of the Barbie Consortium. "She wants stuff and she wants money, but mostly she wants me to get Sarah to tell her what's wrong with the Austro-Hungarian economy."

"So, what *is* wrong with the Austro-Hungarian economy?"

"Hey, I'm the pretty sister. Remember?"

"Not according to the Ken Doll," said Millicent Anne Barnes. "He starts drooling every time he gets near Sarah."

They were just back from a weekend trip to Magdeburg. A long weekend. It took a day each way. So they had taken the sleeper Thursday night and spent Friday and Saturday in Magdeburg with the Wendells, and come back Sunday night. Karl had taken the excuse to go with them and escorted Sarah to the opera. Sort of opera. It was called *A Knight of Somerville*, a new play written in the style of a 1930s Busby Berkeley musical. They couldn't do the full Berkeley experience, but it had lots of dancing and was probably loosely based on the events of the ennoblement of the count of Narnia. In this case, the juvenile princess actually knighted the knight of Somerville herself, rather than have her father do it later.

"So," Vicky Emerson said, "when do you think he's going to ask her?"

"Just because you're engaged doesn't mean everyone has to be," Susan Logsden said.

"I think he's scared," said Heather Mason.

"Of what?" asked Gabrielle Ugolini. "He's rich, he's a prince, and he's not bad looking."

"Of my sister," Judy proclaimed. "As any sane person would be."

"Of the crap that's going to get dumped on them when they actually get engaged," Millicent said. "You know how Catholics can be." She looked pointedly at Vicky.

"I resemble that remark," Vicky said. "Or I would if Bill were Catholic. But he's Lutheran and Cardinal Mazzare says it's okay. I'll just have to endow a church or something."

"Yeah, but will the pope be so understanding? Or the cardinal of..." Judy stopped. "Which cardinal is it who would cover the Holy Roman Empire?"

"It didn't have one," Vicky said. "It was Scipione Borghese till he died in 1633, but the post wasn't filled after that. The Holy Roman Empire didn't have a cardinal, and now there isn't a Holy Roman Empire. There are the Habsburg lands, Austria and Hungary, and they have a cardinal, Franz Seraph von Dietrichstein."

"So how is Dietrichstein going to react?"

"I don't know. But if Cardinal Mazzare gives them permission, there isn't a lot he can do." Vicky said it smugly. She was proud of her parish priest being a cardinal.

Sarah Wendell looked at the plane on the airfield outside Magdeburg. It was a Dauntless, one of the line of aircraft made by Kelly Aviation. The original *Dauntless* had gained fame or notoriety—take your pick—very recently, when it crashed after accidentally bombing Noelle Stull and Eddie Junker. This was a replica, the first one Kelly had made. Bob Kelly's wife Kay was here in Magdeburg lobbying the government to buy some for the Air Force.

At the moment, though, she was still lobbying—and the aircraft was still available. Kay was renting it out on a daily basis for anyone who could afford the steep price.

"Are you sure about this?" Karl asked dubiously. "I've never seen one up close before. It's much smaller than they seem up in the sky."

Sarah shook her head. "I'm not worried about the plane. Bob

Kelly may be the world's worst businessman, but he knows how to build airplanes. The real issue is the *pilot*."

Karl now studied the fellow in question, who was standing next to the plane and chatting with someone Karl took to be the mechanic.

"What's wrong with him? He doesn't know how to operate the plane?"

"No, Lannie Yost is actually a good pilot. The problem is that he's also a drunk." She headed toward the plane. "Luckily, I have a good nose."

As it turned out, there was alcohol on Yost's breath. But the smell was faint—Sarah gauged it as one beer. Certainly not more than two. Given Lannie's capacity, he should be fine.

Not to her surprise, Karl didn't say anything about the smell. Sarah had already learned that people born and raised in the seventeenth century were more lackadaisical about drinking than up-timers were. Given that water was unreliable when it came to carrying diseases, that was probably understandable even if she didn't really approve.

She looked over at Karl. "What do you think?"

"I still prefer comfort." He smiled at her. "But if you'll hold my hand, I'll go up in it."

Holding hands proved to be easier said than done, because of the cockpit's design. There were seats up front for the pilot and someone else—a copilot, theoretically—but only room for one person in the small seat in the back.

At Sarah's insistence, Karl took the front seat. She'd flown before; he hadn't. Her hope was that he'd enjoy the flight, once he got over his apprehension. That was the reason she'd made the suggestion in the first place. Since it seemed clear they would be seeing each other for quite some time and he had lands scattered all over central Europe, Sarah figured that aviation would be a handy thing to encourage.

When they got up in the air, Karl turned around to look back at her. "You promised to hold my hand!" he said, shouting to be heard over the noise of the engine.

Sarah rolled her eyes, but gave him her left hand. It was a sunny day and unseasonably warm, so she didn't object when he took her glove off. Then she felt the cold metal of the ring as he slipped it onto her finger. She turned to look, and he shouted: "Will you marry me?"

Lannie looked at them and grinned. Sarah didn't let go of Karl's hand but she didn't answer right away. She wanted to think about it—and the noise of the engine gave her an excuse to wait until they landed. Besides, she figured after pulling a stunt like this, he should just damn well wait anyway.

The decision took less time than she would have thought. Once the plane was on the ground, she didn't wait for the engine to be turned off.

"Yes!" she shouted.

"What about the religious issues?" Fletcher Wendell asked.

"Karl is talking with Cardinal Mazzare," Sarah said. "There's not going to be that much of an issue, anyway. He's Prince Karl von Liechtenstein and I'm plain old Sarah Wendell, so it's going to be a morganatic marriage. Which is okay. I have enough money so that it's not going to be a problem for our kids. And, as far as I'm concerned his cousin Hartmann can have it. Or Hartmann's kids can. I figure we'll likely outlive Hartmann, unless medical care in Austria-Hungary gets a lot better." While much of the USE had taken to up-time medical practice with a will, that response was hardly universal throughout Europe. "Anyway, we've agreed that we will let the kids choose their religion for themselves once they grow up. Karl has his own confessor, of course, but Father George has a pretty reasonable atitude. He's been on the wrong end of religious persecution in England, so after a few talks with Cardinal Mazzare, he has developed a great deal of respect for freedom of conscience."

"Is Karl all right with a morganatic marriage?" asked Judy the Elder.

"He says he is," Sarah said. "And I think it's mostly true."

"Mostly true?"

"Well, he grew up Prince Karl, heir to the Liechtenstein family holdings, so he's a bit ambivalent about not passing that on to his children. On the other hand, he knows that between us we can set up trusts that will make sure that the kids have a good start. And in the new world we're building here in the USE, that should be enough."

✧   ✧   ✧

The Liechtenstein Improvement Corporation got the news over the telegraph in the private code that Karl had had generated by a computer program in Grantville back in 1633. It was two copies of a notebook, one of which Karl kept, and the other for the board. The reasons for the encoding were two fold. One was the tabloids. The *National Inquisitor* was already printing speculation about when Karl was going to ask Sarah to marry him and what she was going to say. He wanted to inform his family and Emperor Ferdinand III before they read about it in the papers.

But there was a more important reason for codes. Karl was, for the most part, if not sanguine about his marriage to Sarah being morganatic, and least resigned to it. However, he didn't want that to mean that his children's entire inheritance would be from Sarah. Nor did he want Sarah to have to live on her income. Sarah wasn't poor by any reasonable standard. But Karl Eusebius von Liechtenstein was not raised to a reasonable standard of wealth. Instead, he was raised to a *royal* standard of wealth and by that standard, Sarah Wendell was barely getting by. By Karl's standards, a person of reasonable wealth could raise and fund their own army at need. And it was his intent that once they were married, his wife and children should be able to do that if the need arose.

Karl was going to use the LIC to move some funds from the family accounts to private businesses and partnerships that could go first to his wife as her dower, and through her to their children when they came along. And he didn't want his uncles to know about it. For that matter, he wasn't totally convinced that he wanted Sarah to know about it. Judy the Younger Wendell, on the other hand, would do fine administering the fund till it was needed. The LIC had as members Dave Marcantonio and Father George, but also Judy the Younger, Susan Logsden and Millicent Anne Barnes, members of the Barbie Consortium.

"Did you know he was going to ask this trip?" Millicent asked Judy accusingly.

"Naw. I figured he'd chicken out again. He's been carrying that ring around since he got back from Prague. It's Morris Roth's work and the rock's big enough that Sarah's going to have trouble holding up her hand. And her left arm's going to end up a couple of inches longer than her right."

Susan snorted. "How much did the Roths charge him?"

"I don't know. Silesia, maybe," Judy said. Which was, Dave thought, utterly ridiculous.

"Ladies, if we could get to the financial part of the message," Dave said. "I'm a bit concerned about Prince Karl using the LIC for this."

"Why?" asked Father George Hamilton.

"Legalities," Dave said. "He's using the LIC to move money from his family accounts to his personal accounts. I'm worried that it could be seen as malfeasance on the part of the LIC."

"I don't think so," said Father George. "However, I will consult with the lawyers about it. Most of the monies in the LIC were provided by Prince Karl's individual investments, which the rest of the family had no part in."

"That's fine. I'm just not sure that his uncles and cousins are going to see it that way," Dave said. The board had received letters from the Vienna branch of the family, attempting to get the LIC to provide funds for friends of the family. Those requests had been passed up to Karl. Some he had approved, and others not.

"Which is why he's keeping it quiet. It's not so much that he fears he would lose a lawsuit, but that he doesn't want to fight one if he can avoid it."

Two days later, they got the lawyers' report. What Karl wanted to do was iffy, but probably legal. The LIC was in place to give loans and provide startup capital and equipment to companies and businesses on the Liechtenstein holdings, wherever they were. Which of those companies were to receive the loans or gifts of the LIC was at the discretion of the board, under the direction of Karl von Liechtenstein. If he chose to have that money given into hands that would also benefit his future wife, well, there was no rule against it.

The Barbies set up the Dower Corporation, which would be funded by Karl out of his personal funds, then receive equipment and low interest loans from the LIC. It would be managed by the Barbies and would buy things like farms and mines on Liechtenstein holdings, and set up factories, also on Liechtenstein lands.

And in the meantime, the girls were sworn to secrecy. Not just in regard to the family, but especially in regard to Sarah.

They were in the middle of setting that up when Henry Dreeson was killed defending the synagogue in Grantville. Bill Magen, Vicky's fiancé, was shot and killed in some of the distracting riots and it seemed to Vicky that no one really noticed in all the concern over Mayor Dreeson.

Twenty-five Miles North of Vienna

Sonny Fortney took a drink of small beer and returned the canteen to his belt. It was a cold day, but he was working up a sweat in spite of the weather. There were several hundred people here and there were four more camps spread out like beads, each one using Fresno scrapers to build a roadbed to the next and the ones back toward Vienna with wagon after wagon of crushed rock and coal tar to pave the raised mound. Still, it was going incredibly slowly because the ground was frozen about half the time. In engineering terms, the smart thing to do would be to wait till spring. But people needed the work now, and if they waited till spring some of those people would have starved to death in the meantime. Sonny hoped that Prince Liechtenstein came through, because if he didn't they were going to have to shut down.

Vienna

"Well, the LIC sent the money," Moses Abrabanel said, smiling.

"I figured they would," said Dana Fortney. "But we still aren't going to be able to start the rail line. Not enough iron, and it will be four months before the steel mill in Linz will be running."

"I was given to understand it was going to use wooden rails."

"It is. In fact, we're going to use dowels instead of nails and spikes whenever we can. But we still can't avoid using steel for some things. And we need good steel, because to get the same strength from iron would take twice as much.

"No. . . . What we're going to have at first is simply a good road. That, we can do with just Fresno scrapers and lots of labor. That by itself will allow multitrailered steam wagons. Not great, but a heck of a lot better than a mule train. Then, using the road, Sonny figures that a single wooden rail to take most of the weight of the train will let us at least double the cargo capacity. But we won't even start that till next year at the earliest. Meanwhile, it's just a works project. Lots of people earning salaries. Not great salaries, but salaries."

"Well, that will help the unemployment and the level of debt your businesses have been accumulating."

"It should," Dana agreed, though she wasn't at all sure that it would help enough.

Grantville, United States of Europe

Karl Eusebius paced around the room as he dictated the letter to Herr Hofer, who sat at his typewriter. These weren't the easiest letters he had ever tried to write. First, one to the family, telling them he was engaged. Once the inimitable Herr Hofer had the letter in shorthand, he would type them out and give Karl a copy for his signature. Finally, he had the first one written and started the second. This one to Ferdinand III, the emperor of Austria-Hungary, explaining that he would like to come to Vienna for the wedding, but couldn't do it unless he had assurances that he would be allowed to leave again.

It helped a bit that Ferdinand III was a friend, and his younger brother Leopold was a close friend.

Karl debated. Perhaps if he wrote Leopold . . .

No. It had to be faced. His friend, the emperor, was probably somewhat angry that Karl had had to deal with King Albrecht of Bohemia. *Hm. That might be a solution*, Karl thought. Perhaps he could act as ambassador to Austria-Hungary from Bohemia. Perhaps King Albrecht might support him . . . that would give him diplomatic status.

Of course, diplomats did get taken hostage . . . sometimes. . . .

Karl stopped dictating letters and went to the telegraph office. This once, he was glad that the telegraph didn't go to Austria. Yet.

As it happened, King Albrecht of Bohemia was quite pleased with the plan. He had good reason to want a settlement with Austria-Hungary, because he wanted a fairly small chunk of Hungary without a war. Also, he wanted to avoid having the whole issue between the USE, Saxony and Brandenburg sucking in Austria-Hungary, because they would probably be sucked right through his territory. The shortest route from Austria-Hungary to Saxony was right through Bohemia.

So he was quick enough to agree with Karl's request, but it still took a little while to make everything official.

Magdeburg, United States of Europe

"So what do you think the chances are for hostilities to resume between Austria and Bohemia?" Mike Stearns asked his Secretary of State.

Landgrave Hermann of Hesse-Rotenburg pursed his lips thoughtfully. Now that he'd served the prime minister in this capacity for a year, Hermann was a lot more relaxed than he'd been at the beginning. Among other things, he'd learned that Stearns had no objection if one of his ministers took a bit of time to think upon a matter before expounding his opinion. He appreciated the fact, given that it suited his judicious temperament.

The truth was, Hermann hadn't wanted to become the Secretary of State in the first place—and still wasn't very happy with the situation. But he'd had little choice in the matter. His older half-brother Landgrave Wilhelm of Hesse-Kassel was one of Gustav Adolf's primary allies in Germany. He'd been keen to get Hermann a prominent position in the cabinet and refusing him would have been problematic.

Thankfully, Stearns had accepted the situation with good grace. He'd never been anything other than cordial in his dealings with Hermann and, as time passed, the young Landgrave of Hesse-Rotenburg had developed a great deal of respect for the prime minister.

There were many noblemen in the Germanies who considered the up-timers a pack of puffed-up peasants who owed their meteoric rise in status to nothing more than their mechanical skills. (Regrettable skills, to many—but hard experience had by now proven to even the most cast-iron aristocratic minds that the Americans made a huge difference when it came to war.) Hermann might have even been one of them, initially. He could no longer remember clearly what his attitude had been two or three years earlier.

Working as Stearns' Secretary of State, however, had disabused him of whatever notions he'd had then. He'd found that the USE's prime minister was as shrewd as any political leader in Europe, shrewder than most—and probably more far-thinking than any other. He had no intention of telling anyone—certainly not his own family—but he'd already decided that when the time came to vote for a new prime minister, he'd quietly vote for Stearns rather than Wilhelm Wettin. He disapproved of some of the up-timer's policies and had doubts about many others, but of one issue he was now certain—the position of the USE in its dealings with other powers was safer in Stearns' hands than it would be in any other's.

"Smaller all the time," he said. "There are three critical factors, and they all work in the direction of peace—even, I think, toward a final settlement."

"And they are . . . ?"

"First, the threat from the Ottomans. Which seems to be growing again. Second, the advice he's getting from Janos Drugeth."

"Which we know about because . . ."

Hermann grinned. "Drugeth keeps warning him, but the new emperor still has the habit of speaking in front of servants. Some of whom—two, I believe, although Fernando is evasive on the subject—are on our payroll."

Stearns chuckled humorlessly. "It'd probably be better to say, on anybody's payroll. But those two factors have been there for some time. What's the third one?"

"This one is new. It seems—I say this partly from the reports Francisco Nasi gets from Vienna, but also from word that comes to me through my own contacts—"

That meant other noblemen to whom Hermann was related in some way. Which, given the realities of aristocratic intermarriage, included a good chunk of Europe's entire upper crust. Mike Stearns had realized long since that European noblemen were every bit as sloppy about blabbing stuff to each other as they were about blabbing it in front of menials.

"—that the influence of the up-timers who moved—and are moving—to Vienna is growing faster than I'd ever have expected. I'm not sure why, but the fact of it seems certain."

He had a bemused, almost mystified expression on his face. Mike managed not to laugh, or even smile.

CHAPTER 16

𝔚𝔢𝔡𝔡𝔦𝔫𝔤 𝔓𝔩𝔞𝔫𝔰

March, April and May 1635

The Hofburg Palace, Vienna, Austria

Emperor Ferdinand III wasn't thrilled with the letter from Wallenstein. He looked at the two Liechtenstein brothers sitting across the table in the private audience room, and gestured with the letter from Karl Eusebius. "What is your nephew up to, gentlemen?"

"Walking the tightrope?" Maximilian von Liechtenstein said. "When we set up the family charter, it gave Karl and his heirs much of the control over the family estates. Karl Eusebius is trying to follow enough of the rules to keep that agreement from ending up in the courts while at the same time protecting the family's assets. Just in case."

"We can, Your Majesty, convince Karl Eusebius to provide more funds. I'm sure of that," Gundaker said. "But that sort of thing is best done face-to-face."

Moses Abrabanel snorted. "The princes Liechtenstein are well known for their wealth. However, I doubt that every groschen of it is enough to handle the problems we have today."

Ferdinand III said, "Every little bit helps, Moses."

"Yes, Your Majesty. But to solve the problem, we have to start creating money."

The uproar this caused filled the private audience room, but Moses overrode the noise. "I am less concerned with getting Prince

Karl here than I am with getting Sarah Wendell to Vienna. Up-timers still have great cachet, after all. And Sarah is an acknowledged expert in the field of economics. She does work for the USE Federal Reserve Bank and her father is their Secretary of the Treasury."

"You're saying that if we got her to endorse it, we could print more money without a larger silver reserve?"

"Yes, I think so."

Ferdinand III looked at the advisers, Moses Abrabanel, Gundaker and Maximilian von Liechtenstein, and Reichsgraf Maximilian von Trauttmansdorff. "So you all think I should accept Prince Karl's credentials as ambassador from Bohemia?"

The men around the table nodded.

Higgins Hotel, Grantville

"Maid of honor," Judy the Younger squealed. "Me? I thought sure you'd ask someone else."

"You're my only sister," Sarah pointed out, trying to sound regretful. "Now, if I'd had another sister..."

Judy tossed a pillow at her. "You know you love me." She hesitated a moment. "What about your other bridesmaids?"

"I really don't know," Sarah admitted. "Who's going to be able to travel all the way to Vienna? Most people I know are up to their eyeballs in work."

"What about us?" Judy stopped a moment. "The Barbies, I mean. We'd love an excuse to travel, you know."

"*Eek!*"

"Oh, don't be pretending to scream," Judy said. "You know we can be...well, act...really presentable when we want to."

"Yeah, maybe. It's getting you guys to want to that's the problem."

"Seriously, Sarah. I'd really like something for us to do that's out of Grantville. Vicky took Bill's death really hard. And if we don't get Susan away from the old...cats...in Grantville, she's going to explode. Even with all the uproar after Mayor Dreeson was killed, those old bats keep after her about her mom."

Sarah fully understood that, considering Velma Hardesty's reputation as a man-eating slut. "Actually," Sarah said, "having Susan in Vienna might be a very good idea."

"Take one, take us all." Judy laughed, but there was a catch in her voice. Even Judy was shaken by the deaths of Mayor Dreeson and Bill Magen and she knew that.

"Hush. I said that because I know that Karl's family is going to be looking for money. Susan is the best of your crew when it comes to holding on to money."

"I think she's got the first dollar she ever made," Judy said. "She's afraid to let go of any of it. Well, except for what she invests. She doesn't think that's spending it."

"And she's right. But Karl's family isn't looking to invest it. They're looking to loan it to the emperor."

Liechtenstein House, outside the Ring of Fire

"So how are we going to get there?" Susan Logsden asked. "I have no desire to repeat Hayley's trip to the frontier in a covered wagon."

"Vienna is hardly the frontier, Susan," Karl complained.

"You're right. It's past the frontier, well into Injun country," Vicky said harshly. "But my point is, I have no desire at all to spend weeks in a covered wagon, squatting in a field to do my business. I am a child of civilization."

"Well, you can stay home if you want," Sarah said repressively.

"Nope. Got a letter from Hayley. She needs us, so we're going, even if we leave the Ken Doll here in Grantville."

"Not a chance," Sarah said.

"I'll arrange transport," Karl said.

"How?" Sarah asked.

"I have no idea, but I'll think of something."

It took Karl two days to think of that something, and the expense of several radio calls back and forth to the Netherlands. But he got the loan of one of the Jupiters from Fernando, King in the Low Countries. Happily, the royal Netherlands airline had two Jupiters currently in service so they could spare one for a week or so. King Fernando might not have agreed on his own. He tended to hoard his beloved new aircraft the way dragons of legend hoarded gold. But Karl suspected he'd come under considerable pressure from his wife. Part of the arrangement was that Karl would bring letters to deliver to her family from Queen Maria Anna.

Fortney House, Race Track City

"Hey, Mom!" Hayley shouted, tracking mud in. "I just got a letter from Judy. Sarah is going to marry Prince Karl von Liechtenstein. Here! In Vienna!"

"What? What happened to David Bartley?" Dana asked.

"Got me. I always thought he was kind of cute, in an Ichabod Crane sort of way. Nothing to write home about. Maybe he just couldn't compete with the Ken Doll? You know, prince and all that."

"You think Sarah is the sort to go title hunting?"

"Not really, but I don't know her all that well. I mean, she's Judy's sister, yeah. But you know how older sisters are when it comes to their baby sister's 'little' friends."

"Big sisters are indeed cruel and heartless creatures. At least till you're all grown up, and they are never quite convinced that you really are an adult."

"Right. Just like Natasha is." Hayley grinned. "So, anyway, Sarah was always a bit distant and we all had the impression that she didn't approve of the adventurous nature of the Barbie Consortium, but apparently she's gotten over that." Hayley looked back at the letter. "Because Judy and the rest of the Barbies are to be her bridesmaids. Judy's going to be the maid of honor."

"That's great. If we don't go broke before they get here," Dana said. Over the last several months they had been building up a truly massive cache of I.O.Us and slowly spending themselves into bankruptcy to keep goods on the shelves.

"Yes, I know, Mom. I talked to Moses Abrabanel yesterday, and he is getting leery about loaning us money based on the notes we are carrying. He doesn't see how people are going to be able to pay us back, so he doesn't see how we are going to pay his family back. But we can't stop giving people credit."

It had become a matter of increasing worry over the last few months only partly ameliorated by getting into the exports trade. They were now shipping goods manufactured in Vienna up- and downriver, but that was not enough to cover their raw material costs. And even with their labor-saving machines making the goods, production still took labor. And labor had to be paid. "Look, Mom, Sarah is pretty good at the financial stuff. That's why Coleman Walker hired her, in spite of the fact that she is a woman and, in his eyes, still a kid. Maybe she can help. And the Barbies are doing real good in the USE. I can raise some money from them if I have to. We'll work something out." Hayley wasn't real sure whether she was trying to convince her mom or herself. And in either case, she didn't feel like she had done a great job.

Jack Pfeifer's Office, Race Track City

Jack Pfeifer was worried, too. As the lawyer for SFIC, he was aware of the amount of debt that SFIC was owed and he was increasingly concerned that it was going to be unpaid. If the Sanderlins and Fortneys wanted to, they could probably put two or three percent of the population of Vienna in debtor's prison. It was mostly small amounts of debt per individual, but no amount was small if it was more than someone could pay.

He pulled another form from the pile and checked the name, number and the amount against his records. *Three pairs of socks and a kerchief.* He shook his head. The man who had bought them worked on the canal project and was probably going to lose his job in another month when the canal was done. Then where was he going to get the money to pay this off? Jack sighed. He really needed to get a clerk to handle this, especially since it was checking what Mrs. Fortney or Mrs. Sanderlin had already done.

Krause Rooms, Vienna

"I got dinner, Maria," Adam Krause told his wife.

She looked worried. "They took your note again?"

"Yes, no trouble." His boots were muddy from a day behind a Fresno scraper, building the canal that would connect the Danube with Race Track City, and his wife helped out by working as a maid in the apartment block they lived in. They were getting by better, in fact, than they had for the last several years. But they were terrified about what would happen when the canal was finished and they lost his income. "It's all right. I'll find something. I am a good worker and I learn quick. Herr Fortney said so himself." Adam put all the confidence he could in that statement, and his Maria seemed to accept it.

It was a grand canal, too. Wide and deep, lined with stone and mortar. Adam suspected that they were making it grander than they had to, just as a way of keeping people working.

240Z Shop, Race Track City

"How's the canal going, Sonny?" Ron Sanderlin asked.

"Too damned well," Sonny Fortney said. "They work like beavers and we will be opening it in another week. Then what do we do with two hundred workers who are going to be out of a job?"

Sonny sighed. "I dunno, Ron. Maybe ask Hayley which project we ought to take on next?"

"Oh, quit bragging, dammit."

Fortney House, Race Track City

"I don't know, Dad. There are lots of things we could do, but no one has any money to buy anything. We could build a frigging skyscraper next door to St. Stephen's and fill it all, except no one could pay their rent. We could build factories and make everything from sewing machines to steam cars and no one could buy them 'cause no one has any money."

"Well, how are they doing it in Grantville?"

"The American dollar, Dad. They have the American dollar."

"What's wrong with the Austro-Hungarian thaler?"

Hayley looked at him. "Which would you rather have, Dad?"

"All right. But you know they are backed by silver."

"And, unlike most people, I actually believe it," Hayley agreed. "If they were issuing more than they had the silver to back, there would be enough of the thalers. Austria is suffering from deflation."

"I hate when you talk like Fletcher Wendell."

Hayley stuck out her tongue. "Don't blame me. I didn't make this mess."

"I know, but I remember the little girl who dressed her Barbies in overalls and hard hats and had them planning bridges over at Wave Pool."

"That's a possibility Dad. What about a water park? You know, people swim in the Danube during the summer. I bet a water park with swimming pools and stuff would be a big draw."

Through March and April, and into May, workers from the canal project managed to get moved either to the railroad or to the construction of the water park. While SFIC got further and further in debt.

Barclay Engineering, Vienna

Barclay Engineering was the bottom floor of a three-floor town-house rented by the Barclays. They lived on the second floor, and the servants on the third. Peter Barclay looked at the blueprint of the support ring for the concrete mill and tried to concentrate on his work. It wasn't easy. He could hear the servants moving around upstairs and the traffic on the street. Still, they were doing better than a lot of the royal hangers-on. They were *Hofbefreiten*, so they weren't paying city taxes. And he had been able to get quite a bit of paying work consulting on up-time innovations that the down-timers didn't understand or know how to use. All in all, they were getting by.

"What do you know about Karl von Liechtenstein?" his wife Marina asked.

"Only what his uncles say. Gundaker thinks he is a traitor to the Holy Roman Empire."

"There is no Holy Roman Empire and there hasn't been since before we left Grantville. And Prince Gundaker von Liechtenstein has a flagpole up his ass."

Peter snorted a laugh. "True enough on both counts, but he is who Ferdinand III stuck us with."

"Well, at least it wasn't that murderer Drugeth," Marina said, looking over at him. There was a smudge of charcoal on her nose and that had gotten to be a constant since they got to Vienna. No CAD systems here, not that there had been that many available in Grantville after the Ring of Fire. But at least there had been better pencils. It amazed Peter how much work it took to get ready to work here in Vienna. And that was even when they had a down-time staff. Most of whom, Peter was convinced, were spies.

"Well, Prince Karl was involved with David Bartley in that business with the Netherlands guilder a couple of years ago and they say he made millions."

"Financial shenanigans," Pete said. "Not building anything. Just arbitrage, and probably crooked as a dog's hind leg to boot."

Marina was looking at him and he snorted. "All right. I'm not talking about the Partow twins. They're clever enough, especially for untrained kids, but David Bartley and his grandmother are little more than con-artists who got tied into the down-time local power structure. You know that the down-timers do everything through marriage. And I don't believe for a second that Bartley was opposed to Delia Higgins' hotel venture. She got a sweetheart deal, count on it."

"Never mind Bartley. He's not coming here. What about Prince Karl?"

"A rich playboy is all. His family's money plus some good luck. Besides, from what Gundaker said they sent a really bright advisor with him."

"The Wendells seem all right," Marina said.

"The Wendells are tied into the Grantville power structure and that's why they got their positions, and that's why the daughters . . . well, the older girl . . . got her job in Magdeburg. From what they were saying back in Grantville, that whole Barbie Consortium was a bunch of underage femme fatales, using their looks to scam everyone."

"Some of the rumors said they used more than their looks," Marina said. "I heard that that Susan Logsden didn't fall far from her mother's tree and that Velma Hardesty was a slut from way back."

"Engineering takes time, skill, and training. The gambles they take in Grantville, the lack of proper analysis, is going to come back to haunt them," Peter said, just like he had said hundreds of times before. And it was true. He was constantly being pressured to do the same sort of sloppy engineering here, but he wouldn't do it. There were reasons for the regulations they had had up-time and no building or engine designed by Peter Barclay was going to fall down or blow up because he cut corners.

Meanwhile, Emperor Ferdinand was getting impatient and Peter couldn't blame him. It was just incredibly hard to build engines down-time. He had to do everything himself. It seemed that every part to make every machine to make a part of the next machine took more time and cost more than it could have. People always talked about how skilled these primitive craftsmen were supposed to be, but they took forever, and they wasted so much time on curlicues and fancy work that nothing ever got done. And he was sure in his gut that the new up-timers were going to come in with some trick and steal all the credit for all the work he had done.

In a way, Peter was right. But in a lot of ways he was wrong. The big difference between up-time production techniques and down-time production was not quality, but time. It takes a hellacious long time to do almost anything by hand. And if you're going to spend that much time on it in the first place, why not add in a little more to make it beautiful as well as functional? Meanwhile, over the past most of a year in Vienna, he had built up the infrastructure to build internal combustion engines. One piece at a time, because he wasn't good at delegating or trusting, and so required everything to go through him, but it was at least halfway to a finished product.

Peter's unwillingness to listen to the expertise of the down-time craftsmen who did know how to get the most out of their equipment was slowing things down even more.

Water Park, Race Track City

On the other hand, Dana Fortney was getting along quite well with down-timer ladies, teaching them yoga and therapeutic massage at the water park. The water park had evolved into a combination down-time bathhouse and up-time water park, with an up-time beauty shop next door to a down-time barber/surgeon. Well, sort of down-time barber/surgeons. The up-time knowledge of antiseptics had gone a long way to improve their outcomes. They weren't in Sharon Nichols' class—not even close—but they were much better than they had been. In fact, they were getting better results than the professional doctors from the university. The advance of the surgeon from hack to king of the medical profession was starting much sooner in this timeline.

Vienna

The message was terse and less than informative. It had been sent before it was even known whether Pope Urban was still alive, but other messages in the same pouch had confirmed that the pope was alive but had fled from Rome. Cardinal Borja was claiming that Urban had fallen into heresy, and half the priests in Vienna seemed to believe Borja's version. The other half was convinced that Borja was a Spanish pawn who was trying to place the whole church under the Spanish crown.

Over the next several days, the situation clarified some. In fact, there were two versions of events, each very clear and insistent. Even strident. Unfortunately, they were mutually exclusive.

In one version of events, Urban had fallen into heresy, abandoning the true church in favor of the Protestantism that the up-time church had fallen into, and—with great restraint and forbearance—the College of Cardinals had remonstrated with the erring pontiff for as long as possible. But the cardinals had finally been forced to take action to defend the faith against corruption. In this version, the true church had been forced to those measures only by Urban's insanity and the corruption of a faction of cardinals who had abandoned Christ's message.

In the other version of events, Urban had been in the process of weighing the issues brought into the world with the care and deliberation required by his position as head of the church, when a clique of ambitious and venal clerics under unknown influences had attempted to assassinate Christ's vicar on Earth and had succeeded in assassinating a majority of the cardinals. But, through God's grace, the pope had escaped the vile assassins and was continuing to do his duty. He had not decided the issue of the Ring of Fire and, even with the actions of Borja and his mad men, was not going to rush to judgment.

No one knew where Pope Urban was, but wherever he might be, messages from the Father General of the Jesuits confirmed that he was alive. On the other hand, the rump college of cardinals—mostly the Spanish faction—had, in effect, charged Father General Mutius Vitelleschi of the Jesuits with heresy and insisted that he was not to be trusted. They were, at the least, no longer claiming that Pope Urban had been killed in Rome.

Meanwhile, there had been fist fights and even knife fights between priests of the holy mother church. Fights mostly between orders that were not overly friendly with each other to begin with. The conflict between the Dominicans and the Jesuits had approached riots. Neither faction was all in favor of Urban or Borja, but the Dominicans tended to support Borja and the Jesuits tended to support Urban. According to Ferdinand III's confessor, Lamormaini was tending toward the Borja faction because of the raising of Larry Mazzare to cardinal, and was feeling somewhat ill-used by Father General Vitelleschi and Pope Urban.

And in the middle of this came the news that Karl Eusebius von Liechtenstein would be arriving within the week, with his fiancée... and in an airplane.

CHAPTER 17

𝔄 𝔖𝔱𝔬𝔯𝔪 𝔬𝔣 𝔅𝔯𝔦𝔡𝔢𝔰𝔪𝔞𝔦𝔡𝔰

June 1635

Aboard the Jupiter, en route to Vienna

Judy looked at Susan, three seats up and across the aisle. They were all in the Jupiter. It was surprisingly quiet, but not silent, and she could hear the engines faintly.

Susan Logsden needs to get laid, thought Judy with seventeen-year-old certainty. She thought this in spite of the fact that she herself was still technically a virgin and intended to remain one till someone developed a trustworthy means of contraception or she got married. Neither of which looked to be happening anytime soon. But Judy wasn't Susan, or perhaps more to the point, Susan wasn't Judy. Judy looked at the prospect of eventual intercourse with pleasant anticipation, but suffered very little frustration over its present lack. There were, after all, other things you could do.

Perhaps something could be worked out in Vienna. The pilot had just told them that they would be landing in a few minutes.

Vienna

Archduke Leopold Wilhelm of Austria, Bishop of Passau and brother to Emperor Ferdinand III, went over the papers and tried to forget that he was at least nominally a bishop. Leo had never thought of himself as overly religious. The church just was. But now the church wasn't. Urban had retreated from Rome. Borja was butchering cardinals, whether to conquer the church or to save it no one seemed to know. True churchmen, the monks and the real bishops, couldn't decide which side to be on. Order fighting order, priest condemning priest. He tried to retreat into the facts and figures that Gundaker von Liechtenstein and Moses Abrabanel had provided to ready him to meet Karl Eusebius and his bride.

"It's here, Your Grace," Marco said.

Leo looked up from the report. Just as well. There was little good news in it anyway. The treasury was essentially empty. The people who were supposed to be putting money into the treasury wanted things in return. Mostly they wanted products from the United States of Europe kept out of Austria-Hungary. The soldiers wanted to be paid, as did the bureaucracy. "Calm yourself, Marco. Calm yourself," Leo said, trying to sound like a bishop was supposed to. The title was political, a way of keeping lands that were nominally the church's in the family. Not that his father would have ever admitted such a thing, even to himself. To his father, Leo had been something of a human sacrifice, a child given to the church to ensure salvation.

Leo could hear a buzzing from the sky. He kept a straight face as he rose and moved to the window. Keeping a straight face when he was really just as excited as Marco was second nature. Habsburg training. By natural inclination, Leo's preference was for leading armies rather than prayers, but it didn't do to show that to the people surrounding him, any more than it would do to show excitement about the plane.

"But look at it, Your Grace!" Marco was still excited and a bit irrepressible. Leo hid a smile.

The plane had indeed arrived. It was turning, slowly it seemed, making a circle around Vienna before it landed on the hastily-built new airstrip near Race Track City.

"Karl is certainly making an impressive entrance," Leo murmured. When word came that Prince Karl Eusebius von Liechtenstein would be arriving in one of the Jupiter aircraft, Neil O'Connor had provided the information on its needs. Provided it with much bragging. To hear Herr O'Connor tell it, the *Air Cushion Landing Gear* had been wholly his innovation and much of the rest of the plane as well. It didn't need an airfield prepared, just a flat piece of ground or, even better, water. Then a place to park. Markers had been placed on the south bank of the Danube where it was to pull out of the river.

Then, unfortunately, the news had arrived that one of its sister ships had crashed in Italy. It seemed the peculiar landing gear had failed. Apparently there had been many maintenance problems with the landing gear even before the crash. As a result, the Royal Dutch Airlines, which owned the Jupiters, had refitted all of them—more precisely, the only one still in service at the moment—with more conventional landing gear.

So, a landing strip needed to be constructed. Happily, the land around Race Track City had many flat areas and there were now a number of Fresno scrapers on the site. Happier still, from the instructions sent ahead by the airline company, the Jupiter's new landing gear, like the plane itself, was quite sturdy. The strip didn't need to be macadamized, although that would certainly be an advantage in the future. They just needed to make sure the strip was smooth, level, and cleared of any rocks or stones.

Neil O'Connor offered his advice on that subject as well. Maintaining all the while that he'd never trusted that weird ACLG landing gear, nohow.

"Come, Marco," Leo said. "We're the greeting party." Leo headed to Race Track City.

Landing Strip, near Race Track City

"Back, there. Back, back. You want to get run over!" Neil O'Connor had reached the landing strip ahead of them and was shouting in poorly accented German. With the help of half a company of the city garrison, he seemed to be shooing most of Vienna out of the parking place of the aircraft. The guardsmen were having difficulty keeping the crowd back.

"Move," Marco shouted. The crowd parted, mostly because of the guards who surrounded Archduke Leopold. As the path appeared, Leo moved forward. "Would you look at that?" another guard whispered when they got to the front.

The Jupiter was sitting at the far end of the landing strip and slowly turning around in the wide area that had been leveled for that purpose. Then, it began moving slowly back to the strip's beginning where it had first set down and where the crowd was gathered.

"They call that 'taxi-ing,'" said the same guard. "I don't know why. Thurn and Taxis has nothing to do with airplanes."

The approaching airplane looked enough like a monster that the guards had no great difficulty getting the crowd to move back off the landing strip and onto the grounds beyond. Once they'd done so, the aircraft moved the final distance and came to a halt. There was a peculiar noise of some kind and the blurry things on the wings—they were called "propellors," Leo knew—began to slow down. Eventually they stopped spinning, and Leo could now see that they looked like long and twisted oar-blades.

The door on the side of the airplane opened and Prince Karl stepped out onto the lower wing, followed by a pretty young woman. "Leo, ah, Your Grace!" Karl waved, then bowed, and nearly stumbled as the young woman pulled him aside to clear the door. Leo held back a snort of laughter, and moved forward a bit. Others had exited the plane to stand on the wing, including a young man carrying a ladder, which he attached to the rear of the wing.

"Your Grace," Karl said, coming down the stepladder. Leo had known Karl Eusebius von Liechtenstein most of his life, but Karl had been away for several years now.

"Prince von Liechtenstein." Leo nodded, then glanced at the young woman who had followed him down.

Karl took the hint. "Your Grace, may I introduce my fiancée? Assistant Secretary of Economic Forecasting for the Federal Reserve Bank of the USE, Miss Sarah Wendell von Up-time. Sarah, His Grace, Bishop and Archduke Leopold Wilhelm von Hapsburg." The girl, Sarah, performed a small dip of her knees, not a bow, not a curtsy. Just a dip, of sorts. She was much, much different from the young woman who had come to Austria with the defectors. No tattoos he could see, and not a single facial piercing. That was a relief. Leo had begun to wonder about these up-time women after seeing Suzi Barclay.

More young women joined them. "And the rest of our visitors, Your Grace. This is Sarah's sister."

Leo took his eyes off Sarah. He turned his head and suddenly felt like he'd been struck by lightning.

Karl was still talking. "Judith Wendell von Up-time."

"Your Grace," the vision said. "So pleased to meet you. Call me Judy, please. Everyone does."

Beauty incarnate, Leo thought. It was strange, really. She wasn't that attractive by the artistic standards of the seventeenth century. Too thin by half, he would have said if he were looking at a painting. But this wasn't a painting. She flowed, she floated, she waved to the crowd. She smiled and you were welcomed into heaven.

Leo went through the rest of the greeting in a haze. He performed his function in a daze, which proved the value of years of training in protocol. Judy had a soft, furry voice. Leo felt like everything she said was a secret shared with him, and him alone.

The rest of the young ladies came forward. Karl pointed at each. "Victoria Maureen Emerson von Up-time, Susan Elizabeth Logsden von Up-time, Gabrielle Carlina Ugolini von Up-time, Millicent Anne Barnes von Up-time." Leo worked at remembering all the strange names. Then Gundaker von Liechtenstein arrived, and brought Leo back to the present. It was Prince Karl who was important here. More important than the plane, even.

Gundaker had made it all quite clear. The empire was broke. Worse than broke. Without the taxes provided by Bohemia and Moravia, Austria-Hungary didn't have the assets to cover the loans already outstanding. Almost as bad, many of their potential loan sources had instead invested money in the new businesses in the USE. Including the Liechtensteins, in the person of Karl. In spite of which the Liechtenstein family in Austria had, under considerable pressure, made further loans to the royal purse. And that money was now mostly spent to keep the Austrian government from appearing as broke as it was. When asked for more, they had pointed out that there wasn't any more, at least not in Austria-Hungary. They had lost a lot of their income to Wallenstein at the same time the Austro-Hungarian empire had. Karl, however, safe in Grantville in the USE had investments of considerable worth.

"My Lord of the Exchequer." Leo bowed precisely the right amount for a younger brother of the emperor to a member of the highest nobility who was many years his senior. Gundaker was a stickler for protocol. "It's so nice to see you again."

"Your Grace," Gundaker answered, even more precisely than usual. Leo wondered what had him upset. Then he realized it was the up-timer girls. Sarah Wendell von Up-Time to be precise. Gundaker was not one of those who subscribed to the notions of up-timer nobility. Gundaker was a bit of a prick even if he was a highly efficient organizer and quite bright. He had long since appointed himself the job of seeing that no one show the Liechtenstein family *lèse majesté*. Gundaker was happy enough that Karl was making a morganatic marriage. It opened up the inheritance of the Liechtenstein lands to his branch of the family, after all. On the other hand, Gundaker didn't approve of jumped-up peasants. He didn't approve of Sarah Wendell and was only willing to put up with the marriage at all because it removed any potential children from the succession. That, and the fact that most of Prince Karl's money was sitting comfortably in the USE, where the rest of the family couldn't get hold of it, at least not without Karl's acquiescence. The Liechtenstein family and the Austro-Hungarian Empire needed that money. It was a weak bargaining position for Gundaker, a position he found less than comforting.

This was something that Leo had already talked to his older brother Ferdinand III about. The Austro-Hungarian Empire had no particular objection to recognizing the title "von Up-time." Marriages, after all, were significantly cheaper than wars. Ah. Here it came. Karl was introducing his harem, ah, the young ladies, to his uncle. "Sarah Wendell von Up-time, Judith Elaine Wendell von Up-time, Victoria Maureen Emerson von Up-time..." With each introduction Gundaker's face got a little bit stiffer.

"Hi, guys!" came from out of the crowd.

"Hayley!" Judy shouted back. "Let her through!"

Leo nodded, though it wasn't really necessary. Whether it was Judy's voice, which carried a natural assumption of obedience or the obvious fact that several of the nobles gathered around the plane knew Hayley Alma Fortney or some other reason, Hayley was already through the guards. Hayley Fortney, the daughter of one of his brother's mechanics, joined them next to the plane.

"So!" Victoria Maureen Emerson von Up-time asked in English, "how is life in the sticks?"

Leo felt his face stiffen up. Gundaker's was already stone, now it turned to iron. The plays and even movies had spread rapidly—not all of them, but some. Granted, the remark was in English and up-timer English to boot, but sticks and hicks had been translated as slang expressions for villages and villains/villagers.

"It's a translation issue," Judy said.

Leo looked at her, wondering what she was talking about, and she continued, looking back and forth between Leo and Gundaker. "It's one of the most difficult issues we've run into since the Ring of Fire brought us here. It's not the direct meaning of words, though that has been a problem. But the indirect unconscious meanings that people attach. The implications can be quite different than we expect."

"And what was mistranslated?" Gundaker asked.

"I have no idea, but from your expression something was." Then she grinned like an imp and winked at Gundaker. And Leo found himself trying not to laugh.

"Sticks, perhaps?" Leo asked.

"How would you translate it?"

"Out among the villagers, probably."

"And why would that be so very insulting?" Judy asked.

Now Leo was caught. What exactly was so insulting about being called a villager? Were they not as much children of God as the citizens of Vienna? Yet Leo knew that he did feel insulted and he knew why. He was the younger son of the last Holy Roman Emperor, and whatever the Bible might say, he was no peasant and didn't appreciate being thought of as one.

"Perhaps you don't see the insult because you were born in a village yourself," Gundaker offered. "Uncultured, without the benefit of civilization."

"In a way you're absolutely right." Judy grinned. "But not in the way you mean. I was never a 'villain' in the sense it is so often used here and now. I was always a citizen. A citizen of the United States of America. I never met a 'villain' till after the Ring of Fire." Her voice put quotes around villain. "As to the uncultured part... Well, the truth is we have nearly four hundred years more civilization than you do. Great art, great music, great generals, engineering, medicine, mathematics, economics, all sorts of stuff. Things that are available in and near the Ring of Fire, even to an extent in Magdeburg. That part was sort of valid, I guess. But we don't hold their lack against you." Judy smiled again, a thoroughly condescending smile. "At least, we try not to. It would be uncivilized to do so."

Leo had never seen Gundaker von Liechtenstein so thoroughly put in his place.

Hayley Fortney had apparently been explaining to the young ladies what it was like in the sticks. There was quite a bit of giggling going on. Leo suddenly wondered how she knew the other girls. "How is it that the daughter of one of my brother's auto mechanics knows you and your friends, Judy?"

"Because the daughter of your brother's auto mechanic is"— and now Judy's voice became quite cultured, almost a parody of cultured—"Hayley Alma Fortney von Up-time. A member in good standing of the Barbie Consortium." Then Judy's voice returned to its normal friendly, welcoming tones. "And a friend of all of ours since before the Ring of Fire." Then in a whisper, "She's loaded!"

"'Loaded'?"

"Rich."

"If her family is," Leo grinned and whispered back, "'*loaded!*' why is her father working as my brother's mechanic?"

"Oh, her family's not rich. Comfortable, even well off, okay. Quite well off, what with the family money she's been investing for them. But Hayley is the one who's rich. Besides, her dad likes cars."

Which gave Leo a whole other set of things to think about. Not just "what was her father doing here," but "what was the daughter doing here?" It was known, or at least suspected within the family, that Herr Fortney was probably a spy and he was being watched. But if the daughter was the spy, what was she spying on? Neither she nor either mechanic nor their families had made any great effort to insert themselves in the top rung of Viennese society. Instead they talked with the artisans and merchants of Vienna. Which is precisely what one should expect from someone who was keeping Ferdinand III's race cars in working order and building steam engines. But not exactly what you would expect of "Hayley Alma Fortney von Up-time, a member in good standing of the Barbie Consortium." Whatever that was.

CHAPTER 18

𝕿𝖗𝖚𝖉𝖎'𝖘 𝖔𝖓 𝖙𝖍𝖊 𝕵𝖔𝖇

June 1635

Liechtenstein House, Vienna

"Careful with that!" Trudi von Bachmerin's voice wasn't exactly a shout, but it was authoritative. "That is one of less than thirty bottles of up-time bottled wine that still has its original contents. It's worth more than you'll make in a year." It was, in fact, a bottle of $6.95 red table wine named Frog's Seat with a picture of an inebriated cartoon frog toppling off a lily pad. When Gabrielle Ugolini's mother had started to open it to celebrate something two months after the Ring of Fire, Gabrielle had thrown a fit, which was not at all like her. To keep the peace, Mrs. Ugolini put the bottle away. Two years later, after the Barbies had made a name for themselves, Mrs. Ugolini found the bottle in the cupboard and asked about it. Vicky Emerson bought it at auction for twelve hundred dollars and expressed her intent to drink it. That's when Susan Logsden had a fit. "You don't drink an investment!" Vicky had almost drunk it on the spot just to piss Susan off, but calmer heads had prevailed. Susan conceded that it was Vicky's and Vicky had agreed that at twelve hundred bucks a bottle she probably ought to save it for a special occasion. The bottle, still unopened, now resided in a padded teakwood case. The last offer Vicky had turned down was five thousand dollars and the wine aficionado's firstborn son. The boy had pimples. Vicky still planned to drink it someday—in front of Susan.

160

Meanwhile, Vicky had become something of a wine snob. The truth was that Vicky had had exactly one glass of up-time wine since the Ring of Fire but between that and more liberal experience with down-time wines, she was fully aware that the vintners' art had improved over the centuries. The very best down-time wines were way better than the wine in her teak case, but ninety percent of the wines of the seventeenth century weren't nearly as good. Trudi had never had so much as a sip of up-time wine and frankly preferred beer. The comment, while probably true, was mostly to get the attention of one of the upper servants. *Ah. Here he comes now.*

"And you are?" in that snotty Viennese Austrian accent.

"Gertrude von Bachmerin." With this sort, so her mother had always told her, it was best to establish authority right from the start. "*Administrative Assistant* to Millicent Anne Barnes von Up-time."

And so it proved. The guy's accent lost some of its snootiness. "Ah...what is an *Administrative Assistant*?"

So Trudi went into her spiel on up-time socioeconomic ranks. It was guaranteed to leave a down-timer at least as confused as most up-timers were in dealing with German ranks of nobility. It also left the impression that the girls had quite a lot of rank in the up-timer system and so, by extension, did Trudi. She mentioned that Judy had been a junior varsity cheer leader just like "Baroness Julie Sims Mackay, yes, the one with the rifle."

A few hours later, Trudi hid a grin as Vicky started to complain.

"I'm going to raise some serious hell when we get back to Magdeburg." Vicky kicked off her high heels. "That shoemaker didn't get these right yet."

Millicent sniffed. "Maybe if you weren't trying to wear four-inch heels, your feet wouldn't hurt so much. It's not like you aren't five seven in your stocking feet, anyway. You and Judy, both."

"You're just jealous, Shorty."

Before the conversation could degenerate any further Susan apparently decided to step in. "I'd expected Vienna to be a lot more...well, more. It's tiny. And crowded. Did you see all those shacks built up against the walls? I wonder who lives there?"

"Everybody without any money," Hayley put in. "And that's almost everyone who isn't a noble, as near as I can tell."

"When the maid came in, I got her to talking about the place," Trudi said. "She is quite proud of being in the Liechtenstein service. People must be desperate for work here."

"They are," Hayley said. "You would not believe the things I've seen here, Trudi."

Since Millicent was the chief administrative officer of the Barbie Consortium, that made Trudi the Barbie Consortium's administrative assistant. It also meant she won the contest to see who would fly to Vienna and who would ride. More servants and assistants were following by less expensive transport, but what they would need in the first days here was an office manager. It also helped that she was the daughter of an imperial knight. Susan, as usual, put it bluntly. "Rank matters to down-timers."

The reason that the daughter of an imperial knight was acting as servant to the Barbie Consortium had to do with the fact that not all imperial knights were idiots and most of them weren't all that wealthy. Trudi's dad had seen the writing on the wall fairly quickly and put Trudi in Grantville High, where she had met the Barbies. Grantville was a whole other power structure, one that depended a lot less on what your parents were. It was a power structure that the members of the Barbie Consortium were totally plugged into. That had allowed the Consortium to help her family out of what amounted to penury, while making a nice profit on the deal.

Papa, who was already interested in up-timers, became a firm supporter of up-timers in general and the Barbie Consortium in particular. While ranks in the up-timer social structure were less clearly defined, they were still quite real. With the full support of her father, Trudi had attached her wagon to the BC's rising star. She insisted on becoming what she called their "lady in waiting." Meanwhile, she'd also learned English, learned typing, and the basics of bookkeeping. As well, she'd taken up calligraphy and answered any invitations in various elegant scripts.

"What I'm worried about right now is Sarah," Judy said. "I mean, I'm just as glad not to have to attend a formal dinner after that plane ride, but you guys know Sarah. If anybody can open mouth and insert foot, it'll be her."

"I don't think the Ken Doll's uncle liked any of us much," Gabrielle said. "He didn't give me any dirty looks, but the one he laid on Millicent was a lulu."

Judy giggled. "Sarah hates it when we call Karl that."

"Which is why we do it," Vicky said. "Sarah needs to lighten up."

"Not as much as she hates the whole 'von Up-time' thing," Millicent added. "And Mike Stearns hates it even worse."

"Well, you can't drop it," Trudi said. "*Von* Liechtenstein, remember? *Von* Habsburg." They had been all through this and it wasn't the up-timers who had started it anyway. It was down-timers, specifically the *Daily News* and it was on a par with the "Prince of Germany" title that Germany had given Mike Stearns, whether he wanted it or not. Some of the up-timers got all offended by it and others reveled in it, but for the girls of the Barbie Consortium it was a convenience that let von-conscious down-timers deal with them without feeling like they were being forced to demean themselves.

"At least von Up-time is accurate, which is more than most of the vons running around have going for them. You *are* from the future."

They all hushed at the knock on the door and kept quiet while Trudi directed the townhouse servants in laying their private dinner. There was some surprise when Trudi had them set it up as a buffet and informed them that she would handle the service alone.

The girls were in a suite of four rooms, none very large, in one wing of the von Liechtenstein townhouse. Judy wondered just who had been bumped out of the rooms to give them this much space. As it was, the six of them, including Sarah, shared three bedrooms, and this salon would be used for any meals they took away from the family and as an office.

"You know," Susan said, after she'd filled her own plate and sat down, "I don't know how anybody stands never having any privacy. From what we've learned over the last few years, I don't know why everyone isn't stark raving mad from being surrounded all the time. And Vienna is more crowded than anyplace I've ever seen."

"You don't miss what you've never had," Trudi pointed out. "Even during the worst years, I always had a maid in my room at night."

"You lived alone after your grandfather died for too long, Susan," Judy said. In truth, Judy worried about Susan quite a bit. Her experiences in Grantville, due to the gossip about her tramp of a mother, had soured Susan on a lot of things. Men, for instance. While Susan was perfectly happy to deal with anyone in a business sense, she kept any male at arm's length in a personal sense.

Everything Susan did was directed at business and making more and more money.

It ticked Vicky off for anyone to worry about her but that didn't stop Judy. Vicky was a steam roller. All push and no finesse. She was a gun-toting steam roller these days, too, as well as being in mourning for Bill Magen. "Yea, though I walk through the shadow of death, I shall fear no evil, 'cause I'm the meanest bitch in the valley" used to be Vicky's motto. After Bill's death during the Dreeson assassination, Vicky hadn't said it as much. But that worried Judy even more. And now, with the Catholic church seeming to disintegrate before their eyes in the last few weeks, Judy was really worried about how Vicky was going to handle it.

And Gabrielle was here, planning to attend a down-time medical university. Which Judy thought wasn't going to be a lot of fun.

"When will all our stuff get here, again?" Judy asked. "Is it next week, or the week after?"

"Two weeks from tomorrow," Millicent said. "If they don't have too much trouble on the road or with the barges. Though I have no idea where we're going to put it all."

"You can put a bunch of it out by the race track," Hayley offered. "We've got more space out there and it's turning into a decent little town on its own. And we've got houses built out there, too."

"So what's the situation, Hayley?" Susan asked. "I've been reading your reports, and it looks like you're spending more than you're making."

"If you don't count the IOUs," Hayley said. "We've got a whole bunch of them."

"Are they any good?" Susan asked. "A pile of IOUs means nothing if they don't get paid off."

"I really don't know what's wrong," Hayley admitted. "We make good products, we're selling them at a fair price, but if we weren't giving credit we'd be out of business."

"I may know what's going on," Judy said. "Sarah's been talking about it. Austria-Hungary is broke. Not just the emperor. The whole frigging country."

"What do you mean?" Hayley asked.

"You'll have to ask Sarah." Judy shrugged. "I don't really understand it."

"Hayley, other than that little problem, how's the situation?" Millicent asked.

"Dire, but if Sarah can fix the broke problem and if the Catholic church doesn't implode and take Austria-Hungary with it, there could be some major opportunities. Another problem is that corruption isn't just common, it's institutionalized. The local bureaucrats aren't paid at all. They work for tips."

"That's true in Germany, too," Millicent said. "At least sometimes."

"Yes, but Germany was enjoying the benefits of fifteen years of war." Hayley gave the group a sardonic look.

"Benefits?" Trudi asked. There hadn't been much in the way of benefits in her experience of war.

"Sorry, Trudi. But aside from—or perhaps because of—the rape and pillage, war tends to loosen things up."

"I'm willing to forgo my traditional bribe for allowing you to do business in exchange for your not shooting me." Trudi nodded. "Or not taking your troops out of the way so someone else can burn down your town. Which was the subtle stick you up-timers used."

"I don't mind tipping for good service," Judy said.

"Neither do I," said Hayley. "But no one is offering to burn down Vienna, so we can't tip them by stopping it. Besides, a lot of the power structure here in Vienna seems intent on receiving bribes for screwing us over. And that I *do* mind. But unless the Ottomans decide to attack, I don't see what's going to get the burghers and the *Hofbefreiten* to forgo their traditional kickbacks. And there is enough resentment of up-timers and enough just plain old fear of competition that they are being completely unreasonable anywhere they can."

"The *Hofbefreiten?*" Vicky asked.

"The upper crust, the Nob Hill crowd, 'They of Vienna'... you get the idea. The Liechtenstein family are members of the nobility, sort of the *Hofbefreiten*, because they are part of the court. The city council and the guild masters are a competing but intermixed power structure and they both want bribes to get anything done. Partly it's who gets invited to which parties. At the same time, if you're not on the right party list, it's really hard to do business above a pretty meager level.

"Rob Sanderlin and Dad's position as a master craftsmen in unique crafts puts us in the *Hofbefreiten* branch and since Race Track City is outside Vienna, effectively the whole town is *Hofbefreiten* in a way. Which doesn't make the burghers love us. There are some things I could have done on my own in town but with the burghers locking everyone not a member of the club out, it would have caused a fuss. Mostly SFIC has worked out of town."

"So how do we break it open?" Vicky asked.

"I'm not sure we can. There's another problem."

"What's that?" Judy asked.

"There is a real possibility of government seizures of anything we do. We have some political clout because the emperor really likes the cars . . . but it only goes so far. The *Hofbefreiten* and the burghers are holding a lot of royal debt, most of it overdue. And even the *Hofbefreiten* proper, the ones in Vienna, aren't all that thrilled with Race Track City. Unless Sarah's Karl can come through with some counter pressure, His Imperial Majesty might keep the lenders happy by shutting us down."

"So where'd they get the money to loan the emperor?" Millicent asked.

"Vienna has the only bridge over the Danube for a good distance in either direction. It has been able to siphon off a fair chunk of the Danube trade and the cross-river traffic as well. Locally, it's wine country."

"Is the wine any good?" Vicky asked.

"It's white." Hayley shrugged. "Other than that, I couldn't say."

"Barbarians!" Vicky complained. "I'm surrounded by barbarians."

"Do you still have 'The Bottle'?" Hayley asked.

"She does," Trudi said. "I saw to its unpacking this afternoon."

"That may just be a criminal offense," Hayley told them, apparently trying to sound worried but not making a very good job of it. "There is a law against importing wine. It's mainly aimed at the Hungarian wine trade but . . ." Then she continued with the lecture. "Look, Vienna grew up taxing a cut of all the traffic on or crossing the Danube. They have lots of practice at figuring just how much they can skim. That provided them excellent training for becoming a city of government functionaries who know just how much they can charge in kickbacks without making the project obviously unprofitable. They'll charge just enough so that the merchant doesn't go the eighty miles out of his way to get to the next crossing. Or so that the petitioner to the emperor doesn't complain about the bribes he had to pay to get in. Except they are afraid of the up-timer innovations and they don't have any good measuring stick to figure how much the bribe should be. Put the two together and you get an entrenched bureaucracy that consistently overcharges.

"In a way, the crisis over the church has been helpful. People have sort of forgotten about us out at Race Track City while the priests and monks have been fighting each other over whether Urban is still the pope or if he is an outlaw heretic. We got a priest out there late last year and, of course, just about everybody here is Catholic. Father Degrassi is a Jesuit but not a fanatic about it. He's mostly just a parish priest, and he's a pretty reasonable guy. Oh, he tells Mom she's going to burn in hell, but he's mostly just joking and in no hurry to start the process early. So anyway, since the pope booked out of Rome, everyone has been crazy. The issue of whether Race Track City should be forcibly incorporated into Vienna has been put on the back burner. We haven't had any riots out there and the three fights were broken up by our guards."

They continued to talk about the situation in Vienna while they ate.

CHAPTER 19

𝔇inner at the 𝔥ead 𝔗able

June 1635

Liechtenstein House, Vienna

Dinner was going fine, Karl thought. They were using the gold-electroplated flatware from the Wish Book, which Karl found amusing. The tableware was Viennese-made china-style porcelain. The tablecloth was linen, with lace doilies for the place settings. It was surprising how much of the Liechtenstein dinner setting was out of Grantville, in style if not in fact. Conversation was light, mostly about Karl's investments in Grantville and Amsterdam.

Having met Fernando, King in the Low Countries, before he became king, Karl expressed the belief that Maria Anna had made on her own a better match than her father had provided. "Especially since I doubt Maximilian of Bavaria will survive much longer."

"And suppose Gustav oversteps? Perhaps is killed?" Maximilian von Liechtenstein asked, suddenly serious.

"It's possible, I suppose, but I doubt it. And even if he does, it won't make that much difference. The duke of Bavaria has cut himself off from most of his support. He has the USE to the north and Austria-Hungary to the south and east, Bernard's territory to the southwest and no one much cares for him. The USE is the real problem for him. They are both too strong and too rich for him to do more than annoy...and he annoys them at his peril."

"On that subject, how is it that the USE let you take one of their airplanes?"

"Actually, the plane we arrived in is owned by King Fernando," Karl said.

"He bought TEA and converted it to Royal Dutch Airlines this spring," Sarah said.

"The USE doesn't object?" Maximilian asked.

"Not really. About half the ownership is from the Netherlands and always was. People who got out of Amsterdam just before the siege closed in. With the settlement, several of them have gone back to Amsterdam. TEA now has several Jupiters, although they have trouble keeping more than one or two in the air at any one time. Otherwise, it would have been difficult to get the charter flight when we came here, even considering that Karl owns about five percent and the Barbies own another three."

"The Barbies?" asked Maximilian's wife, Katharina, as a maid served soup from her left, just as the up-time manuals said she should. "I thought those were dolls? One of my friends has a Barbie doll that was bought in Venice for seventy-five guilders. It came with a certificate of authenticity, confirming that it was a real up-time produced Barbie doll owned by Delia Higgins."

"Delia's dolls have certainly traveled." Sarah smiled. The serving maid placed a bowl of soup before her. Sarah turned to the young woman and said, "Thank you. It smells delicious," before turning back to answer Karl's Aunt Katharina, not noticing the sudden stiffness in the postures of Gundaker and Countess Aldringer. Uncle Max didn't seem all that upset, but Sarah was still talking. "The Barbies I was referring to are my younger sister and her friends. Like Delia Higgins and some others in town, they had a collection of dolls, mostly Barbie dolls. The girls sold them and used the money to go into investing, starting with a good number of shares of HSMC."

"How is it your parents allowed that?" Gundaker asked.

"Allowed what?"

"Allowed investment in business."

Sarah looked at Gundaker in confusion. "Isn't that what your family does? I mean, Kipper and Wipper and, well, some looting of Protestant lands, is where most of your family's wealth came from, but wasn't it mostly business? Granted, your brother, Karl's father, wasn't very good at it, but that was at least in part because you didn't have the theory to understand what you were doing."

Karl cringed. Gundaker was looking for reasons not to like Sarah and she had just given him two. Karl had seen his automatic distaste for Sarah from the greetings when they had landed. But if there was one thing that Gundaker cared about more than any other, it was the family's reputation as nobility, not mere merchants or tradesmen.

"Are you out of your mind?" Gundaker poured himself a brandy from the table of drinks set out in the library. "The girl is little more than a servant. Cunning and low. And don't give me that crap about up-timers' nobility. The Barclays have been riding that to death. No one believes it, less now than when they arrived."

Karl had been planning on bringing up the miraculous nature of the Ring of Fire, but now didn't seem to be the right time. Opinions about the class into which the up-timers fell varied quite a bit. He walked over and sat in one of the leather-upholstered chairs.

"Calm down, Brother." Maximilian sipped his brandy and leaned back in his chair. "Granted, the Barclays haven't produced that much in the way of results. Yet. But it's been less than a year. And honestly, they have a point about the lack of funding."

"I know and that's not what I'm talking about," Gundaker said. "It's their attitude. They act as though we were some primitive tribesmen. Then they turn around and act like some obsequious tailor, whining about the cost of cloth."

Karl couldn't resist a snort. If that was what Uncle Gundaker was used to from the Barclays and their associates, he was in for a rude awakening. Not that Sarah was all that socially astute, but she was aware of her lack of social skills. And Judy the Barracudy was about as socially skilled as anyone Karl had met short of Dowager Empress Eleonora. Gundaker was looking at him waiting for an explanation of his snort.

"There's an expression I got from David Bartley, Uncle," Karl tried to explain. "'A rising tide lifts all boats.' Grantville, the Ring of Fire, the whole area, is experiencing a rapidly rising economic tide. And while it hasn't lifted all the fortunes of all the up-timers, it's done a pretty decent job. In that environment, the Barclays felt themselves so unsuccessful that they were willing to move to Vienna, where there would be less competition. The Barclays have skills, serious skills even by the standards of the up-timers. So why, Uncle? Why were they available? Why weren't they busy getting rich in Grantville or Magdeburg?"

"Why?" Maximilian leaned forward, looking at Karl.

"Understand, I had met only two members of the Barclay group, and that only once or twice in passing. After they left there was quite a bit of discussion as to why, but most of it second- or third-hand. Just rumors really." Karl shrugged away any personal knowledge of the Barclays or their companions. "The word in Grantville was that they were 'Never Workers.' With almost every project or company that has been started since the Ring of Fire there has been someone, usually more than one, explaining why it would 'never work.' The right tools aren't available. The down-time craftsmen aren't up to the challenge. That's not the way they did it before the Ring of Fire. Sometimes the 'Never Workers' are right and sometimes not.

"But right or wrong, they don't put their money, or their time or energy, into the project. When it does work, they make no profit, because they weren't involved. When it doesn't work, they take no loss but again, they make no profit. Uncle, while I was in Grantville I made fifteen major investments and a host of minor ones. Of the fifteen, six were unmitigated failures and three were 'Grantville failures,' which means they broke even or made only a little profit. The least profitable of the real successes paid for all six failures. From what I understand, the Barclays made no major investments. Partly that was because they were visiting Grantville at the time of the Ring of Fire, so they had very little money to invest. But they also failed to invest their labor, requiring payment up front for whatever services they provided." Karl grinned at his uncle. "In the same amount of time, Sarah went from a child with no money of her own to an independently wealthy young woman."

"I take it you're saying your young lady..." Maximilian von Liechtenstein paused clearly looking for just the right phrase, "...is different from the Barclays."

Karl nodded.

"What about the Sanderlin and Fortney families?" Gundaker asked. "Those girls seemed well acquainted with the daughter of the mechanic that the emperor hired to take care of his toys."

Karl paused. He had not given a great deal of thought to why Sonny Fortney had gone to Vienna while his daughter was getting rich in Grantville. He had just assumed that family necessity had trumped the daughter's preference. But Sonny had been added by the Sanderlins. That was clear, as he thought back on their discussions last year. Why had Sonny Fortney agreed to go? He was a friend of Herr Sanderlin, or at least he had seemed to be, but they hadn't struck Karl as that close. And Karl had wanted him to survey a railroad, but that had come later. Karl pushed it from his mind. He had other matters to deal with. "Hayley Fortney is a member of the Barbie Consortium. She knows quite a bit about the mechanics of up-time tech and a reasonable amount about business. I would expect that she has done well here, hasn't she?"

Gundaker's son, Hartmann, had been to Grantville too, if only for a short time. He laughed. "Someone certainly has, though I had no idea that the girl was more than peripherally involved. I told you, Father, that they do things differently in Grantville."

"They do things stupidly in Grantville, then," Gundaker said. "Those idiots out at Race Track City are giving credit to all the wrong sort of people and they are going to lose their wealth when their debtors are unable to pay."

"I wouldn't count on that, Uncle," Karl said. "Sarah is quite well off, but her younger sister is even wealthier. And a good part of—" Karl managed not to say "my wealth" and converted it to "—our wealth is due to the investments that the Barbies have made for me. I'll have Josef look over the situation out at Race Track City when he gets here, but I suspect that they are in better shape than it might seem at first."

"One hopes," Maximilian said, "that they, or at least your Sarah, can help us to prepare for the Turks."

"I don't think that's likely, Uncle," Hartmann said. "At least not the young ladies. Julie Sims is more the exception than the rule, I think."

"Are there rumblings from the Turks?" Karl asked.

"Yes, there are," Maximilian said. "We're not sure how serious it is yet, but His Majesty is starting to be concerned. Or, at least, his close adviser Janos Drugeth is concerned."

"And you want Sarah's help?"

"Moses Abrabanel seems to think she is some sort of financial genius," Gundaker said, doubt clear in his voice.

"Well..." Karl paused. "Yes. But David Bartley is the real businessman. Sarah is more oriented to the big picture, as she calls it. Understand, no actual economists came back with the Ring of Fire, but copies of economics books did. Sarah Wendell has read every economic book available. Literally, everything that is known in this time about economics, Sarah knows. That is not the same as knowing what they knew up-time, but in at least one way it's better. They have some records of how the economy of the HRE developed in their history and they have the development of the USE since the Ring of Fire to compare it to. That is something the up-timers never had. Sarah has written several papers on comparative economics, focusing on the effect of monetary policy."

While the men were at their brandy, the ladies were having wine and sweet cakes in another room. Sarah Wendell had pled fatigue and escaped to her rooms. Karl's aunt Katharina was just as glad Sarah hadn't joined them, since she would without doubt be the topic of conversation among the ladies this evening. The arrival of Sarah Wendell had brought to mind several things that were bothering her.

Her sister-in-law, Elisabeth Lukretia von Teschen, Gundaker's estranged wife, was living in territory that was now under Wallenstein and apparently quite happy to do so. Most of Katharina's own lands were now in the hands of Wallenstein as well, and at least nominally still in the family as long as Karl Eusebius remained in Wallenstein's good graces.

Katharina started the ball rolling. "Did you see Gundaker's face?"

The ladies chortled or sniffed as dictated by their attitude about the up-timers in general. There was considerably more sniffing than chortling.

"What do you expect? All the up-timers are peasants." Countess Aldringer, whose husband had been made a count by Ferdinand II, was a countess mostly because of her husband's money.

"Careful, dear. From what I understand she could buy your husband out of pocket change," Katharina advised with a certain malice.

Countess Aldringer was clearly less than pleased at that observation. "There are other things than money."

"Yes, there are," Katharina said. "Charity, honor, piety. What I am less sure of by the day is how those things apply to the up-timers. And how they apply to us. When, after all, was it decided that showing appreciation of service lacked in charity, honor or piety?"

"It lacks in both charity and piety!" Countess Aldringer insisted, "because it encourages the sins of pride and sloth in the serving class. It confuses them as to their proper role. It is well known that the peasantry is at best easily confused and must be reminded of their station constantly. She did the serving girl no favor by her condescension." She sniffed. "Not that it was much of a descent for that one, but how is a serving girl to know that?"

"Yet God put them here, and seems to favor their endeavors," Gundaker's daughter Maximiliana Constanzia, called Liana, said.

"Or the Devil," Countess Aldringer countered. "Even Urban has not said they are God's handiwork and Cardinal Borja has made his opinion clear."

"Pope Urban!" Liana said hotly.

Gundaker's daughter by his first wife was, in Katharina's opinion, what the up-timers would call a suck-up. She was surprised that the young woman wasn't parroting her father's attitude toward the up-timers. She guessed that Liana was coming down on the Urban side of the issue. And that was strange. The girl's confessor was a Dominican, after all.

Anna was wondering whether she was going to get in trouble for the up-timer lady talking to her. "I didn't invite it," she assured Stephen, the chief butler, who confronted her in the kitchen.

"You didn't smile at her?" Stephen, who ruled the servant's quarters with an iron hand, didn't seem entirely convinced that Anna was innocent in the affair. "Look her in the eye?"

Anna's head shook like it was about to come off. But Stephen didn't hit her. Which came as something of a surprise.

"I will check with Their Serene Highnesses to see if you are to be dismissed," he warned ominously. And that's what he did.

Karl and his uncles were still discussing the effects of the up-timers when Stephen knocked politely on the door.

"Enter!" Stephen heard Prince Gundaker's voice call. From the sound of it, it seemed unlikely that Anna would keep her position, which Stephen regretted. As harsh as he sometimes was with the under-servants, he did feel a responsibility to them.

"About the incident at supper?" he asked. Normally he would

have dealt with the matter on his own and simply kept Anna out of sight of the nobility for a while. But he wasn't at all sure how the up-timers would react.

"Now see!" Gundaker glared at Karl. "Your girl's lack of manners mean we have a discipline problem among the servants. We'll have to let the serving girl go, and it wasn't really her fault."

"There is no need to discharge the girl, Uncle." Karl snorted. "If you discharge every girl Sarah is polite to, you'll soon run out of servants."

"Maybe it will teach your young woman a lesson," Gundaker huffed. "Let the girl go and tell Sarah Wendell von Up-time why you're doing it."

"Stephen," Karl interrupted. "Tell Sarah first."

As Stephen left, he saw young Prince Karl looking at his uncle and shaking his head.

While Anna was wondering what her fate would be, the young ladies of the Barbie Consortium—now joined by Sarah—were finishing up their discussion. "Come on, Sarah," said Susan. "You're the economic theorist. Industrialization is not a cure for serfdom. If all that is going on is industrialization, it's going to make things worse. Look at what's happening in Poland."

"You need a big consumer base," Sarah insisted, "and without industrialization you can't get that."

"Eventually," Susan said. "But at least in the short run, industrialization means a labor glut, because you need fewer farmers and craftsmen to produce the same amount of goods."

"Yes and no. That same labor glut means you have the labor you need to get new industries off the ground. The real issue is whether you have a class of people ready and able to invest in those industries. In Poland, you don't, because the great magnates would rather plow their wealth back into grain production—and to make sure they have the labor force they need, they've reimposed serfdom. They do some industrialization, but it's more or less an afterthought and they use serfs as a labor force. The political and social situation is different in western and central Europe and the Ring of Fire is giving a big boost to the factors that keep pushing things forward here. It's just..."

"You didn't expect to run headlong into Polish attitudes here in Austria," Judy said.

"It makes sense, though," Susan said. "Information has been flowing out of the Ring of Fire like mad ever since it happened. And for the most part, the lords of Europe have said yes to the technical stuff and a resounding no to the social stuff. So Austria-Hungary has the new plows, but all it means is that the lord of the manor can afford to throw half his peasants out and have that much more profit."

Sarah's expression got exasperated. "*What* 'lords of the manor,' Susan? Land tenure in Austria isn't medieval. The core of the farming population is a class of prosperous farmers—peasants, not nobles, but they're well-off peasants—who hire local labor on an annual basis. They'll replace some of that labor force by adopting new equipment and techniques, sure, but they haven't got enough money to do it quickly. Hell, even back up-time you didn't see a massive mechanization of agriculture until the twentieth century." She remembered the figures because she'd been struck by them at the time. "In 1900 almost forty percent of the American population was still engaged in farming. By the time of the Ring of Fire at the end of the century, that had dropped to three percent."

"And your point is...?"

"My point is obvious. We're a long way from seeing a huge displacement of farm labor. There's enough of a free labor force for industrialization to get started here, but the big problem Austria faces is a lack of capital. The damn idiots—the brains of the nobility *are* still mired in the Middle Ages, most of them—still think in terms of licenses and monopolies instead of investment. There are some exceptions, my fiancé being one of them—Wallenstein's another, up in Bohemia—but there aren't enough yet."

There was a knock on the door and Trudi went to answer it. It was Snooty from this afternoon. Stephen—something or other. Trudi didn't think she had been told his last name. The majordomo, at least among the nontitled servants. Trudi stepped out and closed the door behind her. "Yes?"

"I need to speak with Sarah Wendell von Up-time." Stephen was clearly not happy about his mission.

"In regard to?"

"There was an, ah...incident at table..."

"So I heard."

"Prince Gundaker has decided that to maintain discipline

among the house staff, the serving girl will be dismissed." Stephen paused. "I am instructed to inform Lady Sarah of the dismissal and the reason for it."

Trudi looked at Stephen. Then she turned and opened the door gesturing him inside. Trudi wasn't sure what was going to happen but she had no doubt she was about to see fireworks.

As they came into the sitting room, Sarah was saying, "Barbaric customs. Maybe we should leave Ferdinand III and the whole bunch to stew in their own juices."

Trudi wasn't sure how much English Stephen had but he had apparently gotten at least some of it. She made a sweeping gesture and announced, "Here is Stephen, majordomo of Liechtenstein Palace, with a message for Sarah Wendell von Up-time."

Silence. Every eye in the room was on the unfortunate Stephen. Stephen delivered his message.

"Was Prince Karl there when his uncle gave you your instructions?" Sarah asked, with a chill in her voice that suggested really bad things for the Ken Doll.

Trudi watched as Stephen swallowed. "Yes. It was he who insisted I inform you before dismissing Anna."

"Smart boy," Judy the Younger said.

Sarah looked at Judy with a question in her eyes.

"You were telling Karl all the way here that he wasn't to run interference for you," Judy reminded her sister. "Something about not wanting people to think that you couldn't take care of yourself?"

Sarah nodded.

"So he made sure you would be informed before the servant..." Judy turned to Stephen. "Anna, was it?" When he nodded, she turned back to her sister. "...before Anna got her walking papers. And let you, well, us, deal with the matter as we see fit. He's probably up there right now taking bets on how quickly you're going to rip Gundaker's guts out."

Sarah had calmed down a little while Judy was talking. "Tempting as that thought is, it won't help, ah, Anna. So how do we deal with this? Pack up our bags and move out?"

"Not at all." Judy's grin was very barracuda-ish. "I think it's quite convenient. We were going to have to hire servants anyway. Prince Gundaker is graciously releasing one for us to hire. What is Anna paid?"

When Stephen told her, she shook her head. "That won't do at all. Trudi, would you be a dear and go with Stephen here? And when he fires Anna, hire her. Pay her fifty percent more than she is getting now. It's not like we're short on Austro-Hungarian banknotes." The girls had engaged in a bit of arbitrage before coming to Vienna, buying up Ferdinand's silver certificates in Grantville where they were worth considerably less than they were in Vienna.

Trudi was stealing glances at Stephen while Judy was talking, wondering how he would respond. Apparently he was going to object. Which showed commendable loyalty to his boss, but perhaps not the greatest wisdom.

"With all due respect, ma'am," he said to Judy the Younger, "I don't think that's what Prince Gundaker had in mind."

Sarah jumped in. "I really don't care what Gundaker had in mind," she said coldly.

"On the other hand," Millicent said, "we may want to move out to Race Track City just for the room."

CHAPTER 20

𝔄 Report to the Emperor

June 1635

The Hofburg Palace, Vienna

"So, Leo, were the new arrivals as strange as expected?" Empress Mariana set the china creamer on the table and picked up her hot chocolate.

Leo buttered a roll as he considered his answer. "I only got a few minutes to talk to them before Gundaker hustled them off to the Liechtenstein townhouse."

"Unwilling to share?" Mariana asked.

"Afraid they would embarrass House Liechtenstein," Leo clarified. "And not totally without justification. I am afraid that the up-timer girls who arrived with Prince Karl aren't any more impressed with the seventeenth century than our other up-time guests." Leo turned to his brother. "Victoria Emerson asked your mechanic's daughter how she liked life among the peasantry. 'In the sticks,' she said."

"My mechanic's daughter?"

"Hayley Fortney von Up-time will likely be a bridesmaid at Prince Liechtenstein's wedding. Gundaker is caught between wanting the match for the advantage to his branch of the family and being deeply offended by the whole notion of any Liechtenstein marrying a jumped-up peasant. Judy Wendell told me that Hayley is a Barbie, or something."

"Is that a title?" asked Mariana, "I thought it was a doll."

"You're saying her family has some status among the up-timers?" asked Ferdinand.

"I'm not entirely sure. Judy Wendell said that it was Hayley who was rich, not her family. You know the up-timers count such things differently." Leo shook his head. "And they may be right to do so. Look at what we have. Out of three thousand people, all of whom arrived with no significant rank, we now have two baronesses, a general . . . no, two generals, one of them a former prime minister, an admiral, a colonel of the air force, several other officers, more burghers and merchants of distinction than you can shake a stick at. Craftsmen and healers without peer in Europe. And the village priest makes a short visit to Rome and comes home a cardinal. Three thousand, many still children or toothless with age. And all in less than five years."

"So we are all peasants to them? Or just all barbarians?" Mariana asked. She was clearly more amused than insulted by the idea. But there was some offended dignity in her tone as well.

"Judith Wendell von Up-time, claimed that it wasn't an insult but a translation problem." Leo tilted his head to the side in a gesture of uncertainty. "It may have been, but there is no way they consider us their natural superiors."

"Well, I wasn't expecting to overawe the up-timers with my exalted birth," Ferdinand said. "Sonny Fortney once offered to shake my hand, just as though we were equals. I happened upon him and Bob Sanderlin with no one else about. It must have been a month or so after they got here."

"What did you do?"

"I shook his hand and reminded him not to offer that sort of *lèse majesté* in public. But by that time, I was pretty sure that he was Nasi's agent in Vienna . . . well, at least one of them." Ferdinand shook his head. "We are in a horrible bargaining position. I need to know what I am facing. Do you think that von Trauttmansdorff could persuade the USE to see reason? After all, he persuaded John George of Saxony to support the Catholic powers."

He looked over at Moses Abrabanel as he had looked to him increasingly over the last year. Moses' father had been his father's chief financial adviser. More importantly, Moses had been to Grantville and met Michael Stearns.

"It depends on what you mean by seeing reason, Your Majesty,"

Moses said carefully. "Establish a firm peace with Austria? By itself, yes. Do any of that at the expense of Bohemia or in support of Poland? No. Beyond that..."

"Yes?"

"Gustav Adolf will want concessions in exchange for his help with anything. About Michael Stearns, I can't tell you any more today than I did last week," Moses said. "When I met Stearns, he was the leader of a newly formed independent nation that was little more than six miles across. He was both more desperate and more free to act as he saw fit. Now he has been a prime minister to a king, become a general, and is commanding an army in Saxony. At the same time, he controls—or at least influences—a great deal more. There is also the question of how much he has been influenced by this century. All I can tell you about how he will act as a general is that the man has a phenomenal talent for finding talent. And listening to it. Besides, Michael Stearns is no longer the prime minister. William Wettin is and he, like Gustav, will want concessions."

Ferdinand III nodded. "And the money?"

"Possibly in exchange for concessions that we may well not be able to give."

"So we are back to Liechtenstein's bride and her sister who may or may not think of us as peasant barbarians."

Then Moses smiled. "I have, by the way, met both Wendell girls. Sarah was studious even then, and Judy the Younger a charming child. That was before Judy and her little friends decided to ride through the financial markets like a Mongol horde."

"What?"

"I hadn't realized it till Archduke Leopold mentioned the girl being a Barbie, but Judy Wendell, Vicky Emerson and Susan Logsden along with some others that apparently include the Fortney girl are known in Grantville and Magdeburg as the Barbie Consortium. Investors or profiteers, depending on who you talk to, who..." Moses slapped his head. "...have some sort of financial arrangement with Prince Karl Eusebius von Liechtenstein. I'm sorry, Your Majesty. I should have made the connection." He snorted. "It might be safer to deal with Vasa, or even Wallenstein, than with the Barbie Consortium."

"Well, you're the one who said we need Sarah Wendell more than we need Karl's money."

"I know, and I still think that. I'm less sure about the brides-maids she brought with her," Moses said. Then, getting back to the point he continued. "I need to sit down and talk with Sarah Wendell. I know she is young, but from what Uriel tells me, she, in large part, designed the National Bank of Bohemia, and she does have a reputation as an economist."

"There will be a party in a few days to welcome Karl Eusebius home. You will be invited." Ferdinand III turned to the room as a whole. "Father said he would prefer to rule a Catholic desert than a nation of heretics. Before the Ring of Fire, I was of like mind. But it won't be a Catholic desert. It will be a Muslim des-ert. I am unwilling to destroy what is left of the Holy Roman Empire and leave an open road into Europe for the Muslims to punish heretics that I can't reach anyway. So find me an answer. Some way to fund the government. Get me the money to buy the guns and pay the army that we will need to fight the Turks if they come. Which Janos has been warning me for some time will happen. I'm a bit skeptical, myself, but... Janos is shrewd about such things."

CHAPTER 21

A Visit to Race Track City

June 1635

Race Track City

There was a half-finished air to the streets as the girls left the dock at Race Track City. It was clear that an attempt had been made to create a wide, tree-lined avenue, but the trees were knee-high and the grass was packed down. The street itself was just plain dirt.

"Ew," Millicent said. "Hayley, why the heck haven't you all paved this street?"

"Because we're still negotiating with the turkey who owns the concrete patent."

"Huh?"

Hayley sighed. "This is so, so . . . downright stupid! Back in, oh, '32, I guess, the current emperor's father started selling patents on inventions that came out of Grantville. So if you don't own the patent, you have to pay a fee to the patent holder. See? Now, if the patent holder sees that you've got a major project going, they figure they can hold you up for even more money. They ask ridiculous prices for the use of 'their' process and you can't just do it or they'll take you to court."

"For concrete? That you could buy for a dollar ninety-nine a bag on sale back in West Virginia?"

"Yep." Hayley sighed again. "The way I understand it, when Ferdinand II found out about Grantville issuing patents on new inventions, he decided that since God had placed Grantville in his empire, all the information and technology that came back with us actually belonged to him. So he figured that he could give it out just the way he gave out land. He also needed the money and didn't respect anything that the emergency committee did, so, at least in Austria-Hungary, all the inventions that came back with the Ring of Fire and all new inventions invented anywhere, are the property of the crown."

"Good grief," Judy said. "Talk about a recipe for disaster!"

"The average rich guy here," Prince Karl pointed out, "doesn't see it that way. He figures that having a monopoly on something is the best way to organize it."

"Oh," Vicky squealed. "Look at that!" She went hustling off to a shop window. "They've got blue glass bottles. That's different."

Karl read the sign. "Kreuger's Wine and Brandy. Hm. I wonder if it's worth drinking. Most wines from Vienna are kind of sharp and thin tasting."

Hayley said, "Couldn't prove it by me. All wine tastes sharp and thin to me. Or else sour and, well, icky."

The wine merchant called, "Fräulein Hayley! It's good to see you. Please, bring your friends to try my strawberry wine."

Herr Kreuger, now that it was summer, had taken a leaf from some of the up-time travel guides that had made their way to Vienna. Instead of long tables and benches, he had four-person round tables, with umbrellas. The girls and Karl sat down and he proudly brought out several of his new blue bottles, along with a supply of wine glasses. With a flourish, he poured the chilled wine over ice and topped the glass off with soda water.

"So you got some CO2," Hayley observed.

"Yes, but don't tell the patent holder," Herr Kreuger said. "He'll have me in court."

"Who bought the patent?" Hayley asked.

"Prince Gundaker von Liechtenstein bought the patent on the process for separating CO2."

"Which way of separating CO2?" Hayley asked.

"Is there more than one?"

"Dozens," Hayley said with a sad shake of her head.

"Well, I think the patent that Prince Liechtenstein bought covers them all."

Hayley grimaced. "See what I mean, you guys?"

"Yes, I do," Karl said. "It *is* a disaster waiting to happen. I will check on what patents my family has bought."

After their refreshments, they wandered Race Track City for a bit longer, then met at another restaurant. This one had a private room, which was immediately made available for Fräulein Hayley and her friends.

The restaurateur spoke to Hayley quietly while the others were being seated. He looked concerned, so Judy asked about it when Hayley finally sat down. "What's up, Hayley? Did he infringe on a patent or something?"

"Laugh all you like, Jude," Hayley said, looking a bit depressed herself. "No, he didn't. Yet. What he did have to do was add some more credit accounts. Which means he doesn't have the cash to buy supplies. And with our agreement, that means Sanderlin-Fortney Investment Company is going to have to front him the money."

"What's all this about?" Sarah asked.

"Nobody in Vienna has any money," Hayley said. "At least, none of our customers do."

"Oh, yes. I was meaning to bring that up with you, Sarah. Hayley mentioned it before," Judy said. "You were telling me about how Austria is broke. Could you explain to us what you were talking about."

"Do you remember Mom's 'great sucking sound' lecture?" Sarah said.

"I remember it," Judy said. "I didn't really understand it, but I remember it."

Sarah looked around at the others. "Right after the Ring of Fire, what Mom and Dad were most afraid of was that we would trash the local economy by sucking all the money out of it. We avoided that by introducing the American dollar, but that was just locally. For the past four years almost, we've been sucking money out of the rest of Europe. That's how our economy has grown so fast. Like China's did, back up-time. But the down-time banking system isn't up to shifting the money back and frankly most of Europe doesn't have the credit to borrow the money. So the money goes to the manufacturers in the golden corridor, and all too much of it stays there."

Sarah hesitated, clearly looking for words. "Europe does have stuff to sell and it has people who want to buy that stuff. But, there isn't the cash and that makes figuring out what anything is worth hard. And that's strangling the economies of every country, except the USE. And the Netherlands, sort of. The Union of Kalmar, a bit. Everybody isn't suffering the same amount, but almost everybody is suffering."

"So what is needed is more money?" Karl asked.

"Yes," Sarah said. "But you've got to find a way of introducing it that won't cause more problems than it heals."

"What do you mean?" Judy asked.

"To put it bluntly," Sarah said, looking at Karl, "most of the governments of Europe don't have enough financial credibility to be able to add to the money supply without people losing confidence in the money. Even here, where they aren't materially increasing the money supply, the shift to paper silver certificates has devalued the paper in spite of the fact that it's backed by a consistent amount of silver and the crown claims to have the silver in its vaults to buy every silver certificate out there."

"I think they actually do have enough, or at least close to it," Karl said.

"It's possible. From what I've been hearing, there has been little increase in the money supply, but there has been inflation. That effectively means that there is less money available. And that in turn means that every improvement in productivity makes things worse."

"That makes no sense at all," said Hayley. "Making things better for less has to be a good thing. Especially when there isn't enough money."

"It would seem that way, wouldn't it?" Sarah agreed. "But it hasn't worked that way. Not since the Ring of Fire. As long as the value of money was determined by the amount of silver or gold in the coin, the down-time economists were right. You sold your stuff abroad to get more silver and then used that silver to run your economy. And it was stable because you can measure the amount of silver in the coins."

"Oh my goodness," Judy whispered in pseudo-shock. "Sarah has turned into a silver nut."

Sarah returned a repressive look. "No. Having your economy dependent on whether some miner happens to hit a large vein of silver strikes me as a very bad idea. But full faith and credit are hard to measure. In fact, the only real way to tell is how willing people are to take your paper."

Judy very theatrically wiped her hand across her forehead.

Karl grinned at Sarah, and Sarah grinned back at him in a disgustingly sappy way. Judy grinned. "Stop drooling, Sarah, and explain."

"What you have is sort of stagflation!"

"That can't be. The prices have been going down gradually for the last...well, at least since we got here."

"Inflation is more complicated than it seems in economic-ese—which is as weird as medical-ese or engineering-ese. Inflation actually means 'the devaluation of money,' not simply the 'increase of prices.' What has been happening is a lack of faith in the reichsthaler silver certificates, which is being hidden by increases in productivity."

Judy, in spite of herself, was following this. She couldn't help her upbringing. "So the prices are going down but they should be going down more if the reichsthaler was respected as a currency?"

"Mostly, but if you will notice some prices aren't going down. Eggs, for instance. Anywhere that the cost of production hasn't decreased, the prices are actually going up."

"But the price of wheat and rye are both down," Hayley said.

"Sure. Because they can dump half their tenants off the land and still get in the crop with the new plows." Which was overstating the case somewhat, but not unreasonably. That was why there were so many people in Vienna—because after getting thrown out of their homes, they didn't have anywhere else to go.

"Speaking of which," Karl said. "How are you managing this place, Hayley? It's more active than I expected. There is a strong feeling of industry here."

"Between the cash up front that Ron Sanderlin got for his 240Z and my drawing account with the Abrabanel family, SFIC had the start-up cash. But fairly soon we ran into the same problem everyone else in Vienna has: none of our potential customers had any money. It wasn't that cut and dried. Most people had *some* money, but not enough to keep us going. So we had to offer credit to keep customers. But we are getting close to our credit limit and I am afraid that Moses Abrabanel is going to cut us off if we don't get some sort of cash infusion soon."

Trudi, who had been listening quietly, said, "You've told me before, Sarah, that money is a loan."

Sarah nodded.

"So why don't we make our own loan? Make our own money?"

"Because no one would accept it," Sarah said. "If the governments of Europe don't have the credibility to introduce new money, certainly we don't."

Trudi didn't say anything else, but she had a thoughtful look on her face.

CHAPTER 22

The Reception and the Gifts

July 1635

The Hofburg Palace, Vienna

"Charming," Empress Mariana of the Austro-Hungarian Empire murmured. Judy the Younger curtsied quite well, she thought. Not that the others were bad at it, but it was clear that they lacked practice and seemed a bit uncomfortable. Judy did it with style and not the least bit of embarrassment or pugnaciousness.

As she recovered from her curtsy, the young woman winked at Mariana as if sharing a delightful joke and the empress of Austria-Hungary was hard put not to laugh out loud. The receiving line was dull, but not quite as dull as usual. Mariana had been reminded that these things were supposed to be fun, even if they rarely were.

Prince Gundaker's bow could be measured with one of the new micrometers, it was so rigid. The rumors of a blowup at the Liechtenstein house were apparently true.

Moses Abrabanel was his usual reserved and cautious self. But Mariana could tell that he had things to tell. It was shaping up to be an interesting evening.

The receiving line being finished, some gifts from the new arrivals at court were offered. Bolts of fabric, some of the new paisley prints with the double eagle of the Habsburg crest woven into the fabric. Then it was time to circulate before dinner. Mariana

189

got several versions of the events at the Liechtenstein house over the next fifteen or twenty minutes. She decided to see what the up-timers had to say and spotted Judy the Younger. Not surprisingly, Judy shone like one of the new light bulbs in a dark room. Mariana made her way to Judy, dispersing a bevy of young lords by virtue of her rank. And when she had Judy alone, she simply asked, "What happened that has Gundaker so upset?"

"We're barbarians destructive of the good social order." Judy grinned. "But I'm sure Prince Gundaker has already told you that."

"I don't think he put it quite that way, but that was the gist, yes. So are you barbarians?"

For the first time that evening Judy the Younger put on a serious mien. "It probably depends on where you're standing, Your Majesty, whether it's us or you who are barbarians. I understand that John George of Saxony indicates his readiness for another mug of beer by dumping the dregs of his last one on whatever servant happens to be handy. Did you know that?"

Mariana was surprised by the sudden turn of the conversation. "Yes, I am aware of it. An unpleasant quirk, but John George is an unpleasant man."

"To us, the way John George treats his servants isn't all that different from how you treat yours. Tell me, Your Majesty, were you to find yourself visiting a court like John George's, would you then request a second drink by dumping the dregs of the first on a servant's head?"

"No!"

"Neither would we. Prince Gundaker felt that my sister saying 'thank you' to a serving girl was an offense against the natural order of the world. In order to punish Sarah, he dismissed the servant."

For her part Judy thought Empress Mariana might almost have been a third Wendell sister. An older sister; she was about thirty. Her hair was almost the same shade as Judy's, though curly where Judy's was mostly straight. Her figure was more like Sarah's. Well, almost a sister—she did have the Habsburg lip. "We hired her. Anyway, we brought you some other stuff, just between us girls." Then she told the empress about feminine hygiene as practiced in late-twentieth-century America and which of those products they had been able to reintroduce in the seventeenth century.

❖   ❖   ❖

While Judy was chatting with the empress, Sarah and Karl were buttonholed by Moses Abrabanel. The question was: how can we make money magically appear the way you up-timers do? The problem was that they wanted to do it without accepting the worthless paper themselves.

What they wanted was a Kipper-and-Wipper-like paper money. Everyone else would be expected to take it at face value, but the crown would only accept it at a discounted rate.

That wasn't how Emperor Ferdinand's "financial managers" put it, of course. They talked about crown expenses and the crown's special status. Sarah at least found it an interesting, if infuriating, conversation. Karl was a little bored by it, but you couldn't date Sarah Wendell without learning something about economics, so he rarely got lost. He even winced at all the right times when Moses explained something about finance that was clearly wrong.

When all was said and done, Moses was what Adam Smith would later call a mercantilist, opposed to free trade and a firm believer that a nation needed a great pile of silver to be a great nation.

"No. It just needs a good credit rating," Sarah explained.

"Ferdinand III is the emperor of Austria-Hungary. Of course, he has a good credit rating."

Karl winced visibly.

"Not the emperor. The nation," Sarah insisted.

"The emperor embodies the nation."

"Then Ferdinand has a sucky credit rating," Sarah shot back and Karl winced again.

Moses' face was getting a bit red. Not, Karl thought, because he disagreed, but because he was supposed to disagree and couldn't. The Austro-Hungarian reichsthaler traded at about half its face value, outside of Austria-Hungary, and that was an improvement over what the HRE reichsthaler had traded at.

Count Amadeus von Eisenberg was a wealthy young man whose father was even wealthier. He had spotted the daughter of the emperor's auto mechanic and wondered what she was doing here. She looked out of place. Well, not exactly that. She looked uncomfortable. Partly out of Christian charity and partly out of curiosity, he went over to talk to her. "Miss Fortney, I'm Amadeus von Eisenberg." He wasn't going to use the silly title "von Up-time."

"Good evening, Count."

"I was wondering...do you think you could explain to me how the internal combustion engine works?" He guessed that would be a safe question to put her at her ease. Besides, he really was curious about it.

Miss Fortney gave a slight sigh and started to explain. "It works in essence like a musket. Save that a liquid rather than..."

"Woman, get you to a convent!" Father Lugocie shouted. He was not happy with the guests of this gala. Using up-timer craftsmen was one thing, but presenting them at court was something else. He was also a bit in his cups. When he saw a young up-timer in a dress that left her knees clearly visible, he felt that the dress provided an excellent justification for putting the up-timers in their place.

During the reign of Ferdinand II, the court of the Holy Roman Empire had been dominated by the priesthood. While that was less—much less—the case in the Austro-Hungarian court of Ferdinand III, they were still a faction with considerable influence. Besides, being a bit drunk, Father Lugocie had forgotten the change of status. "Your dress is an offense to God."

The young woman turned to face him. "Really?"

There was no way for Father Lugocie to know it, but he had picked on the wrong girl. Vicky Emerson was fully aware of the audience and had chosen her little black dress to be unique and different, but within bounds. She was also Catholic, and rather more religious after the Ring of Fire than she had been before it. Going through a miracle will sometimes have that effect. So she had become fairly conversant with the Bible and the many and varied ways it was interpreted...and the way bits of it were taken out of context.

Also, Vicky cheated.

"Are you an expert on women's fashions?" she asked.

"You are presumptuous. I am an ordained priest." It wasn't truly an issue of dress. The Austro-Hungarian court was hardly Puritan in nature. It was an issue of religious authority.

"*I'm* presumptuous? God picked me up, and my whole town with me, moved us halfway around the world and three hundred fifty-nine years into the past. Set us down again without so much as breaking a plate. In spite of which, *I* don't presume to know

God's will. Except that, for whatever reason, He wanted me here . . . in this world, in this time. Well, I did learn one other thing from that experience. Do you want to know what else I learned?" Vicky didn't give him a chance to answer, but proceeded to tell him.

"I learned that in spite of all the supposed experts on God's will—ordained or not—the Good Lord didn't see fit to inform anyone in advance of our arrival. No Catholic priest, Lutheran or Calvinist minister, no Jewish rabbi, Moslem mullah, or Buddhist monk was there to greet us. No up-timers knew about it, either. There are a number of people who, after the fact, claimed prior knowledge. But they weren't there when it happened." Neither had she found a single reference to the Ring of Fire in the Bible. At least not one that made any sense without twisting the reference all out of shape.

Father Lugocie brought up Deuteronomy 22:5 and Vicky returned Deuteronomy 22:11 and 12 and added that while her clothing was clearly female dress, his was diverse. He seemed to be about four tassels short. She ended with, "Funny how people pick and choose the rules from the Bible that they decide matter." They traded a few more barbs back and forth before a fellow cleric pulled Father Lugocie away. The main, or at least most immediate, effect was that everyone in that part of the room was reminded that the Barbies had actually experienced a miracle. People got a bit more formal. The title, von Up-time, which had been treated as something of a joke at first became a somewhat more serious appellation.

As Father Lugocie was led away, Count von Eisenberg turned back to Hayley and bowed stiffly. Suddenly the von Up-time didn't seem a joke at all. Rather it seemed a description of the miracle that had brought these strange people into the world to change it—and with it the fortunes of all they came in contact with and more. Spreading out before them like the ripples on a pond when a rock is tossed in, save that this rock was six miles across and tossed by the hand of God. What exactly was the social position of someone delivered by God's own hand?

"Count von Eisenberg?" Hayley Fortney von Up-time didn't seem offended, just confused.

"My apologies, Miss Fortney von Up-time, if I gave offense."

"What?"

"I was curious about how the internal combustion engine worked. I didn't mean any imposition."

"I wasn't offended," Hayley assured him. "But now I'm curious why you thought I might be."

Now the young count was really confused. She wasn't acting like...come to think of it, he had no clue at all what she was supposed to act like. Nor how he was supposed to act around her. It was a most uncomfortable sensation. "Ah..."

"If I promise not to be offended, will you take my word and tell me what's bothering you?"

Put that way he could hardly refuse. "To be...Well, I saw you standing here. Ah. Looking uncomfortable. I...well, I thought it would be nice to come over and..."

Suddenly she was grinning. "Why, Count von Eisenberg! You came to rescue me."

Count von Eisenberg felt his face go hot, but Hayley was smiling and he smiled back in spite of his embarrassment. For the next few minutes, they talked about the internal combustion engine versus steam. And Amadeus learned that though Hayley didn't consider herself a steam head like her father, she did feel that until the supplies of gasoline, refined naphtha, became much more consistent, steam would have a very important place in industry and transportation. "That's why we built a steam engine for the boats that go to Race Track City." Her face lit up when she started talking about building things. It actually lit up, like there were candles glowing through it. At least, that's what it seemed like to Amadeus.

Then another of the young women called her away.

"So, what do you think?" asked Julian von Meklau, another young man of Amadeus' set. They were both sons of the nobility and both their fathers were rich as well as titled.

"I think that we are in the presence of miracles," Amadeus said.

"Oh, come now, Amadeus. I thought you had better sense. Pope Urban has not ruled on the cause of the Ring of Fire. I grant that his elevation of the up-time priest is suggestive, but I think that was a political move, and apparently one that backfired. At least if Cardinal Borja has his way. You think so, too."

It was true and Amadeus knew it. But that was before he had met Hayley Fortney. He had seen her when he went out to the track to watch the emperor drive his 240Z, but she hadn't seemed anyone, just a mechanic's daughter, dressed like a mechanic. Now, though, he had met her, and talked with her, and seen that other up-timer take Lugocie down a peg. All of a sudden he was reevaluating his previous assumptions. Thinking anew about the Ring of Fire and the shining eyes of a lovely girl whose understanding of the eldritch complexity of engines was as easy and natural as a lark's song. "I know I have. But I'm thinking again. Remember right after we heard about the Ring of Fire? Everyone said it was a lie. Especially Lugocie and the Spanish faction. Then, after it was confirmed, they were saying it was the work of the Devil? Then that it was some unknown natural event."

"And that's what it was," Julian said. "Like a volcano, nothing more." There was, Amadeus noted, suddenly a touch of stridency to Julian's tone. "And that up-time girl was dressed like a slut. Her dress was shorter than a common strumpet would wear and her arms were completely bare. Besides, she was wearing it to an imperial ball..." Julian ran down. He was no great fan of the Spanish faction at court. In fact, he was a fan of King Fernando of the Low Countries. Normally he would have been more than happy to see Lugocie taken down, and wouldn't be caught dead agreeing with him.

Amadeus grinned. "Oh come now, are we Puritan prudes, to be shocked at a bit of leg? Granted, the dress was a little risque, but you know as well as I do that Lugocie was only using that as an excuse. I think the juxtaposition of the unadorned black dress with the shortness of the skirt and the fact it had no sleeves probably emphasized the differences between it and what we're used to." Then he paused considering. "I'll bet you a reichsthaler that she knew perfectly well how risque that dress would seem to us and wore it on purpose. Though I don't think she was expecting Lugocie."

"Why?"

"To make clear that they were not going to suit—No...not going to lessen themselves to fit our standards."

"That's pretty arrogant."

"Maybe," Amadeus conceded. "Yes, arrogant. Or at least confident. But then, so are you. So am I."

"But surely they must realize the threat they represent," Julian said. "Shoving it in our face that way...that's crazy."

"You know, I'm not sure they do realize."

"Amadeus, don't be daft, man."

"No, really. Hayley may realize it, but the others...the girl in the black dress...her name's Vicky Emerson, by the way. Hayley told me. From the rumors, things are very different in the USE. And they are up-timers. Maybe they *don't* realize."

Liechtenstein House, Vienna

"You know what she did last night?" Father Lamormaini said to Gundaker von Liechtenstein at lunch the day after the party. "She contradicted and publicly embarrassed a member of the Society of Jesus and a consecrated priest. 'Women are not to speak in church, nor dispute with men over the word of God.'"

"I quite agree, Father, but there is little I can afford to do right now. Vicky Emerson, in her own person, is inconsequential and I would not care at all if she were to fall down a well. But she is a bridesmaid of my nephew's intended, and Sarah Wendell— much as I would love to see her beaten like the peasant whore she is—is simply too valuable to my family for now."

"How?" Lamormaini's tone was both accusatory and confused.

"First, she will be acting as witness for the family in several of the cases brought against my family in regard to the whole Kipper and Wipper business. Something the up-timers call an expert witness. She is an acknowledged expert in matters of finance. Second, Moses Abrabanel has convinced the emperor that she can provide credibility to paper reichsthaler, which is a source of income that the empire needs desperately to counter the wealth of the USE, and Bohemia. She was involved in forming the Bohemian National Bank a few months back. So her expertise is internationally recognized."

"Do not let the material utility of these vipers of Satan blind you to their spiritual corruption."

"I'm not, Father. But you know as well as I that material tools are needed in the material world. You have gotten those tools from me often enough." Lamormaini had, in fact, sold his advice to Ferdinand II to Gundaker von Liechtenstein several times during the old emperor's reign. "Besides," Gundaker continued, "with Karl Eusebius married to the Wendell girl in a morganatic union, and with Maximilian not having any children, nor likely to, the wealth of House Liechtenstein will, soon or late, pass to my line. Karl Eusebius has already been corrupted by the up-timer's heretical beliefs. Would you have House Liechtenstein's wealth and influence arrayed against the true church permanently?"

Lamormaini's expression was not pleased, but neither was it truly hostile. The priest knew how the world worked, after all. As long as marriage to Sarah Wendell removed any children that Karl might have from the succession, she was too valuable to Gundaker for him to consider any action against her.

CHAPTER 23

𝔄fter the party

July 1635

Liechtenstein House, Vienna

"Her Majesty is on board for the feminine hygiene." Judy grinned. "She wants a copy of that paper you wrote up, Gabrielle."

They were in the Liechtenstein townhouse. Sarah watched her sister and the rest of the Barbies plot the overthrow of Austria-Hungary with a sort of bemused enjoyment. Gundaker hadn't gone out of his way to make her welcome, and even Maximilian was pretty distant. She looked over at her new maid and saw that Anna was trying to follow the girls' Amideutch.

"Good," tiny, curly haired Millicent said, making a note. Then she turned back to the conversation that had been going on.

"There are coal and iron deposits, some of them along the Danube, especially in Hungary. Austria-Hungary has resources," Hayley said.

"So what do they need here aside from a good dose of morals?" Vicky asked. "What will they buy?"

"Living space," Hayley said. "Susan's right. Vienna's crowded, even by down-time standards. There are laws preventing anyone from living in the free-fire zone just outside the walls. That's part of why the race track is so far out."

"But there are people living in shacks up against the walls," Judy said. "I saw them."

"Sure. Mostly they are soldiers, but a lot are just poor people. They aren't supposed to be there, but the people in the shacks don't have anyplace else to live and unless Ferdinand III wants to order his troops to burn out their own wives and children, there isn't much they can do. Not that some people, including your soon-to-be Uncle Gundaker, aren't pushing for that," Hayley explained.

"Anyway, about the only people with the money to buy anything are the very wealthy. Austria is in the midst of a depression. People are hungry and no one can pay them. The cost of bread has gone down in the last two years but there isn't any money to speak of and what there is, isn't worth crap. People are still going hungry and we are buying flour on credit and selling bread on credit and I'm not sure how much longer I can keep it up."

"Yeah. We talked about that already," Gabrielle said.

"But what do we *do* about it?" Hayley asked.

"What about meat and wine?" Sarah asked. "The price of bread has been trending down even in the USE. More people can afford to eat, but many of them can afford to eat better, too. More vegetables, even more meat and eggs in their diet, less bread and porridge. That means the net market for bread has decreased, even as the new farming methods are pushing down grain prices. The price of bread goes down as it's marketed toward people who would have been living on the edge of starvation a couple of years ago. So beef and pork are almost twice as much as they were in 1631, but bread has dropped by an average of fifty cents a one pound loaf. That's an average over the whole USE and it's a wild-ass guess, because we just don't have data for a lot of the USE."

"It's not like that here." Hayley bit her lower lip. "At least I don't think it's the same. Since we moved here the prices of bread, wine, peas, and a lot of the other daily needs have gone down a lot. Beef is about the same, pork is a little less, lamb is a bit more. But what's really gone down are wages. We have people who have lost their place in the farms and villages in the area, and other towns all over Austria-Hungary are facing the same problem."

"No, the wages are trending up over most of the USE."

"Meanwhile, it seems all the money in Austria-Hungary is going to buy products from the USE," Hayley said.

"It's not just the money Grantville is sucking out of the economy," Sarah said. "It's the plows. Didn't Judy ever tell you my dad's story of the Fed Fairies?"

"Sarah!" Judy whined, sounding like a twelve-year-old. "Can you imagine Coleman Walker in a tutu with a magic wand? Yuk!"

Which produced general laughter and a lightening of the mood.

"What about the plows?" Hayley asked.

"Not just the plows, but they make a good example," Sarah continued. "A farmer can plow more fields in the same amount of time. It's easier to arrange his furrows to minimize run off. The crops come in fuller and the next year he plows fifteen acres rather than ten and adds a bit of fertilizer. Now that farmer is producing twice as much grain as he was two years ago, but the amount of money available to pay for the grain is just the same, or even less, than it was two years ago.

"Since the price of grain has dropped, the farmer down the way who was a bit slow to take up the new ways or just had a bad year can't make the rent. His family gets thrown off the land and they come into town looking for work. But there is no work. The carpenter has a drill press that he got from the USE and not only isn't hiring, he's laid off a couple of journeymen who are also out looking for work. Meanwhile, the money that might have been spent on the price of wheat went to the USE and there is even less available to pay anyone for anything. Causing unemployment and the lower wages you talked about. Unemployment must be even worse than we thought back in Magdeburg."

"It is," Hayley said. "We've been hiring people just because we couldn't stand seeing them out of work. In fact, that was the whole basis for SFIC."

"That won't work on a large scale." Sarah shook her head sadly. "We don't have enough money. Not all of us put together."

"Then we get the money. Get others to put it up," Judy said. "We need a project . . . something impressive. Then we get investors."

They tried to talk her out of it. Susan for business reasons, Sarah for economic reasons, Hayley for political reasons, Gabrielle because it looked like a lot of distraction from getting a better understanding of down-time medical science. But Judy had an impulse of iron. It was an impulse to do good, but it wasn't a real plan.

"How do you form a corporation in Austria-Hungary?" Susan asked.

"They have a lot of laws, but not all that much in the way of corporate law. Moses Abrabanel has been pushing for limited liability laws, but with very little success. I have a lawyer who is familiar with the state of corporate law."

"Good." Judy commanded, "Susan, you and I will go talk to Hayley's lawyer and set up a stock corporation agreement with the best protection we can get for potential investors. Then we need a project, something to excite people, get them interested and involved."

"Well, like Hayley said, they need living space," Trudi said. "How about a tram like they have in Grantville to make the land outside the walls more accessible?"

"I've been testing the waters about that. There's not much interest and considerable opposition," Hayley said.

"Why opposition?" Sarah asked.

"They don't want to make it easier for the hoi polloi to get to town," Hayley said. "It's the whole peasant villager versus citizen thing. And the ferry boat to Race Track City hasn't helped, either."

"That's stupid!"

"Stupid or not, it's real," Hayley said. "I don't see them getting excited about a few miles of track till they see it in operation, and maybe not then. I do see the city council stopping the trams at the city gates and searching the passengers to make sure that they aren't smuggling in bread or beer to sell in competition with the city bakers. They've occasionally done that to the ferry boat."

"A building then, like the Higgins or some of them going up in Magdeburg," Trudi said. "Only bigger. A combination hotel and office building. Prince Karl is getting to be a pretty good architect, isn't he?" She looked at Sarah.

"Oh my God!" Sarah complained. "Don't get Karl involved in this."

"Yes!" Judy said. "Karl is crazy for architecture! And he's actually good at it, too."

Two days later, at the meeting with Hayley's lawyer, Jack Pfeifer, it was pointed out that there was no law against selling stock in a corporation registered in the USE in Austria-Hungary. And, not to put too fine a point on it, the girls owned all or part of several. In fact, they had American Equipment Corporation... just sitting there. With Prince Karl already owning several million dollars worth of preferred shares.

"We better talk to Ken Doll," Judy said.

"Ken Doll?" Jack asked.

"Prince Karl Eusebius von Liechtenstein," Judy said in her snootiest voice. "Otherwise known as the Ken Doll of the Barbie Consortium."

"Oh," Jack said, sounding confused.

Trudi, who was with them, giggled. "By majority vote of share-holders, AEC can issue as much preferred stock as it chooses to. That's in the charter, right?"

"Yes," Susan said. "What about it?"

"Susan, what exactly is the difference between a preferred stock certificate and a dollar bill?"

Susan started to answer, then stopped. She didn't have a clue what the difference between a dollar bill and a preferred stock certificate was. Neither did anyone else in the room. They were all quite sure there was a difference, but when they actually thought about it, they couldn't think what it was.

This was a job for Sarah.

"That's a good question, Trudi," Sarah said, pleased. "There are a couple of differences. I guess the first is that money is issued by governments. There have been exceptions to that, company scrip that's only good in company stores, but the results are usually bad. I'd say universally bad, but I can't prove it. It ties people into a single supplier, the company that issued the script because who else would take it? Money issued by governments is—or at least can be made—legal tender for all debts public and private, so if you have a debt measured in that money, they have to take it. The second difference is that preferred stock is an investment that is generally expected to pay dividends. Interest of some sort anyway. After all, why would someone loan you money if they weren't getting interest?"

"Like the AEC preferred that the Ken Doll has," Susan said "He's made a bundle on that."

Which was true enough, Sarah had to admit. "That's *participating* preferred. If you guys do well, he gets extra dividends, but if you don't, he just gets more paper. You've been lucky so far."

"Don't confuse skill with luck, Sarah," Vicky said. "Sure, we were lucky at first, but we've gotten good at it."

Trudi interrupted before the conversation got totally derailed. "Why do people loan governments money for no interest? That's what money is, a loan. You've said that lots of times."

"Another good question," Sarah said. "Because money benefits everyone . . . well, everyone who has it. It *is* a transferable debt on the government, true enough. But the key there is it's transferable, which lets it act as a medium of exchange. A dollar in your pocket is a dollar in your pocket, whether you got it from the government or from the local bookie."

"So if we issued preferred stock in AEC, it would work like money."

"No," Sarah said. "People wouldn't accept it. Not if they had any choice in the matter. You wouldn't know about company scrip, at least not the term. But when a company out in the boonies paid its employees in company scrip, it was because that was the only job available and it locked them into using the company store where prices were jacked up. It was a way of keeping people locked in perpetual debt. It didn't work in cities where people had other options."

"It's not so different from a village shop that gives credit," Trudi said. "It's not like you can take your credit to another shop. Shopkeepers often act as local banks, loaning people money that goes on their account and is paid when the harvest comes in."

"Sort of," Sarah acknowledged. "But the loan is going the other way. It's the shopkeeper giving the loan, not the company getting it. It's always easier to get people to accept a loan than to give one."

"Not always," Trudi said. "Often enough the shopkeeper will pay people in credit at the shop. Sometimes my father paid people in credit in local shops. My father wasn't a cheat, but after Kipper and Wipper, we didn't have the cash. Almost no one did and the shopkeepers knew we were good for it."

"Didn't the banks issue money way back when?" Vicky asked. "Back in colonial days?"

"I knew someone would bring that up," Sarah muttered, feeling cross. "Yes, and that's more like what the local shopkeepers Trudi was talking about were doing. Acting as local banks with their own money, just without the cash. Just the accounts on their books. People will always find a way around the lack of money. The trouble is they generally don't work that well. And usually the problem is that the pseudo money ties people down in some way. Bank money worked fine locally, as long as the bank was solid, but the money lost value as you got farther from the bank."

"Heck, Sarah," Judy said, "American dollars lost value once you got out of the area right around the Ring of Fire. At first, anyway.

USE dollars lose value outside the USE and in some places inside it." Judy grinned. "I learned as little as humanly possible from you, Mom and Dad arguing about economics around the dinner table, but no one could avoid learning something."

"What are you suggesting, Trudi?" Karl asked.

"I think we should use AEC to issue preferred stock, maybe participating preferred stock, then trade that stock for the licenses we need to do a project. Maybe build a big building here in Vienna. Maybe several projects, sort of like your LIC. When it makes a profit, the profit gets shared out among all the people holding the preferred stock, then the people with common stock," Trudi said, bouncing in her seat.

"Wait a minute!" Susan looked shocked. "A lot of our money is tied up in AEC. I don't want it diluted to pay a bunch of people bribes just to be able to use stuff we brought back with us in the Ring of Fire."

"We're going to have to pay *licensing fees*," Trudi said. "I just think it's better to pay them in stock than in reichsthaler."

"And that's just the wrong attitude, Trudi," Sarah said tartly. "The same attitude that Moses Abrabanel and company were talking about at the party. What if you don't trust the stock like you trust the reichsthaler? Why should anyone else?"

Trudi flushed. "That's not what I meant." Then she paused, clearly trying to figure out how to express what she did mean.

Judy came to the rescue. "Sarah, you said we didn't have enough money to do much good, not all of us put together. You also said that Austria-Hungary was broke. All Trudi is talking about is the fact that we'll run out of reichsthaler but not stock, because we can print up as much as we need."

"That's almost worse. You can't go around printing up money just because you feel like it. Or just because you need it. Mr. Walker is right about that. There has to be something to back it."

"So we let people starve?" Karl asked.

"No, but..." Sarah stopped and looked at her betrothed. She didn't want Karl to see her as cold or cruel, but there were limits on what they could do. "Karl, I understand that you want to help. But if we just start printing money, no one will trust it. Or worse, they will trust it for a little while, then lose faith in it. That's what happened in France, later in this century in our timeline. It put the introduction of paper money back a hundred years."

"And we'll be left with loads of AEC that we have to take at face value. I'm not going to be poor again to rescue what's left of the Holy Roman Empire," Susan said.

"Susan, I grew up here," Karl said. "There are a lot of decent people in Austria-Hungary. And many of them are going to end up in something as close to serfdom as makes no difference if we don't do something. More than a few will starve in the next few years."

"That's right," Hayley said. "Good people, who just want work. I've met a lot of them. And we've barely scratched the surface out at Race Track City. There were ten people looking for work for every one that we could find a job for."

"Fine," Susan said. "I'm not saying I won't help, but not with AEC. We all have too much invested in it. And by now it's turning a really nice profit."

"Well, AEC still owns Up-time Financial," Karl offered. "We could use that."

"It won't work." Vicky tossed her head in a gesture reminiscent of Veronica Lake. "People will have to see that we have some skin in the game or they won't buy in." It was clear from her posture that Vicky wasn't thrilled with the idea, but from conversations with Judy, Sarah knew that if the others decided to do it, Vicky would go along.

"Vicky's right," Judy said. "The up-timer rep is not nearly as strong here as it is in the USE. And sorry, Karl, but your family's rep sort of sucks."

Karl grimaced. "I know. One of the sticks that Ferdinand III is using to try to get money from me is threatening to come down on the other side in the lawsuits. It's not as big a stick as it would be without King Albrecht holding Bohemia and a lot of our family's money quietly shifted to the USE, but it's still a pretty good-sized stick."

"And it gets bigger with every dime you invest in Austria-Hungary," Sarah pointed out.

"Which makes it a pretty counterproductive stick," Susan said. "Because it almost forces your family to move as much of your money out of Austria-Hungary as it can."

Karl nodded. "That's one of the reasons that money keeps flowing into the USE. A constitutional monarchy is less likely to, ah, insist on loans. Which, oddly enough, makes it easier for Gustav to *get* loans."

"Back to the point," Sarah said. "Anything Karl invests in Austria-Hungary is potentially subject to seizure. For that matter, once we're married anything *I* invest here is potentially subject to seizure. Unless we are real careful, anyway. If Judy and Vicky both think it won't work without heavy investment from us, then it won't work without that investment. So I don't see a way of doing it."

"Keep your money in the USE, darling," Karl said. "We may need it if we end up having to run for our lives." He grinned. "Besides, I sort of like the idea of being a kept man."

"That's right, Sis," Judy said. "That way if you get bored, you can trade the Ken Doll here in on a more anatomically correct model."

"Don't call him that," Sarah said. "Besides he's fully anatomically correct."

"Do tell!" Hayley said, "and I want all the juicy details."

Sarah felt herself turn bright red.

"Help me, Trudi!" Karl put his hands to his cheeks in an overdone imitation of a melodrama ingénue. "These lascivious up-timer girls are treating me like a piece of meat."

Trudi snorted. "Up-timers are prudes.

"The point is, Vienna *needs* this," Trudi said, clearly trying to bring the discussion back on the track that Sarah realized the down-time girl had been pushing for since the first question. Trudi, Sarah realized, was a very bright young woman, probably brighter than she was. "Vienna needs it bad. Not Emperor Ferdinand, not the upper crust of Vienna, whatever they call themselves, although they will benefit too. But Vienna needs it. The small crafters. The people coming in from the farms, the tailors, the bakers. All of those need this. They need work. We can provide work."

"All right. Trudi's right," Karl said. "And if it requires me to put skin in the game, as you girls call it, I'll put skin in the game."

Sarah saw that Trudi had won the point. "All right. If you're going to do this, you're at least going to do it right. Susan, I'm going to need your computer and I'm going to need price points..."

Sarah went through what she was going to need to determine how much stock they could issue, money they could create, based on what they were going to have to sell. In a number of ways it was like figuring out how much you could afford to borrow for a capital investment like a house or a tractor. But it also had to involve how much of an influx of money the local economy could absorb. Over the next days and weeks, that second assessment would increase by an order of magnitude. It wasn't the Viennese economy that was a constraining factor. Vienna was on the Danube and a major north/south trade route. New cash introduced in Vienna would be absorbed by the greater economy, just as had happened around the Ring of Fire in 1632 and 1633 . . . but faster. All that would come later, though.

"Wait a minute," Judy said. "All that's fine, Sarah, but in the meantime we need to make sure that people will take it. The American dollar went over so well partly because people looked at it as a piece of artwork, an engraving. They didn't know Abe Lincoln from Abe Vigoda or George Washington from Curious George, but they could see the quality of the engraving. They could see the detail. You guys have seen the gold backs." She was referring to the paper money printed by the Holy Roman Empire, now the Austro-Hungarian Empire. The printing sucked. They were printed in yellow and black ink on beige paper, and the yellow ink was barely visible. That applied to all of the notes, the reichsthaler, the goschen and the pfennig. It even applied to the new "mark" note that was to be the worth of a Cologne mark of silver. "We can't have that. We need something that will be really hard to counterfeit, and we need it to be visually impressive."

"So what do you want to do?" Susan asked.

"I want to let Heather Mason back in Grantville know what we want and have her come up with designs. You know she's tied into the whole art community. Then we'll have plates made up of the hardest steel they can make and have them cut at one of the up-time machine shops."

"That's going to take time," Hayley said. "I'm not all that sure how long Moses Abrabanel is going to continue to take our IOUs."

"I'll talk to Moses," Karl said.

"I'll write Heather," Judy said, and the rest took their assignments.

Over the next weeks, the girls of the Barbie Consortium did what they did best. They shopped. They bought cloth, they bought jewels, they bought bread and cake and buttons and bows. They bought flour by the ton and coal and bronze. Every purchase was recorded and went into Sarah's database, and a picture of what the Austro-Hungarian reichsthaler was worth began to emerge. People like to think that one currency translates into another in terms of a simple exchange rate, but it's not really true, any more than one language translates perfectly into another. An exchange rate is an average and that average will be accurate enough for some products, but way off the mark for others. Like the German word *Weltanschauung* can be translated as "world view," but that translation is not completely accurate. In terms of money, it depends on where you are and what you want to buy. What Sarah developed wasn't so much an exchange rate for the reichsthaler versus the American dollar, but a picture of what the reichsthaler was good for.

It wasn't a pretty picture.

Abrabanel Offices outside Vienna

"Hello, Moses." Karl Eusebius von Liechtenstein smiled as he was ushered into Moses Abrabanel's tiny office. Then the smile died as he saw the yellow circle on Moses' doublet. Jews in Grantville were not required to wear special signs on their clothing, and with Morris Roth as a major noble of Bohemia, they weren't required to wear them in Bohemia either, though many still did. But here in Austria-Hungary, it was still a legal requirement. Quite to his own surprise, Karl suddenly realized that he was offended by it. The news out of the USE was full of the CoC and Operation Kristallnacht. Much as he knew and understood the political motivation, he remembered Henry Dreeson's body, and was for the most part in sympathy with the CoC and Mike Stearns on this.

At the moment, he could see concern blooming on Moses' face and wondered what his looked like. "I'm sorry, Moses. I have been living in Grantville these last years, and, well, sometimes I forget that the rest of the world has not changed as much as we would hope. It was the yellow circle. No one wears such things in Grantville unless they choose to. And not every one that wears one is Jewish. They are all the rage among a certain faction of the CoCs recently."

Moses didn't look especially reassured by Karl's comments. "I've been concerned that there might be a reaction to the CoC operations here."

"You think that likely?" Karl asked. "It's not Jews stringing up the anti-Semites in the USE."

"That's a distinction not commonly made in the midst of a pogrom." Then the Jewish banker shook his head. "Never mind, Your Serene Highness. What can I do for you?"

"You have been loaning the Sanderlin-Fortney Investment Company money for the past several months, I understand?"

"Your Serene Highness, with all respect, our dealings with the SFIC are a private matter and it would be inappropriate for me to discuss them with you. You wouldn't want us bandying about any dealings we might have with your family, would you?"

"No, and that's fine. I got the information, including the numbers, from Hayley Fortney. I'm here with her knowledge and consent to buy the debt."

"Why?" Moses blurted, then blushed all the way to his receding hairline.

"Because Hayley is approaching her credit limit, and her fellow Barbies are coming to the rescue. I'm the Ken Doll, I'll have you know. And the Ken Doll is supposed to stand around looking good and giving the Barbies money. Judy says it's a rule."

Moses Abrabanel blinked and his mouth fell open. Karl found himself laughing out loud. "The Barbies are backing the SFIC, and the Liechtenstein family is backing the Barbies. SFIC's credit may now be considered as good as any in the Austro-Hungarian Empire, and better than most."

Now Moses was giving Karl a very sharp look. "Why?" he said again. This time it wasn't shock, but calculation.

"Because it's a good investment," Karl explained. "Yes, they are carrying people, but most of those people are hard-working and if some of them will fail to pay the SFIC back in full, most will. The SFIC can afford the loss of the occasional default or forgiven loan better than the loss of business."

Moses nodded, slowly at first, but then with more vigor. "I see, and if I could I would extend them more credit. But with the loss of Bohemia and the rest, the empire has been leaning on its other sources of income with more force than might be entirely wise. To put it bluntly, Your Serene Highness, the Abrabanel family in Austria-Hungary is teetering on the edge."

Karl pulled out a check book. It was printed down-time, but in the up-time style and it was on the First National Bank of Grantville. He then took a gold inlaid fountain pen, also down-time made to an up-time design, and used it to fill out a check with several zeros in the amount line. It somewhat more than cleared the debt owed to the Abrabanel Banking house by the SFIC.

"And the rest?" Moses asked.

"A drawing account."

"I'll implement it today, Your Serene Highness." It would take about two weeks for the check to reach Grantville and clear, but apparently Moses didn't doubt that it would be good.

Liechtenstein House, Vienna

"You did *what*?" Gundaker's face was as red as Moses' had been, but it wasn't from embarrassment. It was from anger.

"I bought twenty percent of the Sanderlin-Fortney Investment Company," Karl repeated.

"Have you lost your mind?"

"I find myself wondering the same thing," Maximilian said, rather more cautiously.

"No, Uncles. My mind is right where it ought to be. However, there is a real difference between a loan to one individual and the same amount loaned to many people. It is less the level of risk than the measurability of risk. Some of the debts will not be paid, some will be, with interest. This will average out to either a slight gain, or at worst a slight loss on the loans. If it turns out to be a loss, the interest in the many businesses will cover the loss over time. It's actually much safer than, say, investing in armies. After all, armies sometimes lose the war."

Grantville, July, 1635

"Judy has gone nuts," Heather Mason told Els Engel.

"Don't be ridiculous, Heather. To *go* nuts you have to start somewhere else," Els told her. They were at the studio, recording a new record. "All you Barbies live in crazy."

Heather stuck her tongue out at Els, then looked at the tray of foods in the green room and decided that she had better pass. She was having trouble keeping her weight down, especially since she could afford chocolate these days. "Fine. The still-crazy Judy the Younger Wendell wants me to get printing plates designed to print preferred stock certificates for a company called BarbieCo. In denominations of one pfennig, six pfennig, one groschen, twelve groschen, one reichsthaler and one mark denominations, no less. And one more, on which the amount is filled in when it's issued. I'm supposed to decide what goes on which denomination. There's a rough drawing of a building that's supposed to go on the back, and some legalese."

"So which Barbie goes where?" Els asked. "You ought to keep the really big one for yourself."

"I was thinking about the puns. You know . . . the buck and the dough and the picture of Johnny Cash."

"No." Els shook her head. "Don't try to make it look like a copy of American money, or people will think it's a fake."

"*Hmm.* Maybe," Heather said as she continued to read through the documents. "Hey, wait a minute. BarbieCo is American Equipment Company. They renamed it by stockholder vote. This really is crazy." She continued to read. They were going to issue lots of preferred stock. Sarah and Susan were still working out how much, but at least several million dollars worth, possibly a lot more. Heather was to contact their other investors, warn them, and offer to buy them out. AEC was pretty closely held. Aside from the Barbies and Karl, there were maybe twenty people who had stuck with the company.

And Judy admitted it was a really risky venture.

Heather looked up from the bundle. "Els, you don't really need me for the rest of this record, do you?"

Els eyebrows shot up. "But you love . . ." She gave Heather a look, then said, "No. It's okay, Heather. This is serious, isn't it?"

The latest take of Els' down-time Amideutch version of "The Battle Hymn of the Republic" was playing over the speakers to get the levels right. It was for *Robin of the CoC* and they were doing it with Els as Marian, starting as a lone voice singing quietly as they marched along, then Rod Friedman who played their unit commander joining in, then more and more people, till they had an army of voices. Which took laying down tracks of the same singers several times. It was all about the CoC's attack on the anti-Semites. And Heather felt a chill go down her spine that was only partly the music. "It could be, Els. It could be very, very serious."

✧   ✧   ✧

All the way to the Higgins Hotel, Heather Mason considered. By the summer of 1635 there was a large and growing contingent of top-flight artists in Grantville. They came to visit, and stayed for the suite of artistic tools that didn't exist anywhere else on Earth...and wasn't going to for the next twenty years at least. Digital cameras, computers with graphics software, computer-controlled cutting and shaping tools. And Heather knew a great many of them. It went with being Trommler Records, because it wasn't just the records themselves. She was also in charge of the sleeves and album covers.

So she knew who to talk to and, most importantly, she knew who would keep the job secret.

The artists of the seventeenth century would have been right at home at Disney Studios in the thirties and forties. They understood schedules and working to them, and there was darn little of the later nonsense about "prostituting their art." They painted what the client wanted and they did it as quickly and efficiently as they could manage. When they were privileged to work for Heather Mason, they also had access to digital photographs and computer-aided design. The photographs they used were the high school dance photos and, for Hayley Fortney, a year book photo for the last year she was in Grantville High.

They knew what they needed to do and they—for altogether too much of the time—had Heather Mason looking over their shoulders and encouraging them to hurry up.

Two weeks after she got the notice, Heather delivered into the hands of Dave Marcantonio a floppy disk containing twenty-eight image files. Then, for a truly exorbitant fee and as a personal favor, Dave used those image files to cut twenty-eight high carbon steel printing plates.

"Interesting thing here, Heather," Dave Marcantonio said, grinning as he examined the image files. "I see Susan, Hayley, Judy, Vicky, Gabriel, Millicent and even Trudi, but I don't see a picture of Heather Mason."

Heather put on a look of great dignity. "I made an executive decision. It's time and past time that people started realizing the Barbie Consortium is not just an up-timer club, so I put Trudi in."

Heather sniffed. "We only needed the seven denominations." Then she laughed out loud. "Judy figured I'd be using bucks and fins and stuff. But Els was right. We don't want these to look too much like the American dollars. Besides, the reichs money uses a picture of Ferdinand II, Ferdinand III on the new ones. So if they have people's pictures, they will look more like money to the Austrians. I considered using the Ken Doll, looking all regal like he can, but I figured that might cause problems with Ferdinand III. Heck, putting just one face on the money would have caused problems. This was the best choice."

"And you think your co-conspirators aren't going to notice that you are the only one not on a bill?"

"Oh, they'll notice all right." Heather Mason smiled like a naughty five-year-old who just got the very last piece of cake at the birthday party. "Think of it, Mr. Marcantonio. I got the bunch of them."

Dave Marcantonio laughed and went back to work. Two days later, those plates were on a plane to the Danube. Three days after that, they arrived in Vienna. But all that would take into August. In the meantime, the Barbies were still learning about Vienna.

CHAPTER 24

The Wall around Race Track City

July 1635

Race Track City

"What is all this business about a wall around Race Track City?" Judy asked, looking around at the road and the canal. "It's all anyone is talking about." They were back at the wine shop.

"We're quasi-official," Hayley said. "We have a deal with the emperor. But while the businesses that the emperor set up out here are *Hofbefreiten,* the businesses that we set up are sort of semi-*Hofbefreiten.*"

"Why did he go along with it?" Vicky asked.

"At first he just wanted a place to drive his 240Z," Hayley started to explain.

Gayleen Sanderlin interrupted. "But there were so many people looking for work, any kind of work...we had to do something."

"We know," Vicky said. "Hayley wrote us about it. But why was the emperor willing to give you guys even quasi-*Hofbefreiten* status?"

"For the money," Hayley said. "In this case, for the money it would have cost him to build the canal on his own. The deal was we would pay for half of it. As it worked out, we paid about three-quarters of it and he owes us the money for the rest of his half."

"But why build the canal in the first place? It's a road, ah, canal to nowhere."

"No. The race track is a real attraction. The place is jumping

214

every time the emperor comes out and now that Dad has finished
the Sonny Steamer, we can do runs even when the emperor is
busy. Then there are the gardens of the emperor's hunting lodge.
Brandon cut a deal with the lodge's chief gardener, and a bunch
of up-time flowers and—"

"So that's what that was all about," Judy said, "I was there when
Delia got the letter about needing flower seeds."

"Right. Between the extensive gardens they already had and
the flowers, the royal gardens are a big draw. It's a half pence to
take the tour which lasts about an hour. It's all 'look, no touch'
but it is pretty and it smells wonderful."

"We'll give it a go sometime," Judy said, "but go on."

"Between the race track, the water park, the gardens and the
shops, this is a great place to spend a day if you live in Vienna.
We get a lot of people out here most weekends. It didn't happen
all at once, but just sort of grew.

"These days the royal family mostly takes the royal steam yacht.
It makes it like a twenty-minute trip and Ferdinand can even
hold a sort of mini-court on the yacht."

"Royal steam yacht?" Vicky asked.

"Yep. A catamaran with a steam engine. It will do about fifteen
knots, which makes it a really easy commute, so the emperor
comes out here a lot. That brings members of the court and once
they are here they buy stuff. Honestly, it's the members of the
court who have kept us as close to in the black as we are. The
speed runs are really popular. They get to see the emperor and
the 240Z going really fast. I have to say, the people here are as
addicted as any up-time NASCAR fan. I don't see it myself, but
it seems to strike a chord with the down-timers."

Judy nodded. They had all seen the track with its raised ends
and the bleachers on either side of the straightaway.

"We get lots of foot traffic between the canal and the track.
The emperor's real *Hofbefreiten* mostly have the area between the
canal and the gardens at Schloss Neugebuade. They get just as
much of the traffic, but they aren't as willing to give credit, which
means they are probably making out like bandits. It's something
between a duty free shop and a mall, and we control almost half
of it," Hayley explained.

"You mean the Sanderlin-Fortney Investment Company?" Vicky
asked.

"Yes. Ferdinand's *Hofbefreiten* have the rest of it and more snob appeal than we have, but our stuff is cheaper and, more often than not, better quality. Partly that's because through you guys we have been able to save on the imports from Grantville and Magdeburg. Lathes, clocks, sewing machines, that sort of thing."

"I like the way Race Track City is laid out," Karl commented.

"Thanks. I'll tell Dad you said so," Hayley said. "He drew up the layout and the roads and stuff."

Sonny Fortney had designed Race Track City starting with a two-lane street with a twenty-five-foot median in the middle with turnarounds. It was designed for cars but aside from the cars they had brought or built here, there weren't any, so it ended up as a wide open parklike road between the docks and the race track. On either side were shops, restaurants, anything that Hayley, her parents and the Sanderlins could come up with to make money. And anything Ferdinand's courtiers could come up with, as well.

The courtiers tended to look down on the clients of the Sanderlin-Fortney Investment Company, but that was nothing new. For the most part, the Fortneys and Sanderlins let it roll off their backs.

And Race Track City was making money. Enough money that even with the majority of its customers buying on credit, it was still almost running in the black. The problem Hayley had was that a "little bit in the red" from eighteen separate businesses is a lot in the red. The problem the upper crust of Vienna had was that Race Track City was competition for them. Just barely so far, but it was growing. The people in charge in Vienna wanted Race Track City brought to heel. Well, what they really wanted was it shut down, but that was unlikely to happen. They argued that it was unsafe, being outside the city walls. They argued that the proprietors of shops in Race Track City were avoiding city fees and taxes, which was true. They argued that the goods sold in Race Track City were of inferior quality, which was not.

"So how is that all connected to the wall around Race Track City?" Millicent asked.

"It's all connected to the 'forcibly incorporate Race Track City into Vienna' business. Which is still working its way back and forth between the burghers of Vienna and the emperor's court. The burghers are insisting that it's unsafe out here without the protection of the city walls and that we are not really *Hofbefreiten*. And some of the *Hofbefreiten* out here are arguing on the burghers' side. So far the emperor isn't buying it, but he is planning to put a wall around Race Track City and use the river and the river boats to connect the two in case of attack."

"And," Dana Fortney added, "once a wall is around Race Track City, the burghers are going to argue that it's all part of Vienna and we need to get their permission to do business."

"Which they will gleefully deny," Susan said. "We know the drill by now. Getting the burghers of Vienna to agree to blow their noses when they have a cold is the next best thing to impossible, as we have learned to our regret." She was talking about the roadblocks that the burghers of Vienna and the courtiers as well, had put in the way of building anything in the city proper. Problems that would, of course, all go away if the right hands were properly greased with large amounts of silver.

Meanwhile, Ferdinand III was having his own conference with Moses Abrabanel, Reichsgraf Maximilian von Trauttmansdorff, and Georg Bartholomaeus Zwikl, his official spymaster.

"What do you think will happen with John George?"

"He's gone, Your Majesty. Probably October, perhaps November."

"We could send support," Ferdinand offered instantly. But his tone made it clear the suggestion was tentative.

"That would be most unwise, I think," Georg Bartholomaeus said. "Gustav always moves fast and he is apparently taking advantage of up-time techniques in surprising places, which are letting his army march even faster. By the time we could move much of a force around Silesia and through Poland into Saxony, it would probably all be over."

"What do you think will happen when they meet?" Moses Abrabanel asked.

Georg laughed bitterly. "John George will either die or escape. If he escapes, he may well end up here, asking us to help him retake Saxony."

"And the USE?" Moses asked.

"After Saxony, Gustav will go after George William of Brandenburg. Depending on how much of a fight John George puts up, that will be late in this year's campaign season, or early next year. I suspect late this year. But next year, Poland."

Ferdinand shook his head and changed the subject. "What about Murad?"

"They are coming, Majesty. Not this year. He is going to have to reorganize and consolidate his forces. But next year or the year after, at the latest."

"Maybe. I am still not convinced. Baghdad will not be so easy to take. Even if that is what Murad plans."

There was silence.

"Never mind. Tell me about the railroads."

"Wallenstein has started a railroad from Prague to Cieszyn. He is using the single rail system that Herr Fortney recommends and wooden rails. Even if we don't allow the line to Cieszyn, his railroad will still connect the Baltic to the North Sea by way of the Olga River. He already has the Elbe and the railroad will connect the two rivers. He is building other rail lines, one to Grantville from Prague and one to the Danube. It won't cut us out of the Black Sea trade, but will cut us out of much of the Baltic trade. Even though they are wood lines, they will still carry a massive amount of cargo at very low cost," Moses Abrabanel said. "And Elisabeth Lukretia von Teschen is building her part of the rail line to the—" Moses paused, clearly looking for a nonoffensive way of saying it.

"To the present border between Silesia and Austria," Ferdinand III offered.

Moses nodded and continued. "Most of the cost is being borne by the Liechtenstein Improvement Corporation."

"Which will also allow him to ship thousands of troops, fresh and ready to fight, from his capital to our border in hours. And if we extend the line to meet their lines, the railroad will allow Wallenstein to ship an army all the way to Vienna in just a few more hours," Georg said.

Ferdinand nodded at Georg's point. "I know Karl insists that the railroads are for trade and defense, but Karl has no military experience. He's a good boy, but not a soldier."

Reichsgraf Maximilian von Trauttmansdorff added, "He's also sworn to Wallenstein, not to you."

CHAPTER 25

The Expansion of Race Track City

July 1635

Race Track City

Before the printing plates got to Vienna, the staff and stuff had arrived. Three more personal assistants, plus a machinist, an electrician and a chemist. All down-timers, and three of them girls. They included one more "von" and four were former students at the university in Jena. They all moved out to Race Track City.

The equipment included things like a movie projector for the new down-time-made celluloid movies. Down-time-made machining equipment, typewriters, and anything the girls could think of. For the most part, that equipment also went to Race Track City. Both the people and the equipment increased the capabilities of Race Track City greatly. They were still selling more on credit than for cash, but you could almost hear the sucking sound as the money flowed out of Vienna. The biggest draw was the new movies.

Not all of those movies were exactly down-time made. A clever chap had figured out a way to project and photograph video tapes from up-time. It wasn't perfect by any means, but it was considerably cheaper than shooting a new movie. Especially when special effects were considered. So there was a stock of movies, like a version of *Casablanca* dubbed in German, and Elvis would be known in two universes. Not that there weren't one-reel wonders shot on soundstages in Grantville. Drawing room comedies, mysteries and small scale musicals. But it was *Star Wars* and the heretical notion of the Force that would cause them problems. All that would take months, and in the meantime the plates arrived.

Hayley read through the notes that Heather had sent with the plates. There were twenty-eight plates, but the base four of the plates were to be used on all certificates regardless of amount. They were for the black and red ink. Black for the contractual information on the back and outlining and emphasis on the front. The red to combine with the white of the background to make pink, as well as orange and purple when combined with yellow and blue. Together they formed surprisingly effective blend of down-time engraving techniques with up-time newspaper and comic strip coloration. Which produced almost photorealistic images of the Barbies, with backgrounds that were clearly drawn. It took Hayley and the printers three days of trying before they got the inking and placement just right. All the rejects were burned.

Hayley laid them out in order.

Millicent was on the one pfennig, They were going to be printing a lot of those. Heather's letter to Hayley explained that she figured Millicent wouldn't mind. Also, she didn't want to put Trudi on the lowest denomination bill because people might interpret that to mean they thought less of Trudi than the up-timer Barbies.

A milli would buy a half pound loaf of day-old bread. Three of them would buy a meal at one of the stalls on Canal Street.

Heather put Trudi on the six pfennig bill. A trudi would buy a shampoo at the beauty shop.

Gabby got put on the one groschen. A gabbi would buy you a day at the water park, riding all the rides as often as you wanted. Two gabbies were a day's pay for unskilled labor.

Vicky was on the twelve groschen. And now they were into real money. A week's pay for a day laborer, a day's pay for a master craftsman, a full day at the spa with massage, steam, pampering and primping. Or a new skirt, or a blouse, or a new pair of shoes. A month's rent at Frau Krause's boarding house, without meals.

Judy on the reichsthaler, because it was Judy's sister who was marrying Karl. A judi would rent a room at the boarding house with meals, or just the month's rent on a nice two bedroom in Race Track City.

And there, looking back at Hayley, was her own face on the

one mark bill, because Heather said Hayley was the one who had been in Vienna the longest. Also because there would be fewer of the one mark bills in circulation. And a hayli could buy a cow, something that Brandon was sure to note.

Susan Logsden was on the face of the variable denomination bills. The ones that would have the amount filled in by hand at the time of issuance. In essence, a check written on the BarbieCo account. Those would be used when they bought a village or a building at one shot. Heather had chosen Susan for that because those bills had to be signed to be good. And most of the time it would be Susan who was doing the signing.

A few days later, Trudi was talking to the Liechtenstein upper servants about the Barbie Consortium when the issue of investments came up.

"Is it true," Anna asked, "that regular people in the USE can buy into companies, even servants?"

"Anna!" Stephen remonstrated.

Trudi lifted an eyebrow and Stephen flushed, clearly remembering that Anna was no longer under his authority.

Anna shrank back for an instant, then relaxed, apparently remembering the same thing.

"As it happens," Trudi said, "Anna is quite correct. Anyone can invest in publicly traded companies in the USE. Well, anyone who has the money. But it's not always wise."

"Why not?" Stephen asked. "I mean, from what we hear, people make money all the time. In fact, I heard that Prince Karl was heavily invested with the young ladies of the Barbie Consortium."

"He is, and he's made a very good profit," Trudi agreed. "In fact, so have I."

"Could I invest?" Anna asked. Clearly, Anna was looking ahead at a dowry and a full hope chest.

"I'll have to ask, but I suspect so."

"Is that wise?" asked Stephen. "I mean, in the USE they have the ear of the Secretary of the Treasury. That's where the real money comes from, surely."

"Not at all. Fletcher and Judy the Elder Wendell are not particularly wealthy by up-timer standards. Sarah's money comes from the HSMC, ah, Higgins Sewing Machine Company and OPM which is a mutual fund. Its official name is Other People's

Money. Plus, she has other investments. Judy the Younger and the other members of the Barbie Consortium got rich through a series of astute investments."

Trudi listened to the disbelieving snorts with no great surprise. She could hardly believe it herself. She hadn't for the first few months after she got to Grantville High School. But it was true. The elder Wendells stayed scrupulously out of business. Nor did they help their daughters with insider information. Not that the Barbies didn't get insider information. They knew every mover and shaker in Grantville and were past masters at getting information out of them.

But no one here was going to believe that. She shrugged it off. They would learn. Just not too soon, she hoped. Instead, she told of her father's problems after Kipper and Wipper and the arrival of the Ring of Fire. "He sent me to Grantville just after they ratified their constitution. So I attended the Grantville high school."

"Why would he do that, especially with a daughter?" asked Stephen. He was the senior servant here and seemed to feel it was his responsibility to put into words what the others wanted to ask.

"Well, I have no brothers. They were killed in the war in 1625. We were close enough that we could make the trip and see the Ring of Fire. Father felt that the Ring changed everything. Besides, I had always been interested in books. Anyway, that's where I met Judy Wendell. I got onto the junior varsity cheerleading squad. A lot of down-timer girls were unwilling to do so because of the short skirts of the cheerleader's uniform." Trudi stood up and gestured on her body where the skirt fell, to gasps of disbelief and titillation. There were condemnations, but she defended the practice and pointed out that they weren't all that much shorter than the dress Vicky Emerson wore to the emperor's ball. Then she told them about the various financial adventures, including the acquisition of American Equipment Corporation. "After that, the Barbies were very short on cash till Prince Karl got back to Grantville from the Netherlands." She explained that Judy and Karl had made a deal and the Barbies had been funded since then by Karl, through the American Equipment Corporation, and had made him a lot of money.

From there, the stories about the "Barbie" company spread through the upper servants and the lower nobility. It was all part of Trudi's plan. They were going to introduce BarbieCo Preferred as an alternative to reich money, and to do that they needed a whisper campaign, not a proclamation. That was also the reason for the change of the name from AEC to BarbieCo. Barbies were expensive and valuable, so BarbieCo Preferred must be the same.

Anna, the new maid who was getting more money and getting paid on time, asked about getting some of her pay in stock from the Barbies. The girls said "sure." The Liechtenstein under-servants asked about the availability of stock as well, apparently having heard about it from Anna.

But mostly the investors were the upper nobility. They had more money to spend. They got the word from Judy and Vicky.

The Hofburg Palace, Vienna

Karl Eusebius looked around the meeting room. It was small for the group, and crowded, and Karl was almost regretting bringing the Barbies. The rectangular room had thick walls with the windows set back to the exterior walls. There were two windows set high on the walls, and two lower. The cloudy day insured that the light was not particularly bright. A polished oak table sat in the center of the room, surrounded by chairs and covered with papers and reports having to do with balance of trade and the proposed railroad.

"We need to stop these imports from the USE," Moses Abrabanel insisted.

Karl hid a wince.

"Just how do you figure on stopping them?" Sarah Wendell asked. "Are you hiding an industrial complex in your back pocket, by chance?"

Uncle Gundaker slapped a hand on the table. "We need to introduce sumptuary laws to counter the flow of silver to the USE."

"What are you going to do? Make it illegal to own sewing machine-made trousers?" Susan snorted.

"If everyone will just calm down," Karl tried.

It didn't do a lot of good. Duke Leopold was representing the royal family in this meeting and being wisely quiet.

Gundaker, representing the court, and Moses Abrabanel, representing the mercantile interests of Vienna, were both pushing for the mercantilist viewpoint. The proposed railroad was fully mapped-out and construction had started in Silesia, but was being delayed in Vienna because of fear of even more silver flowing from Austria-Hungary to the USE. This time through Bohemia, with still more silver in fees and taxes going to Wallenstein. All in exchange for manufactured goods that the USE seemed to be producing at an ever-increasing rate.

"The Swede is trying to destroy the Holy Roman Empire by bankrupting it with cheap machine-made goods and the railroad will just make it work faster. Trainloads of silver will be going from Vienna, through Bohemia, to Magdeburg as the Swede gets stronger, Wallenstein gets stronger, and we get weaker," Gundaker complained.

It was all very overblown. Yes, the balance of trade between the USE and Austria-Hungary was more than a bit one-sided, but it was far from the deadly dangerous problem that Moses and Gundaker were making it out to be. Even with the rail line, it wasn't going to become killing.

"Look," Judy Wendell said. "All you really need to do is come up with stuff that they need in the USE and Bohemia. And, well, you're farther south. Can you guys grow oranges and stuff?"

"No. It does freeze here in the winter," Hayley told her.

"But they grow citrus fruits in the Ottoman Empire," Karl pointed out.

"Marvelous. You wish us to provide Murad the Mad with the silver to pay his armies by shipping oranges from Istanbul to Magdeburg by way of the Silesian railroad?"

"That's not a bad idea," Susan Logsden said. "We already get coffee from there. Why not orange juice to go with it? In exchange, we can sell them aspirin and machine-made boots and shoes. Vienna isn't rich because of what it produces. It's rich because of what flows through it."

"You need the railroad," Sarah Wendell said. "You need it more than Bohemia does, and in the meantime you need steam barges on the Danube up to Regensburg and down to the Black Sea. But you also need native industries for value-added products."

Judy moaned theatrically. "Value-added," she whined. "The buzz words are attacking."

"That is what I have been saying," Gundaker said.

"No. What you were saying was that you wanted to prevent

imports from the USE, not that you wanted to encourage local production," Sarah said. "It's not the same thing."

It was, Karl thought, the next battle in the ongoing war between Sarah and the more conservative economic theorists of the Austro-Hungarian Empire. Sarah was chipping away, but they were holding out for a regulation-based structure that tried to protect their industries from foreign competition by outlawing that competition. Sarah, on the other hand, wanted the government to invest in local businesses to encourage development of industry, as was being done in the USE, because some of those businesses wouldn't develop without government intervention. At least, she was convinced that they wouldn't, and Karl was willing to take her word for it.

Race Track City

Days later, in Race Track City, the fourth showing of *Singing in the Rain*, dubbed in German with Els Engel voicing and singing the Debbie Reynolds part, was sold out. The machine shop was up and running with the new equipment, and the howling of Vienna's merchant class could almost be heard over Els' singing.

Father Lamormaini enjoyed the movie, though he found the music strange and a little disquieting. What he resented was where it came from. More and more, the Ring of Fire was getting its hooks into the world, spreading something that his agent in Grantville had described as humanism. Placing humanity above God. Repeating Satan's sin of pride, and feeding it to every peasant.

There was a natural order in the world that reflected the order of Heaven, with God at the top and the choirs of angels ranked below. So, on Earth, the emperor above, and below—ordered by their natural ranks—the great nobles, then the lesser nobles, the merchant classes, and at the bottom of them all, the peasant. But the up-timers would reverse that order, overturning it like Satan tried to overturn God's order.

It was the job of the church to prevent that from happening, and that was the answer to Maria Anna's vexing question, "Is it more important that the Church regain all the temporal worldly goods that she once held? Or that she be free to practice her faith unhindered in Protestant territories? If these were placed before a Catholic ruler as a choice, which way should he go?" It was a false question for it still allowed the Protestant heretics to lead others into heresy, and not just in Protestant lands, but in Catholic lands as well. The restoration of property to the church was not for the church, but to give the church the power to enforce God's will on the ungodly. It was to the ultimate benefit of the heretic that he be forced to renounce his heresy, and if his renunciation was not heartfelt it still protected another from following him into heresy, and so condemning another soul to perdition.

Hence, Father Lamormaini watched a pleasant movie and resented not the movie, but those who provided it. He managed to justify again the Edict of Restitution...and take a further step along the road to fanaticism.

Liechtenstein House, Vienna

A few miles away in Liechtenstein House, Gundaker von Liechtenstein was taking a similar trip by a different road. Karl's investments in Bohemia were extensive and confusing, but Gundaker was nothing if not thorough. The Liechtenstein Investment Corporation would spend a fortune on building a railroad from Vienna to Cieszyn, then give that rail line to the Liechtenstein Railroad Company, which would be given to Sarah Wendell as her dower right. It was obvious that the great expense of the railroad was the building of the line. The grading of the line was expensive enough, and even using wood rails instead of steel, the cost of the rails were impossible. But once the rail line was built, the railroad would be profitable. Highly profitable, if not so profitable as to pay for the building of the rail line in the first place. But Sarah Wendell would not be paying to build a rail line. She would pay just to run the trains along the line that the family would pay to have built.

He wasn't yet willing to stop the marriage. After all, a morganatic marriage's advantages were still there. But Gundaker would find a way to prevent this LIC from wasting the family fortune on building a railroad.

He started working out further arguments against the railroad.

Eisenberg House, Vienna

Amadeus walked into his father's office, noting his father at the table and, in passing, his father's secretary, Hans, in one corner at an up-time designed desk, pen in hand. "Father—" Amadeus ignored Hans. "—how would you feel about me courting the daughter of the emperor's mechanic?"

"Hayley Fortney? The girl at the party? She's not the one who took Father Lugocie to task, is she?"

"No, Father. That was the one called Vicky."

"A shame, that. I was rather impressed. Still, she is the daughter of Sonny Fortney. You know he's a spy, don't you?"

"Who?"

"Sonny Fortney. Janos Drugeth is convinced that Herr Fortney works for Francisco Nasi and is sending him regular reports. Nasi is a Jew and Fortney is an up-timer. How is a man supposed to judge the true rank of either? Especially with this inverted pogrom that the Committees of Correspondence seem to be carrying out in the USE."

Amadeus ignored the reference to Jews and just said, "Von Up-time."

"Oh, don't be silly. Just because..."

"Just because God picked them up and put them here. It seems enough to me to justify a von."

"Perhaps. But what sort of a von? A minor nobility or a duke? How many princes in the Ring of Fire?"

"I don't know, Father, but Hayley Fortney is quite wealthy. I have been looking into things out at Race Track City since the party. And I think she, more than the Sanderlins, is the one who financed the whole project."

"They got thirty-five thousand reichsthaler for that car, and they get fifty reichsthaler a month. That's quite a lot of money." Peter paused. "No. You're right. It's not enough to pay for the canal and all the projects that they have out there. But you're saying it's the girl, not the father? Nasi is no spendthrift, but he is not ungenerous to his agents. I hadn't really thought about it." Peter paused and rubbed his nose. It was a mannerism that Amadeus knew well. "I should have, though," Peter continued. "In fact, I should have even more if it had been Sonny Fortney financing the project."

"What? Why?"

"Because: Why is a spy for Francisco Nasi financing a whole city just four miles from Vienna? Would it not be nice for Gustav to have a fortress next door to Vienna?"

Amadeus laughed. He couldn't help it. "Race Track City? There is no wall. No fortifications of any sort. There are fifteen soldiers that the emperor sent and a bunch of craftsmen. It's a lovely place to spend a summer day, but it couldn't hold off a tercio for an afternoon."

"Except that until this news about the pope there was increasing agitation among the They of Vienna to put a wall around Race Track City, or even to extend the wall to surround it and make it part of Vienna proper. The argument was that it would put them under the city's authority. The emperor was, of course, opposed to the idea because he has found placing imitation-*Hofbefreiten* there both convenient and profitable. But a likely compromise might have been a wall around Race Track City, and some sort of separate city status, like Buda and Pest."

"Which would put a walled city just a couple miles from Vienna, with a large part of the population loyal to their patrons, the Sanderlins and the Fortneys. Then Gustav invades and Race Track city declares for him." Amadeus shook his head. "No, Father. It's a flight of fancy. It would never happen. Yes, the Sanderlins and the Fortneys are popular, but so is the emperor. His drives are a major draw and the making of many of the businesses in Race Track City."

"You're probably right. Almost certainly right. But even a slight chance of such a coup would be worth a considerable risk of funds. Especially if there was a good chance that the investment would make an ordinary profit."

"I think you're hunting monsters in my wardrobe, Father."

"Probably. Particularly if it's the daughter, not the father. Still, I think I will have a talk with Moses Abrabanel about the wealth of the Barbies and where it comes from."

"Fine, Father, but about my courting Hayley Fortney...?"

"You were serious about that?"

"Yes, Father, I am very serious about that."

Peter held up a hand, then examined Amadeus carefully. "All right. I won't say yes right now, but I will talk to Moses. Depending on what he says, I may have a talk with the girl's parents on the matter."

Moses Abrabanel's Office, outside Vienna

"I don't believe it, Moses," Peter von Eisenberg said. "It's really the *girls*? Francisco Nasi has nothing to do with it?"

"Nothing we could find," Moses said. "I wouldn't be shocked to find that he provided information to the Barbies at some point, in order to make sure that Sonny Fortney's family was provided for. But, frankly, we haven't been able to find any financial connection between Sonny and Don Francisco. What letters to Uriel did reveal was a solid connection between Karl Eusebius and the Barbie Consortium. He has been their backer and their bank. In return, they have brought him into dozens of ventures that have increased his wealth dramatically."

"So, how wealthy is Hayley Fortney?"

"That depends on the fate of Race Track City," Moses said. "It took me much too long to realize it. In fact, it wasn't until the rest of the Barbies arrived that I truly saw what was going on. Hayley financed Race Track City out of her own pocket. If the place is a success, if the debts owed to Sanderlin-Fortney Investment Company are made good, she will be richer than you. If not, she could be a pauper in a year."

Peter shook his head again, not in negation, more like a fighter who had just taken a blow to the head and was trying to shake it off. "What do you think, Moses?"

"I think . . . no, I know . . . that the rest of the Barbies have come to her rescue. And they bring House Liechtenstein."

"Yes, that makes sense. A great deal of sense."

"So what are you going to do," Moses asked, "if you don't mind my asking?"

Duke Peter von Eisenberg looked at the Jew. For just an instant he was all injured dignity, then he rubbed his nose and smiled. "I, sir, am going to have a talk with Sonny Fortney. On the subject of courting and the combining of fortunes." Another pause and more nose rubbing, then, "But first I will have a talk with my wife about the inevitability of change. And children growing up."

As it turned out, he couldn't have a talk with Sonny, because, as was often the case, Sonny Fortney was out of town, working on the surveying of the road that would—if the agreements were ever worked out—become the Vienna-Cieszyn rail line.

Fortney House, Race Track City

Dana Fortney stepped into her daughter's office. "And just who is Amadeus von Eisenberg?" she asked severely.

Hayley looked up from her homework, clearly confused. "Huh?" Then, apparently, the penny dropped. "Amadeus? Oh, he's that nice count I met at the party just after the girls got here. Why? What did he do?"

"I got a visit from his mother."

"Really? What's she like?" Hayley asked, sounding confused again.

"She's concerned that her darling little boy isn't being led astray by a succubus from the licentious north."

Dana tried not to laugh at Hayley's expression.

"Mom, will you please talk sense?"

"Well, it took some working out, but it seems that your young count was pretty impressed with you. He went to his father to ask if he might court you."

"He did *what*?"

Dana watched her daughter carefully, but couldn't tell if Hayley was pleased or offended. Which wasn't unreasonable. Dana wasn't all that sure how she felt, either.

"He went to his father, who is apparently a court duke. He has lands, but his primary title is a court title." By now they all knew how it worked here. "And he asked if the Noble Family Eisenberg would have any difficulty with an up-timer being married into the noble lineage."

"Well, he didn't mention it to me," Hayley said. "We met at the party, like I said, and he came out to the track a couple of times. But, well, he hasn't even asked me out yet."

"But you expected him to?"

Hayley blushed a little. "It was starting to seem like it might happen."

Dana nodded. "But, being a loyal son of a noble house in Austria-Hungary, he first went to his dad to clear it. His dad apparently decided it was at least potentially an acceptable match, and brought the matter to his wife's attention. Then Mom came out here to check out the family and I was in the middle of a yoga class when she showed up.

"I get called out of the class and sat down to have tea with her, and then half of Race Track City comes in. Mostly, I think, to find out what's going on." Dana grinned, recalling the last couple of hours. She thought that Duchess Eisenberg had ended up a bit intimidated by all the people showing up and asking Dana what they could buy or who they could give credit to. "Anyway, we are invited to dinner with them next Wednesday, and the duchess barely even flinched when I thanked Gloria for the tea. So, do we go or do we beg off?"

Hayley considered. She hadn't been old enough to date when her parents had brought her here. And once they got here, she had just been too busy. They all had. "I guess we should go . . . though he should have asked me before he did anything like this."

"I disagree," Dana said. "You know that it's entirely possible that his parents might have gone ballistic over the very idea of an up-timer in the family. Not that you're going to be in the family any time soon. You're not even sixteen yet."

"Which is another weird thing. What is he doing, wanting to court me at this age?"

Dana knew what she meant. After they hit the seventeenth century, they had been surprised by how late people waited before getting engaged or married. "Nobles, Hayley. The reason that the commoners wait so long is because they can't afford it earlier. If things work out, you'll be able to date . . . but keep things light for the next couple of years anyway. For your dad's blood pressure, if for no other reason."

CHAPTER 26

𝕷𝖔𝖔𝖑𝖘 𝖆𝖓𝖉 𝕽𝖚𝖒𝖔𝖗𝖘

August 1635

Liechtenstein House, Vienna

Johannes Koell, the bookkeeper for the Liechtenstein family, was in love. Not with Susan Logsden, but with her computer. It took a few weeks for the love affair to blossom. At first he had looked at the whole thing askance. The "desktop computer," the battery pack and transformer, the pedal-powered generator to provide power. The down-time-made from a combination of up-time parts dot-matrix printer. It all seemed like expensive gewgaws, designed to disguise the basic lack of mathematical skill of the girl. However, young Prince Karl had insisted, so Johannes provided a room and guards and a kitchen boy to pedal the generator and change the batteries.

He objected when Prince Karl insisted that he provide Millicent and her assistant with copies of the account books. There was private Liechtenstein information in those books. That was some weeks ago.

In those few weeks, Millicent, her assistant, and one of his apprentice accountants had been doing something called "data entry." It wasn't a long time. They had, in fact, barely scratched the surface. But by concentrating on one set of transactions, they had enough for a demonstration. The transactions selected were the rents paid by both the crown and the regular tenants of an apartment building on Market Street, placed against the costs of upkeep. The picture wasn't heartening. The crown rents were in arrears by more than a year and private rents were far from up-to-date. In response, the upkeep—basic repairs that any building needed now and again—had been put on hold. With the consequence that what would have been minor fixes had gotten worse to the point that they were now going to cost twice to three times as much as the regular repairs would have cost.

Which, as it happened, was what Johannes had been arguing for the past several months but had been unable to prove.

"While we're happy to help out," Judy Wendell informed him, "the computer is not owned by the Liechtenstein family, but by Susan. And using it just for one family's books, even the Liechtenstein books, would be a horrible waste of resources. So what we propose to do is open an accounting firm. When Susan isn't using the computer for her investment strategies, the accounting firm will have access to it for use in keeping the books of various businesses around Vienna. Sometime soon, the Liechtenstein family, with your advice, will need to decide whether or not it will engage the services of our firm."

"Perhaps I should rent time on the emperor's aqua computer."

Johannes was a bit surprised when the up-timer girl nearly rolled on the floor laughing. For rather a long time.

Between gasps, she said, "Be my guest. I promise you, that old desktop of Susan's, as antique as it was up-time, has about a hundred times more power than the aqualator. At least. You'll pay the emperor twice as much and wait four times as long for the results."

"Don't get me wrong," Judy continued, wiping her eyes. "I actually love the aqualator. But they are not as fast, they are not as powerful. And if you're going to go that route, you'd probably be better off buying your own in a year or so. I'll bet you a couple of reichsthaler that in a year, just like computers up-time, they'll have a better, faster model."

After some consideration, Johannes recommended to House Liechtenstein that they use the Barbies' computer. Besides, there was no point in having the family accounts put at risk of exposure by going to an outside firm.

Race Track City

Anna was spending her Sunday afternoon at Race Track City. Word was that the emperor would be doing speed runs at the track and it seemed like half the city of Vienna was out enjoying the midsummer air.

"Oh!" Anna stopped dead in the street. "Oh, would you look at that." She wasn't speaking to anyone in particular, since she'd come alone. But the words just flew out.

It was a bra. A lace bra. "Oh." On a mannequin. "Oh, my." In the window, with a sign. "Oh, I want one. I want two."

She hesitated. Bras were the very latest thing. Everyone who was anyone had one.

She made her way to the window. And stared. "Oh."

"Would you like to try one on?" the shopkeeper asked, knowing a sale when she saw one.

"Oh." Anna hesitated some more. "Oh, yes. But I know it's going to be too expensive."

"Oh, we can work something out."

After the fitting, still wearing her new acquisition, Anna began turning out her bag to see how much money she had. In the process, she pulled out her latest purchase of BarbieCo stock.

The shopkeeper asked, "What's that? It's pretty fancy printing."

Anna explained, while continuing to check inside her bag. She didn't have enough money.

"Let me send a runner," the shopkeeper said. "I'm curious about something."

A boy was called over and sent on an errand. Anna said, "I guess I'd better take this off. I just don't have quite enough money on me. Can you put it back for me? I'll be back next week to pick it up."

"Surely, if that's what you want. But let's wait just a few minutes, until the boy comes back. We do sometimes give credit, if your reputation is good and your employment steady."

Anna laughed. "I work for the people who issue these stock certificates."

"In that case, your credit is probably pretty good. At least here in Race Track City."

The boy came running back and passed the shopkeeper a note, which she read aloud. "This is from Mrs. Sanderlin. It says 'BarbieCo stock certificates are to be accepted at par value, good as cash. The par value is written on the stock certificate.'" She looked at Anna. "So you do have enough money, after all."

Liechtenstein House, Vienna

As soon as Anna got back to work, she began telling about her purchase, and even showing the lace off a bit. Anna was just a bit vain about her looks.

"Where did you get the money? I saw one of those and it was too expensive."

"Race Track City. Frau Krauss' shop."

"Yep. That's where I saw it. Did she give you a special price? I'll go there tomorrow and insist on the same one if she did."

"No. But she took my BarbieCo stock certificate. Said it was as good as cash. She even gave me change."

That started the story of BarbieCo money. It wasn't as planned as they might have preferred, but it wasn't unplanned either. Word spread from servant to workman, from tavern to shop. And the Barbies went to considerable effort to convince people that they would really prefer not to let any of the stock out of their control.

The shopkeeper Anna had talked to got her bras from a four shift "sweat shop," which, in turn, made them using the Higgins sewing machine brought by the Fortneys. By now everyone in Race Track City had heard about Hayley Fortney being one of the Barbies. Based on that, the shopkeeper had been considering taking the stock in trade. She was doing well now and the notion of a bit of investment for the future appealed to her. But she wanted to hear what Frau Sanderlin thought about it first. The "good as cash" from the note had been a bit of a surprise, so once race day was over she headed for the Sanderlin house—stock certificate in hand—to find out what was going on. The maid let her in. Frau Sanderlin was usually willing to talk to the merchants and craftsmen of Race Track City, and today was no different, except a little busier. Race days always were, especially since they added horse racing to the 240Z and Sonny Steamer laps.

There were half a dozen merchants who were bringing in IOU's they had gotten from customers. And Frau Krauss, the shopkeeper who had taken Anna's stock certificate. The others were a bit concerned because SFIC was getting more strict about who they would let the shopkeepers give credit to. They had to be. Frau Krauss was simply curious. She already had approval.

Frau Sanderlin wasn't all that helpful. "I don't really understand, but Hayley was here when the boy came with the note. It's one of the Barbies' business deals. I understand Susan Logsden doesn't want their investment diluted by too many shareholders, so they buy them back whenever they can get them."

Frau Krauss didn't know it, but Gayleen Sanderlin didn't understand what Hayley had told her even as well as Gayleen had thought. The Barbies weren't in any great hurry to buy back BarbieCo stock. But Hayley realized that reputation was important, so the Barbies would, at least for now, buy them at par value in reichsthaler. To Gayleen, the important part had been that Hayley said they were as good as cash. Frau Krauss was left with the impression that they were better, since you could spend them if you wanted to, but if you held onto them they would grow at two percent a year or more.

The next morning, there was a sign by the door of the shop. WE ACCEPT BARBIECO STOCK. GOOD AS CASH. That led her neighbors to question her, and Frau Krauss explained the situation, adding her own interpretation and not clarifying what came from her and what from Frau Sanderlin.

The next day there were similar signs on half a dozen shops in Race Track City. And still more the day after.

Tuesday morning, before having the Fortneys over to dinner the next day, Duchess Eisenberg and two other ladies of the court were in Race Track City. They intended to buy some of the strawberry wine that was becoming quite popular with the very upper crust of Vienna after the dowager empress had come out to see her stepson race around the track and discovered it.

The wine had quadrupled in price in the last week and Duchess Sophia Eisenberg wasn't at all sure that her servants would have the clout to get some. Besides, any excuse to go out to Race Track City was a good excuse. After it had been learned that she had invited the Fortneys to her home, she had found herself the center of a storm of curiosity. So, along with her servants, this trip had her accompanied by Katharina Schembera, Maximilian von Liechtenstein's wife, and Gundaker von Liechtenstein's daughter, Maximiliana Constanzia, called Liana, who had married Johann Baptist Mathias von Thurn und Valsassina about five years before.

The trip was quite fun. They chatted as the pontoon boat carried them down the Danube to the canal, and up the canal to the docks. The emperor wasn't racing today, but the Sonny Steamer would be making a few laps this afternoon, driven by Bob Sanderlin. Which Liana, in particular, was looking forward to. She was trying to get her husband to have such a car built.

The weather was warm and the flowers were blooming. There were smells of baking bread and sausages from the shops along the street. They reached the wine shop and swept in. Duchess Eisenberg proclaimed to the air, "I will have ten bottles of the strawberry wine." She knew about the fad of addressing servants and merchants directly, but it made her uncomfortable. Not so much with her own servants, whom she knew, but with a clerk in a wine shop such familiarity might lead to who knew what. The next thing you knew the fellow would be asking her for an introduction at court or a loan.

"I am most sorry, but there is no more."

"What? Why not?"

"It was an experiment suggested by some of the texts that young Brandon Fortney von Up-time brought with him," the shopkeeper explained. "We only made a gross of bottles and we almost didn't make those. We used strawberries from the imperial gardens and mixed the juice with the grapes from..." He apparently saw her expression because he stopped explaining how the wine was made. "Well, anyway, we could only make a little. The strawberries in the imperial garden plots were not extensive before last year and this year's crop will make next year's wine. Most of our limited stock went to the imperial cellars and Victoria Emerson von Up-time bought several bottles as well."

"What else do you have?" asked Liana.

"We have a pear and spice wine that uses cinnamon. Here, let me get you ladies glasses." While other clerks took over the serving of the rest of the wine shop customers, the owner himself served them.

The pear and spice wine proved to be a bit cloying. The sweetness overwhelmed the other flavors. Then they tried a brandy that had been made from the same wine and it worked. The bottles of the brandy were expensive, and when the change came it wasn't all in reich money.

"What are these?" Duchess Sophia asked the owner, startled into speaking directly to him.

"Those are BarbieCo money. If you would prefer we can give you reich money. It makes no difference to us."

She examined one of the bills. It was mostly pink, with other colors in the background. She had seen the young woman at the reception the emperor had held for Prince Karl Eusebius' intended. She had also seen faces on money before. In fact, two of them. One was the face of Ferdinand II, and the other was the face of Ferdinand III. She pulled another bill out. Orange dominated this one and the portrait was the young woman who had been so rude to Father Lugocie. The bill's printing said that it was worth twelve groschen of BarbieCo stock. She looked back at the first one. One pfennig. She read more carefully. The bill itself didn't say it was money, but stock. She wasn't sure what that meant, but she doubted that it had much to do with cattle or sheep. Sophia suddenly felt a chill run down her spine. Here was something that looked a lot like the new paper reich money, except for the fact that it was clearly better. The colors were vibrant and the engraving was neither smudged or scratched. Sophia knew quality work, and this was quality. "Please," she said to a shopkeeper for the first time she could remember, "may I see the other sorts of bills of this BarbieCo money?"

"Yes, I would like to see it as well," Liana said.

"Of course," the shopkeeper said. "Is anything wrong?" He went back to his cash box and dug out several bills.

He brought them back and said, "There is one more bill, but I have none. The susans are for large transactions and the value is set when they are issued." He handed Duchess Sophia a stack of bills and Sophia went through them quickly, noting the color and denomination of each bill. The green thaler note had a picture of Judy Wendell, the sister of Sarah Wendell. And then there was the purple note. It had the face of Hayley Fortney on it, looking like a younger version of Dana Fortney, and it said "One Mark." She held it up to the shopkeeper. "What is this worth?"

The shopkeeper blinked. "One mark, a Cologne mark. Not silver but it's worth the same, except it earns interest too. They all do."

"Interest?" she asked. Sophia hadn't read the back of the bill.

"It's on the back. One fiftieth of the value of the bill every year, from the date on the bill." He reached over and pointed to the date.

Sophia nodded. There was Hayley Fortney's face and One Cologne Mark. Further, this was the largest of all the bills. To Sophia the obvious conclusion was that Hayley Fortney was the most important of the Barbies.

Katharina spoke up. "We would like to buy all these bills." She looked over at one of the servants. "Pay him."

The shopkeeper, clearly very nervous but sticking to his guns, would not take one pfennig less than the marked amount on the bills.

"No," Sophia said to Katharina. "You can take the others to show Maximilian and the emperor. I will be taking the hayli." They were on the pontoon boat, heading back to Vienna.

Katharina looked at her. "All right, but you owe me a Cologne mark." She laughed. "Though if your son's suit should prosper, that will be nothing to you."

"I note that Sarah Wendell is not on a bill, and that Judy is only a thaler."

"And I note that Sarah and Karl are engaged and your son hasn't even walked out with Hayley," said Liana.

The Hofburg Palace, Vienna

"It's not actually illegal," von Trauttmansdorff said. "Not, at least, unless you say it is. I think we could make a case for outlawing them by claiming that they intend its use as money. But I have read the paragraph on the back describing it, and it is preferred participating stock. It doesn't promise that it will ever be exchangeable for reich money."

"The shopkeeper—" Peter von Eisenberg started, and von Trauttmansdorff interrupted.

"I know, but that was the action of the shopkeeper. No different than insisting that he be paid for any other thing he was selling. If he had insisted on a Cologne mark for a bottle of wine, that wouldn't make the wine money."

"We can't have them printing money, whatever they call it," Maximilian von Liechtenstein said.

"Why not?" asked Moses Abrabanel.

"Because they aren't paying for the privilege," Gundaker insisted. "The minting of money is a prerogative of the crown that the crown delegates to the minters of money in exchange for silver."

"We are under no obligation at all to accept their stock in payment of taxes, nor for anything else. But we've known for over a year now that we needed to introduce more money into the economy. Let them issue their stock. If it fails, it won't reflect on us."

Emperor Ferdinand snorted. "That's a weak argument, Moses."

"With all due respect, Your Majesty, we are in a weak position. With the USE sucking the silver out of Europe, our economy is on the edge of disaster."

"And what happens when others copy them?" Gundaker asked. "When some imperial knight from the back of nowhere starts trying to pay his debts in stock certificates?"

"Who's going to take it?" Moses asked back. "Certainly not me."

"Are you going to take this BarbieCo stock?"

Moses stopped, clearly considering the question. "I honestly don't know. But even if I don't, the shopkeepers in Race Track City are. And not just the ones that are partly owned by the Sanderlin-Fortney Investment Company."

"My *Hofbefreiten* are taking it?" Ferdinand III asked. He had been busy in the capital for the last week while all this was happening. He hadn't known a thing about it till this meeting.

"Most of them," Moses said. "Why not? At most they need to walk across the street to exchange it. And, besides, it earns interest."

"You honestly think I should endorse this, Moses?"

"No, Your Imperial Majesty, not in the least. I think you should take no official notice of it at all."

"And if I am having linzertorte at the cafe and am offered a Barbie in change?"

"Take it," Moses said. "As long as you don't take too many of them, I'll buy them from you. I don't know if this will do any good or not. But if it all goes wrong, we get no blame. And if it works, it might help the economy. On the other hand, if we shut them down, we *will* get the blame for that."

Eisenberg House, Vienna

Duke Peter von Eisenberg looked at his wife. "The emperor isn't going to shut them down, at least not now. Neither is he going to endorse it."

"What does that mean? We have that whole family coming here this evening. She has her face on money! Is it good money?"

"I don't know! No one knows if the Barbies don't. Moses Abrabanel thinks it might work. Gundaker thinks it will fail. Karl Eusebius wasn't in the meeting and I would give three villages to know what he thinks." Peter's tirade cut off as though by a knife. For a very long fifteen seconds, he just stood there. "It's good money."

"What?"

"I do know what Karl Eusebius thinks about it, because there's no way that they are issuing this BarbieCo stock without his consent."

"Kipper and Wipper," Sophia said.

"Karl Eusebius is not his father."

"Welcome to Eisenberg house," Sophia said, looking past her guests at the carriage on the street.

"We were going to come in the Steamer," Sonny Fortney said, "or maybe the Range Rover. But they are made for the track, not the streets of Vienna. So we borrowed Bob's carriage."

"It looks like the emperor's new carriage," Sophia said.

"It should. It's basically identical to it, except for the crest on the doors and some of the interior touches. It has the same air shocks and lamps."

Sophia and Peter looked out at the carriage again. On the door were painted crossed wrenches, a monkey wrench crossing a crescent wrench. Not that they could tell what kind of wrenches. They were just tools done in silver on a red shield background.

"Are you allowed a crest?" Peter asked.

"The emperor didn't seem to mind. He got a good laugh out of it. Started calling Bob the knight of the monkey wrench."

Peter looked at Sonny Fortney and tried not to show his shock. If Emperor Ferdinand had named Bob Sanderlin a knight even in jest, how long was it going to be before the joke was made legal reality? "Well, please, come in," Peter said with a gesture.

They all went into the house. It was a mix of condescension and curiosity that had brought Peter and Sophia to the door of their town house. They knew that greeting your guests at the door was the custom in Grantville, where servants were still much less common than elsewhere in the USE, much less the rest of Europe. And after seeing the hayli bill, Peter and Sophia were being careful not to give offense.

"So what are you working on now, Herr Fortney?" Peter asked once they got settled in the receiving room.

"The railroad—mostly the road part at the moment, not the rail part, because the permission for a railroad in Austria is still held up in committee so far. But we don't need permission to do the grading and preparing. All that is, is road improvement."

"There are serious concerns about the railroad, as you are no doubt aware. And it's not just the potential military threat, but concerns over Austrian silver pouring into Bohemia at an even faster rate."

"Well, Hayley..." Sonny Fortney turned to his daughter.

"Even if that were a problem, all the railroad would do is make it quicker. What you need are your own industries, so the silver will flow the other way."

"What sort of industries?"

"All sorts. Mining, manufacturing, farming..." Hayley and Peter talked about the potential industries in the Austro-Hungarian empire for a while. Peter was impressed and a little terrified. Especially when Hayley ended with, "But you really need to talk to Susan Logsden and Sarah Wendell about that. I'm mostly a tech geek."

"What is a tech geek?" asked Sophia.

"I mean, I mostly handle the mechanical parts of the industries. How to make things."

"So, how do airplanes work?" asked Count Márton von Debrecen, the von Eisenbergs' son-in-law. He had been married to Polyxena, their daughter, and wasn't sure to what extent the uptimers were responsible for the death of his wife at the hands of Maximilian of Bavaria's executioners.

Hayley looked at him, surprised. Peter couldn't tell whether it was the question or the challenging tone. He was about to apologize, but it proved unnecessary. The girl, after only a slight pause, explained. "Lift is a function of the shape of the wing and something called Bernoulli's Principle. Bernoulli lived in the eighteenth century in our timeline, and will probably never be born in this one. But he figured out how air flowing over a surface or through a pipe acted, and later people used that to figure out how to shape wings and get lift out of them without flapping. I have the figures at home and can show them to you, if you're interested. In fact, Dr. Faust, our tutor, and my little brother are building a glider. Just to test the principles."

"You're building an airplane?"

"Just a glider," Dana Fortney said. "It's to teach Brandon the theory of aeronautics and it's based on a design that Hal Smith has vetted back in Grantville. Frankly, I would have been more comfortable if they hadn't ever started the thing. And I am thankful for the farm, and the up-time plants, and even the bugs, that keep distracting him from the deathtrap."

"It's not a deathtrap, honey. It's quite well built," Sonny said.

"So it's a well-built deathtrap," Dana said with some heat, apparently going over a long-running argument. "You know perfectly well that the danger is pilot error and with no qualified pilots to teach them, pilot error is a virtual certainty."

Peter looked at his wife, and his wife looked back at him. He sympathized with Dana Fortney's concerns, but at least no one was going to chop her daughter's head off. Then he thought about the BarbieCo stock that was just starting to circulate and realized that that wasn't necessarily true.

They had a five course meal and the Fortneys politely thanked the servants with every course, often asking them to carry their compliments to the chef. It made Peter feel boorish not to be doing so, especially since first Amadeus, then Márton, started copying them.

Discussion was wide-ranging. Politics and engineering, economics and medicine, nutrition and vegetables. Sophia was surprised when Dana mentioned that her family had a vegetarian meal at least once a week, which often included beans and cornbread, made from corn imported from Spain.

"But surely you can afford meat if you are paying for maize from Spain."

"It's not a matter of cost, but of health. Too much fat is bad for you and the occasional vegetarian meal helps clean the system."

All in all, it was a confusing evening, vaguely uncomfortable, but highly intriguing. The stock certificates were brought up and

Hayley Fortney rolled her eyes, then the boy Brandon said, "Moo," only to be admonished by his mother.

Then Dana turned to Sophia and asked, "Was Amadeus as silly as Brandon is when he was eleven?"

"I don't understand?"

"Brandon has noted that a hayli is the price of a cow or close to it. And, not yet being civilized, he has latched on to that to tease his sister. And it wasn't her fault. Heather Mason, back in Grantville, decided who went on which bill."

"Which one is Heather Mason?" asked Peter. "I thought they were all in Vienna. Which certificate is she on?"

"Heather, the rat," said Hayley, "isn't on any of them. But she's going to be. I've written Dave Marcantonio a letter insisting that we need a half-pfennig coin and Heather would be perfect for it."

"Coin?" Márton asked. "I thought you disdained silver."

"Yes, we do, mostly. But this won't be a silver coin. It will probably be made of iron or copper, maybe bronze. No more metallic value than the paper. Just a marker like the rest of them are."

Sophia was running the conversation through her head and suddenly she laughed. Everyone turned to her and she said, "Yes, as it happens, Amadeus was just as silly as Brandon when he was eleven. He put a garden snake in Polyxena's bed one time."

Suddenly Hayley was looking very severely at Amadeus. Sophia laughed again, and almost decided she liked the young woman. "That was the first time I have been able to laugh like that since it happened," she said.

"Since what happened?" Dana asked.

"My wife..." said Márton, "...was a lady in waiting to Princess Maria Anna when she went to Bavaria to be married to Maximilian. She was executed after Maria Anna ran away. I don't see how she was implicated in that escapade. Polyxena could be a bit silly about social position, but she wouldn't have done anything so insane."

"I'm sorry for your loss," Dana said. "We were on the road when all that happened, so we never learned what was going on."

That put something of a damper on the evening for a while. Still, Márton did promise to go out to Race Track City and see the glider.

CHAPTER 27

𝔅uying 𝔓atents and 𝔅ribing 𝔓eople

August 1635

Moses Abrabanel's Office, outside Vienna

"Because the people like calling it 'BarbieCo.'" Susan grinned. "I know the name sounds silly, but that doesn't stop people from liking it."

"Actually, Ms. Logsden," Moses Abrabanel said, "it doesn't sound that silly. Not here in Vienna. What most people know about Barbies is how expensive they are, not that they were cheap toys up-time. At least not the cheap part. And, of course, the rumors of the Barbie Consortium . . . they've all heard those. So what did you want to see me about?"

"Well, we want you to endorse Barbie preferred." She hesitated, then said, "The way you did the American dollar back in '31."

Moses felt like he'd been hit with a brick. This was not what he had in mind when he counseled the emperor not to shut them down a week ago. "Endorsing the money of a nation, is one thing. Endorsing the stock of a private company, well, that's quite another, ah, thing."

"We're aware of that, believe me, Herr Abrabanel. But we are planing to build a skyscraper here in Vienna. Such a building would act as a long-term income source."

"So?"

"So, acquiring BarbieCo stock—which guarantees a two percent annual income but can, if our projects prosper, become a much better investment—is a good idea."

"Well enough. I will look into it, and if we decide we are interested, we will acquire some BarbieCo stock. But that's not what you're asking for. You're asking our family to guarantee the value of your stock with our money."

"Yes. Which doesn't cost you anything at all unless you are forced to buy it, which you won't be, because it's going to be circulating throughout the community."

"You hope," Moses said, shaking his head. "I hope so too, even though what you're doing is too close for comfort to usurping the crown's right of creating money."

"Not at all. It's stock in a corporation. I admit that it's negotiable and fungible, so that under certain circumstances it can act like money. But in no way are we claiming any endorsement or legal recognition by the government of Austria-Hungary or any government, for that matter. What it is, is limited liability part-ownership in BarbieCo, formerly known as American Equipment Company, a stock corporation registered in the State of Thuringia-Franconia.

"Meanwhile, the Austro-Hungarian reichsthaler is losing ground against the American dollar, even faster than silver bullion. You don't have enough money to run your economy and you can't introduce more without a panic. Besides we think introducing our—" She shrugged. "—sort-of-money is necessary . . . and not just for us. Your family has a lot invested in Vienna and Austria-Hungary in general. If this malaise keeps up, those investments are going to be seriously damaged. Frankly, sir, even if Prince Karl was to invest every penny he owns, it wouldn't be enough."

"I'm aware of that," Moses agreed. "But there is still the danger of inflation and you're still asking us to risk getting stuck with thousands, perhaps millions, of reichsthaler worth of prettily printed paper."

"That could happen," she acknowledged. "But I don't think it's likely, for a couple of reasons. First, given any reason at all to feel confident in BarbieCo preferred, people will use it. Also, if we can buy up enough of the patents that Ferdinand has been selling, we can break the industrial logjam." She stopped for a moment. "And that's about the dumbest thing I've ever heard of, even if he is your emperor."

"His father started it," Moses put in. "And his clerks have continued selling patents on up-timer inventions as a matter of course. Honestly, Ms. Logsden, we haven't had that much choice. The government simply needed the money."

"Maybe. But you were killing the goose that would have been laying the golden eggs. You know, and I know, and your emperor ought to know, that it's just plain stupid..."

"I heard you the first time, Ms. Logsden. And by now I tend to agree. But it wasn't so cut-and-dried at first. After all, you up-timers offer patents, do you not?"

"Limited patents, to the people who invent things, yes. Not just to anybody who's willing to cough up a few bucks." Then Susan visibly paused and contained herself. "I'm sorry, Herr Abrabanel. I didn't come here to criticize either you or the emperor. The fact is, if we're going to do any good here at all, for ourselves or for Vienna, or for the Austro-Hungarian Empire, we need to be able to introduce more money than we can afford to ship in from Grantville. But if we can do that, and we can free up some of those patents, there is a very good chance that we can set up a boom like the one that's going on in the USE."

"That sounds very attractive..." Moses paused. The girl herself was...very attractive. It was invigorating to be discussing matters of business and finance with such a young and attractive woman. So very, very...attractive. He pulled his mind back to the conversation with an effort. "But, how do you plan to do it?"

"First, we license a bunch of patents. Not preventing the patent holders from using them, but allowing us to use them as well. Then we do a major project that will employ a lot of people. We can spend some money on this. Money for salaries, for instance. But most of the expense of the project is going to have to be paid for in stock. In BarbieCo preferred. That will get money and BarbieCo preferred out into the economy where it can circulate, funding other businesses. We're going to do it basically the way Sarah says FDR did it, with what amounts to a big public works project that will eventually pay for itself."

"FDR? What is FDR?"

"Franklin Delano Roosevelt," Susan said. "The President of the United States, back...ah, up...in the twentieth century, in our Great Depression."

"Ah. I have indeed heard of the Great Depression. Still, when my family endorsed the American dollar back in 1631, we put the floor considerably below what we expected the American dollar to be worth. We had every expectation that even if we were forced to buy up a great many of them, we could then spend them on Grantville goods and either make a profit or at worst only take a fractional loss. I guess we could see our way clear to offering to buy your stock at half the face value."

Susan shook her head. "I don't disagree, but we can't afford to do it that way this time. We need a base of the face value."

"Then I don't see how I can help you. The two percent interest you're offering on your BarbieCo stock is not enough to justify the risk. Not nearly enough."

"I can make you one of two offers and let you take your pick. One hundred thousand thalers in BarbieCo as an up-front fee for the endorsement, or at the end of 1637 we will promise to give you half again the BarbieCo stock you already possess. Or buy it back for reich money at face value at that time, our choice. We don't want you trying to buy up all the BarbieCo in the world in the last half of 1637. This way, if you drive it up against the reichsthaler, you will lose money."

"Which would you recommend?" Moses asked, curious to see what she would say. If BarbieCo was good, then the best deal was the up-front thalers, because all the Barbies would have to do to pay them off would be buy up the necessary reichsthaler using BarbieCo and pay the Abrabanel family in reichsthaler.

She looked Moses straight in the eye and said, "If you're smart, you'll take the thalers up front."

The discussion continued for over an hour as they talked out the details of the Barbies' proposal. It was a risky venture and Moses might not have gone for it, in spite of being quite impressed, but for the fact that Prince Karl had invested considerable silver in it.

Office in Vienna

"I most certainly will not!"

"Very well, sir. Thank you for your time," Vicky Emerson said. Then she got smoothly to her feet, turned on her heel and walked out the door.

"Well, that was a disaster," she told Millicent. "He's not going to accept BarbieCo preferred. Not ever, apparently."

"Yeah, I heard," Millicent said. "And I really liked that location, too. Oh, well. The next on the list is in the old Jewish Quarter."

"We'll send Susan to talk to Moses on that one," Vicky said. "I think he likes her, anyway. Did you see his eyes glitter the last time we had a meeting?"

"I think she likes him, too." Millicent giggled. "I just don't think she's noticed it yet."

The old Jewish Quarter, Vienna

"Ick," Susan said.

"The aftermath of a fire in this city is never pretty," Moses pointed out. "And do be careful. You don't want to fall into an open basement."

"I'll be careful. The burnt part doesn't really matter," Susan said. "We were going to have to bulldoze the place anyway."

"Bulldoze?"

"Like the Fresno scrapers. Only bigger. I meant that we'd have to tear the building down to the basement level anyway. So we can get the whole block?"

"Oh, yes. But it's going to cost a great deal."

"They'll take Barbie preferred?"

"Yes," Moses said. "They've agreed to that, though quite a bit of it will be coming to my family, I suspect. So..."

"I understand," Susan said. "It puts you in an uncomfortable position. You want to get the best deal you can for your friends, but you're concerned that we'll pay too much and put your family out of pocket. Don't let it worry you. I don't intend to let any more of the Barbie preferred out of my hot little hands than I have to."

Hot little hands. Moses had to forcibly bring his mind back to the business at...hand.

Susan was still talking. "...I'm going to send Judy and Vicky after them."

And that's just what she did.

Beauty Shop at Race Track City

"Fräulein von Up-time," Frau Lechner rushed up and gave a rough curtsey. "Welcome, welcome."

Trudi was so shocked it took her a few moments to react, by which time she had been *gently* hustled to the head of the line. "Wait! I'm not von Up-time. I'm Gertrude von Bachmerin."

Everything stopped. Suddenly Frau Lechner was looking at her like she was a fraud or a liar. She examined Trudi's face then looked at the wall, then back at Trudi, then back at the wall. Trudi followed her gaze to the wall, where there was a list of services. And tacked next to each service were bills. BarbieCo stock certificates. Several of them were the six pfennig notes with Trudi's face on them. A shampoo was one trudi, a set was one trudi, coloring was a trudi and three millies.

Trudi tried to explain. "Yes, that's me. It's my prom picture from the senior prom. I did attend school in Grantville and I am a Barbie, I guess. But I'm not an up-timer. I was born in 1617."

Everyone was looking at her.

Frau Lechner asked, "How can you be a Barbie and not an up-timer?" She sounded quite suspicious, and from the mutters around the room she wasn't the only one.

"Because the up-timers don't care!" Trudi blurted. There was silence again. Trudi looked around the room at the shocked faces, and she was back in Grantville on her first day in high school. Being shown around the school by a girl who spoke the most atrocious German that Trudi had ever heard, but still managed to get across the basics and introduce Trudi to the rest of the little group of girls who were not yet known as the Barbie Consortium. The girl suggested that she should try out for the junior varsity cheerleading squad. Being accepted by the Barbies had meant the world back then. Not all of the up-timers had been so accepting.

"At least, the good ones don't," she continued. "The ones like General Stearns and the Barbies. The up-timers are people. Some are mean and some think too much of themselves. But mostly they are good people who will look at you, not your blood lines. Just like they accepted the daughter of an imperial knight who barely owned a village into the Barbie Consortium."

"What is the Barbie Consortium? Is that the BarbieCo on the money?"

"No," Trudi shook her head. "BarbieCo is an investment corporation. A consortium is sort of a partnership. Judy Wendell found out how much the dolls were worth from her older sister Sarah and told her friends. When I met the Barbies, they knew how much their dolls were worth but hadn't sold them yet. They were holding onto them, waiting for the right opportunity. That opportunity came when the Higgins Sewing Machine Corporation went public.

"I didn't have any Barbies." Trudi paused a moment at their confused looks. "The up-time-made dolls, I mean, and I didn't have much money. But when Judy and the rest decided to invest, I managed to scrape together enough to buy a few shares. Not that I was part of the Barbie Consortium back then. I was just sort of on the outskirts of it. I was teaching them German and down-time social conventions and they were teaching me English and cheerleading and stuff like that.

"Over the next several months, I got invited into several deals. Some I could afford to invest in, others I couldn't. But they had enough stuff going on that it took some keeping track of and that job mostly fell to Millicent. And she hired me to help her because I'm good with accounts."

Every face in the beauty shop was turned to Trudi as she reminisced. "The wedding between Karl Schmidt and Ramona Higgins was a big deal for the Barbies and Millicent got me into it. After that I had some money. And there was the germanium." Again she had to explain. "Germanium is a material like iron or copper. It's used in electronics. Anyway, there was a small deposit of it on our family lands, tailings from a worked-out mine. The Barbies found a market for it and that got my family out of debt.

"For the last couple of years, I have been investing with the Barbies in most of the deals. But I'm not the only one. I don't know why Heather decided to put me on the stock certificate, not one of the others."

Actually Trudi did know, or at least could make a good guess. This whole "preferred stock as money" was her proposal and it was a safe bet that when Judy had written Heather she'd made that clear. The Barbies had never had a truly fixed membership. Each deal was a new arrangement and none of the Barbies had been in on all of them. For that matter, very few of the deals included only the Barbies. Still, she wondered how the rest of the down-timer Barbies were going to react. Trudi took a vicki from her purse and handed it over, collected her change, and sat down for her wash and set. And through it all, she talked about the Barbies and the up-timers.

Not that the conversation remained one-sided. These women weren't ignorant of up-timers. While most of the customers were from the Them of Vienna, some of them lived and worked in Race Track City, and all of the staff lived here.

But a combination of circumstances had locked the Sanderlins and Fortneys into a sort of pseudo-lords of the manor role. They owned, or owned in part, many of the businesses in Race Track City, including this one, and people had been coming to them indirectly for loans for the better part of a year now. Besides, they were the emperor's representatives, so far as the race track and the 240Z were concerned. At the same time, there were only a few up-timers here, so they had to be more careful about offending the powers-that-be than up-timers did in Grantville or Magdeburg. So whatever their preferences might have been, the up-timers were treated as upper *Hofbefreiten* or lower nobility.

This was a complete up-time style beauty shop. Gayleen Sanderlin had insisted on that. They provided washing, setting, perms and dye jobs, with the chemicals and dyes shipped in all the way from Lothlorien Farbenwerk in the Ring of Fire. By now, after a year of practice, they were pretty good at it. They also did manicures and pedicures with clear or colored nail polish. There were eight chairs and a waiting area. The shop had six hairdressers and fifteen customers either getting something done or waiting to have something done.

Trudi had expected to wait, but had been rushed to the head of the line. Seated now, in the shampoo chair, with her neck on the neckrest and one of the hairdressers using what amounted to a watering pot to wet her hair with warm water, Trudi proceeded to tell them how up-timers acted in the wild. So to speak. As she was describing Grantville High and TwinLo Park, she in turn learned about the founding of Race Track City and the up-time style beauty salon that Gayleen Sanderlin had insisted upon, and who came here and how often.

Princess Maximiliana von Liechtenstein was a regular with a

weekly appointment, as were perhaps half a dozen others. The salon was a place where ladies of high standing could, literally, let their hair down and chat. It wasn't good to get too familiar, whatever Frau Sanderlin said, but it was acceptable for the staff, with all proper deference, to share the latest gossip and express their opinions.

Trudi realized as they talked that this place was another center of revolution—not overt like the Committees of Correspondence— but a whisper here, a wink and a nod there, repeating opinions along with reporting on the latest scandal. A place where the female They of Vienna could exchange information and affect opinion without ever meeting.

"I was at the beauty salon and I heard that von Dorkfish was having it on with his wife's maid," followed by "Did you hear the emperor is going to shift troops to the south? Sadi von Linden said her husband is being sent to Hungary, rather than the border with Bohemia," followed by "The Sonny Steamer can be used as a model for a bigger engine that will pull several wagons behind it, if they get permission for the railroad," followed by, followed by . . . for a year now. Juicy gossip, politics, technology, and attitudes, especially attitudes shared by the woman washing your hair repeating and reinterpreting what she has heard.

By the time Trudi left the salon, she had a much clearer view of what had been going on in Vienna since even before the Ring of Fire. And the women in the shop had a much clearer view of how up-time investment worked and the value of BarbieCo stock. If that view lacked some of the mathematics and scholarly accuracy that Sarah Wendell would have insisted on, it was still much more reassuring for these women, shop girls and great ladies alike.

"Gresham's law says that bad money drives out good," Trudi explained, "because people hold onto the good money and spend the bad money. Well, in the USE people hold onto American dollars and spend silver."

Von Hatch Apartment, Vienna

"You turned them down?" Elena von Hatch shouted at her husband, "They offered you BarbieCo for that damned useless mine and you turned them down! My mother told me you were an idiot and she was right!"

"It's not like it was American dollars. It's just paper."

"It's ownership in BarbieCo, so it's ownership in everything that BarbieCo owns! All the factories, all the businesses. Just like reichsthaler notes are ownership of silver in the royal vaults."

"But how much ownership? With a reichsthaler, it's a ninth of a Cologne mark of silver, but how much is a BarbieCo thaler? Tell me that."

"A ninth of a Cologne mark of silver's worth," Elena insisted, going a bit farther than Trudi had, "but it's backed by buildings and machines, so as they build more buildings and machines it can be worth even more."

Another Apartment, Vienna

"How was your day, dear one?"

"I'm not entirely sure," Jäger said. "Ludolf came in for some licensing and gave me these instead of reichsthaler." He showed his wife the green and orange sheets. "I didn't want to argue. Ludolf is mostly fair, if a bit stiff. Do you think he was cheating me?"

"No, those are fine. I was out at Race Track City getting my hair done and there are signs all over the place. These are as good as cash, and they pay interest as well. Not a lot. Well, maybe not a lot. It depends on how well the company does, because they are participating preferred. But a minimum of two percent annual interest. That is written on the back."

"What are you talking about?"

"Viveka was explaining it to me." She took the money from his hands. "No, you didn't get a hayli. A judi and two vickies." She pointed at the writing that curved around the bottom half of the portraits in the center of the sheets. One of them said, "Judith Elaine Wendell." The other said, "Victoria Maureen Emerson." Then she continued. "Apparently, Gertrude von Bachmerin—that's the six pfennig BarbieCo note—was in the shop to get her hair done yesterday morning and explained it all. Anyway, Gertrude is sort of a von Up-time by adoption, even though she was born in this century. And the BarbieCo stock is just like American dollars, except in the normal denominations instead of that weird system that the up-timers use."

Jäger let it wash over him, at least for the most part. The important point was the bribe he had gotten from Ludolf was good money. That, and the fact that he was going to be very very polite to up-timers in the future, even this Gertrude von Up-time by adoption. A smart man didn't offend people who could wave their hands and make money appear out of nowhere. He also wondered why the up-timers out at Race Track City hadn't done it months ago.

CHAPTER 28

A Concrete Problem

August 1635

Concrete Plant

Baron Johannes Hass looked at the young women who had come to look at his concrete plant with a mixture of hope and resentment. Baron Hass couldn't say which was the larger component of the mix. Not that he had any choice, however it came out. He had been told to provide the tour by no less a personage than Maximilian von Liechtenstein. The emperor was not pleased with the time it was taking to get concrete into production, in spite of the fact that he had shown them the designs and reports that Peter Barclay had provided. Baron Hass was building the rotating kiln just as fast as humanly possible. It was simply a very large project. So he took the young ladies around and showed them the sights, explaining as he went.

After the tour, while they were setting down to dinner, the auburn-haired girl, the one whose sister was going to marry Prince Karl, asked him. "Where are the little kilns?"

"What little kilns?"

"Oh. You know." She waved rather vaguely. "The little ones like they have all up and down the Elbe and Saale rivers. The ones that just make a batch at a time."

"Little ones are very inefficient. They waste fuel and time."

"Told you so!" said the short, curly headed one. "It's long past time to shoot the engineer."

256

Istvan Janoszi looked at Millicent, the short one. And for a moment Baron Hass was very glad that he wasn't Herr Barclay. "Do you think..."

"No," Judy said. "Tempting in this case, but no. Millicent was just talking about an up-time business quote. 'In every project there comes a time to shoot the engineer and put it into production.' She's not literally talking about shooting the engineer. It's just a comment on the fact that if given their heads, an engineer will end up costing you millions to save a few pennies." Judy tilted her head and gave a half smile. "They aren't doing it on purpose. It's just the nature of the beast. Considering what's already been invested in that monster—" She waved at the half finished rotary kiln. "—it ought to be finished. But eighty percent or more of any savings it generates in production costs is going to be eaten by transport costs, even if it is located right on the Danube. If you'd gone with beehive kilns, you'd have been in production a year and a half ago, before Pete Barclay and his crowd ever got here, just by modifying kilns you were already using for making quicklime and pottery. Which would have meant that Baron Hass here would have already been making money off his patent and this thing wouldn't be pushing him into receivership."

"So it's too late to use the beehive kilns?"

"Not at all. Sure, this thing will produce twenty or thirty times the concrete that a beehive would, but the rotary kiln and a hundred beehive kilns together won't produce enough to meet demand. Concrete was everywhere up-time because it was so cheap and flexible. The stuff you'll be able to make in the beehive kilns won't be nearly as cheap or quite as flexible, but it's still going to be one of the cheapest, most flexible materials available. Baron Hass here will even make a reasonable profit. As long as he's not too greedy!" Judy the Younger looked over at Baron Hass. "If you try for too much profit by holding down production and jacking up prices, you'll lose your market, or most of it, to other materials. Stone, brick, wood, plastics when they get into production, composites like resin-impregnated fabrics, iron and steel. You have the exclusive right to produce one building material, but it's not the only one. The reason it was so common up-time was that it's cheap to produce and easy to use."

"But that means I should be building a dozen of the big ones," Baron Hass protested. "Just like my spies and Herr Barclay told me."

"If the only factor involved was engineering," said the little one, while opening a spiral notebook. "If all you had to worry about was turning rawmix into clinker. But it's not. You have to make the rawmix, you have to powder the clinker, you have to ship in the fuel, the limestone, the shale or clay, package and ship out the Portland cement. You need to provide instructions on the mixing of the Portland with water and aggregate, on the pouring and how long your customers will have to make the pour after mixing. So you're probably going to have to train concrete consultants to send out to major customers, if you don't want to be sued because the customer did something wrong and is blaming your cement instead of their error for the problem. You'll probably win those lawsuits but they will still cost you money. A lot more money than consultants to keep the problem from happening in the first place would."

"The transport will be more expensive than the consultants anyway," said the tall one, looking over the short one's shoulder. "Cement works out to be less expensive to transport than quarried stone or brick, when you figure in the weight of the concrete against the weight of the stone wall, because you can usually get the water and aggregate closer to the job site. But you're still shipping lots of tonnage. Meanwhile, if you had beehive kilns in operation you would be working out your other issues, and making money, while the big rotary kiln is being built. And once it is built, it's still not going to satisfy all the demand. So the beehives will still be in operation. Still making you money, if not quite as much as the rotary kiln will."

Baron Hass looked between the girls and Istvan Janoszi. The girls were consulting their notes in light of what they had seen here and the agent was giving Baron Hass a crooked smile. For the past several months Baron Hass had been putting off Ferdinand III and his advisers with the reports from Herr Barclay. That option had just disappeared. Besides, the girls were right. Baron Hass was not by any means ignorant of business, though it was true this was by far the largest undertaking he had ever attempted.

"How many tons of clinker will the rotary kiln produce in a day?" Millicent asked. When given a figure she started calculating, giving figures for the amount of coal used each day, the amount of limestone, the amount of shale or clay. Each week, each month. There was quite a bit of limestone clay and coal already on the site. But after a couple of minutes, she pointed out that there was only enough on site to run the kiln for a month or so. Baron Hass knew it had taken three months to get the supplies there. So it was starting to look like he was only going to have enough fuel and raw materials to keep the rotary kiln running about a third of the time.

"But I can't! I don't have the money for small kilns. It's all invested in the rotary!"

Got him right where we want him, Judy thought. "We might be able to help you out there."

"How?"

"Well, you still have the patent you bought from the emperor. And that's worth something. If you can get into production soon enough that he doesn't get disgusted and revoke it—"

"Soon enough would be right now," Janos said, somewhat sternly. "The emperor's patience is not...unlimited."

"It so happens we have access to several beehive kilns," Judy said. "And if we can come to an agreement, we can both get into concrete production."

"You want to infringe on my patent? Is that it?"

"Not at all," Judy said. "We want to license it. We have projects of our own, you know, and we're willing to let you in on them, in exchange for a nonexclusive license to produce concrete. You'll still be able to produce it once your rotary kiln gets up and running, and you can sell nonexclusive rights to other people. Meanwhile, you'll be getting in on the ground floor, so to speak, of the Liechtenstein Tower."

"Liechtenstein Tower?"

"Yes. We've already bought the land," Judy said. "It's in the old Jewish quarter. The tower is going to be fifteen stories tall, with elevators and electric lights. Plumbing. All the modern conveniences. And we expect it to fill fast, since living space is at such a premium in Vienna."

"It sounds very interesting," Baron Hass admitted. "But what I need is money."

"I understand. But, you know, BarbieCo preferred stock is fully negotiable. The Abrabanels are accepting it at face value." She opened a bag and pulled out a set of papers exactly the same size as the reich banknotes. Judy doubted that the possibility of the similarity in size being coincidence ever even crossed his mind. Baron Hass was not, after all, an idiot. He looked the bills over and seemed to be impressed. He should be. The printing on the bills was both more subtle and more vibrant than on the reich money. He looked at a judi then looked up at her. Judy smiled at him. He clearly recognized her face on the BarbieCo one thaler note, and the faces of the other girls who were here. Judy continued as he looked over the notes. "That means you can sell it, trade it, you can do whatever you want with it."

Baron Hass continued to look over the bills. He was concentrating on the susan. The one bill that didn't have an amount printed on it also had a different format. The cameo of Susan was over on the left side of the bill to leave room to fill in the amount and for the signature, with a list of names who were authorized to sign. That list did include Karl Eusebius von Liechtenstein, but it did not include Gundaker or Maximilian. It included Judy Wendell, but not Sarah Wendell, but for different reasons.

"Also, we do like that ball mill you have for turning the clinker into fine powder. Transport is expensive, but it still may be more profitable for us to ship the clinker here for grinding than to set up grinding mills at every beehive kiln up and down the Danube. Assuming, of course, you're reasonable about the price and are willing to accept BarbieCo stock. I assume you're using good high-chromium steel balls in your ball mill?" Judy asked, though to the best of Judy's knowledge there was not a single chromium steel ball in the universe.

"What? It's taken me almost two years to get the high carbon steel balls." He looked over at Istvan. "You know I have been trying for years to get some of the steel. You can't import it from the USE at any sane price. And with the explosion of the Bessemer plant, there have been major delays in getting good steel at anything approaching a reasonable price."

"What about crucible steel?"

"We have had difficulty finding the right clays and the duke has been most unreasonable about licensing."

"Mad Max of Bavaria is most unreasonable about most things these days," Judy said. The duke of Bavaria had bought the patent for crucible steel before his first wife died and he went totally off his rocker. They were even using it in Bavaria at the moment, though his lawyers were suing anyone in Austria-Hungary who tried to use it. And having sold him the patent, the government of Austria-Hungary was stuck with it unless they wanted to give the money back...and they didn't have the money.

The rest of the day was spent talking with Baron Hass about how his facilities, half-finished as they were, might be integrated with beehive kilns that could be adapted from other uses or built much more cheaply and quickly to produce concrete in a reasonable time.

Race Track City

Herr Buschen counted out four reichsthaler notes, then a Barbie preferred, then another reichsthaler, nodded sharply to confirm that the payment was right. "Good day, Herr Krause. The same again next week?"

Herr Krause shook his head. "I need more linen next week. Bring more linen."

"How much more?"

"Half again as much," Herr Krause said.

"I think I can do that," Herr Buschen said. Then he stuck out his hand and the deal was done.

Neither one of them paid much attention to the fact that part of the payment was in Barbie preferred rather than the silver-backed reichsthaler. It was all money. When the girls had started trading stock, they had set the stock values to match the local currency, reichsthaler, not American dollars. The price was set at Race Track City. The shops that the SFIC owned a piece of took it at face value. The shops in Race Track City that they didn't own—any of those shops set up on the part of Race Track City kept by the emperor—were right next door often as not to the SFIC shops, and it really wasn't any trouble at all to take their BarbieCo stock next door and trade it for reichsthaler. Not that they bothered, unless someone insisted. They just kept it in their cash boxes and used it for change or to buy their next batch of supplies.

✧   ✧   ✧

Father Lamormaini bought the small casein crucifix. It was a beautiful piece, painted and detailed, only about three inches tall and quite inexpensive. He bargained a little, but not much. The thing was quite lovely for the price and he had a half reichsthaler note. He offered it to the shopkeeper. The woman took it and placed it on the counter while she opened her cash box and counted out his change. There was quite a lot of it. The standard bills were printed in yellow and black, the royal colors. But here were other bills. Pink bills and purple bills, green and blue bills. "What are those?"

"Oh, those are BarbieCo preferred. They are as good as reichsthaler." In a half whisper, she added, "Better really. They pay interest every year."

"I will not take those," Lamormaini hissed. The words came out without any conscious control, and that wasn't something that normally happened to him. He had been working in the halls of power for most of his life and had not survived there by letting his tongue run wild.

The shop woman looked up at his tone, then quickly said, "That's fine, Father. I'll make sure that your change is all in reich money."

Father Lamormaini now realized that the mark of the beast had invaded Austria-Hungary in the form of this BarbieCo stock money. The poison of the Ring of Fire that made peasants think they were the same as kings—the same poison that made Lucifer think himself the same as God. The corruption had arrived. The mark of the beast was upon them, and it was more subtle and more deadly than he had ever imagined. Pride, vanity, the arrogance of infinite wealth... made from nothing. Sarah Wendell, whatever Gundaker said, was Satan's handmaiden.

CHAPTER 29

Riverside Entertainments

September 1635

Sanderlin House, Race Track City

"Would you like to go on a picnic?" Jack Pfeifer asked Trudi von Bachmerin. They had met several times since the Barbies had arrived, and it was clear that she was high in their confidence. Honestly, Jack was a little nervous about asking her out, but since the family's fortunes had increased, his mother was making matrimonial noises. And Trudi was someone he could talk to. Besides, she was very pretty.

Trudi looked over at him, eyes wide, and Jack wondered what she would say. Then her eyes narrowed, and then she smiled. "That's a lovely idea. I'll get the girls and we can do it Saturday afternoon."

Jack wasn't sure whether to be thrilled or disappointed. He had three days to work it out.

Fortney House, Race Track City

"We have to invite Amadeus," Hayley said, as soon as the notion of a picnic was brought up.

Judy hid a grin. She approved of Amadeus for Hayley. He seemed like a nice guy.

With a smirk and a sidelong look at Susan, Millicent said, "Well, in that case, we'd better make sure the food is kosher, because we'll be inviting Moses Abrabanel."

"Why?" Susan asked.

"If you don't, I will," Millicent said.

Susan blushed, then said, "I'll ask him, you little..." Susan apparently found the right insult hard to find.

Good job, Millie, thought Judy.

"If I don't get Moses, who do I get?" Millicent pouted. "Hayley, have Mozart bring some of his friends."

"He's not Mozart," Hayley said. "I don't think he even plays an instrument."

"And somebody ought to invite that cute Dr. Faust," Judy said.

"Yes," Millicent chimed in. "He's kind of cute."

"What's with you, Millie?" asked Vicky. "Did you finally reach puberty?"

Millicent stuck out her tongue, but didn't say anything. They were all a little careful of romantic discussions around Vicky. Bill Magen's death was only a few months ago.

"That's not enough men," Judy added. "We have Amadeus for Hayley, and Dr. Faust for Millie. Jack for Trudi, since he started all this. Moses—"

"I don't know about that. I may want Amadeus instead," Trudi said.

"You keep your paws off Amadeus," Hayley said.

"In that case, you need to invite a couple of spares. Moses for Susan, but what about Gabrielle, Vicky, and Judy? Oh, I know. Have Amadeus invite Bishop Leo. You saw the way he looked at Judy at the plane and again at the party. I don't think he's that committed to the church."

"I can find my own fellows, thanks," Judy said.

"And I'm not interested. So you only need six," said Vicky.

"I'm not sure I'm interested either," Gabrielle said. "I grant that the rubbers that are available now will probably work well enough, but I have school and I don't need the distraction."

"I didn't mean you should wrestle them to the ground and have your way with them," Millicent said. "Just that it's better to have enough guys around to match the number of girls. It makes the seating arrangements easier, if nothing else."

"Right. So we need three more guys?" Judy asked. "Hayley,

have Amadeus round up some extras. Not Leo Habsburg. He's probably too busy anyway. Make it four more guys. Let's invite Carla Barclay too."

"What about Suzi?" asked Millicent.

"No, she's involved with Neil O'Connor, and I don't want to invite him," Judy said. "He's a jerk."

Fortney House, Race Track City

"So I need you to round up some of your friends," Hayley finished her explanation.

"Moses Abrabanel?" Amadeus said, almost scandalized.

"What's wrong with him?" Hayley asked, sounding like Amadeus had better be careful what he said. "Is it because he's Jewish?"

Honestly, it was at least a little because Moses was Jewish. But Amadeus was a fairly socially adept young man, so he didn't say that. Instead he said, "He's almost thirty!"

Hayley shrugged. "I guess she likes them older."

Amadeus considered and said he'd see what he could do. He would have to discuss it with his father, and his mother was probably going to want some sort of chaperone, especially when she found out that a Jew was going come along. So he wondered . . . Well, if he could get his brother-in-law Márton as a chaperone, he would also be one of the guys he was supposed to round up.

Eisenberg House, Vienna

Márton wasn't thrilled with the idea but Amadeus called in a favor. And besides, Márton had several deals going with the Jewish banker. So while Amadeus talked to Julian von Meklau and Rudolf von Kesmark, Márton talked with Moses. As it happened, they discussed it with Archduke Leo, the emperor's younger brother, in the room.

"You're going on a picnic? Where are you going?" Leo asked.

"I don't know. Maybe the water park out at Race Track City," Moses said.

"And why were you invited?"

"I think the idea is that Hayley Fortney wanted company to

keep Amadeus from pressing his suit too vigorously, and Moses is there as extra company," said Márton.

"Well then, a bit more extra company will not be amiss. I'll borrow the steamboat and we can steam up the river to the family hunting lodge." The Habsburg family had several properties near the vicinity of Vienna. Race Track City was located on one a few miles downriver from Vienna. The one Leo was talking about was not a lot farther, but upriver, on the north side. It was a hunting lodge in the sense that the up-time Taj Mahal was a tomb, but it did have plants and animals and outdoors.

Márton didn't know what to say. He wasn't at all sure that the young ladies were going to be pleased to have the duke along. But then, how did you tell the brother of the emperor of Austria-Hungary that he wasn't invited?

Julian von Meklau wanted to know, "Which one do I get?"

"You don't get any, Julian. You ass. You'll be lucky if you don't get stepped on. Have you noticed that they have their own money?"

"I've seen it, but I haven't taken any," Julian said. "Father says it's worthless."

"That's because your father is an idiot," Rudolf von Kesmark told him. "The Abrabanels are taking it at face value. That means they think it's worth more than the reich money."

"The reich—" Julian started.

"Never mind. Take it or don't, as you like. I know my father is taking it at face value and so is Márton." Amadeus' brother-in-law was a count because he had enough money to buy a county, and had. Ferdinand II, and now Ferdinand III, depended on Márton for financial acumen as well as cash. He held no official post in the government, but he was listened to.

Julian looked stubborn, but dropped the matter. Julian was not stupid but he was influenced by his parents, who were very much of a conservative nature.

"I think Judith Wendell is the prettiest," Rudolph said, laying his claim.

Amadeus just shook his head. He was pretty sure his friends were in line for a rude awakening and he just hoped they didn't embarrass him too much.

Fortney House, Race Track City

"This is turning into a circus," Trudi complained. "All I wanted was a little company to keep things cool while Jack and I got to know each other."

"It's your own fault," Susan said, with not much in the way of sympathy. Susan was uncomfortable about the whole thing. She had no idea what she and Moses would talk about in a social situation.

She looked over at Judy, who seemed to think the whole situation funny, and for just a moment she hated her long-time friend for the way she was always so comfortable in social situations. Judy was never at a loss for how to behave.

"Well, on the up side, there are going to be enough men to go around," said Millicent. "We may even have a couple of spares."

Vienna docks

Saturday morning dawned bright and crisp, but with not a cloud in the sky. It looked to be a hot day by afternoon and Moses Abrabanel was wondering what he was doing. He wasn't working on a Saturday and the Jewish community in Vienna was fairly cosmopolitan anyway. But he was going on a social engagement with a gentile and he wasn't Rebecca, to marry a gentile. Not that that had stopped his father, his mother, and his sister from teasing him over the matter. Teasing gently, because he had only lost his bride a year ago. Still, his mother had commented that the mourning period was more than over, and his little daughter needed a mother, not just a hired wet nurse.

Those were the thoughts running through his mind as he walked up the gangplank to the royal steamboat that would take them to Race Track City. Amadeus and a couple of his young friends were already there, as was Jakusch Pfeifer, looking pretty uncomfortable in the august company.

Márton was fiddling with a rifle that he had bought from a gun maker in Suhl. It was a copy of a Cardinal and fairly expensive. Márton was an avid hunter when he had the time, but he had bought that rifle right after he heard about Polyxena, and Moses didn't doubt that it was royal—or at least ducal—game that Márton wanted to hunt. He had loved the silly girl. It hadn't just been a social marriage.

On the other hand, Márton had always liked guns. They were his hobby.

Archduke Leo waved to Moses as he rode up and left the horse with a retainer to return to the stables. Then he bounced up the gangplank, all youthful energy. "Are we ready to go?"

"Yes, Your Grace. Dr. Faust is out at Race Track City," Amadeus offered.

And they were off. Jakusch Pfeifer stayed diffident during the trip, not speaking unless spoken to. Amadeus and his friends were boisterous, but somewhat restrained by the duke, who wasn't restrained much at all.

Márton tried to bring out Jakusch with some success, talking about the businesses out in Race Track City and the Liechtenstein Tower, which was in the preconstruction "dig up the lot" phase. The value of the Tower, and the number of tenants. The tower would be expensive, but Jakusch was convinced it would pay for itself in ten years, and in the meantime it would be a major status symbol for the Liechtensteins . . . and for the Barbies, of course. Clear evidence of the value of their shares.

Moses tried to stay out of that conversation. It was Saturday, after all. And he did try to avoid doing business on a Saturday.

Carla Ann Barclay had lied to her parents to come here this morning. They knew she was coming to Race Track City, but not that she was going on a picnic with the Barbie Consortium and a bevy of local nobles. For some unfathomable reason, Mom seemed convinced that every down-timer with a title—any title—was just waiting to get her alone to practice *droit du seigneur*. Well, she was going to be with the Barbies and no one was going to mess with them. She hoped.

The barge pulled up to the docks and everyone piled on, carrying baskets. There were thermoses of coffee and coolers with chilled wine and cold meats, bread and fruits. It was to be a well-stocked picnic and everyone was apparently in a good mood, even the guards.

Judy Wendell was busily introducing everyone to everyone, even the people she didn't know. Carla wished she knew how Judy did it.

Then Vicky Emerson saw the rifle. "Is that a Cardinal?"

One of the older down-timers—*He must be over thirty*, Carla thought—said, "Yes. I bought it from the gunsmiths of Suhl last year."

"I bet it's from U.S. Waffen Fabrik."

"Yes. How did you know?"

"Oh, Vicky's a gun nut," said Judy. "Knows all about guns and who makes them. She brought her own arsenal. Won't leave home without it."

"Is she like that other up-timer?" The old guy paused, like he was trying to remember a name.

"I'm not the markswoman that Julie Sims is," Vicky said, "but I'm better with pistols." She opened her purse and pulled out a six-shot handgun that would have made Dirty Harry proud.

"I recognize that. It's also made by U.S. Waffen Fabrik."

"Not this one. I had it specially machined in Grantville. It's match quality. But, yes, they make one much like it. I like mine. It has more stopping power."

Carla drifted away a bit, uncomfortable with the turn of the conversation, and left Vicky and the old guy to their discussion of murder and mayhem.

Judy Wendell was talking to Gabrielle Ugolini, Archduke Leo and Dr. Faust, with no regard for their ranks, and managing to get them to talk to each other. Dr. Faust was building a glider and Archduke Leo was very interested in flight. Gabrielle was talking about biochemistry and the use of vitamins to prevent deficiency diseases.

Carla drifted on again. There was Hayley, surrounded by three guys about their age. Carla guessed that one of them was Amadeus. Probably the blond. He was giving the other two "get lost" looks. He had a beard, though you could barely tell, it was so light. The other guys weren't taking the hint. Both had long noses and one had black hair, the other brown. Carla drifted in their direction, then Hayley was waving her over. Apparently glad of reinforcements.

"Gentlemen, this is Carla Ann Barclay von Up-time." Turning to Carla she added, "We were just talking about that Shirley Temple movie, the one where she tap dances. What was the title, do you know?"

"*The Little General*?" Carla asked. "That's the one they were showing at the theater this week. But Shirley Temple danced in most of her movies, I think."

"That's the one," the guy with black hair said. "Those clicks. Rudolph says that it was the black man clicking the heels of his shoes, not the sound track."

"It was the toes of his shoes," Carla said. "That was Bill 'Bojangles' Robinson. He was one of the greatest tap dancers in history."

"Maybe. But no one could do that. They added the sound later, like they do the German voices. I saw *Singing in the Rain* and it said right on the screen that the voices and singing had been done by down-timers."

"They do do that. In fact, it was Els Engel who did the Kathy Selden voice and singing. But in terms of the taps, it's all Bojangles. I saw that movie up-time before the Ring of Fire in Baltimore. It's just the same. I know, because it's famous among tap dancers."

"Are there any tap dancers?" asked the brown-haired guy, probably Rudolph. "I mean, in this century."

"Well, I know tap. I took it for years before the Ring of Fire," Carla said.

Carla was wearing a calf-length pleated skirt and regular shoes. Not tap shoes. In fact, she didn't have tap shoes anymore. Her last pair of taps had been left in Baltimore. And she was way out of practice, though she still tapped some, just for fun. She lifted her left foot and did a quick staccato toe tap. It wasn't the dance part, but then Carla wasn't that into the dance part. She had focused on the musicality.

"Carla helped Dad with the layout of the movie theater," Hayley added. And Carla blushed.

"How do you do that?" The black-haired guy asked, pointing at her feet.

"This is Julian von Meklau—" Hayley point at the black-haired one, "—and Rudolph von Kesmark." Hayley pointed at the brown-haired one. So the blond was her Amadeus, but she didn't introduce him. Carla took that to mean that so far as Hayley was concerned, she could have either Julian or Rudolph, but not Amadeus.

"It just takes practice," Carla told Julian. "I did it every Monday, Wednesday, and Friday after school for years. Just part of the social graces we were supposed to learn."

"Ah, like riding and swordsmanship," offered Julian.

"Or sewing for the ladies," added Rudolph, who apparently thought that would earn him points.

"Yes, but we had sewing machines up-time," Carla said. "And retail."

"What?" Rudolph asked, as Hayley laughed.

"What's so funny?" asked Millicent, coming up to join them.

"Shopping therapy," Hayley said. "Rudolph was talking about ladies learning to sew."

"We have sewing machines now," Milly said, and everyone but Rudolph laughed.

"Are they teasing you, Rudy?" asked Millicent, and Carla wondered how she had known his name.

Rudolph gave Julian a look. "Any chance they get."

"Rudolph always says the wrong thing," Julian added.

"Me too," said Millicent. "What were you talking about before Rudy stuck his foot in his mouth?"

Julian and Amadeus looked blank for a moment, then started laughing. "Stuck his foot in his mouth. That's clever."

Amadeus, Carla noted, had a laugh like a horse braying, but Julian had a nice laugh, sort of a happy guffaw. She didn't know why, but she liked Julian's laugh.

They continued to talk as the boat made its way upriver and reached a dock about noon. After debarking, they walked over to a lovely little grassy knoll where sheep had kept the grass at a comfortable height, found places where the sheep hadn't left little presents for them to step in, and put down their blankets.

Archduke Leo had enjoyed the chat with Dr. Faust and Judy, though he had found Gabrielle Ugolini's monomaniacal focus on biochemistry a bit wearing. On the other hand, Dr. Faust seemed entranced by the girl. He would leave the doctor to her tender graces and look in on the glider that Faust was building another time. Besides, he would rather see the thing than talk about it.

By now some of the mystical charm of the beautiful Judith Wendell von Up-time had worn off. He had been thinking about her since she arrived. She was very pretty and vibrant in a very attractive way. But as the day wore on the almost spiritual image he had of her began to get a bit frayed around the edges. She was, frankly, less well-informed on a number of matters than Leo had expected. "I just ride the things when I need to go somewhere fast," she'd said. "I don't need to know how to build them. That's someone else's job."

That comment, along with several others where Judy Wendell admitted ignorance of finance, chemistry, engineering, politics and a host of other fields. She was still very attractive and he was intrigued by her, but he was much less in awe of her as the day wore on. He was watching the pairing up. Dr. Faust was completely enraptured by the chemist Ugolini and Pfeifer by the one down-timer to make her way onto the BarbieCo stock certificates.

The mechanic's daughter seemed quite taken with young Amadeus, and Julian was following the Barclay girl around. Leo smiled. There was something about the way her calves moved when she was doing that tap dancing that was quite enticing.

Even Moses seemed relaxed. He and Susan were discussing the roast beef, which was kosher. There was a small Jewish contingent at Race Track City. Apparently a kosher delicatessen was one of the businesses that the up-timers had helped to finance. Because, according to Susan Logsden, the kosher practices got you part way to up-time sanitary practices.

Leo looked over at Márton von Debrecen and the tall young woman in slacks in time to see the woman toss a stick out onto the river.

Márton held up a hand, then called out, "Everyone, be at ease. Vicky and I are settling a bet." The others all looked their way, and suddenly Vicky dropped her purse and fired her pistol, hitting the stick that had floated downriver. At least, Leo thought she had hit it. The splash had certainly moved it, but it was still in one piece.

"Fine," Márton said. "I'll grant that was a hit and a very fast draw," but still he put his Cardinal to his shoulder and after a quick sighting, fired. Now the stick was in two pieces, carefully bisected in the center. Then Vicky fired again and one of the pieces was bisected. Then, while Márton was still reloading, she fired a third time, this time missing the other piece. But not by much. If it had been a man, he would have been hit.

"Oh, no!" Judy complained theatrically "Vicky's found another gun nut." Everyone laughed, mostly at Judy's tone.

"Connoisseur!" Vicky corrected. "A gun connoisseur."

Judy put her face in her hands, histrionically, then laughed. "Fine, but go downriver a little way, so we can hear ourselves think while you assault innocent trees."

Márton looked up. "You know that's an excellent idea. Your Grace, may we borrow your boat for an hour or so?"

Leo was surprised at the request. Still, it was more than a year since Polyxena had been executed by Maximilian of Bavaria. He looked at the girl again, noting that she was the one on the twelve groschen note. She probably wasn't after his money. And as for his title, he had effectively bought it. "Certainly, Count. Enjoy yourselves."

As it happened, Rudolph and Millicent went with Márton and Vicky, so propriety was mostly observed.

They spent the afternoon nibbling and chatting. All the while, Leo watched Judy. She was amazingly graceful and the sun shone on her auburn hair. Her short sleeves showed her arms to advantage. She had a wide smile that no painting could capture. It lit her face and seemed most inviting. Leo was more and more anxious as the day wore on to accept that invitation.

His eyes were drawn to her when, three hours later, the boat got back, and they trooped aboard to head back to Race Track City. Leo's eyes were captured by the motion of her bottom as she climbed the gangplank.

On reaching Race Track City, as the girls were disembarking, Leo grabbed Judy Wendell and pulled her in for a quick kiss, more in the way of a promise of things to come than any—

Suddenly he was bent over, with his gonads screaming at him, and from what seemed a very long way away, he heard Judy Wendell saying, "I am not one of those cases where it is better to ask forgiveness than permission. I do hope you will remember that in the future." Then she turned and walked away. Down the gangplank, one of the guards made a move to stop her, but there was Vicky Emerson with her gun out, not pointed at anyone right now, but that could change in an instant, as she had demonstrated that afternoon. All this was no more than peripheral to Archduke Leo's universe, which was still quite concentrated on the pain emanating from his groin.

Royal Steam Yacht, the Docks at Race Track City

The men—young and old—who had been on the cruise were all agog, Carla noted. The women, on the other hand, had immediately formed into an almost military solidarity. And Vicky wasn't the only one holding a gun. Millicent Anne Barnes was too, and so were Hayley Fortney and Trudi. Gabrielle wasn't showing one, but she had a hand in her purse and so did Susan Logsden. Not knowing what else to do, Carla put her hand in her purse. Not that there was a gun in there, but female solidarity was clearly the way to go here. She followed the rest as they walked down the gangplank and headed for Race Track City. Carla didn't look back, as tempting as it was.

Marco Vianetti, who commanded the Archduke's guard, almost ordered the young women arrested. He didn't for several reasons. First, of course, was the fact that at least two of them were showing arms—and quite deadly arms at that. He wasn't sure that an arrest attempt would be met with force, but it would be really easy for things to get out of hand if the young women were pushed. That kept him from acting for long enough for his brain to catch up. He knew that the young ladies were of such a status that arresting them would cause problems for the crown, even if no one ended up dead. They weren't being any sort of threat to anyone. Not even the archduke anymore. All the damage there was already done. While he was thinking that through, the others reacted and he saw that, too.

Dr. Faust looked at the brother of the Austro-Hungarian emperor, who was bending over and holding his balls, and had a decision to make. This was his stop. He was the tutor to Hayley Fortney, and if he didn't go ashore he would be arraying himself against her. On the other hand, it was quite likely that following the girls down the gangplank would be seen as aligning himself with them against the imperial household, and for a man in his position that could be horribly dangerous. All that ran through his mind in an instant and the decision was made before he even knew it. He was walking after the girls, not because they were his employers, but because they were right. Archduke or not, Leo bloody well should have asked.

He was pleased to see his friend Jack Pfeifer walking beside him.

He didn't see Archduke Leo standing up, but the rest of the men in the party did.

Count Márton turned to Archduke Leo, bowed and shrugged, then turned and followed the girls off the boat. Amadeus, seeing his brother-in-law's action, suddenly realized that if anyone tried to arrest these girls in a foreign land like Maximilian had arrested and executed Polyxena they would have to go through Márton to do it. He remembered Polyxena. Flighty and irritating as she could be, she was his sister and he wished someone had been there to stand by her. He followed his brother-in-law off the royal steamboat almost hoping someone would try something. He didn't even notice Rudolph and Julian dithering.

Moses Abrabanel didn't dither at all. He didn't even bow to the duke. He simply left the boat. Had he done otherwise, he was convinced that his deceased wife would come back to haunt him.

Archduke Leo was embarrassed, in pain, and more than a little pissed off at the public humiliation more than the pain. He turned to the captain and said, "Let's go."

In moments the boat was steaming back for Vienna.

Docks at Race Track City

"Are you insane?" Hayley hissed at Judy. "That guy you just kneed in the nuts is two heartbeats from the Austro-Hungarian throne!"

"Calm down, Hayley," Judy said. "I know what I'm doing." Which was, in a way, perfectly true. The action hadn't been planned, not at all, but Judy did have an instinct for social situations. And, after the fact, she was even pretty good at figuring out why she had done what she did. She hadn't exactly figured it out yet, in this case, but she was sure she had a good reason. And suddenly she knew what that reason was. Her reaction wasn't even mostly about Archduke Leo, who aside from the Cyrano de Bergerac nose and the pale blotchy skin, wasn't even bad looking. Well, not *that* bad looking. But he had grabbed her without asking, in public, as though he had a right to. And her reaction was a precedent. A precedent that was going to affect all the Barbies. She had had to make it clear that *no one* had the right to mess with a Barbie unless she gave prior consent.

"It's a status thing. We aren't peasants." Seeing the look on Hayley's face, Judy quickly expanded on her first simplified thought. "I'm not endorsing the down-timer attitude toward peasants, Hayley. No more than I'd endorse a hurricane or an avalanche. But refusing to endorse something doesn't make it cease to exist.

The down-timer attitudes are there whether we endorse them or not, you know that. So like the hurricane or the avalanche, all we can really do is get out of their way."

"What down-timer attitudes are those?" asked Márton von Debrecen, who apparently had good hearing.

Judy turned to him. "The whole notion of good blood and not good blood, the judgment by blood that is common in this century. We can't make that belief go away because everyone we have met in this century has had it, at least to an extent. The reason that Archduke Leopold felt that he had the right to grab me was the belief that his blood and birth *entitled* him. But, he wouldn't have tried it with another archduchess, because her blood and birth would have protected her. I can't change that. All I can do is make it clear that he's not entitled to me. He's going to interpret that to mean that my blood protects me." Judy shrugged. "There's not much I can do about that. But Trudi's a Barbie too, so she gets some of that protection. And Gretchen Richter, in her own way, is making it plain that her something—certainly not blood, but something—makes it unwise to start feeling entitled to her. It chips away a bit at the entitled notion. It will be a generation or more before it's seriously diminished. In the meantime, I have to look out for myself and my friends. That means making sure that when someone draws a rank line, my friends and I are on the right side of it."

"I don't think Gretchen sees it that way," Vicky Emerson said. "And frankly Judy, I'm not sure I do either."

Judy looked back at Vicky and shrugged again. "I'm not sure I do either, Vicky. But the only other option is to start the revolution right here and right now, and we don't have the muscle for that. We can't even be really sure that we have the muscle to pull off what I did. It was just the minimum that I could live with."

"We really are barbarians to you, aren't we?" Amadeus said about half to Judy and half to Hayley. He sounded chagrined and at least a bit resentful.

"No!" Hayley said quickly.

Judy considered him for a moment. "Yes. A little bit, at least. But don't feel too bad. You're the noble barbarian sort. The sort that can be civilized."

"Judy!" Hayley objected.

"Don't be rude," Millicent chimed in.

"Judy is rude whenever she wants to be," said Vicky. "And I wish I knew how she gets away with it."

"It's because I'm not rude when I *want* to be, only when I *need* to be. There's a difference. So, since you gentlemen were unwise enough to rank yourselves with the evil up-timers, why don't we go up to the Fortney house and try to figure out how you're going to survive the contamination?"

Fortney House, Race Track City

Amadeus had known he was in over his head before he had left the boat. But what else could he have done? Over the next few hours he mostly kept his mouth shut as Márton and Judy and, increasingly, Vicky Emerson talked about reasons and consequences. He learned that Vicky had been engaged to a town guard in Grantville and that the town guard had died doing his duty when Mayor Dreeson was killed. He learned that, in Vicky Emerson's mind at least, Bill Magen was as noble as any man born. He saw that the mutual loss shared by Vicky Emerson and Márton had somehow produced a bond between them.

He wasn't sure what it all meant, but somehow as he listened he came to believe, to know, that getting off the boat had been the smartest thing he had ever done. Because he was on the right side.

Royal Steam Yacht

Archduke Leopold was having a very different experience. No one was even talking to him. The truth was they were frightened to do so, lest it be taken as *lèse majesté*, but it seemed like they were condemning him and he resented it. He even more resented the knowledge that dozens of people had seen him bending over in agony after that puffed-up peasant had kneed him in the groin. Normally Leo would have been more understanding, but normally his balls weren't distracting him. It took the boat around twenty minutes to get back to Vienna from Race Track City, and by the time it docked he was coldly furious at the up-timers and their arrogance. He went directly to his rooms and didn't speak to anyone he didn't have to for the rest of the day.

The Hofburg Palace, Vienna

"What on earth were you thinking?" Ferdinand III asked his little brother the next morning.

"It was nothing. Or it should have been, if that up-timer slut didn't have delusions of grandeur."

"I hardly think slut is the appropriate term," said the empress of Austria-Hungary, "considering the events as they were relayed to me."

Leo didn't say anything. Not only was there little he could say, it wasn't the sort of thing he wanted to talk about with his sister-in-law.

"My question is 'what do we do now?'" Ferdinand III said.

Leo stayed silent. If the emperor insisted he apologize, he would. He was a loyal member of the family. But he very much didn't want to.

"We can't apologize," said his stepmother, Eleonore. "It would be seen as a sign of weakness."

"Well, we can't throw them in the dungeon either," Empress Mariana said. "We need Karl Eusebius' support and we aren't going to get it by imprisoning his prospective sister-in-law. For that matter, Judy Wendell is the daughter of the Secretary of the Treasury for the USE."

"And Márton von Debrecen got off the boat," Cecilia Renata pointed out. "So did Moses Abrabanel."

"The problem goes deeper than that," said Ferdinand. "I just received a new report from Janos Drugeth. He says it's now definite: Murad IV is marching on Baghdad. If he takes it and makes peace with the Persians—which is what he did in the American universe, only three years from now—then his forces will be free to attack Austria. If all that comes to pass, that means we have little time any longer—a year; maybe two—to generate the funds we need to bolster the army." He gave his younger brother a hard glance, which Leopold shied away from. "And the best source we have for funds at the moment and for the immediate future are the Barbies. Indirectly, because of the effect they're having on all Austrian finance and commerce, even more than directly from the taxes and fees they pay us. The very *last* thing we can afford to do right now is cause a major breach with them."

It was rare that Ferdinand III put on his emperor's voice in these family meetings, but he did so now. "We will take no official notice of the incident. In the future, Leo, if you meet the Wendell girl or any of the up-timers, you will be polite and keep your hands to yourself."

Leo nodded unhappily, but was obedient to his brother and his emperor.

Tavern in Vienna

"I was standing right there," Julian said. "I mean, it wasn't any big thing. The archduke just grabbed her a little. But it was him that did it. It wasn't like she just walked up to him and kneed him in the balls." He couldn't help it. He giggled a little at that. It was funny, at least in retrospect. At the time, it hadn't seemed funny in any way.

"Why are you taking their side?" asked his friend, Frederick.

Julian had been getting that reaction all morning, and by now he was wishing he had followed Amadeus off the royal steamboat. Carla probably wasn't even speaking to him. And, well, you could tell just by watching them that the up-timer girls weren't peasants. The archduke should have seen it and been more discreet about his advances. "She said that she was not a case where it was better to ask forgiveness than permission," he told Frederick and the other young men in the tavern. "And I'll tell you, you'd better have permission before you try anything with an up-timer girl. And that's a fact."

"They don't scare me," Frederick insisted.

"You haven't seen Vicky Emerson shoot," Julian said. "I have. You remember that western, *High Noon*? Well, she's like that sheriff. I mean . . . the gun was in her purse then it was in her hand, faster than you could see."

Now interest took the place of outrage, as it will when something as strange as a pretty girl who can shoot is brought to the attention of teenage boys. All their interests rolled into one.

For the next half-hour, Julian was called on to describe Vicky Emerson's shooting and quick draw. He was forced to admit that he hadn't seen most of it because Vicky and Márton von Debrecen had taken the steam boat upriver.

"Well, why didn't you go?" Frederick asked.

"Carla didn't want to," Julian admitted.

"So it's just luck that you're not the one who got kneed in the balls," Frederick said, laughing.

Julian turned a bit pink even under his tan complexion. The boys laughed and elbowed him in the ribs.

"Now we know why he was taking the up-timer's side." Frederick snickered. "Lust before honor. Tut tut tut."

"It's not like that," Julian insisted, thinking that it very much was like that.

To a great extent, it was Julian's version of events that made the rounds of the young men of the nobility and that acted as a further embarrassment to the archduke over the next few weeks.

Restaurant at Race Track City

"I saw it myself," said a dock worker the day after the event. "The archduke grabbed her like she was some peasant girl, and she kneed him in the balls."

"There's going to be trouble!" said an older dock worker. "You don't embarrass an archduke like that."

"They're up-timers," said a waitress.

"So what? Sonny Fortney is an up-timer and he's just a regular guy. It's not like he's noble."

The waitress pulled a BarbieCo stock certificate out of her pocket. It was a trudi, the best tip she had gotten that morning. She waved it at him. "Does Sonny Fortney have his own money?"

The dock worker laughed. "That's a trudi," he said grandly, "and she's not an up-timer."

"Fine. You go grab her and see what happens to your balls," the waitress shot back.

"Not me, lass," he said, reaching for her, but not at all suddenly, and she slipped away. "I like my women with a little maturity."

She sniffed, but smiled a little as she headed for the next table. She was a decade older than the Barbies.

The social status of the Barbies and the up-timers became a major topic of conversation all over Race Track City. It was clear that you could be an up-timer and not a Barbie, or a Barbie and not an up-timer. It was also clear, given that the Barbies weren't arrested, that Judy Wendell was of a rank that could, given provocation, knee the emperor's brother in the balls and get away with it. But what gave her that rank was a matter that was entirely murky. Was it being a Barbie or being an up-timer?

St. Stephen's Cathedral, Vienna

"I told you," Father Lamormaini said to Gundaker von Liechtenstein. "They have no respect for the natural order of things, no sense of their proper place at all. It was intentional. I'm convinced of it. She enticed the archduke in order to embarrass the emperor and his family."

Gundaker's experience with Archduke Leopold didn't indicate that he needed all that much in the way of enticement. The boy had a weakness for pretty things, though he was usually more discreet in the matter.

Still, Gundaker nodded to Father Lamormaini. The man was moving farther and farther into fanaticism and that might be useful at some point. Even so, after agreeing Gundaker added, "But we must be careful, Father. We can't let them tempt us to rash actions."

CHAPTER 30

𝕸𝖚𝖉, 𝕭𝖑𝖔𝖔𝖉, 𝖆𝖓𝖉 𝕭𝖊𝖊𝖗

September 1635

Liechtenstein Tower Construction Site, Vienna

The scraper was down six feet below street level now and they were running into real problems.

The basement was a well.

Johann's foot sank into the mud and the ox he was following wasn't doing much better. The scraper was sinking into the mud. "Leonhard, we have to do something about the seepage!" Johann shouted.

He was overheard by no less a personage than Karl Eusebius von Liechtenstein, who was here observing the construction preparations for the Liechtenstein Tower, in preference to observing the towering rage of his uncles.

Gundaker was much the worst, but Maximilian wasn't happy either. Sarah was taking the attitude that Leo got what he was asking for and if the emperor didn't like it, they could all go home while the whole Austro-Hungarian Empire sank into its massive debt. That threat was pretty effective, more so because Gundaker really wanted Karl and Sarah's marriage to happen. He wanted Karl's children out of the succession, and wanted it badly. It was reassuring in a way, in spite of Gundaker's recent association with the Spanish and Borja faction.

The whole city had been tense since Pope Urban had been

forced out of Rome. There were clear fault lines over the crisis in the church, and while the royal house was tending toward the Urban faction, they had not declared for him. Judy's knee might just move them to the Borja faction. Certainly, the Dominicans seemed to be flocking around Leo.

What possessed the girl?

No.

Karl knew exactly what had possessed her. The exact same thing that possessed all the up-timers. That up-timer sense of self-worth. It was what he expected from his fellow aristocrats, "the best bloodlines in Europe," but it had come as quite a shock when he had first gotten to Grantville and realized that all the up-timers had it. And a whole bunch of the down-timers that associated with them were developing it.

Damn it, what possessed Leo?

No.

Karl knew what had possessed Leo too. He simply hadn't realized what he was dealing with. *What if he had done that to Gretchen Richter?* She'd have used a knife, not a knee.

He would have to find a way to talk to Leo, try to explain. Karl had gotten used to up-timer attitudes over the years, and had moved the up-timers into the category of nobles in his mind, without even realizing it. That was Gundaker's trouble with Sarah. Well, most of it anyway. That he hadn't moved up-timers into the category of noble.

Another call pulled Karl's mind from his mulling. Another scraper was sinking into the mud. It seemed all of Austria-Hungary was insisting on following it. "We'll need to dig some wells and pump the water out!" Karl shouted over to the foreman.

The water would have to be pulled away long enough for them to get concrete walls and a floor in, and even then there was going to be serious seepage. They would have to design for it. Meanwhile, he would have to find a way to convince the nobility of Austria...not that there were no nobles. That was impossible, whatever Mike Stearns thought. No. The trick was to convince them that everyone was noble. Karl snorted. Even that was the work of Sisyphus. But at least that way he could move a boulder at a time. First, convince them that the Barbies were nobles—that *all* up-timers had to be considered noble—and then that they'd better learn to treat Gretchen Richter and her like as noble.

He figured he should reach that point about the time his grandchildren were doddering old fools.

The Hofburg Palace, Vienna

"Thank you for seeing me, Leo," Karl said, holding up a bottle. It was fortified wine from the shop in Race Track City. Karl knew that Leo had not been to Race Track City in the two weeks since the incident. The Barbies hadn't been invited to the palace either, but they didn't seem particularly bothered by the fact.

"Welcome, Karl," Leo said without any particular rancor, but with less real welcome in his tone than Karl was used to from Leo. Still, he did wave Karl to a chair.

Marco Vianetti was standing by the door, like he had been for years. Before the trip to Grantville, Karl would have barely noticed the man. Just one of Leo's retainers. He would have been perfectly willing to say anything to Leo in front of Marco, because he just assumed that Marco was trustworthy as Leo's man. And, in truth, Marco probably was trustworthy. But he was also going to talk to the other servants and not all of them would be.

Karl sat down and handed the bottle to Marco. Once the man had poured for them, Karl said, "Marco, with the archduke's permission, I would like to speak to him privately. Would you mind waiting outside?"

It was hard to tell which of them was more shocked by the suggestion that Marco's presence might matter. But it was Leo who spoke up. "Marco is completely trustworthy, Karl. How can you doubt it?"

"I don't, Your Grace. It's more a matter of good practice. It's what the up-timers call the 'need to know principle.' The question isn't whether someone is trustworthy, because anyone can slip. The question is: do they need to know? If they don't need to know private information, it's better if they don't know. If, after our talk, you decide Marco needs to know, then by all means tell him. This way you have the choice, that's all."

"Well, you've certainly made it all seem most mysterious," Leo said, sounding intrigued.

"I didn't intend to, Your Grace," Karl said, thinking of a talk he had had with Melissa Mailey and Prince Vladimir of Russia on the subject of serfs, slaves and espionage. Mary Bowser had been Miss Mailey's prime example, Ivan Susanin had been Vladimir's. Karl had found himself in the middle and seeing both sides, yet less able to persuade anyone of his point of view, because he was convinced that they were both right and wrong. Servants were, in Karl's experience, in the main loyal to their employer and that was the larger part of the trust that members of the nobility had in their servants. On the other hand, there was an unthinking assumption that the lower classes lacked the wit to engage in the sort of subtle subterfuge necessary for betrayal. The attitude was all mixed together with a belief that the nobles were treating their servants quite well and so there was no reason for the servants to be disloyal.

Karl had no idea how he was going to make clear in an afternoon's chat what had taken him three years in Grantville to learn. But he didn't say anything and waited. After a few moments, Leo shrugged a little and gave a little wave. Marco left the room with no objection.

"So, what is this so private of private talks, Karl? If it's about the Wendell girl, Marco might as well have stayed. He was there when she attacked me."

This wasn't shaping up to be an enjoyable interview, Karl thought. "Do you think that Sarah agreed to a morganatic marriage because she accepts our notions of rank?"

"Why else?"

"She accepted it because she doesn't care. No, not even just that. It's because she is condescendingly willing to allow us our barbaric beliefs as long as we don't spit in the soup or piss on the sofa. You have no idea how arrogant up-timers are. To Sarah, marrying a court prince of the Austro-Hungarian Empire isn't marrying up. It's marrying down. Different in no important way from David Bartley's mother marrying a minor burgher from Badenburg or any of the up-timer women who have married peasants."

Leo blinked in shock, then actually seemed to consider what Karl was saying. "So when the Emerson girl asked the Fortney girl how she liked life among the peasants, it wasn't a translation problem at all. That's what they really think of us."

Karl winced. "Not exactly. Else there would have been no consideration of marrying me at all. It isn't that they consider us inherently less than them, just...poorly brought up.

"Let me ask you, Leo. What would you have done if Marco

had handled Cecilia Renata as you handled Judy Wendell? What would you have done if the man handling her had been a peasant you didn't know well?"

Leo went pale.

Karl shrugged. "She didn't react that way, did she? Instead she reacted the way you would have expected Cecilia Renata—or more likely, Maria Anna—to act if a person of our own class had handled her that way."

Leo winced, but then said, "However, Judy Wendell is not Cecilia Renata or Maria Anna, whatever she may think."

"Isn't she, Leo? Is it me or Sarah that Moses Abrabanel wanted here?"

They talked some more, but Archduke Leopold wasn't convinced.

Race Track City

Two weeks later at the brewery in Race Track City, Hans Fischer finished unloading a barge of barley for the brewery. He loaded up on casks of the lager beer which had become a specialty of the brewery with the introduction of refrigeration by the up-timers.

Once the barley was unloaded and the beer loaded, Hans was due one and a half cologne marks of silver, or the equivalent in paper money. In the office Hans had a stein of cold beer while Schwarz counted out his money. The beer came down and Hans spoke. "Wait, Wolfgang. I want barbies."

"Why?"

Hans was caught without a good reason but he was a quick thinking fellow. "They give interest," he said, trying to sound virtuous and frugal. Hans wasn't an overly frugal fellow, so it wasn't an easy sell.

Wolfgang looked at him doubtfully but started digging through his cash box. "That's odd," Wolfgang said.

"What?"

"Being right here next to Race Track City, we usually have a lot of barbies. But I only have two judies and no haylies at all. I have three vickies, and a dozen gabbies, but not one trudi and not all that many millies."

"Don't take all his money, Hans. I've got to get paid yet," shouted another man.

Wolfgang made a rude gesture. "I have plenty of reich money. It's just the barbies I'm short on."

"That's not what you said when we were bargaining," said another merchant.

Wolfgang made another rude gesture. No one paid that much attention to which bills were in short supply. They just noted that barbies were hard to come by. Harder than reich money, and reich money was none too easy to get.

The truth was that Hans' hadn't wanted the barbies for any reason of frugality or long-term planning. No, Hans wanted barbies so that a few miles upriver he could show his friends a judi and say "That's her. That's the girl who kneed Archduke Leopold in the balls and got away with it." He wanted to be able to show them a hayli and say, "She's the one who has been living out at Race Track City for over a year." He wanted to show them a trudi and explain that "she's the down-time Barbie." He didn't have that many specifics about the other barbies, but he wanted those, too—just to fill out the set. And he wanted extras, because he figured that his friends would want their own Barbie money.

Liechtenstein Tower Construction Site, Vienna

Back at the Liechtenstein Tower, a steam-powered water pump was pumping out the wells by now, and digging had resumed. Millicent Anne Barnes, escorted by a squad of mercenary soldiers, parked her armored wagon by the work site and directed the soldiers in setting up her pay table. Then she waited for the whistle to blow. She had boxes of money in the wagon and a book with the names of all the workers. Each worker would come up, show her his ID, collect his pay, and sign the book. Millicent was good with names, but there were over two hundred workmen at the site.

The first payday they had ended up paying most of the men in reich money. The workers weren't entirely sure they trusted barbies, and the Barbies didn't insist, though they always offered barbies first. That first week it had been only the most desperate and least assertive men who had taken barbies. Even at that, some of those men had shown up over the week asking for reich money because their landlord or food seller wouldn't take the barbies. Policy was to always take the barbies at face value and exchange with no trouble.

The second week had actually been worse. They had paid the men almost entirely in reich money, but things had evened out. A lot of the workers spent quite a bit of their money out at Race Track City, which had become the Coney Island of Vienna. And it was common knowledge that the businesses at Race Track City took barbies, even before the first shovel had touched dirt at Liechtenstein Tower. And the fact that the Abrabanel clan— and therefore most Jewish money lenders—would take barbies at face value hadn't hurt at all. So for the first month of work at Liechtenstein Tower, they had ended up going about half barbies and half reich money.

Then Judy kneed Archduke Leopold in the balls and by the next Friday, it was pretty clear that no one was going to be dragged away in chains. At that point, the requests for reich money had decreased markedly.

The tables were set up, the whistle blew, and the money started changing hands. Millicent noted a name. It was one of the men who had always been most insistent that he get "real" money. She reached for the reich money box without even asking and he said, "I'll take barbies."

"Are you sure?" Millicent asked. "It's no trouble to pay you in..."

"I'll take barbies," he insisted rather belligerently.

Millicent shrugged and paid the man in barbies. Half an hour later, they ran out of barbies. Just in case, they had had enough reich money to pay off all the workers every payday, always hoping that they wouldn't use too much of it. But they hadn't expected this many of their employees to want barbies and they hadn't brought enough. The last twenty-five people were told that they were out of barbies and would have to take reich money for their pay.

Millicent knew the policy, "Always be willing to give reich money and whenever possible make it seem you would rather take barbies." So when a worker asked, she refused to promise that he could exchange his reich money for barbies. Instead she said, "I'm sorry, but we only print the barbies when we have enough product to back them."

"What does that mean?"

"Well, it's all very technical, but what it comes down to is we'll always give you reich money for barbies, but we won't always be able to give you barbies for reich money." Millicent tried to sound regretful, but it was hard because inside she was dancing around and capering like a monkey. This was the precise phrase that Sarah had explained meant they were in. And before she finished the pay parade, she had repeated it at least fifteen times.

All the way back to Race Track City, Millicent Ann Barnes hummed—but carefully did not sing.

> *Where have all the barbies gone? Pink notes passing.*
> *Where have all the barbies gone? Green notes they go.*
> *Where have all the barbies gone? Gone to lock boxes*
>   *every one.*
> *When will they ever learn?*
> *When will they evverr learn?*

It was almost a shame, because Millicent had a decent voice. But then, those last lines might not have gone over all that well. Besides, she knew that not all, or probably even most, of the barbie money was going into lock boxes or other hiding places. But barbies were now being taken in favor of reich money. Gresham's law was coming into play. The barbies would start being saved, while the reich money was spent. The next thing they would see would be people charging a surcharge to take reich money in exchange for barbies. She could feel it.

Fortney House, Race Track City

"No," Sarah said flatly.

"But, Sarah..." Judy whined.

"You agreed," Sarah said, looking around the room. "When I agreed to this you all agreed that I would set the amount of BarbieCo issued. We all agreed that the amount would be limited by two factors. First, not so many barbies that it would disrupt the economy. *And* second, no more barbies than the goods and services that BarbieCo could supply to support them. I grant that with the barbies going into lock boxes, the threat of inflation is shifted to the reich money. But that doesn't mean that Liechtenstein Tower or the other projects have suddenly become twice as valuable."

In truth, Judy wasn't arguing for herself. Judy had been able to afford just about anything you could buy with money since she was fourteen. But unemployment in and around Vienna was still hovering around twenty percent.

"What about the Liechtenstein railroad?" Karl asked. "The Vienna-Cieszyn line is a decent road most of the way, even if it only has the rail over about ten percent of it."

The railroad Sonny Fortney was building was a thoroughly hybridized mishmash of technologies. The rail, where it had a rail at all, was a single wooden rail that went right down the center of the roadway. The train that ran on it had outrigger wheels that ran on hard track next to the rail—packed dirt would do, although macadam was better—which maintained the vehicle's balance while most of the weight was carried on the rail. That rail was low enough that with a bit of effort the normal wagon wheels could roll over it in order to move over to the side and let others pass. The tricky bit was the rail wagons, which had a set of rail wheels that could be cranked down onto that center rail and take up most of the weight of the wagon. While they were down, the wagon acted like a rail car. While the rail wheel was cranked up, the wagon acted like a wagon on a good road.

This arrangement had an added advantage. It meant that where there was no rail yet, the railroad became a normal macadam road and the "train car" became a wagon. But if your wagon had the rail wheel, anytime you ran into rail you could crank it down and for as long as the rail ran, you had a much happier team, be they oxen, mule or horse. All of which, taken together, meant that even though the road was still mostly without rail, those stretches that did have rail were making transport easier and cheaper along it. That, in turn, was pulling traffic from other routes.

"It's already figured in," Sarah said. "It's true that Sonny's innovations have allowed it to start paying dividends sooner and the rail wagons are selling well. However, I think the LIC should consider keeping the rail line, rather than granting it to the railroad company. The way Mr. Fortney has set it up, the rail line is going to be a lot easier to get onto or off of than they were uptime. That's going to make it easier to use and it will be harder to restrict that use. I think you should consider keeping it as a state-owned road that is available for use by anyone, and make your money back on taxes, which will increase with the increase in trade and industry. At the very least, you ought to consider keeping it a public line and just charging tolls for its use."

"I'm not sure that would be fair to Herr Fortney or all the other people who have invested in the railroad company in the expectation that they would have a proprietary interest in the rail line."

Considering that the railroad company was a big part of what he had in mind as a dower for Sarah and inheritance for their morganatic children, that didn't strike Karl as a great idea. But he couldn't say that to Sarah. It would look too much like "the not exactly illegal but certainly questionable" transfer of funds from the Liechtenstein coffers to hers. And Sarah was rather unreasonable about potential conflicts of interest.

Abrabanel Offices, outside Vienna

Moses Abrabanel poured his father a beer. "I'm considering releasing some of the barbies that we received in exchange for our endorsement."

"Why?" Abraham Abrabanel asked. He'd been less than thrilled by Moses' accepting a bribe in barbies in the first place, and Moses had been expecting him to be happy to be rid of them.

"We have a chance to buy into a freight line that is using steam on barges to go up the Danube."

"You mean those Pfeifer people?"

"Yes. Jack Pfeifer was talking to me about it on the picnic."

That earned his father's scowl. Abraham Abrabanel was not comfortable with socializing with gentiles. You did business with them, you had to. But you didn't go on picnics with them, even if the stuff in the baskets was supposed to be kosher. Moses was aware of his father's attitudes, and the reason for them. In the Empire, Jews could often rise high—but they weren't allowed to be close. Not without converting, at least. Moses, on the other hand, had been a little corrupted by his trip to Grantville, then more corrupted by his dealing with the Fortneys and Sanderlins. And, recently, thoroughly corrupted by Susan Logsden—and had decided he rather liked it. So he ignored his father's disapproval and started discussing the economic advantages of the relationship. The Pfeifers knew the trade, and the steam engines had made their river boats much more efficient in terms of cost per ton mile. They were gentiles, Catholics, but they, like Moses, had been corrupted by the Fortneys and the Sanderlins, to the extent that Jack was getting serious with a Lutheran girl. And Jack was the most corrupted of the family. He was busily trying to turn the family shipping business into a stock company that could expand. What he was offering Moses was a significant share in the new company, in exchange for financing and they could provide the financing without having to spend any reich money, just using the barbies. He went over the proposal with his father, and his father was ambivalent.

"The barbies are cash on hand, Moses, fully negotiable and we can loan them out without any difficulty. I don't know about this boat business. We aren't shippers or shopkeepers. We're bankers. And you know we can get a good interest rate from the crown."

"We're more money lenders, Father. At least, that's what we have been. And, frankly, I'm getting nervous about how much the crown owes us already. I don't want Ferdinand III getting any idea of eliminating the loan by getting rid of the lender."

"Ferdinand III is an honorable young man."

"I agree, Father. But he's also under a lot of pressure and too deeply in debt for my peace of mind."

Two more beers and his father was still not convinced, but did agree to look over the proposal.

The Hofburg Palace, Vienna

The beer at the Hofburg was cold, with beads of sweat on the stein as Ferdinand read the latest reports. "I would not have believed that Gustav could move so quickly."

"I wouldn't have believed that he would have divided his forces like that," said Maximilian von Liechtenstein. "It worked out this time, in spite of his General Stearns being an idiot, but talk about arrogant!"

Maximilian was referring to the recent battle of Zwenkau, where the USE army under Torstensson's command had defeated Von Arnim's Saxon forces. The turning point in the battle had come when the inexperienced American general Michael Stearns foolishly advanced his division too far ahead of the rest of the USE forces. In the event, it had all turned out well for him, but it was the general assumption among Austrian analysts of the battle that Stearns had triumphed despite his blunder.

"Some people are saying that was a trap set by Torstennson," Leopold said. "That it was all planned that way."

"That's what I'd say too, if I had a political general who bungled that badly," Maximilian said. "I guess it's possible. But I certainly wouldn't trust a virgin general with an assignment of that nature."

"You think we should support King Wladislaw, if—when, I should say—the Swede attacks Poland?" Ferdinand asked.

"No, Your Majesty," said Maximilian immediately. "Gustav Adolf may be arrogant, but he's also good and he has a very good army, in spite of Stearns. Besides, I don't recall any favors we owe Wladislaw at this point."

"We're probably going to need the Poles if Murad comes," offered Archduke Leopold. "Which he might well do, considering that he is apparently going after Baghdad this year, instead of waiting for the appointed time from the encyclopedia. If he rushes Baghdad, why not have the 1683 attack on Vienna early as well? And we needed the Poles in that history to fight him off."

Ferdinand had considered the same factor himself—many times, now. But the advice he'd gotten from Janos Drugeth still seemed sound. Sending Austrian troops to aid King Wladislaw simply couldn't be done without risking a renewal of the war with Wallenstein—whose Bohemian forces stood between Austria and Poland. Poland would probably still be defeated by the USE and all Ferdinand would have accomplished was to bloody his own forces to no purpose.

"No," he said. "We have no choice but to wait for developments."

CHAPTER 31

Fractured Reserve Bank

October 1635

Liechtenstein House, Vienna

"Theoretically it's a full reserve bank," Sarah explained, "but in fact it operates as a fractional reserve bank." She was talking about the Bank of Amsterdam, but the servant didn't hear that part.

"What's a fractional reserve bank again?" the lawyer asked. Over the past months since Sarah had been in Vienna, she had found herself with an extra occupation. And it was all Karl's fault. He had introduced her as an expert witness in several of the cases against his family that were based on the Kipper and Wipper panic, which happened ten years before the Ring of Fire. Mostly, what she had done in those cases had been to explain that Liechtenstein, Wallenstein, and the others hadn't known any better because no one had known any better. But to do that effectively, she had had to demonstrate that she did know better and was recognized by the financial community as an expert in financial matters.

Based on her proven expertise, she had been asked to testify in all sorts of cases that involved finance in some way. This case involved the Bank of Amsterdam and its double bank structure, which gave the illusion of being a full reserve bank, but with many of the advantages of a fractional reserve bank. The servant put the hot tea with lemon and honey on the table and Sarah thanked her, then answered the lawyer's question. "They don't have enough silver in their vaults for the amount of money they issue."

The servant left the room and the lawyer asked how they got away with it. Sarah explained, but by then the servant was down the hall, convinced that the Royal Bank of Austria-Hungary didn't have enough silver in its vaults for the reich money issued. This information, she repeated with great confidence. Then added that as an employee of the Barbies, *she* got paid in BarbieCo.

The maid was by no means the first person to suggest that the full reserve Royal Bank of Austria-Hungary didn't, in fact, have enough silver to pay off all the people who were carrying around and circulating bank notes. The level of confidence in that claim had never been great, and the unwillingness of the crown to allow independent confirmation had done nothing to reassure the financial community. Abraham and Moses Abrabanel's reassurance had helped some, but Gundaker's somewhat strident insistence had actually hurt confidence.

Now, according to rumor, Sarah Wendell, in a deposition, had said there wasn't enough silver in the Royal Bank of Austria-Hungary. Sarah Wendell was both engaged to marry Karl Eusebius von Liechtenstein and a recognized up-time expert on money. In the course of a couple of days, the rumor had turned the deposition into a "secret" deposition.

BarbieCo Preferred traded on the Grantville exchange, the Magdeburg exchange, the Amsterdam exchange and the Venice exchange. In all those exchanges, it traded as a stock, not a currency. The price quoted for a full share of BarbieCo Preferred—also known as a judi—was, according to the last September issue of *The Street*, thirty-one American dollars. The price of a reichsthaler was twenty-two American dollars. It wasn't an obvious thing, since the prices were listed in different sections of the paper.

The difference in price wasn't any big secret. Moses Abrabanel had discussed it with his father, with Gundaker von Liechtenstein, and Susan Logsden. However, the new issue of the financial paper had an article about the difference in prices and what they meant in terms of money versus stock and bonds. The article was a "thought piece" and encouraged readers to invest in the market, and in most of Europe that was how it was taken. However, in

Vienna, its main effect was to make Grantville's view of the relative value of a judi versus a reichsthaler obvious to anyone.

Beauty Parlor, Race Track City

"What do you mean, it costs more if I pay in reich money?" Liana asked. Maximiliana Constanzia von Liechtenstein was so obviously put out by the sign that Frau Lechner pulled out her copy of *The Street* and handed it to Liana. But she didn't wait for the noblewoman to read it. She pointed out the specific passage and the line that followed it, about the writer's belief that the difference in price was simply going to increase.

As it happened, Liana had both reich money and BarbieCo stock in her purse. She did quite a bit of shopping here and often got barbies in change. She glanced over the article, but didn't really follow it all that well. She was literate and reasonably bright, but not particularly well-versed in business. However, she got the point and paid in reich money. After all, the barbies were going to get more valuable. It said so, right there in *The Street*.

Barbies were disappearing at a remarkable rate all that day, and the next. By Thursday, it was hard to find one even in Race Track City and essentially impossible in Vienna.

Frau Winkler's Boarding House, Vienna

"Herr Maier, you get paid tomorrow, don't you?"

"Yes, Frau Winkler?" Herr Maier wasn't behind on his rent, not since his third week working at the Liechtenstein Tower construction project. It was hard, dangerous work, but Karl Johann Maier didn't mind that. They paid well and on time, every week.

"Well, I want my rent in BarbieCo, so just you make sure you get barbies."

"There's nothing in our agreement that says I have to pay in barbies." Karl Johann wasn't all that happy with the landlady. She had been a constant pain while he was behind on his rent and not much nicer since he had gotten the good job. Besides, there were rumors that a barbie was worth more than the reich money.

Frau Winkler's blotchy face got even blotchier, but he had her and she clearly knew it. "I will give you a discount for barbies," she said grudgingly.

And they were off. The bargaining took fifteen minutes and he would save two trudies on a week's rent. Karl Johann left the apartment building with a spring in his step and a song in his heart.

Frau Winkler was worried. Not all her tenants worked for the Liechtensteins or the Barbies. She had no idea why reich money wasn't worth as much as barbies. She just knew that it wasn't.

Royal Bank of Austria-Hungary, Vienna

"We need to open the second vault," whispered Franz Traugott to Karl Lang.

"This is crazy," Lang whispered back. "Why are they all here?"

"Didn't you hear? Sarah Wendell reported to the emperor that there wasn't enough silver to support reich money. No one trusts paper money anymore."

"Don't be silly," Lang said, starting to get a really bad feeling about this. "How could she know?"

"Her up-time computer worked it out, the one she brought with her from the Ring of Fire. You know that they can calculate anything."

Karl Lang didn't know a thing about what computers could or couldn't calculate. But he did know that the vaults weren't as full of silver as they were supposed to be.

Another customer came up to the window with a stack of reich money. "I will have silver, if you please," the man said. He didn't look like a silversmith.

Lang went toward the second vault while his mind whirled. It was the silver. All that silver, just sitting there. And he'd had expenses. And it wasn't fair! The emperor was always late with the pay. Maria was expensive. A man liked to give things to his lady love and Maria was so grateful when he got her a new dress or shawl. Besides, his wife needed stuff too, even if she wasn't so grateful. There were the children to think about.

It had seemed so simple. They never used the second vault. The first vault was mostly left open, so the bank could provide silver for people who had some reason to need it, mostly silversmiths.

They brought in paper reichsthaler and bought silver to use in their craft. And, of course, when people brought in old silver coins to have them assayed, they went in to the first vault. It was only after they had been melted down, refined and made into silver bars that the silver went into the second vault. The second vault was just for storage.

Storage for stacks of silver bars that never got used for anything. And it was easy enough to stack the silver bars so that they looked like there were more of them than were actually there. For someone with the key to the second vault, it wasn't that hard to make the switch now and then. Lang was almost sure that he wasn't the only one doing it.

Those thoughts had taken him to the door of the second vault. He unlocked the vault, then stopped. He had only taken just a few bars from the second vault. There might not be a problem . . . but if this kept up it would be noticed and Lang was one of only three people who had keys to the second vault. He would be discovered. Karl Lang wasn't a brave fellow and he didn't like to gamble, not at all. It had taken six months of the second vault only being opened at the beginning and end of each business day before Karl had worked up the nerve to take his first bar.

Lang turned the key the other way and slipped out a side door of the bank. He managed to keep from running till he was a block away. It was the hardest thing he had ever done in his life, but he did it. Once he rounded the corner and was out of sight of the bank, he ran. And, at least in the figurative sense, Karl Lang would never stop running as long as he lived.

Franz Traugott was getting worried. Karl should be back by now, pulling a cart of silver bars. He motioned over a guard. The Royal Bank had a gracious plenty of those.

"Go to the second vault and see what's keeping Herr Lang, please."

The guard went back to ask and returned quickly. "He left out the side door," the guard told Franz. "Georg saw him."

"Why didn't Georg stop him?" Franz hissed.

"Why the fig should he have? Herr Lang didn't even open the second vault. He put the key in, then pulled it out again and went out the side like he had just remembered something. At least, that's what Georg told me."

Franz looked at the line of customers and at the shrinking pile of silver and was very tempted to make a run for it himself, in spite of the fact that he had done nothing wrong. But he was made of sterner stuff than Karl Lang. "Listen, send a runner to Herr Maurer's house. Tell him that we need him and his key down here now. And you'd better send another to Liechtenstein house and tell Prince Gundaker von Liechtenstein that we need his key as well."

"What's going on?" the guard asked.

"I don't know. Maybe Karl had a good reason to leave, but what I'm afraid of is that he had a very bad reason to leave. Whatever the reason, if we don't get a key to the second vault here soon, we are going to have a run on the bank."

The guard paled. There had been seven bank runs that had made the international press since the Ring of Fire. In five of them, someone had ended up executed. In one, twenty-three people involved with the bank had been executed.

By the end of the day there had been eight bank runs. Gundaker was at the palace and Herr Maurer was enjoying his day off at the water park at Race Track City. The bank ran out of silver hours before either of those worthies were found. Word spread like wildfire and the Royal Bank of Austria-Hungary had to close its doors. By the time Gundaker von Liechtenstein got there, the building was surrounded by guards and there was the next best thing to a riot out front. It wasn't a riot of poor people. The upper crust of Vienna—burghers, masters, *Hofbefreiten*, and nobles—were up in arms. They had put their silver in the bank and they had been promised that they could get it back when they wanted it.

Gundaker von Liechtenstein, whatever else, was a brave man. He went out to face the rioters, pistols in hand, and backed by the bank guards.

He fired a pistol into the air to get the attention of the rioters. Once the shouting died down, he roared, "What is wrong with you people? Is this any way for the greatest nobility in the world to behave?"

The uproar started again. "Where's our money?" came a shout from the crowd.

"It's in the bank!"

"Then why can't we get it?"

"Why would you want to? What has caused this unseemly demonstration? Where is the courage of our noble blood? Where is the trust in our emperor?"

"It's not the emperor we don't trust! It's his banker." Which was a direct shot at Gundaker. As the chancellor of the exchequer, he was the official head of the royal bank, which was why he had the third key. For political reasons, the Abrabanels were officially simply depositors in the royal bank, though Moses was present at the board meetings and had much to do with its design, using information from his family in Grantville.

"The bank is closed while we inventory the silver stocks and will reopen day after tomorrow."

"Why do you suddenly need to run an inventory?" came from several voices.

The one thing Gundaker didn't want to say was that they were afraid some of the silver had gone missing and didn't know how much. He considered saying they needed to assay some of the recent silver deposits, but that would only cause more panic and he knew it. Finally, he just got stubborn. "Because I'm not going to let a mob of peasants into the emperor's bank," he roared at the crowd.

The roar that came back was unclear, but not at all difficult to interpret. The mob didn't care for being called peasants.

"Then stop acting like base-born villagers! Go home, get some sense. Let us do our jobs and come back when you have some reason other than panic to need your silver." With that, Gundaker turned his back on the mob and went back into the bank, followed by the guards. They prudently barred the doors. With no one to shout at and not quite ready to burn the place down—or go into open revolt against the crown—the upper crust of Vienna went home. At least, some of them did. Rather a lot went to the palace to complain to the emperor about their treatment at the bank.

The Hofburg Palace, Vienna

"It's Sarah Wendell's fault," said Gundaker. "How did she know that there had been pilfering?" The audit of the bank had in fact found that there was silver missing. However, it was less than five percent of the amount that was supposed to be there. Of greater concern was something they had discovered after the printer for the royal treasury had turned up missing the day after the bank closure. It turned out that the man had been printing a little extra money with every print run. He had been paying two guards to look the other way. One was under arrest, the other was also missing. It still wasn't a massive amount, not even a percent, but it was enough to set all three men up for life. Set them up in luxury.

"It's not her fault," said Moses Abrabanel. "For one thing, in the rumor I heard the secret report was made to Your Majesty and myself. That's why I was asked about it. When I told them that there had been no such report, all I got was warned that they were going behind my back. So tell me, Prince von Liechtenstein, why wasn't I informed of the meeting in which Sarah Wendell informed you and the emperor that half the silver in the national bank had been siphoned off to buy off Wallenstein?"

"There was no such meeting," Gundaker said.

"Precisely my point."

"Is the bank opened again?" the emperor interrupted.

"Yes, and there are lines around the block," Gundaker said. "No one is taking paper reich money, just silver and barbies."

"Sarah Wendell is not the cause, but she may be the solution," Moses offered.

"You've been pushing that since she got here," Gundaker told him. "And I will even grant that she does have a good understanding of the art for someone her age. But she is a girl and a peasant. No one is going to take the word of a peasant on matters of this import."

Moses looked over at Gundaker in frustration and suddenly a demonically delightful thought occurred to him. Moses felt himself smiling. He turned to the emperor. "Ennoble her, then. If it's her lack of title that causes the problem, give her one."

Gundaker went pale. He despised Sarah Wendell and most of the up-timers, but he also found them useful. If they were ennobled, especially Sarah, that would mean that a marriage between her and Karl wouldn't be morganatic. At least, the marriage wouldn't have to be, and knowing Karl, he would insist that it not be.

✧   ✧   ✧

Ferdinand III was aware of the issues involved and, under other circumstances, he would have been in sympathy with Gundaker's attempt to ensure his family's property. Gundaker was sworn to the empire and Karl Eusebius was sworn to Wallenstein, so Ferdinand would prefer Gundaker's branch of the family to inherit control of the family wealth. But not now. Not today, when his people were lined up around his bank demanding silver.

"Gentlemen, I need money. I need it to pay my armies and to run my government. I wish to speak with Sarah Wendell. Arrange it."

"It might be better if you let me talk with her, Your Majesty," Moses said.

"Why?"

"Well, there is the matter of Duke Leopold and her sister, and the rumors about her comments on the banks. If it looks like we are arresting her or attempting to coerce her or her sister there could be a reaction. It might be better to have someone else talk with her at first."

Ferdinand considered. "I think I will have Mariana talk with her." He shot Prince Gundaker a look. "Someone she will be more comfortable with."

The Hofburg Palace, Vienna, the next day

Sarah wasn't happy with the summons. It had been phrased as a request to visit the empress but Sarah had heard the rumors too, and was a little afraid that the emperor was going to have her arrested.

She had had no involvement in the Austro-Hungarian Imperial Bank. And every time she had commented on it in the presence of Gundaker, he had, in essence, told her to sit down and shut up as much because she was female as because she wasn't of the nobility. She had given up trying over a month before.

So she approached the Hofburg with no joy in her heart. She was surprised to be met by the empress. Even if it was an ordinary visit she would have expected to be met by a functionary and put somewhere to wait on the empress's pleasure.

Empress Mariana was very friendly and reassuring. "We just need you to explain to us how you make the barbies work."

Sarah looked at the empress. "I'm not sure what to say."

"Well, nothing right here. Follow me and we'll find some place comfortable and not quite so public."

A few minutes later, seated in a richly brocaded chair in a room full of candles and golden ornamentation, Sarah was asked the question again.

"How do you make people accept the barbies?" Mariana asked. "I could understand if it was just your employees. After all, it's a job, even if it's only paying in paper. It's still better than no job at all. But a day after you pay your workers, you can't find a barbie anywhere."

"Your Majesty, imagine you have two coins. They are both of gold, they are the same weight and purity. But one of them has a note on it that says if you keep it for a while, it will grow by a silver pfennig. There is something you want to buy that costs a gold coin. Which coin will you spend and which will you save?"

"I'll spend the one that won't grow a pfennig. But they aren't both gold. One of them is paper."

"No, Your Majesty. Both of them are paper," Sarah said. "One is backed by silver, and the other by the goods and services owned by BarbieCo, but both are paper, backed by perceived value and both have the same value marked on the front of the bill. So people save the barbies and spend the reich money."

"But they aren't spending the reich money. They are trading it in at the bank for silver."

"Yes. What happened with that?"

"A sneak thief we think." Mariana's expression was sour. "At least he's gone missing and quite a bit of silver is missing from one of the vaults. We discovered the situation because there was a crowd at the bank and Herr Lang panicked. What we don't understand is how the rumor got started that you said there wasn't enough silver in the bank to cover all the money."

"I have no idea. I've made no comments at all about the Royal Bank of Austria-Hungary. I've commented on the Bank of Grantville, the Federal Reserve Bank of the USE, the Royal Bank of Bohemia and the banks in Venice, Amsterdam, Paris, and Moscow. It's my field of expertise, but Gundaker von Liechtenstein won't talk to me about your bank. It's come up in a couple of depositions, but all I've ever said is that I don't know anything."

"Perhaps that's the problem . . . ?" Mariana tapped a finger on the table and Sarah noticed that she was wearing red nail polish. "Could someone have taken your silence to be hiding something?"

"I guess... but I don't know how they get from that to 'there isn't enough silver in the bank.'"

"I don't either. But however it happened, the run on the bank and the closure have left very little confidence in the reich money. We desperately need you to wave your magic wand and make our money good again."

Sarah blinked. There was no answer to that. Well, there was... but the answer was *I can't*... and Sarah couldn't say that. Not because she was scared of imperial retribution. No, what froze the words in Sarah's throat was the sudden realization that she had probably destroyed Austria-Hungary. That the presence of the BarbieCo money had exposed the weakness of the the reich money, and in exposing, magnified those weaknesses to the extent that it was likely that the reich money would not recover. Without any trusted money supply, the sputtering Austro-Hungarian economy would collapse entirely and depression would be the least of their problems. There would be blood in the streets of Vienna in months.

"Is it that bad?" Empress Mariana's face had gone a bit pale, apparently from seeing the expression on Sarah's.

Sarah wished she had Judy's poker face. "We need Judy!" it came out as almost a shout.

"What?"

"We need my sister Judy. The rest of the Barbies, too, especially Trudi. But most of all, we need my little sister Judy."

"But I thought you were the economist?"

"I am. But what we really have here is a perception problem. There are major economic aspects to it and economic constraints that will limit the options, but when it comes down to it... what we have is an image problem and Judy does image better than anyone I know." Sarah paused. "Please don't tell her I said that, Your Majesty. She'd never let me forget it."

Sarah saw Empress Mariana's mouth twitch up on the left side.

CHAPTER 32

You Ain't Got a Thing
If You Ain't Got that Zing

October 1635

The Hofburg Palace, Vienna

"Sarah has gone to fetch her sister Judy and the Barbies," Mariana told the emperor and the gathered nobility in the room.

"Why?"

"She says what we have is an image problem and I tend to agree."

"An image problem?"

"We have vaults full of silver, and no one trusts our money."

Heads turned as the movers and shakers of Austria-Hungary looked at each other.

"So why the sister?" asked Duke Leopold, and Mariana looked at him. His expression was even more sour than his tone had been. He continued. "From what I have heard her say, she has very little true understanding of economics or any of the other up-time sciences. She said she has no need to understand how airplanes work, she just hires one when she needs to go somewhere. She made similar comments about medicine, steam, internal combustion and, specifically, economics."

Mariana was actually fond of her brother-in-law, at least most of the time. Just at the moment, however, he was acting like a spoiled three-year-old. "According to Sarah, Judy understands the making and managing of image better than anyone Sarah has ever met. Considering that Sarah knows Mike Stearns, Gustav Adolf, Els Engel, not to mention Wallenstein, Pappenheim, the Roths and who knows who else, I think we must assume that that the young woman you chose to grope in public is the greatest expert on style in Christendom."

"Leo," Ferdinand said, "go to your apartments."

Leo looked shocked, but after a moment he stood stiffly, bowed to his brother and left the room.

Ferdinand watched him go, then looked around the room, his eyes resting for some time on Gundaker and Maximilian. "There will be no suggestion in this meeting that the young ladies who are coming here are peasants or even lesser nobility. Assume for the time that they are my sisters or cousins. If you can't do that, leave now."

Mariana knew that Ferdinand was not comfortable with the von Up-time rank and she realized that he was being as harsh as he was on the subject to counter his own doubts. She was more comfortable with the notion of von Up-time than he was, because she believed that God was talking to the world though the Ring of Fire. Pope Urban had not gone to the USE, but neither had he come to Austria-Hungary. Her faith had not had a strong anchor in Rome. Instead, there was the miracle of the Ring of Fire, and whatever the judgment of the clerics, she found herself clinging to that.

Fortney House, Race Track City

"So what's up at the palace?" Judy asked as Sarah hurried in the front door.

Sarah looked around at the curious faces. "Judy, Trudi, Susan, we need to talk."

A few minutes later, in Hayley's private office with the door closed, Sarah began. "How do we restore faith in the reich money?"

"Why do we want to?" Judy asked.

"Why do we need to?" Trudi asked at the same time.

"Because there aren't enough barbies to run Austria-Hungary," Sarah said.

"Well, we could print more barbies," Judy said.

"No. Liechtenstein Tower and all the other projects are still only a small fraction of the Austro-Hungarian economy. They're becoming a vital fraction but even that's more because of the perception rather than the percentage of GDP."

"Well, we could print barbies and buy reich money," Trudi suggested.

"No way," Susan said.

"So we turn around and buy silver with the reich money," Trudi said.

Susan shook her head. "No. We pay two percent a year on every barbie we issue and you know it. Besides, silver is going down against BarbieCo."

"But silver is going to go back up someday. Isn't it, Sarah?"

"Yes, some day. Probably starting in about ten years." Sarah shrugged. "The economy is going to grow much faster than silver stocks, but that's not the only factor. Right now, silver is a monetary metal that is losing its status. That decreases its value, producing a glut which decreases its value even more. Eventually, that will turn around, but not any time soon."

"There is no way we are blowing barbies on silver." Susan's voice was very firm.

"Okay, okay," Trudi said. "But then we need some way to prop up the reich money."

"No," Judy said. "That won't work. The reich money is dead. We killed it. Not on purpose, but we killed it."

Sarah looked at her sister in shock. Judy was looking as grim as Sarah had ever seen her. "Judy, there has to be an answer."

"I think I have an answer...but all the Barbies will have to agree." Susan took a deep breath. "And I do mean all the Barbies. Every investor in American Equipment Corp, here or back in the USE."

"What?"

"We have to sell the Austro-Hungarian Empire BarbieCo." Susan sounded sad.

"It won't work," Judy said. "It's us, the Barbies, that they have faith in. If we sell Ferdinand III BarbieCo, who will trust Barbies? No, just like before, we will have to have skin in the game and everyone will have to know it."

"We can accept payment in BarbieCo," Sarah said.

"Sarah, I don't want the Austrian economy to collapse, but that doesn't mean I'm willing to let Ferdinand III turn BarbieCo into waste paper and pay me in that same waste paper." Susan shook her head. "I won't do it."

"No. We will have to keep control," Judy said, "and not just for Susan, but for everyone. If the people out there are going to have faith in our money, then it's going to have to stay our money." Judy had an abstracted air as she spoke. "Trudi, would you go ask Hayley what's the fastest way to get a message to Grantville?"

"A steamboat up the Danube will reach Regensburg in three, maybe four, days. Then radio to Grantville." Trudi knew that answer.

"Fine. Go tell Hayley to order a boat. We are going to offer a buyout of BarbieCo stock at ten percent over face value in silver. And, Trudi, when you tell Hayley, make sure that there are servants in the room."

"No one is going to take ten percent," Susan said. "Not in silver, not in Grantville."

"I really don't care. We're offering it, so if they don't take it, it's their own look out."

"What are you planning?" Sarah asked Judy.

"I'll tell you once we get to the palace."

"No, I don't think so, Judy," Sarah said. "Tell me now."

"I haven't got it all worked out, Sarah." Judy grinned. "But basically, you . . . well, you and the Barbies . . . are going to become the national bank of the Austro-Hungarian empire."

As it happened, Trudi was in the process of stepping out the door when Judy said that.

In the living room, where Hayley and Dana Fortney, Gayleen and Ron Sanderlin were waiting—along with half a dozen servants, merchants, and shopkeepers—there was a sudden and profound silence.

"Hayley," Trudi said into that silence, "can you arrange the fastest boat possible to go up-river to Regensburg? We have some instructions for Heather Mason." Trudi paused and looked around the room with a little grin on her face. "Oh, and can someone run tell the royal yacht to get up a head of steam? We'll be going to the palace directly."

The Hofburg Palace, Vienna

The Barbies made an entrance. Sarah and Judy were in the lead, heads together, apparently arguing. "No," Judy said. "I think we should get Carinthia."

"I don't want Carinthia," Sarah responded. "I swear, Judy, you're getting downright medieval in your outlook. Besides, we're doing this to save the economy, not to make you and your gang even richer."

"I don't mind saving them, Sarah," Susan piped in from behind them, "but I expect to get paid."

The doors to the council room opened just as Susan said this, and the young women filed into the room, still talking about the empire of Austria-Hungary as though it was a gown they were considering buying.

Once the girls were all in the room, Judy looked around. "Where's the Ken Doll? We can't do this without him. He's going to have to agree."

Then she turned to the emperor and curtsied very low. She made it both respectful and graceful. "Your Majesty, you called and we are here." She looked around again. "I don't doubt the faith or discretion of your servants, Your Majesty, but even the most loyal and trusted retainer may make a slip. And there will, I suspect, be things discussed that you will not wish the world at large to know. So I beg your indulgence, that we might discuss these matters with only your closest advisers present?"

Ferdinand III had been ready to explode at the casual *lèse majesté* that the Barbies had displayed, and then that curtsey had stopped him. He looked at Judy Wendell von Up-time and found himself wondering how much of what he had just seen was theater. He looked around the room. It held more servants than advisers. Ferdinand made a gesture. Quickly, the servants left.

"So how much of that was real," he asked, "and how much pageant?"

"Is there a difference?" Judy said more than asked. "Perception affects reality, which in turn affects perception. Sarah will tell you that the value of money is the end of some formula, and no doubt she's right...as far as that goes. But you and I know that the value of anything is the same as royal authority. It's there if people think it's there. Right now, today, the value of BarbieCo stock is tied up with the rank of the Barbies." Judy waved at herself and the others. "You can destroy that with raw power, call in the guards, have us dragged out into the public square and executed. That will destroy the value of BarbieCo stock, and I don't doubt that some of your advisers have been advising you to do just that." She looked over at Gundaker. "But wiser heads have pointed out that destroying BarbieCo will not restore reich money. Some will see it as firm, but more will see it as desperate. So it will, on the whole, only weaken reich money still more."

"And," Vicky Emerson said, "it will offend your northern neighbors, making rapprochement and alliance more difficult. And leaving Austria-Hungary in much the position that Bavaria is in today. A worse position, actually. Bavaria has you between them and the Ottoman Empire whether you want to be or not. All you have is an open road."

"No one is contemplating execution!" Ferdinand III said truthfully.

"Well, that's good," Judy Wendell said. "With execution off the table, all the lesser punishments are even worse options. They will be seen as even more desperate, without the advantage of decisiveness. They will hurt the reich money worse than the BarbieCo. Lock us up, and people will hold onto their BarbieCo all the harder for their uncertainty."

"What do you suggest?"

"It's been said that the Habsburgs would rather wage marriage than war. What we need to do is wed the BarbieCo stock to the reich money, to produce one *trusted* money. And for that you need the Barbies to have the status that we can produce. Sarah will examine your economy and its prospective growth and tell us all how much money Austria-Hungary can have in circulation. Then, you and I together will figure out how to present it so that it will be trusted.

"The first step to that will be to make the production of that money completely independent of the..." There was a knock at the door.

"Come," said Ferdinand.

The door opened and Karl Eusebius came in. He bowed and said, "I got word I was needed."

"You did?"

"He's the Ken Doll," said Millicent.

"What, pray tell, is a Ken Doll?" Peter von Eisenberg asked.

"He stands around looking pretty and giving us money," said Vicky Emerson.

"I am told that that is the natural function of men, Your Majesty," Karl said with a slight smile.

"What a lovely notion," said the empress of Austria-Hungary. "I quite approve."

Ferdinand saw the expression on his wife's face and felt a bit uncomfortable.

"My wife had a similar attitude," Márton von Debrecen agreed. "But why the Ken Doll?"

"Well, you know that the Barbies were dolls made for little girls. There were several sorts of Barbies. Malibu Barbie, Princess Barbie, Doctor Barbie, Astronaut Barbie . . . but there was just the one Ken doll. This occurs because the Barbies do things. The Ken Dolls, however, stand around looking pretty and giving us money," Millicent explained.

Sarah groaned. "The dolls were designed for preteen girls, with a childish view of relationships. Which my little sister maintains, even though she should long since have outgrown it. In fact, Karl is a major investor in many of the projects of the Barbie Consortium and the largest single stockholder of common, ah, voting stock in BarbieCo. So if we are to make any changes, he will have to agree."

"So again, the prince of House Liechtenstein holds the purse strings of the Empire," said Márton von Debrecen. He didn't sound overly pleased.

They talked, sent for food, talked some more, rested, got up, and talked some more. All the while, Vienna waited, and a steam boat made its way up the Danube.

Grantville Stock Exchange

It came up on the ticker, just like all the trades. BCPP + 10% SLV A. The brokers on the floor could read it. BarbieCo Participating Preferred at ten percent over the face value in silver all comers. Anyone with BarbieCo PP could sell it. Ten haylies would bring you eleven Cologne marks of silver.

There was a rush, but it was a small one. It dried up almost before it began. By the end of the day, the Barbies had stabilized at forty-three American dollars to the judi, about eleven percent over the face value price. And the Barbies weren't trading at all. Everyone who had one was holding onto it.

Heather Mason wasn't on the floor. She had called in the offer to the Barbie Consortium's broker. When he called her back at the end of the day, it was to inform her glumly that he hadn't managed to get more than a few percent of the BarbieCo stock in Grantville.

"It's okay, Jacob," Heather said. "It was just Judy making sure that anyone who didn't want to play could get out with their skin intact."

"What's the game?"

"I'm not sure. All the radio message said was that they were going all in."

Heather heard Jacob swallow.

"Anyway," the radio operator in Grantville said to his friend, "the rumors in Regensburg are that the Barbies are buying Austria-Hungary."

"That's crazy."

"Yeah? What else is new?"

Over the next several days, the price of BarbieCo stock went up. Everyone who wanted out had gotten out that first day, and quite a few hearty souls decided that they wanted to gamble.

The Hofburg Palace, Vienna

The *Regensburg Weekly News* printed the stock quotes from Grantville and Magdeburg that they got over the radio. It took three days for the steam barge carrying the latest price for BarbieCo Preferred to reach Vienna.

When it did, Ferdinand and the Barbies were still in conference.

"No." Karl didn't say it loudly nor particularly belligerently, but he did say it firmly. "I know that Sarah doesn't care about rank. Prince or peasants, it's all the same to her. But, much as I love her, *I* am not Sarah. I was willing for it to be a morganatic marriage, given the circumstances that held sway. But the circumstances have changed. You need her. Both Judy and Moses have pointed out that giving Sarah imperial rank would help this work. Yet Gundaker insists that she not receive that rank till after the marriage, and that any issue from the marriage be excluded from the family inheritance. I won't have it.

"I will not consent to the merging of our stock into reich money unless Sarah is elevated now, and the marriage contract is adjusted to reflect her new rank as an imperial princess."

There were no up-timers in the room. It was just Emperor Ferdinand, Gundaker, Maximilian and Karl.

Gundaker was pale. "She's not Catholic."

"Which Catholic? Urban's or Borja's?" Karl countered. "If our children decide to become Protestant of some sort, then the issue of their faith may be raised. But for now we don't even have a single Catholic church."

"Very well, Karl. I'll bring up her elevation at the next general meeting. You're probably right that it will make things easier. Come to think of it, we might as well elevate her sister as well. What about the rest of the Barbies?"

"If you elevate any of them, Your Majesty, I recommend you elevate Trudi von Bachmerin. If you just elevate the up-timers, the up-timer Barbies will have a fit."

"By denomination, do you think?"

"No. The choice of denomination was almost random."

Ferdinand waved a hand. "Fine. We will make them all imperial princesses. It will simplify things. Considering the rest of this arrangement, they are going to be among the richest young women in the empire anyway."

Fortney House, Race Track City

"So, what's the latest word?" Annemarie Eberle asked Dana Fortney. After her failure to realize that Hayley Fortney was the money behind the SFIC and the raking over the coals that she had gotten from Janos Drugeth, Annemarie had taken to simply asking questions. It worked surprisingly well.

"I don't know. They have agreed to back the reich money, but they are still working out how it's going to work. Last I heard, the barbies are going to be gradually pulled from circulation, replaced with a new kind of barbie that doesn't provide interest but is legal tender for all debts in the Austro-Hungarian empire."

"What about people that already have barbies?"

"I don't know. I can't see Hayley letting them do anything unfair, though, so don't let it worry you."

"I heard at the beauty shop that the Barbies are buying up BarbieCo stock for ten percent more than the face value in silver. At least in Grantville. Do you think we'll be able to sell ours that way?"

"I would imagine so."

"Do you think I should?"

"How should I know, Annemarie? Do I look like Susan Logsden?"

Annemarie set out the coffee service and left. But the question didn't depart. It simply spread.

St. Stephen's Cathedral, Vienna

"I warned you," Father Lamormaini said, and took a certain satisfaction in Gundaker von Liechtenstein's clenched jaw. It was as much Liechtenstein's fault as anyone's. He should have been fighting against the marriage from the beginning, but his greed had blinded him to the threat. Just as Urban's greed for the up-timers' tools must have blinded him. The wisdom of Cardinal Borja—the new and legitimate pope, rather—was now obvious to any who were not blind.

"The question is what can be done about it."

"The infection must be burned out, root and branch." It was the first time Lamormaini had said that—even in his own mind—but as the words came out, he knew they were true. Ferdinand III had betrayed father, state, and church in his desire for transitory advantage. "The crown of the Holy Roman Empire must be wrested away from this unholy traitor to the faith, else the Holy Roman Empire will decay into permanent separate states. That was Satan's goal in bringing the Sphere of Fire. They weaken us and destroy the natural order so that Islam can conquer Europe and put an end to the true church, condemning all mankind to heresy and perdition. It will take planning, Prince Gundaker, planning and care. But it must be done, and God will understand."

"I have given oaths—"

"An oath to a heretic is no oath at all. Urban has fallen into heresy. He is followed into that heresy by the Father General of my own order and by Ferdinand III, and the royal house in Austria."

"Leopold?"

"I don't know, but can we risk it? The infant is too young to have been infected. Given a proper upbringing, Ferdinand IV will be the emperor. But in the meantime he will need a strong regent and the Liechtenstein family, once it too is cleansed of the infection, will make the perfect bulwark for the infant emperor." Lamormaini let his voice shift from reasonable to severe. "But to be made ready, House Liechtenstein must itself be purified. Karl Eusebius must be eliminated."

Lamormaini hid a smile. That was what Gundaker wanted now, most of all. Making it his duty, giving him the excuse, would make him accept the rest.

The Hofburg Palace, Vienna

The room still had the same expensive wallpaper and furniture, and each night the staff had cleaned. But it was midafternoon, and the tables were covered with papers and dishes of half-eaten food. Coffee, beer, and wine servers were out, and no one's finery was still in good repair... except Judy's.

There was a knock, and a servant came in with a note that was handed to Susan Logsden.

Susan read it and passed it to Judy, who passed it to Sarah, who passed it to Karl.

Karl read it.

> People are asking if the offer to buy BarbieCo for silver at 10% over face value in Grantville applies here? What do I say?
>
> Gayleen Sanderlin

Karl looked over at Susan and said, "I think we have to, don't we?"

"Yes. But in Grantville we can buy plenty of silver out of funds on hand. It will take a while to get the silver shipped, unless..."

Susan tuned to Moses. "Moses, how much can we borrow on BarbieCo assets in Grantville?"

"Excuse me, but what is in that message?" Gundaker asked.

Susan looked at Gundaker, but didn't say anything.

"It's a request for clarification, Uncle. When this all started, we sent Heather Mason instructions to buy up all the BarbieCo for silver at ten percent over face value."

"Why?" asked Ferdinand III.

"To give people an out in case things blew up in our face," Judy explained. "After we do that, those who don't take us up on the offer have no complaint if it doesn't work out."

"And the clarification?" Ferdinand III asked.

"Gayleen Sanderlin is getting questions about whether that offer extends to people holding BarbieCo here."

"And you feel you have to give them ten percent over the face value in silver?" Gundaker asked. "That's insane!"

"No, Prince von Liechtenstein," Sarah said. "That's why barbies are considered better than reich money."

"Let me get this straight. You are going to buy silver from my vaults, and pay it out at ten percent over the face value?"

"If we can borrow the reich money from Moses to do so, yes, Your Imperial Majesty," said Susan Logsden. "If not, we'll have to ship the silver in from Grantville." Susan shrugged. "It will take a week or so."

"Aren't you going to run out of money?" Ferdinand III asked.

"No," Sarah said. "Most people won't take the buyout. It could be as high as fifty percent, but what we are really doing is setting the base." She looked over at Moses. "Well?"

"One million reichsthaler. Will that be enough?"

Susan nodded, wrote out a note, which she handed to Judy. Judy read it, smiled, and handed it to Sarah, who handed it to Karl. Karl read.

> *Yes, we will buy. Take the barbies to the Abrabanel bank and get reich money, or wait a few days for silver. Make sure they understand that we won't be accepting silver for BarbieCo at that rate. That they will have to pay us more to get BarbieCo. In fact, for now, we are not going to be accepting any amount of silver for BarbieCo stock.*
> *Susan Logsden von Up-time*

Karl snorted a laugh.

"May I see it?" Emperor Ferdinand asked.

Karl didn't care, so he passed it over with a shrug.

Emperor read the note. He looked at Karl "This will work?"

"I'm betting my fortune that it will, yes, Your Imperial Majesty," Karl said formally.

The emperor looked at Karl, then he looked at Sarah. Then he looked at each of the young women. Then he bent to the desk and wrote three notes of his own. When he had finished with the notes he called for his seal.

He looked around the room again. "I have spent too much time on this as it is. Gustav Adolf is incapacitated and may die or be rendered unfit to rule. But Poland is still at war with the USE, and as long as that is the case we can get aid from neither of them. Murad is marching on Baghdad, which is well and good so far as it goes, but Janos Drugeth thinks he will then make peace with the Safavids and come at us. Maximilian of Bavaria will sit in his mountains and watch the world burn. My cousin in Spain is supporting Borja. My cousin in the Netherlands is supporting Urban. And Austria-Hungary is an edifice whose mortar is made of silver, and there is not enough of it to hold the edifice. The only nations in Christendom that are in any position to send us aid are ruled by usurpers."

The seal arrived and the emperor took it and stamped the three notes.

"May I see?" Karl asked. The emperor passed them over. The first was to the Imperial bank instructing them to accept BarbieCo at ten percent over face value in silver or paper reich money. The second was a note to Gayleen Sanderlin. Nothing special, it simply informed her that people who wanted to cash in their BarbieCo stock they could do so either at the Abrabanels or at the Imperial bank. The only interesting thing about it was that it had Ferdinand's signature and the imperial seal on it. The third . . .

The Barbie Consortium is hereby granted control over the issuing of money in the Austro-Hungarian Empire and responsibility for the valuation of all paper currency.
Ferdinand III, Emperor of Austria-Hungary

Karl felt his the blood draining from his face, and passed the note to Sarah, who passed it to Judy and the rest of the Barbies.

Ferdinand III turned to Count Peter von Eisenbach. "Make the deal." Then he stood up and left the room.

The last note, which was an Imperial proclamation and had the force of law, was passed around the room. After reading it, Uncle Gundaker got up and left.

After everyone in the room had seen the notes, messengers were called, and were sent off to the appropriate locations. Along with another note Susan Logsden sent to Race Track City, to go to all the merchants: *The Barbies are now in charge of the reich money, so it's good now.*

CHAPTER 33

𝕭uilding 𝕻lots

November 1635

Lichtenstein Tower Construction Site, Vienna

The work site at the Liechtenstein Tower was a happy place over the next few days. The royal proclamation that the Barbies were in charge of money in the empire meant that their pay was pretty much assured to be on time in the future. The same was true for the suppliers, so anything they needed that could be had was now available. The rotating kiln that would make massive amounts of concrete was still not operational, but hundreds of little ones, all up and down the Danube, were making up the lack, and the ball mill was busily turning clinker into powder. The basements were dug by the end of October and the workers were learning how to mix concrete under the guidance of Bob Sanderlin, a cheat sheet, and three doctors of natural philosophy from the University of Vienna.

Within a couple of weeks, the workers understood the process just fine and started pouring the basement walls. They also put up tents over the work sites to keep out the increasingly cold and wet weather.

The Hofburg Palace, Vienna

"I never asked to be made an imperial princess," Sarah Wendell said, putting down her coffee cup.

"I know, my love, but it's necessary," Karl said. "First, you must have a rank that the great of the empire will recognize, and most of them don't recognize von Up-time, not in any real sense."

"Besides," Judy added, "if you're not going to be an imperial princess, how do the rest of us get away with it?"

"Judy, you don't give a flying fig about being an imperial princess and you know it."

"Yes, I do," Judy said, then laughed. "Why, I've dreamed of being a princess since I got my princess Barbie when I was eight."

"Along with being an astronaut and a ballerina and..."

"Sure. But I don't see a lot of space shuttles looking for pilots, so why not a princess? I'll get myself a little tiara and wear it to fancy dress balls."

"And swearing an oath of loyalty to Ferdinand III?"

"It's a nonexclusive oath."

Which is true enough, Sarah thought. It turned out that there were all sorts of oaths of allegiance, and several of them were nonexclusive. You could be a noble in the Austro-Hungarian Empire, and in Bohemia, and a citizen of the USE, all at once, and the oath they would have to swear recognized that. Karl was a noble, sworn to King Albrecht of Bohemia and Emperor Ferdinand III of Austria-Hungary, and he wouldn't have to decide which side to fight on until one side or the other asked him to raise an army. Meanwhile, the deal that was shaping up would make Sarah and the Barbies—including Trudi—serene highnesses.

"Look, Sarah. We are in the seventeenth century and it's not just the nobility that has problems with nonnobles in positions of authority. President Stearns isn't the Prince of Germany because the nobles call him that, and Wettin won for a reason. Peasants as well as princes are uncomfortable with a lot of the CoC's rhetoric, and they are a lot more uncomfortable with it here than in the USE." Judy got up and walked around the table to squat next to Sarah's chair. "I know that a lot of people in Grantville are going to figure we've gone native, and for all I know they may be right. Some of them are going to be convinced that we have betrayed the principles of America. But I don't believe that. I think we can do more for those principles with Her Serene Highness in front of our names than we can without it. And I know if you're going to reform the money of this nation, you *need* the title."

"And what about our children? What if they don't want to

be serene highnesses? What if they want to be rodeo riders, or painters, or auto mechanics?"

"Then they can abdicate the title," Karl said, "and it will go to the next branch. In the meantime, we need to finalize the designs for the new reich money. I still think that it should look as much like BarbieCo as we can make it."

"I want members of the imperial house on the bills," Sarah said. "The empress and Cecilia Renata, if not Ferdinand III. However it happened, money with women's faces on it is more trusted here in the empire. But it doesn't have to stay just the Barbies."

And the negotiations continued.

An Inn in Vienna

It wasn't Gundaker's sort of place and even less Father Lamormaini's, but the third man at the table was quite at home here. Adorján Farkas was a squat man, with a scar on the right side of his face that went from his eyebrow to his beard. "I don't care. As long as I am paid in silver, not this paper that people use here."

"That won't be a problem," Gundaker said. And it wouldn't. Gundaker still had a key to the vaults, and in the last weeks there was more and more silver in the vaults as trust in the bank was restored. He would have to be careful because the security precautions at the bank had been strengthened ... but he was in charge of those procedures.

"We will need many men, and they will have to be dependable," Lamormaini said.

"What will they do?" Adorján Farkas scratched his graying beard,

"Each group will have a target," Gundaker explained. "And I don't want any group to know the other's targets. You will coordinate for us."

"I will need to know what they are to do."

Gundaker passed over a note. "Start with these names, but don't act. I'll have another list in a few days." The list Gundaker gave the man had the names of the Barbies and Sarah, but not Karl or the imperial family. "The timing will have to be precise. They will all have to be ..." Gundaker would not obfuscate. "Killed, and at the same time, else the death of one increase the security on the others. For now, have them watched and learn their habits."

Adorján Farkas finished his beer then, while going over the list. "It will be expensive, but you can afford it, right? And you'll want to wait till after the wedding, no doubt, so that your family inherits."

Gundaker felt dirty as he left the squalid tavern, but in a strange way also invigorated. He was committed now. There was no turning back...but then, there never really had been.

Leopold sat in his townhouse in Vienna and brooded. His brother had effectively endorsed Judy Wendell's position. She and all her Barbies were to be ennobled. Even Trudi von Bachmerin, the daughter of a minor imperial knight from the back of nowhere, would become Her Serene Highness Trudi von Bachmerin. Granted, a *Fürstenstand* was a considerably lower rank than *Erzherzog*, the rank Leo held. Leo felt his lips twitch. *Gundaker must be having a fit. Damn it, even their expressions are creeping in.* But it was true. The Barbies and, importantly, Sarah Wendell now held exactly the same rank that Gundaker, Maximilian and Karl Eusebius held. So all Gundaker's plans had crashed on the reef of Sarah's sudden elevation. He could at least take comfort in the fact that the Wendell girls were publicly humiliating more than just him.

He looked over at one wall where hung centerfolds and images from the up-time magazines *Playboy*, *Penthouse* and *Hustler*. They were carefully framed and had cost a pretty pfennig. He found himself wondering how Her Serene Highness Judy Wendell von Up-time would look posed as the April 1994 playboy centerfold was. Judy didn't look anything like the model, but something about the pose brought Judy to mind.

He called for more wine and Marco brought it.

Fortney House, Race Track City

"Why," Bob Sanderlin asked Brandon, "is a serene highness 'serene'?"

Hayley rolled her eyes and waited for the punch line.

Grinning, Brandon said, "I don't know, Uncle Bob. Why is a serene highness serene?"

"'Cause they ain't got nothing to do."

Brandon snickered. Ron shook his head in amusement and Gayleen Sanderlin gave her uncle by marriage a look. And Mom, the traitor, hid her smile behind a napkin.

Hayley groaned and, though it didn't sound it, the groan was complicated by the fact that it was starting to look like she wasn't going to be a serene highness after all. Just a highness. What Bob said was true. A serene highness didn't rule a principality. It was a court title, and most of the Barbies were going to be serene highness. But the way it was shaking out, Race Track City was going to become a postage-stamp-size principality, and one with Imperial Immediacy, meaning that the ruling prince—or in this case—princess, would have a vote in the imperial diet.

Since she was going to be the ruling princess, and she wasn't at all sure how her mom and dad and the Sanderlins were going to take the news—much less the citizens of Race Track City—serene was probably not the right word to describe her mood. "About that...you remember how the Barbies bought up our debt and traded it for a twenty percent share in SFIC?"

"Yes?" Gayleen said.

"What's wrong, Hayley?" Dana Fortney asked.

"Well, they didn't really want part ownership in Race Track City, and the emperor wants our status regularized. I tried for *burgrave*, but Judy's gone all political on us and wouldn't hear of it. So, for a whole bunch of barbies switched from my account in the reich bank to the accounts of other girls and the emperor... well...you see..." Then in a rush she blurted out, "Race Track City is going to be a principality and I am going to be the ruling princess. Or at least the reigning princess. We can work up a constitution so that the rights of the people here are protected, freedom of the press, freedom of assembly, the right to bear arms, the whole works."

There was silence for a bit and they could hear the people out on the street. It was a busy street.

Then Ron Sanderlin asked, "Isn't Race Track City a little small to be a principality?"

"Yes. According to Amadeus's dad, it's going to be the smallest principality in Austria-Hungary."

Suddenly Gayleen Sanderlin was laughing. Everyone looked at her and she said "Downtown Dallas," then went back to laughing.

Hayley was totally confused. She knew that Dallas was a city back up-time. She was even pretty sure it was in Texas and she knew it had had a really good football team, but that was about it.

"Gayleen," Ron Sanderlin said, "if you don't tell us what's so funny..." Mr. Sanderlin stuttered to a stop, apparently unable to come up with an adequate threat.

"It's an old joke," Gayleen said. "It seems that these three Texas ranchers were taking a jet back to Texas from somewhere. Well, being Texans, they were bragging about their spreads. 'I own the Circle W, fifteen thousand acres up near Brownsville.'

"'That's a right spread,' says the second rancher. 'Myself, I own the Bar X, thirty thousand acres up in the Panhandle.'" Hayley was surprised at how well Gayleen Sanderlin was doing the accents, but she was pretty much totally lost. Gayleen continued.

"'That's a fine spread, pardner. Fine indeed.' Then he turned to the third man and asked, 'What about you, pardner? How big is your spread?'

"'It's only a touch over ten acres,' the third Texan said.

"The other two began to wonder if the fellow had snuck into first class, but they were friendly and didn't want the man to feel bad, so the first rancher said, 'Well, a small place can be right nice. What do you call your spread?' The third rancher smiled a slow Texas smile and said, 'Downtown Dallas.'"

All the adults cracked up but Hayley looked at Brandon who shrugged his incomprehension.

As the adults settled down, Gayleen continued. "I sometimes think in strange ways, so I always wondered how the richest rancher on the plane had ended up owning downtown Dallas. I guess now we know." She looked over at Hayley, and seeing the confusion said, "You need to have a talk with Herr Doctor Faust about what he's teaching your kids, Dana. Hayley, Dallas was the biggest city in Texas...at least, I think it was. In any case, downtown Dallas was probably the most expensive real estate in Texas. Race Track City is actually bigger than Vienna, and we're building it using up-time tech from the outset. Most of the buildings don't have electricity, but all the ones that have been built since we got here are electric ready, plumbing ready, and natural gas ready. And even the ones that were already here, like our house and your place, have been retrofitted to handle them once we get them. So it's a safe bet that this place is going to be really valuable in the next few years, and by the time your heir inherits the title, he or she is going to be like the owner of downtown Dallas."

"That's, in essence, what Susan told Amadeus' dad while they were working out how to arrange things. You guys will have to agree, but let me tell you what Count Peter von Eisenberg suggested. First, Ferdinand III will be making you and Ron, as well as Mom and Dad, counts. And your place, and Mom and Dad's, will be tax exempt from local taxes. After that, it's your choice whether to take a buyout of the Sanderlin-Fortney Investment Company or to maintain your ownership in it. Considering what you just said, keep your share. The income will be considerable over the years. Brandon will inherit Mom and Dad's countship, and Bob is going to be getting an imperial knighthood, which will also make his place tax exempt. Ferdinand is keeping the race track itself, and the stands and the shops. I, or rather the SFIC, keep the water park, and all the land extending southeast at right angles from the end of the canal to where it connects up to the river. That gives us a bit over one and a half square miles. Then there are your places in Simmering, and if the residents of Simmering agree, the whole village of Simmering and its environs. But they have to agree."

"They will," Dana said. "You know perfectly well that the villagers in Simmering have been calling us all von Up-time since a week after your gang arrived. They will love it." Then Dana stopped and got a pensive look on her face. She reached over to the table and picked up a little silver bell and rang it.

Annemarie must have been waiting by the door considering how fast she arrived. "Annie, would you call Jack Pfeifer in? I think he's going to go down in history."

The maid blinked, then rushed from the room.

"What's up, Mom?" Hayley asked.

"Well, the principality is going to need a constitution. Who else are we going to get to write it?"

It didn't take long for the word to get around. It was barely evening before a delegation from Simmering arrived, requesting to be included in the new principality. Jack Pfeifer, not one to miss an opportunity, snagged the brewmaster of the Simmering brewery to be the Simmering representative to the constitutional convention. They based their constitution on two documents, the

New U.S. Constitution with the modifications involved in changing it to a state in the USE, and the Magdeburg Charter, on which the status of imperial cities was based. Jack wanted to give Hayley a major role in the government of the new principality, but Hayley was having none of it. It all sounded like a lot of work, and she had other things to do with her time, she told them, thinking about Amadeus.

Liechtenstein House, Vienna

Gundaker von Liechtenstein didn't react noticeably to the news that Hayley Fortney was going to be given that status he and his brothers had been working for their whole lives. That lack of rage bothered Karl. It made him nervous and troubled his thoughts. But there was a great deal going on. He had to get back to the Hofburg for the next round of meetings.

Sarah had left the negotiations to Karl, Judy, and Susan while she tried to figure out how much money to introduce to the Austro-Hungarian empire and how to do so. Karl thought she ought to use the money to buy back the patents that the empire had been selling since a few months after the Ring of Fire, but Sarah was thinking more in terms of low-interest loans to new businesses.

Karl said goodbye to his uncles and headed back to the palace.

"It does make sense," Maximilian von Liechtenstein told his younger brother.

"No doubt it does," Gundaker said. "Just one more perfectly logical betrayal of our family by the crown. We will be good little courtiers and kowtow to the daughter of a mechanic. I need some air. If you will excuse me, Maximilian." Gundaker rose and bowed stiffly to his brother and left.

Maximilian watched his brother go with the same itch of suspicion that, had he known it, his nephew had had. But his reasons for not paying attention to that itch were different. It wasn't that he didn't have time. No. Maximilian simply didn't want to know. Truth be told, he wasn't a lot happier about the situation than Gundaker was.

CHAPTER 34

Silver and Paper, Honor and Stone

November 1635

Silver Depository, Vienna

Gundaker sat in the small office, going over the books. The sun had set and he was working by one of the up-time-designed down-time-made Coleman lamps. This one was made right here in Vienna by a burgher who had bought the patent. The factory that made them had been redesigned by Peter Barclay, who had wisely accepted payment of an interest in the shop. None of which mattered to Gundaker at all. What mattered to him was that he had excellent light to cook the books, and make it look like Lang had stolen quite a bit more than he had. It wasn't all that hard. Change a couple of threes to eights, that sort of thing. Then the silver could wait in the vault till he needed it. There would be an audit after the new year, but by then he would have moved the money. Gundaker shivered from the cold and set back to work.

Streets of Vienna

The wagon made its way down the cobbled street, carrying a ton or so of gravel. It was before dawn and aside from supply wagons like this one, the streets were empty. But they were well lit. There was a Coleman lamp on each street corner, with enough fuel that each would last most of the night. Besides, the wagon had one too, with a curved mirror behind to send the light out ahead. The wagoner shivered in the cold, and flicked the reins to encourage the horse to pull a little harder. He wanted to get back to the docks so he could get inside. He turned a corner and headed for the work site for Liechtenstein Tower.

Reaching the tower, he pulled up behind another wagon, which carried a load of sand. He couldn't see the work under the tent, but he knew that the basement had been finished. They were now working on the ground floor, which was supported by a set of interconnecting arches that were based on the work of some up-timer who used chains to design buildings. It was funny looking but at the same time it had a sort of grace that was almost like a church.

The sand cart moved out and he flicked the reins again to move into its place. The crane, a set of pulleys and a framework, was shifted by a team of workers. The wagoner climbed back into the bed of the wagon and helped. He wanted to get back to the docks and in out of the cold. It took almost an hour to get the wagon unloaded, but the work kept him warm except for his hands and he had good canvas gloves. He would rather have been sleeping, but it was a good job...and even bad jobs were hard to come by.

Race Track City

Gayleen Sanderlin held Ron the Latest on her lap while the nanny, Lisa, kept a wary eye on three-and-a-half-year-old Carri. They were all in the imperial box, but it was still a cold snowy day. The crowds scared Ronny, but Carri was excited, all bundled up in her little fur coat and constantly trying to get a look at the two-year-old heir to the throne. Not because he was heir to the throne, but because he was a potential playmate.

Meanwhile, the sound system was playing records from the Magdeburg Opera House. The emperor was crazy for music. The stands were packed, even on a cold and blustery day like today, because once the music was over Ferdinand III would read out the agreement that the Austro-Hungarian crown had worked out with the Barbies over the course of the past several weeks. Her Serene Highness Sarah Wendell von Up-time was made the chair of the Imperial Bank and the right to issue money was moved to her and her heirs or appointees. The emperor had insisted on the heirs and Sarah had insisted on adding appointees. At the moment, Moses Abrabanel was the appointed heir to the chair of the imperial bank, which took Karl Eusebius off the hook.

The song ended. Sarah and the emperor went out onto a raised platform at one end of the race track, where Sarah knelt and received her tiara and bank book.

They went back to their seats, and Sarah sat down muttering dire imprecations about Judy and her overblown sense of theater. Personally, Gayleen thought it all looked rather splendid. From the applause, so did the audience.

Millicent then went out on the platform and got her crown and a gavel. She was going to set up the Vienna stock exchange.

Trudi von Bachmerin was next. This was all as new to Trudi as it was to any of them. This ceremony was as much the child of Judy the Barracudy's imagination as it was a product of the seventeenth century. Trudi got a bank book like Sarah's, but smaller and trimmed in silver, not gold. Her tiara was silver, with an amber stone in the front.

Gabrielle would have been next but she had declined the honor. Gabrielle wasn't interested in any title other than "doctor."

Vicky Emerson was next and she was a little stiff, which was a considerable improvement over her initial response to the idea of swearing an oath to a foreign potentate. Vicky was an *American*, not of the Club 250 sort. Bill Magen had been a down-timer, after all. But Vicky hadn't approved of the New U.S. joining the CPE, much less becoming a state in the USE. Márton was working on that and she swore her oath as required. Besides, the news out of the USE was starting to get scary. It looked like a civil war might be coming. Emperor Gustav Adolf's condition meant that Chancellor Oxenstierna was able to run wild.

Next came Judy, playing it for all it was worth. The tiaras had been made by Morris Roth in Prague and flown in. They had more in common with a beauty queen's crown than a down-time crown. Judy's was gold—well, electrum—and had a huge emerald in front. She really did look like a princess. She got a bank book, too.

Susan went up next and got her tiara and bank book. She didn't carry it off with Judy's grace, but she wasn't as stiff as Vicky had been.

Then Emperor Ferdinand called up Ron and her. She gave little

Ron to Lisa and took Ron's hand as they walked out onto the platform. At which point Carri abandoned her examination of the heir to the Austro-Hungarian throne and ran after them on her stubby little legs, only to be caught up short by Lisa. "I wanna go too!"

Little Ron, upset by the sudden movement or his sister's shout, started crying.

Ron grinned ruefully. "Well, so much for solemn state occasions."

Gayleen wanted to slug him. They walked on out to the platform and swore their oaths into the microphone and the emperor invested them as imperial counts. On their way back to the imperial box, Ron sneezed.

The Fortneys were counted too, then it was Hayley's turn. The whole morning standing out in a blizzard had been leading up to this. First, the emperor read out the agreement making Race Track City an imperial principality. Then Hayley read out the constitution, which included a bill of rights right in it, and called on the assembled people to accept or reject it. There was a great shout of acceptance from the audience. After which the emperor went down and got into the 240Z and the newest princess went down and got into the Sonny Steamer. Gayleen, Ron, and the kids got into their truck and the Fortneys into their Range Rover, and all of them, in a parade, drove the bounds of the new principality.

Liechtenstein House, Vienna

Of course, they all caught colds. Emperor and empress, all the way down to scullery maids, everyone caught a cold. The Hofburg Palace and Race Track City were as drippy as leaky faucets, and it spread to just about every noble house in Vienna.

"If you indend that we get married in duh streed, I will no—*Aaahhchooo!*—be adending," Sarah told Karl.

Karl, eyes puffy and long nose red as a beet, just looked at her. Anna, outside the room, blew her nose loudly and then brought in a silver service with tea, lemon, and honey.

"*Dno.*" Judy was, for once looking just as raggedy as any normal human, agreed. "Ub-time we did weddings id church. 'Id' being duh impordand poind."

"Dere are a couple of reasons we can—*Aaahhchooo!*—cannod do id dat way. De most impordant is that id's looking like St.

Stephen's is leaning toward Borja—*sniff*—and if we give Anton Wolfradt an excuse, he's likely do make an issue of id."

"Wad aboud cidy hall?" Sarah sniffed, and it hurt.

"Don god one," Karl said.

"Din you to can jusd wade dill da dower—*Aaahhchooo!*—tower is finished."

Karl sneezed again, then held his head like he was trying to keep his brain from falling out. But after a minute, he said, "Wade a minid. We can pud the roov on de first do floors, radder din wade."

Sarah tried to think through the pain. The first two floors of the Liechtenstein Tower were two stories of shops surrounding a large mezzanine. The third floor was planned to cover over the mezzanine, to act as support for the higher floors. The first floor and about half of the second was done. If they put in the floor of the third floor before extending it, they could have a functional roof over the center area in a month. "Id's gonna be darg, dark."

"No. God in the generader. We can have elecdric lighds and steam heed."

A week later, with Vienna mostly recovered, the new order for construction on Liechtenstein Tower was given. They would focus on getting a temporary roof over the central mezzanine and stringing lights. The next priority was the pipes to take the steam to the first two floors.

The emperor was pleased with the arrangement, and wanted to see the tower in operation, even if only limited. After all, once it was finished, the Liechtenstein Tower was to become the Imperial Tower. Part of the deal that left the honking huge bank accounts in the Barbies' names in the imperial bank was that Liechtenstein Tower was to be completed by the Barbies and then transferred to the emperor.

Tavern in Vienna

Gundaker and Adorján Farkas were in the same chairs as before. The Hungarian mercenary wasn't happy.

"You agreed to pay my people." His face was flushed, bringing his scar into sharp contrast.

"That was when they were going to be doing the job," Gundaker hissed. "I don't pay for what I'm not buying."

"You're the one changing plans, not us."

"Circumstances have changed."

"What circumstances?"

"None of your business," Gundaker said. "I've paid you and your people for your efforts up to now. I don't owe you any more money, nor any explanation."

There was an expression on Farkas' face and Gundaker waited for the threat. But the threat didn't come, and after a minute Gundaker nodded sharply. So Farkas knew enough to realize that a man of his station didn't threaten a man of Gundaker's, ever, under any circumstances. He gave one more sharp nod, got up and left.

If he had thought it through, he still wouldn't have realized that Farkas was a man unimpressed with rank and as willing to kill a king as anyone else. Gundaker didn't think that way. And the Barbies weren't real nobility, so didn't count. He didn't see the expression on Farkas' face as he left. Besides, Gundaker had his mind on other things. He needed to figure out where to get several hundred pounds of gunpowder, and a good excuse for not attending his nephew's wedding.

With hatred in his heart, Adorján Farkas watched the man go. He had been used by nobles to do their dirty work from the time he was a boy. He hated them all with a kind of cold passion that made people like Melissa Mailey seem models of conciliation. But he was a practical man, who believed in very little. Certainly not the twaddle of wild-eyed idiots like the Committees of Correspondence. He drank his beer and tried to figure away to get some of his own back from Gundaker von Liechtenstein. Then he got up and went to give the bad news to the boys. They had been following the Barbies around for weeks now, learning their patterns. Maybe something could be done with that.

"No, Captain. They are too well guarded. And they are armed. All of them. You know the shooting range at Race Track City? I have seen them all shooting. Mostly they are not that good. Not bad, but not really skilled. However, they all carry guns. Every one of them. And all the guns are the up-time style that shoot several shots. I wouldn't want to try for them without a dozen men. Even then, we would likely just end up with a body, not a hostage."

It wasn't news. That was consistent with all the reports. Even the one who wanted to be a doctor carried a gun and trained with it at least once a week. And they were all accompanied by guards everywhere they went. It was hard enough to get close enough just to watch them.

"Fine then. But keep watching them. We may get lucky and I want Fredrich on His Serene Highness Gundaker von Liechtenstein."

"Good enough, Captain. But remember, we aren't getting paid. If we don't get lucky soon, we're going to run out of money."

"I know," Adorján agreed with his long-time friend. "I know."

Word rapidly spread through the men of Adorján's company, and disappointment bred sloppiness, as it so often does.

Water Park, Race Track City

"I like ice skating," Her Serene Highness Trudi von Bachmerin said, as she leaned back into Jack Pfeifer's embrace. Jack liked ice skating too, especially if it caused Trudi to lean into him like this. He just wasn't sure what to do next. Everything had been going along swimmingly, till the emperor had gone and made Trudi an imperial princess. His parents had approved of the match. She was wealthy, and the daughter of an imperial knight was a step up for the family, but not an unreasonable step. A serene highness was a completely different matter.

"Trudi, ah, Your Ser—"

"I'm still Trudi, Jack. And I'll always be Trudi. To you, at any rate."

"But you—"

"Yes, I know. But I spent the last several years in Grantville. The difference in our rank doesn't really bother me. The bigger issue is the difference in our bank accounts. How are you going to deal with that?"

"What do you mean?"

"I am probably the poorest of the Barbies. I had the least to invest from the beginning, and haven't been able to afford to get in on all the deals. But BarbieCo was sort of my idea, so I got a bigger share than the money I had would have justified. When the empire bought BarbieCo...what it amounts to is, I'm now as rich as Judy Wendell was before the BarbieCo deal. How are you going to deal with that?"

Jack just looked blank.

"I mean, how are you going to deal with me being richer than you?"

"It doesn't bother me."

"Really? Vienna doesn't need seven imperial banks. Susan is probably going to be staying in Vienna with Moses. So that means if I'm going to set up a bank, I'm going to have to do it somewhere else. Maybe back in Grantville, maybe Magdeburg, Venice, or Amsterdam I'm not sure where yet, but not Vienna. That would mean you'd have to move. How would you feel following me around?"

That was something Jack hadn't thought about. He looked around, and as he did he saw a man and something about the man caught his attention. He'd seen him before recently. "I wouldn't mind. I know a law professor who would be better qualified to manage the legal requirements of SFIC and the new principality than I am. You'd give me a job, wouldn't you?" He asked trying to sound winsome. "After I finished my law studies?"

They turned and headed for the open-air refreshment area at the side of the skating rink. As they did, Jack saw that same man again. He shifted Trudi in his arms, and the man turned away. When he turned, Jack saw a patch on the back right shoulder of his cloak. That was it. He had seen the man earlier that morning across the street from the Fortney house. For that matter, he had seen him before that, but he wasn't sure where.

It wasn't that patched cloaks were unusual. Patches were the rule, not the exception, all over Europe. This one was a faded red, and Jack remembered it. He seated Trudi and kissed her gloved hand. "I'll be back in a minute, okay?" She nodded and he walked over to Felix, one of the guardsmen, and quietly pointed the man out. "Let me know what you find out, Felix? Something about him bothers me."

"He's a mercenary, Herr Pfeifer," Felix said. "I know the look."

"But who's he working for and what's his interest in Princess Trudi?"

"I'll find out," the guardsman told him. Then Jack went back to Trudi.

"What was that about?" Trudi asked.

"Maybe nothing." Jack said. "I saw a man that I recognized. He's been hanging around and I don't know why. Likely he has a perfectly legitimate reason and it's all just a coincidence."

Trudi pulled out her compact and examined her makeup while she said, "Where is he?"

Jack told her and she adjusted the mirror so she could see the man. One thing Jack really liked about Her Serene Highness was how quick on the uptake she was.

"Yes. I think I've seen him around too. Three days ago when I was at the beauty shop, he was across the street. I remember the patch on his jacket."

"Well, Felix knows about him now. We should get a report."

"Good enough. What were we talking about before you went all paranoid?"

"Susan Logsden and Moses Abrabanel."

"He finally introduced her to his baby daughter and his family, you know."

"No, I didn't. How did it go?"

"Quite well. You know that each of us gets to set the rules for how our families handle differences in rank. Not completely. Susan can't make Moses an imperial prince by marrying him, but any kids they have will be imperial princesses or princes, and if she adopts his little girl, she will become one, too.

"Apparently, when Moses' mother found that out, she suddenly decided that, gentile or not, it was time for Moses to get married again. The thing is, Susan isn't used to being on that side of the social equation. She was looked down on in Grantville, even after she got rich, because of her mother." Trudi giggled. "Having people thinking of her as Her Serene Highness is freaking her out a bit, but I think she likes it. But you know that wasn't what we were talking about. We were talking about the fact that I will be moving after the wedding. The only question is where will I go."

"It's fine, Trudi. I will follow you." Jack reached over and touched her cheek. "I'll follow you wherever you go. I doubt you will be setting up your branch of the Imperial Bank of Austria-Hungary in a village that doesn't have a law school. And with the change in my family fortunes, I will be able to finish my schooling. Besides, I have been involved in the writing of a constitution, so I can probably get a place on the faculty of a law school at this point."

Trudi covered his hand with her own, pressing his palm against her cheek. "You really will?"

Jack nodded his agreement. "I can be replaced here."

"That's right. You said you have a law professor who can take over for you. Why is that?"

"Partly, it's a good job. But also because, in this principality, there is freedom of faith in the constitution. Doctor of Jurisprudence

Aigner is a Catholic only because you have to be Catholic to hold that position in the University of Vienna. I expect that Lutheran and Calvinist groups will be applying to Princess Hayley for permission to set up churches."

The waitress brought them hot chocolate and strudels, curtsying after she placed it on the table.

"Good," Trudi said, once the waitress was gone. "The churches, I mean."

"I'm not so sure. There are a lot of people who are upset about the freedom of faith in the principality constitution. They are going to be even less happy."

"As it happens, I'm Catholic. But I became one after the Ring of Fire, because of Father Mazzare. My father is Lutheran, and my brothers fought for Gustav. I would be the last person to try to force anyone to change their faith."

"I don't object," Jack said, which was almost true. "I'm the one who put the clause in the constitution, after all. I'm just worried about the political fallout. Hayley and her family were pushing things pretty hard even before the rest of the Barbies got here. And since then—" Jack shook his head at a loss for words. "There's going to be a reaction. Just like there has been in the USE."

Trudi shivered and Jack wanted to scoot around the table and hold her protectively, but they were in public and it was still early in their relationship.

Guard Station, Race Track City

"I know him, at least by reputation. He's one of Adorján Farkas' men."

"What would one of Farkas' men be doing at the water park?" Captain Erwin von Friesen, the newly made chief constable of the Race Track City principality, scratched his graying hair. "That's not the sort of entertainment that Farkas' men usually prefer. Put out a list of all his troop. I want them watched for."

"Herr Pfeifer asked me to tell him what we learned." Felix said.

"I'll have a talk with Jack," Captain von Friesen said.

Jack Pfeifer's Office, Race Track City

"Welcome, Captain. Or should I call you Constable?"

"Just don't call me late for dinner," Erwin said, and Jack felt himself smile.

"So what brings you here? You need a warrant?"

"I might. I'm still not sure how that part is supposed to work," Erwin said.

"And even less sure you approve of it, I would imagine," Jack agreed. "The best I can tell, those laws are designed to make it difficult for the police to do their jobs. But Her Highness insisted."

"The reason I came by is one of my men recognized the description Felix gave of the man you saw watching Princess Trudi."

"Who is he?"

"I don't have his name yet, but he works for a man named Adorján Farkas. Farkas runs a smallish mercenary company and they take odd jobs between campaigns. His bunch and others like them are why a lot of people find it hard to distinguish between soldiers and criminals. I will say that Farkas has his own sort of honor. He does what he's paid to do. But if you have the money, he will do just about anything."

"Thank you, Captain," Jack said. "What do you think we should do?"

"Not that much we can do with the constitution. A year ago I probably would have dragged the man with the cloak in and beaten him till he told me what he was doing. Now?" He shrugged, indicating that he wasn't sure.

Jack felt real regret, but he shook his head. "I've talked to the Fortneys and the Sanderlins enough to know that Princess Hayley wouldn't stand for anything like that. Look, get me descriptions of the rest of—what was his name, Farkas?"

Erwin nodded.

"Farkas and his men. I'll give them to Moses, Amadeus, Márton, and Prince Karl. Perhaps one of them will have a suggestion. And I'll tell Hertel about them, too. He has a good eye for detail and might have some ideas. Meanwhile, just keep your eyes open for them."

Márton von Debrecen's Townhouse, Vienna

Over the next few days, several of Adorján Farkas' men were spotted in places where they could observe the Barbies or Sarah. Those sightings led the gentlemen to have chats with the Barbies on the subject of direct action and law.

"No, Márton," Her Serene Highness Vicky Emerson von Up-time said seriously. "Bill talked about this a lot. Not all the down-time cops liked the up-time laws protecting citizens' rights, but a lot of them did. Mostly the ones like Bill, who had seen the results of their lack. I don't care how noble you are, if there aren't any laws like that on the books, it ends up bad. Mostly, people like you and me are protected by our wealth. And now rank, I guess," she added with a grimace. "But everyday people? Before you know it, every shop owner is being shaken down."

Márton listened politely, but he wasn't convinced. "But I am not a police officer. I have no judicial position at all. If I were to hire some people to go have a chat with this Adorján Farkas, how would that be a violation of his rights? Twice in the past four days, I have seen members of his troop watching you. I respect your beliefs, but I will not stand idly by while what happened to Polyxena happens to you. I can't!"

Vicky looked at him and he could see her weighing her words. "Just go ahead and say it," he told her.

"What happened to Polyxena was *perfectly legal* and an excellent example of why those protections were instituted in later centuries. Maximilian had a suspicion and he was the duke, so he wasn't required to prove it—at least not with the rigor that should have been required of him. If Bavaria had had a constitution like Race Track City's, Polyxena would never have been executed. She would have had a lawyer and there would have been a court and rules of evidence. What you're proposing is just the strong brutalizing the weak. Your strength, in this case, is hired—but that doesn't change what it is."

"What about whoever hired Farkas? Are they to be allowed..."

Vicky reached out and took his hands. He felt the strength in her hand and wrist that allowed her to use her pistol with such speed and accuracy. She squeezed hard. "Let me tell you something that Bill told me. He got it from Dan Frost. 'The difference between the good guys and the bad guys isn't who's wearing the badge.'"

Apparently she saw his confusion, because she explained. "The difference between the good guys and the bad guys is not who has the title or the legal right. It's not even entirely what you're fighting for, because every despot in the history of the world has been convinced that he was on the side of right. The way you tell the good guys from the bad guys is by how well they follow their own rules."

"If you say so." Márton was still unconvinced.

"I know that sort of restraint is hard and, truthfully, most of the time I want to just go ahead, kick ass, and sort it out later," Vicky said. "In fact, Bill and I argued about it all the time. After he got killed I pretty much gave up on the idea of civil rights for assholes. You want to know what changed my mind?"

"What?" Márton asked.

"Your Polyxena. You're convinced that she was innocent. Amadeus is convinced that she was innocent. And even if she'd been guilty, execution is totally off the wall for helping someone duck out on a wedding. But what happened to her was all perfectly legal, and things like that happen all over the world, all the time. But they don't happen in Grantville. You don't need to worry about the cops busting in your door because someone next to the mayor or the president is pissed or wants something you own. What happened to Polyxena and what it did to you is what convinced me that we must be ruled by laws, not the whims of the powerful."

Márton looked into those eyes glowing with conviction and wanted to believe. He even agreed that that was the sort of world there ought to be. But it wasn't the world they lived in. So, instead of agreeing or continuing to argue, he simply lifted her hands to his lips and kissed them.

CHAPTER 35

𝕿𝖍𝖊 𝕾𝖊𝖈𝖗𝖊𝖙 𝕬𝖚𝖘𝖙𝖗𝖎𝖆𝖓 𝕲𝖔𝖔𝖉 𝕲𝖚𝖞𝖘

December 1635

Márton von Debrecen's Townhouse, Vienna

"Our young ladies have very noble beliefs, but they are not alto-gether practical," Amadeus complained to Márton.

"Their up-time world must have been populated by saints," Márton agreed. "Vicky gave me chapter and verse on the rights of the accused."

"We need to talk to Jack Pfeifer, you think?"

"Do you think we can trust him not to go running to Princess Hayley? He's her lawyer, when all is said and done."

"I think he'll respect our privacy. And I think that he can give us some practical limits. The thing is, Márton, I would prefer to stay as close to Hayley's rules as we can. There is something that is just right about them. I'm not quite sure what, but something."

"Me, too." Márton agreed. "While we're at it, though, we should have a talk with Dr. Faust and Moses Abrabanel. And what about your friends, Rudolph and Julian?"

"Not Rudolph. He's a good and honest man, but he doesn't think before he speaks. As for Julian...he's more circumspect, but Carla is the only von Up-time who didn't get offered noble rank, and Julian's parents are..."

Márton waved off the explanation. He knew about the von

340

Meklau family, and was sure that, within just a few more generations, they would accept fire as a useful tool.

"On the other hand, Julian is always up for intrigue," Amadeus stopped. "You know who we really need to involve in this?"

"Who?"

"Hayley's father."

"He's an up-timer and likely to have the same prejudices as his daughter."

"Father says that Janos Drugeth says that he's probably a spy for Francisco Nasi."

"Is he in town?"

"No. He's back along the rail line, negotiating rights-of-way and surveying routes. But he's expected back at the end of the week."

"Fine. In the meantime, I am going to go talk with Moses Abrabanel and Jakusch Pfeifer, and I want you to go have a chat with Dr Faust. Maybe the up-timers have some kind of magic technology to help them arrest criminals and Dr. Faust knows about it."

Fortney House, Race Track City

"In a way they do," Hertel Faust said. "They have what they call forensic science, which is a way of gathering evidence from the scraps and tiny bits people leave behind. Some of them we can do, and some we can't. Brandon and I put together fingerprint kits last winter, and the barber surgeons at the water park hospital have learned to type blood."

"What good does that do?"

"It can narrow down the number of your suspects." Dr. Faust went over to a bookshelf that was too full by any reasonable standard. "I have a subscription to the Mystery of the Month book club." Dr. Faust blushed a little. "Also the Romance of the Month book club and Science Fiction and Fantasy of the Month book club and Cheat Sheet Compilation book club." Dr. Faust pulled a book from the shelf. "*Dr. Quincy, M.E.* This is a story about a medical examiner who helps the police solve crimes by examining the bodies of murder victims. He can determine who killed them by the marks left by the weapons on the bodies of the victims."

Amadeus looked at Dr. Faust skeptically.

"Frau Fortney says that it's fiction and only loosely based on actual up-time forensic techniques. But it's fun to read about and I have done some of the things in the book to see if they work and they do, at least sort of."

"What sort of things?" Amadeus was curious in spite of himself.

"Blood spatter, for instance. When a pig is stabbed, you get one kind of blood spatter. When it's shot, you get another. And you can tell things about where the shooter was standing from where the blood spattered."

Suddenly Amadeus was less curious. "That's all very interesting, Herr Doctor, but we're trying to find out what's going on before—for instance, Gabrielle—is harmed."

"Oh, yes. Quite right." Faust scratched his head. "None of these seem to focus on determining what someone is up to before they do it. I will see what I can find, though."

Moses Abrabanel's Office, outside Vienna

"Honestly, I've been sort of expecting some type of reaction like this for months," Moses Abrabanel said. "The changes are frightening and the up-timers are the center of them. While it was just Race Track City, the complaints were political and because the emperor liked his car, no one wanted to push their objections to extremes. Now, though, it seems that the Barbies are intent on subverting the social order."

"Do you really think that?" Márton asked.

Moses put his hands to his forehead and rubbed his face for a moment. "Yes, in a way I do. But I'm not sure the Barbies are wrong. I think a world without pogroms would be an improvement."

Márton closed his eyes for a moment. Moses certainly had a point, at least if you were a Jew. "My concern is that someone is going to try to kill the Barbies."

"They have guards and they are armed," Moses offered.

"And someone is having them watched. I want it stopped before the attack."

"Then have your people pick up one of the mercenaries." Moses shrugged. "I'm not going to tell Susan about it, and I'm not going to object."

A Tavern in Vienna

Adorján Farkas felt an itch between his shoulders. It wasn't the first time he'd had such an itch and he had learned to pay attention to them. Someone was after him. He could feel it. He looked over his shoulder and hid every time he turned a corner. Normally he drank in the common room, but he'd paid extra for an alcove because of his itch. When he saw the guardsmen entering the tavern, he slipped out the back before they saw him. There was a guard out back, but he wasn't really expecting Farkas. The moment Farkas saw the guard, he attacked.

He jumped forward, pulling his knife as he moved, and shoved it into the guardsman's belly. The guard screamed like a girl, but Farkas didn't really care about that. All he'd been interested in was getting past the man. He ran out into the street, bloody knife in hand, to the accompaniment of more screams, and ran. For three blocks and two alleys, he was followed. Then he found a place to hide. It was a soldier's shack near the city wall and unoccupied at the moment. Farkas waited half an hour, then left the shack, wearing the clothing of the soldier. It didn't fit, but it was a different color than his own clothing, and the hat was a different style.

He wasn't sure what had gone wrong, but with the probably dead guard, he couldn't afford to hang around to find out.

That night, Farkas was on a barge going downriver.

Basement, von Debrecen Townhouse, Vienna

"I didn't do anything!" whined Rácz.

"You were watching Princess Millicent Anne Barnes von Uptime, and you work for Adorján Farkas."

"I wasn't watching anyone and what business of yours is who I work for?"

Johannes hit him. Rácz was tied to a chair, but Johannes didn't care. Erwin was in the hospital out at Race Track City and probably going to die, because this fuck's boss had wanted a clear way to run.

Rácz spit blood and a tooth, then tried to pull loose. It didn't work and Johannes smiled. Then he got himself a little under control.

"Your boss cut up a friend of mine when he ran for it. So I want him in that chair and I want to take my time with him. But until I get him, I'll make do with you. In the meantime, do me a favor and lie to us. Because every time you do, I get to hit you."

Rácz looked at Johanne's face, then at his hand, then back at his face. "Look, I don't know anything about that. I don't tell the captain what to do."

"What did Farkas tell you to do?"

"Just watch."

Johannes hit him again.

Two Nights Later

"We caught three," said the commander of Márton von Debrecen's guard. "The rest got away."

"Why so few?"

"We didn't have the men to go after them all at once. And Farkas made quite a scene when he ran. That warned the others. The men we got were mostly far enough away so that they didn't hear about it before we found them."

"Did they know anything?"

"Not much. At least not individually. When we put it all together with the help of Herr Pfeifer and his clerks, we ended up with a bit more than I was expecting.

"Farkas was hired by some noble to kill the Barbies, but not until after the wedding. We are assuming that they meant the wedding of Prince Karl Eusebius von Liechtenstein and Princess Sarah Wendell von Up-time. And then, a week or so ago, the contract got canceled."

"Then what were they doing, still watching the women?"

"Apparently, Farkas wasn't happy with the cancelled contract, so he was looking for some other profit to gain from the observation. A kidnapping, perhaps. None of the men we caught actually know. What we do know is that they lost the contract after the Barbies got ennobled."

"That doesn't make sense."

"If someone was offended by the Barbies and felt that having peasants killed, but not nobles..."

"You're talking about Archduke Leopold!"

"Not necessarily," the captain said, but Márton could hear in the man's voice that he did think it was the archduke. "It could have been someone in the They of Vienna who decided to back off after the Barbies got ennobled."

"That doesn't make much sense, either. We knew they were going to be ennobled before they were, but the contract didn't get called off till after the ceremony. Correct?"

"Yes, My Lord Count."

"I'd suspect one of the Liechtensteins, but I don't see them backing off just because Ferdinand III hung a title on the girls. In fact, with Gundaker, the title would just make him more angry." Márton shook his head. "None of this makes sense."

Liechtenstein House, Vienna

Gundaker von Liechtenstein almost canceled his plans when he heard about Farkas. After considering the matter, however, he decided that he was too far in to get out, save on the other side. He did hire a mercenary to bring him Farkas' head. He wanted Farkas dead because the man could answer questions that Gundaker didn't want answered, but at the same time he had a perfectly good excuse for wanting the man dead, in that the Barbies, two of them, were about to become family. It was almost his duty to kill their attacker, whether the attack had actually happened or not.

He rang the bell and had the steward bring in some of the carbonated wine. Then he went back to his paperwork and to his thoughts. Farkas had been a mistake . . . and possibly Lamormaini as well.

No, he decided. At least for now, he wouldn't have Lamormaini killed. *Too much risk for not enough gain.* Besides, Lamormaini and the Spanish-leaning Jesuits were just the cats' paws he needed. What was the up-time term? A cutout. The thing about a cutout was that it eventually had to be cut out. After the bomb had gone off. At that point, Lamormaini would be nothing but a liability. He would make arrangements.

He got up and went to see Karl Eusebius.

"What can I do for you, Uncle?" Karl looked up in surprise as his uncle came in. Uncle Gundaker hadn't been in any hurry to talk to him for over a month now.

"For now, we still own the Liechtenstein Tower?"

"Yes. The imperial government won't get it till mid-January."

"What about contracts for long-term storage?"

"What do you mean?"

"You know that the cost of storage is still quite high, in spite of the new warehouses planned for Race Track City?"

"Yes, I know." Karl nodded.

"I want to rent one of the basement rooms in the Tower for the next four or five months, till they finish those warehouses. I have acquired a large consignment of apples for a specialty wine. But I need a place to store them that is dry, cool, and secure. And not too expensive."

"Yes, there is a grandfather clause in the transfer because we had already sold some apartments. But we're talking about prime real estate. Are you sure you want to store barrels of apples in that?"

"Only if I can get a good deal."

Karl didn't push the price very hard. This was the first sign of rapprochement he had gotten from Gundaker.

Debrecen House, Vienna

Jack Pfeifer looked around the room. Márton and Amadeus were at one end of the table, and Sonny Fortney at the other. Jack, Hertel Faust, and Carla Barclay were arranged along the sides. They had all been seated and they all had drinks. There were snacks on the table. Something the up-timers called donuts. Márton had just asked Sonny about the laws against forcing people to give evidence against themselves.

"The girls are right, you know, as far as the laws are concerned," Sonny Fortney told the group. "There's a reason Moses didn't get into the Promised Land."

Moses Abrabanel looked over at Sonny Fortney in surprise. "And what reason is that?"

"Because sometimes, when your job is leading your people out of bondage, you have to cheat a bit. After all, Moses is the guy who called down the plagues on Egypt."

"God delivered the plagues," Moses said.

"Yep, that's true. But the point is that calling them down had an effect on Moses. Sometimes there are not any good answers and someone has to do something iffy—or even downright evil. It's never something to be proud of, and there is a moral cost. Also, if you do it enough, you end up one of the bad guys, no matter how noble your motives."

"What about spying?" asked Amadeus.

Sonny Fortney looked over at Amadeus like he had no clue what he was talking about. Then he gave a twitch of a shrug. "Yes, that would be one of the things that leaves a mark on the soul. You're making friends with people with the full intent to betray them as necessary for your cause."

"What sort of a cause would justify that sort of betrayal?" Amadeus wondered aloud.

"I'm not sure 'justify' is the right word. Necessitate, maybe. 'We hold these truths to be self evident, that all men are created equal and endowed by their creator with certain inalienable rights. That among these are life, liberty, and the pursuit of happiness.' There's also a moral cost to standing around doing nothing while those rights are being denied to your fellow men. Like I said, sometimes there are no good answers, just a choice between evils. The scary bit is how easy it is to convince yourself that those necessary evils aren't evil because they're necessary."

There was something in the up-timer's face and voice that Jack couldn't quite identify. A hardness...or a tiredness.

"Then what do you think we should do?" asked Carla Barclay.

"Break the law," Sonny said. "But don't kid yourselves that what you're doing is good or just."

After that they got into ways and means. Hertel and Jack were assigned to coordinate the information they gathered and—especially in Jack's case—give them what legal cover he could. Carla would, in essence, spy on her parents, who had fallen in with the Spanish faction at court. That was a group of conservative nobles and clergy, mostly Dominican, but including about a fourth of the Jesuits.

"Do you think we should include Julian?" Amadeus asked Carla.

"Not yet. I'll see what I can find out from him." Then she looked over at Sonny. "Yeah, this really sucks."

Jack could sympathize with the young woman, but the reason she was here was because they needed an information source into the Spanish faction. As well, Carla's name had been on the list of people Farkas was going after. Which was another reason to suspect Archduke Leopold.

Liechtenstein Tower Construction Site, Vienna

The concrete arches gave the interior of the tower a forestlike look. It was as though the ceiling was held up by flowers or smooth trees. There were pipes for gas lighting that ran beside channels for wires, once they had enough light bulbs to light the place. And the place had an unfinished look. Bare concrete columns, and bare concrete floors.

The shops around the edge of the building were mostly finished and they were putting a wooden roof over the center plaza. Karl Eusebius von Liechtenstein, in a yellow fiberglass and rosin hardhat, was standing at a table with the construction foreman, going over the placement of the load-bearing arches. "The idea is to use as little steel reinforcement as we can get away with."

"Yes, Your Serene Highness, but I think we should go ahead and use reinforcement in this section. It will let us skip this whole set of supports." He pointed to the central open arches that honestly looked like a cross between the acropolis of Athens and a forest of almost gothic arches. The arches were slightly different in shape and started about halfway to the two-story ceiling.

"It's not the money, Heinrich," Karl said. "It's just that steel is really hard to come by at the moment. It would probably cause a delay and Sarah has instructed me to have the two floors ready for the wedding by mid-January or she's going to start looking for a more efficient suitor." Karl looked over at the foreman, saw his expression, and said, "Oh, go ahead and laugh, Heinrich. But believe me, you'd rather have Judy the Barracudy angry at you than her sister Sarah."

Heinrich squeezed his legs together in unconscious reaction to that comment and Karl tried not to laugh.

The Hofburg Palace, Vienna

"Are your parents going to be able to attend?" asked Her Imperial Majesty, the Empress of Austria-Hungary. The room was cozy by Hofburg standards, but incredibly plush. Aside from the empress, her mother-in-law and sister-in-law were there, along with Sarah, Judy, Vicky, Hayley, and Millicent. Susan and Gabrielle had both ducked out on the preparations. They would show up at the bridal showers with gifts, and at the wedding.

"Yes," Sarah let herself smile but continued gravely. "Dad got fired from the treasury when Wettin came in. And considering the guy Wettin put in at treasury, the Austro-Hungarian thaler is liable to become the preferred currency in the next few years."

"Really?" asked the dowager empress.

"Well, they couldn't fire Coleman Walker. He has another two years on his term before he has to be reconfirmed. But if the head of the Fed as well as the head of treasury are Wettin appointees, I would expect confidence in the American dollar to diminish."

"I don't know whether to be upset or pleased," Her Imperial Highness Cecilia Renata said. "I mean, I don't wish your family any bad luck, but it's to our advantage to . . ." She looked around and sort of ran down.

"Actually, no. The USE is running a couple of years ahead of the rest of Europe in industrialization, and it will be easier for you guys to gear up if you can buy crucial parts from the USE. Things like water pumps to make mining possible at greater depths."

"Enough," declared the dowager empress. "We're here to talk about wedding plans, not dreary economics. You said your parents were coming, too?"

"Yes. We've gotten the king in the Low Countries to loan us a Jupiter again. In fact, there is a possibility that Their Majesties will come to the wedding. The thing is, a Jupiter can't make it all the way from the Low Countries to Vienna in one hop, so they would have to stop in Grantville. Which, as it happens, is right on the way. But the politics involved in King Fernando landing in the USE, both on the way here and on the way back . . . there would have to be some assurances from Ed Piazza that no one would interfere with them. Bohemia isn't a problem, because they will be at five thousand feet all the time they are over it."

"I'd love to see Maria Anna again," said Cecilia Renata.

"So would I," said Empress Mariana. "I'll mention to Ferdinand that he should perhaps write a letter to the President of the State of Thuringia-Franconia on the matter. In the meantime, tell me more about this up-time custom, the bridal shower?"

Sarah listened as Judy, Vicky and Hayley told the highest noble ladies in Austria-Hungary about bridal shower and the sorts of gifts that were given at the different types of showers. The "kitchen" shower idea brought forth quite a bit of laughter, but the "lingerie" shower was given more approval.

Liechtenstein House, Vienna

"Well, Nephew, are you getting a bit nervous?" Uncle Maximilian asked with a smile that seemed to Karl less than completely kind.

"Yes, Uncle, a bit. But overall, I am quite happy." And he was. He even felt more than a little sympathy for both his uncles and most of the rest of the people in his class. He had, after all, gotten to choose his own bride, and he hadn't had to do it based on establishing or maintaining control over lands for the family. He picked up his fork. It had four tines and was electroplated in gold. It was very nice flatware, but it was flatware that most prosperous burghers could afford. He speared a piece of roast beef from his plate and popped it into his mouth. After he swallowed, he continued. "I have been incredibly lucky. First in finding Grantville on my grand tour, and then in finding Sarah Wendell. I feel a bit guilty about the limits our family's position put on the rest of you and, at the same time, incredibly fortunate that my choice of bride was allowed to be mine."

Gundaker ate in silence.

Liechtenstein Tower, Vienna

"What have you got?" the guard asked the carter.

The carter pulled out the paper work. "Barrels to go in the cellar."

The guard took the paperwork and read it over. Everything was in order. It was to go in room B-27, one of the mid-size basement rooms. A load of apples.

They used a powered winch to lift the barrels off the wagon and lower them to a pallet on a trolley. That, in turn, was used to shift them to the room where, pallet and all, they were left in the corner. Then another pallet, and another after that, till B-27 was loaded with barrels.

Debrecen House, Vienna

"What have you found out?" Márton von Debrecen asked Jack Pfeifer.

"Nothing of use. We managed to tag one more of Farkas' men and we're now convinced that there was a priest involved."

"Oh, come now. If there is evil done in Vienna, there's a priest involved."

"I know. That's why I said nothing of use. We know that there was a plan to kill the girls, and we know that it was called off, but we don't know if the plotters gave it up as a bad job or switched to a new plan."

"Is there any reason to believe that they went to another plan?" asked Amadeus.

CHAPTER 36

Wedding Preparations

December 1635

Roth Jewel Emporium, Prague, Kingdom of Bohemia

The clerk took one look at Beth and sent for his boss, and, ultimately, for Morris Roth himself. For almost half an hour, the duchess of Cieszyn was fed wine and sweet chocolate, while she got to look at hundreds of jeweled rings, necklaces, bracelets, chokers, tiaras, and the like. It was enough to bring great covetousness to a girl's soul. Not, however, enough to even consider any sort of rapprochement with Gundaker von Liechtenstein.

Finally, Morris arrived. "What brings you to our little shop, Your Grace?"

"I've been asked a favor by Empress Mariana and several other ladies of the Austro-Hungarian court, as well as the new imperial princesses, the Barbies...?"

"I know them all well, except for Trudi," Morris said. "And I imagine that she's much like the rest. And what is this mission?"

"Apparently there is an up-time custom called a bridal shower. And, in this case, they have decided to do a jewelry and clothing shower. Lingerie?"

"It means undergarments, specifically for women, and implies attractive and perhaps a bit naughty," Morris explained without even a hint of a blush.

Beth didn't blush either. Instead, she opened her case and

352

brought out several documents with seals from the Emperor of Austria-Hungary and Abraham Abrabanel. The documents, each with a price limit listed, empowered her to buy jewelry to give to Sarah Wendell, and smaller gifts to be exchanged among the ladies attending the party. All together, the letters of credit came to just over two million dollars.

Morris Roth looked them over and smiled. "I suspect that we're going to have quite a good day today, Your Grace. Fun for you, and quite profitable for my little shop."

Morris was completely correct. Beth had a blast. Morris even found several young women who had similar shapes and the coloring of the Barbies and the royal ladies. There were other shops in Prague, some in the Jewish quarter and some elsewhere, and runners went and found lingerie and other small items. Still, Morris' shop got most of the two plus million dollars.

At the end of the day, a thoroughly sated and satisfied Beth ordered that all of the purchases be shipped to the Hofburg in Vienna.

And Morris ordered a company of guards to escort it.

Private Sitting Room, Palace of the King in the Low Countries in Brussels

"We're going." Maria Anna's voice was not loud, but it was very firm.

Fernando, King in the Low Countries, felt a smile twitch his lips. His submissive "Yes, dear" earned him a sharp look from his wife, but the truth was his financial advisers, including William of Orange, wanted him to find out how stable Austro-Hungarian money was going to be and the wedding was an excellent opportunity to judge the situation for himself.

"Why are you so willing?"

He explained, then added, "Besides, it will give us both a chance to talk to your brother and my sister. And since relations with my brother in Spain seem to be...less than cordial...having good relations with your family are especially important."

Maria Anna nodded, nibbling a fingernail. She was an astute judge of the politics of Europe and the Hapsburg family that ruled much of it. "Yes, I see. Do you think that your sister might be able to help with your brother?"

"I don't know. With Olivares whispering in his ear, and now Borja. But anything we can do to forestall open war with Spain is worth a try."

Grantville Airport, State of Thuringia-Franconia

"Yep, Clive, it's official. A Jupiter will be arriving on January eleventh for refueling. It's to be considered a diplomatic flight."

"What's that mean?"

"Nothing much, in this case. Just that everyone on it is going to have diplomatic immunity, so we don't get to search the plane looking for contraband."

"Pete, have we *ever* searched a plane looking for contraband?"

"Not that I recall, Clive. Not that I recall."

Wendell Suite, Higgins Hotel, Grantville

"We have a ride," Fletcher said, holding up the telegram. "King Fernando and Queen Maria Anna are picking us up on the way to the wedding."

"How crowded is it going to be? The Monster is pushing it to hold fourteen."

"It doesn't say, hon. But probably pretty crowded. There are going to be Fernando and Maria Anna, probably Doña Mencia, and at least one of Fernando's retainers. I doubt that William of Orange will be coming. He'll probably be holding down the store in the Netherlands. But there is a fair chance that they are going to bring at least a couple of their advisers—financial, political, something. And probably gifts. So pack light."

"What about my gifts?"

"I think both our budget and our weight allowance are going to limit us in that regard. I'll bring the digital and take wedding pictures, but that's probably going to be all we can manage."

Fortney House, Race Track City

"Say, Karl, if we got a couple of fast horses do you think we can make a run for it?" Sarah Wendell asked, only half-joking. "I knew this was going to be a circus. I even realized there would be royalty in attendance. But now it's looking like an international peace conference, as well."

"What?" Karl's show of surprise didn't impress Sarah at all. "Has Ferdinand invited Murad the Mad to our wedding? It will be all right, as long as we don't have Philip and Fernando seated next to each other."

"Okay. From now on, no one gets to complain to me about their in-laws. Ever!"

"They aren't actually Karl's relatives," Gayleen Sanderlin said, laughing. "Just friends of the family and what...business connections? You should meet *my* mother in-law."

Sarah gave her a look, then looked over at Ron, who was looking a bit shame-faced. "Okay, you have a point. But how many heads of state attended your wedding?"

"Just one." Gayleen sniffed haughtily. "Mike Stearns was there, and he was Chairman of the Emergency Committee at the time."

Sarah blinked in sudden realization. Mike Stearns had attended a lot of weddings since the Ring of Fire. Heck, he probably attended a lot of weddings before the Ring of Fire as a union leader. She considered. "I still say this is over the top, even for post Ring of Fire weddings," she insisted, but with considerably less heat. "But okay. At least the so-called 'Prince of Germany' won't be coming."

"Welllllll..." Karl said in a tone of exaggerated musing. "Unless I invite King Albrecht. He is my liege lord, you know. And I understand that General Stearns is going to be visiting him."

"You know, Mrs. Sanderlin, if I were to just shoot Karl it would solve all the wedding problems."

St. Stephen's Cathedral, Vienna

"They are going to endorse Urban," Father Lamormaini told Father Montilla. "It's confirmed. I still have connections in the Hofburg." The last part of the statement was true, and he was almost sure that the first part was true as well. The decision hadn't been made yet, but if things continued as they were now, Lamormaini didn't see any other outcome. "They have to be stopped before they make the public announcement, which will be shortly after the wedding of Prince Karl Eusebius and the Wendell peasant girl."

"It is a hard thing you ask, Father," said Montilla, but his tone didn't bear him out. There was an excited light in the chubby little Spanish Jesuit's eyes and the quaver in his voice was of excitement, not doubt.

"You saw the documents," Lamormaini said. "*The Omen* clearly documents that the Antichrist had already arrived in that other history, before the Sphere of Fire transported the seed of evil into our world. The vile satanic rites that Friedrich Babbel sent us, confirming the evil that they allowed under the guise of secularism. *Rosemary's Baby. Left Behind. The Satanic Bible.* The truth of the up-timers is there in their libraries. They tried to hide it, but a careful study of their archives proves it beyond doubt. The 'force' from their movie *Star Wars* that we have seen right here in Vienna. Trying to make God into a mere field of energy. We talked about all this. You have seen the proofs."

"Yes, Father Lamormaini, and I would willingly burn every up-timer at the stake! But the Holy Roman Emperor—"

"He has rejected that duty. Quailed from it like a startled rabbit running from a fox."

"Very well. I will need some equipment. I don't want to use a slow fuse. It is too likely to be smelled. Besides, there is a certain justice to using Satan's tools against his minions."

"What do you need?"

"I will need wires. Insulated copper wires. A battery. It can be lead acid, zinc-carbon or really anything that will produce the juice. And a spark generator. Or, if you can get one, one of the blasting caps. If you can't get me a blasting cap, get me some light bulbs and I can rig something from them."

"From a light bulb."

"They make light though heat. Remove the glass container, surround the filament with gunpowder, and when the electricity flows, it heats the filament, which burns. That's all you need."

"I'll get them for you."

"Just make sure your man can send them to us before the wedding."

Dressmaker, Race Track City

It was white silk, a bow to the up-timer custom. Floor length, with gold-embroidered lace cap sleeves, a low sweetheart neckline, a full skirt with gold-embroidered lace insets.

"That's about the most princessy dress I've ever seen," Judy remarked airily. "Too bad it's wasted on you."

Sarah stuck out her tongue.

"Ahh, the the true Platonic form of ladylike maturity," offered Imperial Princess Cecilia Renata, giggling. Cecilia had declared herself a probational Barbie during the negotiations and nobody had objected. All the Barbies liked her.

Judy's dress was the same style, but in emerald green with gold embroidery. Cecilia Renata's was grass green with gold, Susan's was dark blue with silver embroidery. Millicent was in red with silver. The rest of the girls had similar dresses in all the colors of the rainbow, even Gabrielle and Trudi. Of course, none of them had quite as much gold embroidery as Sarah's. It was her day, after all. And Judy, as much as she might tease, wouldn't allow any of the rest to outshine Sarah on her wedding day.

Instead of a veil, Sarah would wear her tiara, which was gold with green jewels.

The next couple of weeks were caught up in wedding preparations and Christmas celebrations. However, during that time Moses managed to propose and Susan accepted. When Susan told Judy, Judy suggested that they have a double wedding with Sarah and Karl.

"No!" Susan said. "First, I want a quiet ceremony, and second, I am not going to be a part of your political machinations."

"Oh. You spotted that, did you?" Judy said.

"I agree that having the wedding of a Jew attended by half the crowned heads of Europe would be a good thing in the long run. It's just not going to be mine."

"It's also too soon," said Trudi. "What we are seeing in the USE now and what we saw in front of the synagogue when Mayor Dreeson was murdered, is proof of that."

CHAPTER 37

𝖂𝖊𝖉𝖉𝖎𝖓𝖌 𝕻𝖗𝖊𝖕𝖆𝖗𝖆𝖙𝖎𝖔𝖓𝖘

January 1636

The Vienna airfield, near Race Track City

The Jupiter made its landing on the Danube with no difficulty. In the months since its first visit, the airfield had been considerably improved. The runway was now macadamized.

First off the plane was Fernando, King in the Low Countries, followed by Queen Maria Anna, Doña Mencia, and her brother. Four more counselors, and, finally, the father and mother of the bride.

The next day, Mike Stearns arrived, flown in on a *Gustav* aircraft by the head of the USE Air Force himself, Colonel Wood. General Stearns and his Third Division were now stationed in the southern Bohemian city of České Budějovice.

His visit was unofficial, however. In theory, this was purely a personal trip to attend the wedding of a daughter of old friends. Never mind that the Wendells had never been more than casual acquaintances, and especially never mind that Stearns hadn't bothered to ask permission from the USE government.

And whose permission would he ask, anyway? Word had just arrived that Prime Minister Wettin had been arrested in Berlin at the order of the Swedish chancellor Oxenstierna—who had precisely no authority to give such an order in the first place.

Not to mention that the Swedish general Banér had just placed Dresden under siege, despite being ordered not to do so by Ernst Wettin, the administrator of Saxony appointed by the emperor himself before his incapacitating injury. For all practical purposes, the government of the USE was now a vacant abstraction. The nation was dissolving into civil war.

Liechtenstein Tower, Vienna

"Karl? You do know that a tower is supposed to be taller than it is across?" Fletcher Wendell asked with a sardonic smile, and Karl hid a grimace.

He had gotten along quite well with Fletcher Wendell before he started courting Sarah, but since then Fletcher never missed an opportunity to call Karl's abilities into question. Sarah's mother was bright and helpful, if a little awkward around people she didn't know. Judy the Younger was was charming, if manipulative. But Fletcher Wendell was snide. "Yes, Fletcher, I do know that," Karl said, as he led the way up the three steps to the main entrance.

"Have you considered changing the name? Liechtenstein Lump, perhaps."

"We did consider that, Dad," Karl offered, with a certain emphasis on "Dad." "But there's all that bureaucratic paperwork involved, so we thought we'd simply add fourteen more floors." The doorman opened the door for them and they walked in. The generator and the steam heat plant were both installed in the basement. At this point, neither of them was working at anything near capacity, but that was because it wasn't needed yet. There was plenty of heat and power for what they did need. They also had enough light bulbs to light the shops on the first two floors and the grand indoor plaza.

The grand indoor plaza was sixty up-time feet across and the ceiling was held up by two rows of concrete trees with trunks a yard wide. They started branching at nine feet and reached their full extension twenty-three feet above the floor.

Fletcher Wendell looked around and whistled, and Karl started to smile. Then Fletcher said, "This place is going to need an army to keep it clean."

Karl led the way into the plaza, pointing out the various shops that surrounded it. There were quite a few and about half of them were already open. They would stay open even as the floors above were built.

In the basement of the tower, Father Montilla walked down the hall, carrying an ordinary lantern with the wick so low it sputtered. He needed just enough light to see, and the light sockets in the basement were empty of light bulbs. There weren't yet enough electric lights to go around, and the shops on the first floor were getting what there were.

He angled the lamp so that the light fell at his feet. He didn't want to call attention to himself.

He made his way to the door of Gundaker von Liechtenstein's storage room and pulled out the sheet of paper that held the combination. It was a down-time-made multiple-dial lock based on a bicycle lock. It didn't take him long to get it unlocked and go into the storage room.

Once inside, he closed the door, turned up the lamp and looked around. The room was twenty by twenty up-time feet and packed high with pallets of barrels marked as holding apples. Father Montilla knew that the barrels held fine grain black powder. There were four barrels to a pallet. The pallets were stacked two high and three deep, in three rows.

Father Montilla moved along one wall to the back of the room and took off his back pack. From the back pack, he took a lead acid battery, ceramic but based on an up-time motorcycle battery. Then a fifteen foot roll of insulated wire, copper multistrand, tight wrapped in linen thread, made in Magdeburg. Then a small hand-powered wood drill, again made in Magdeburg, this time based on an up-time spring-powered screwdriver. Also a twenty-four-hour clock made in Halle from an up-time design. The fact that it was a twenty-four-hour clock was important because security on the actual day of the wedding was going to be tight. He could slip in the day before the wedding to do the final prep.

First, he got down on his knees and, snaking his arms around, managed to drill a small hole in a back barrel, out of sight. It shouldn't matter, but this was important, and he didn't want some idiot knocking things awry by accident or noticing gunpowder leaking out of the barrel. The hole was a little bigger than the blasting cap, so he wrapped the cap in a piece of cloth before shoving it into the hole.

Carefully he stripped insulation from one end of his wire and attached it to one of the leads to the Grantville-made blasting cap. He unrolled the wire and cut a length of about three feet, then carefully threaded the wire between the slats of the pallet and the bottom of the barrel, then snugged the wire tight. He stripped the other end of that wire and attached it to a stud that he had placed at two P.M. on the face of the clock.

He attached a second length of wire to the hour hand so that when the the hour hand reached two o'clock in the afternoon, the two wires would come together. He measured out that second length so that it would reach to one pole of the battery but didn't attach it.

He measured off a third length of wire, leaving himself a fair amount of slack, and stripped the ends. He threaded this wire under the barrel and attached one end to the blasting cap's other lead. Again he made sure the other end of the wire would reach the battery, then cinched the wire in against the slats of the pallet and the staves of the barrel.

He wiped his brow with the sleeve of his cassock. That had been hot work, and he was a scholar, not a tradesman. But he was also a man of God, doing his duty.

"You know you can still get out of this," her dad said, and Sarah wanted to kick him. They were in the Goldberg Candy Store, just off the main entrance to Liechtenstein Tower, waiting for the final wedding rehearsal to begin. The plaza was filled with chairs and benches for the invited guests. Liechtenstein and BarbieCo guards were at each and every entrance. The generator in the basement was running and the lights were on.

In just a few minutes, assuming she didn't kill him first, her dad was going to walk her down the aisle to meet Karl and they would practice getting married. What made the all-too-predictable offer even more irritating was that a tiny part of her wanted to take him up on it. Not because of Karl, but because of the baggage that came with him.

This would be the final lock on the cage for her. Court princess, the head of the banking system for the Austro-Hungarian empire, princess of the House Liechtenstein, countess of this, baroness of that, the wife of the head of government of territories in two countries. Sarah Wendell was about to be swallowed by Princess Sarah, and as much as she loved Karl, it scared the hell out of her.

"We're ready," said Countess Fortney.

Three hours later, as the guards were leaving, a priest came wandering in, ostensibly looking for a Book of Hours. When no one was looking, he slipped down the stairs into the still dark basement. He lit his lamp using a Magdeburg-made Zippo lighter, then made his way to the storeroom rented by Gundaker von Liechtenstein. He unlocked the door and slipped in. He turned up the lantern and went to work. He wound and set the clock using his Hamburg-made pocket watch. The minute hand on the clock he bent outward so that it wouldn't bind the hour hand that was going to slowly drag the wire into contact with the stud. He checked the battery, getting a shock, and attached the leads. Then he left. It wasn't till he was back upstairs that he realized that he still had the lock in his pocket. He considered going back down but decided against it.

CHAPTER 38

𝕬 𝖂𝖊𝖉𝖉𝖎𝖓𝖌 𝖙𝖔 𝕽𝖊𝖒𝖊𝖒𝖇𝖊𝖗

January 15, 1636

The Hofburg Palace, Vienna

The morning was cold and crisp, but the sun had come out and there wasn't a cloud within a hundred miles of Vienna. They wouldn't dare, not today. Empress Mariana looked out the window at the beautiful day and made a decision. "There will the one more royal at the wedding. We'll bring the baby," she pronounced.

"Ferdinand the latest?" the emperor asked. "Are you sure?"

"Yes. It's a beautiful day and by the time we go to the wedding it won't even be that cold. Besides, the tower is lovely, what there is of it. On the inside, at least. I love the arching concrete pillars."

The emperor of Austria-Hungary shrugged acceptance and rang for the servants. It was best to get the preparations underway.

St. Stephen's Cathedral, Vienna

"They are taking the heir?" Father Montilla hissed. The bomb was in place, the clock running, and there was no way at all to get back into the the Liechtenstein building, not today. "You have to stop them!"

"How would you suggest I do that?" Father Lamormaini hissed back. "Shall we walk up to the Hofburg and tell them there is a bomb? Or perhaps we should kidnap the imperial prince?"

"No. God is talking to us here. It falls to us to understand his meaning."

"Are we then to destroy the House of Habsburg entire? The Austrian branch, and Netherlands branch, leaving only the Spanish Habsburgs? I admit that has a certain appeal, but with France and William of Orange in the way, it will be difficult at best for Spain to reassert control."

"No. Aside from everything else, were King Philip to put forward a claim, suspicion would fall on him," Lamormaini said. "No, we need at least one surviving Austrian Habsburg. If we can't save the son, the brother will have to do."

"Leopold has been ordered to attend the wedding by the emperor. He won't ignore that."

"But he's not happy about it. The enmity between him and the Barbies, including Sarah Wendell, has not decreased one bit with their elevation."

"Happy or not . . . You don't plan to tell him?"

"Not unless absolutely necessary."

Liechtenstein House, Vienna

Gundaker von Liechtenstein wasn't happy to be interrupted. He liked the news less. "What is Lamormaini doing at the archduke's townhouse?"

"I don't know, Your Serene Highness, but he seemed in a great hurry."

"Wait here," Gundaker told the man. Another one like Farkas, but this time he had been more careful. This man didn't know why he was watching Lamormaini. And wouldn't until it became necessary to act. Gundaker stepped into the office of the chief butler. "Has there been any change in the schedule for today."

"No, Your Serene Highness. Nothing that affects us."

"What about things that don't affect us?" Gundaker growled.

"Only that the Imperial Family has decided that Imperial Prince Ferdinand will be going to the wedding too. He will be in the daycare with the other toddlers. We were told because of—"

"Never mind." Gundaker turned and stalked out.

Now he knew what had happened. Realizing he couldn't save the babe, that idiot Lamormaini was going to tell the prince not to go to the wedding. And he knew of Gundaker's involvement directly. By the time he got back to his office, Gundaker had decided that he couldn't wait.

"I want you to kill Lamormaini," he said. "And if he has spoken to the archduke, you will kill the archduke as well."

"That's the sort of thing that can leave a man running for the rest of his life."

Gundaker went to a chest and pulled out a sack of gold coins. "There is another one of these for you when I know it's done."

Townhouse of the Bishop of Passau, Vienna

Archduke Leopold was going through his wardrobe. He didn't want to go to the wedding. The wardrobe search was partly to delay the inevitable and partly to find the clothes that would show absolutely the least respect for the Barbies he could get away with.

Marco Vianetti tapped on the door and announced, "Father Lamormaini would like a word."

Leo winced. He could almost agree with a lot of his father's former confessor's attitudes, but the man had become increasingly strident since the church had broken in two.

"You must not go to the wedding, Your Grace," Father Lamormaini said. "It is an offense against God and the true church."

"Father, I am a man compelled by duty to both my brother and my emperor. It you have a reason that my brother, the emperor of Austria Hungary will accept, I'm more than happy to hear it."

"Ferdinand doesn't matter."

"That is a preposterous statement."

"It is true!" Lamormaini insisted. "He will be but dust by two o'clock. Do not go to the wedding or you will join him."

"What do you mean?"

There was a pause. Not long, just a few seconds but long enough for Leo to realize that it wasn't hyperbole or priestly nonsense. That there was a plot of some sort. Long enough for the realization that if he did nothing, he might well be emperor soon.

Leo didn't call the guards. He listened. Relations with his family had been going downhill since Judy Wendell had publicly humiliated him. All of them had sided with the up-timers against their own blood.

"There is a bomb in the basement of the Liechtenstein Tower. A room filled with gunpowder."

"If I am not there, suspicion would fall on me. Who arranged the room? The Spanish faction couldn't have. Anything they tried to put in the tower would be scrutinized."

"Not all the Liechtensteins are corrupted by the up-timers."

That meant either Gundaker or Maximilian. Probably Gundaker. Maximilian was a good general and loyal, but pragmatic. Leo looked over at the clock. It was what the up-timers called a grandfather clock. It used a new sort of escapement and was more accurate. Currently, the hour was twenty-seven minutes past noon. He had time. Not much, but time. "Tell me about it, Father Lamormaini."

Then he listened as Father Lamormaini laid it all out. All the way back to Ferdinand III forcing Ferdinand II to revoke the Edict of Restitution. Plus a bunch of nonsense about the number of the beast and up-time movies.

Through it all, Leo listened and weighed risk and advantage, while images of his brothers and sisters, his father and mother, and stepmother ran through his head. Cecilia Renata, who in that other timeline would go to a horror of a marriage in Poland. No wonder she was in favor of the Ring of Fire. Images of Ferdinand in that car of his, of the few times that Leo had been allowed to drive the thing. Images of Judy Wendell as she had come off the plane.

His decision was a foregone conclusion, of course. This priest was insane to think that Leo would betray his own brother—his entire family, in fact. Yet, oddly enough, it was the thought of Judy Wendell being slain that made the decision come immediately. As resentful as he still was at her humiliation of him, Leo did not want her dead. The thought of the girl being murdered, in fact, was what was finally enabled him to admit that his own behavior had been at fault.

Leo looked at the clock again. It was almost one. He pulled the cord that would call Marco.

The door opened and a guard entered. Leo rose and pointed at Father Lamormaini. "He is to be placed under close arrest and held for my brother's pleasure." He looked back at Lamormaini. "The brother you would murder in the name of God."

He left to get his horse. Hurrying.

Rotenturmstraße, Vienna

They came out of nowhere. Marco, Archduke Leopold, and four of his guardsmen were riding down the street and what must have been a dozen men on horseback came out of Lugeck Street. Someone shouted, "At them," and they charged. Marco managed to draw and fire, but didn't hit anyone. He had a six-shooter on order, but it hadn't arrived yet, so he had three single shot pistols left and that was it. It didn't matter, though. There wasn't enough time to even draw the next one. He pulled his sword.

"Ride, Your Grace!" Marco shouted. "Ride for your life!"

He never saw the shot that hit Leopold in the side. He was too busy fighting for his life and trying to buy Leopold the time he needed to get away.

He failed in the first, but succeeded in the second.

Leo felt the blow and then the sharp agony. He stayed in the saddle and rounded a corner, then he was riding for his life, every hoofbeat an agony as a broken rib stabbed him with every jounce. It made it really hard to concentrate on where he was going.

Outside Liechtenstein Tower

Amadeus was stationed in front of the tower. There were several late arrivals, some of them of high station, so a noble was needed to direct them and Amadeus had gotten the job. A horse came galloping around the corner and several guards rode out to halt the rider, then backed away and let him pass.

Leopold actually rode up the steps to the entrance and almost fell off the horse into Amadeus' arms.

"Your Grace, are you drunk?" Amadeus hissed at the archduke. Then he felt the wetness, and looked at his hand. It was bloody.

"Have to get to the basement."

"What? We have to get you a doctor."

"No. No time!" Leo slurred.

"You need a doctor."

"Now, God curse you. That's an order!"

Amadeus knew he should get a doctor, but this was the arch-duke. He turned to the guards. "You, go find us a doctor. A barber-surgeon, mind, not one of those philosophers from the university. The rest of you, watch the door."

He led Leopold to the stairs down to the basement. There was a guard at the staircase but Leo bulled through him, stopping only to get a couple of lanterns.

At the bottom of the stairs was an office. It was empty. There would be no deliveries during the wedding.

Leo looked around at the halls and turned to Amadeus. "Which one is the Liechtenstein's?"

"They're all the..."

"No, Gundaker!" Leo said. Then he fainted.

About then there was a clattering on the stairs and three men came down. One of them had the black bag that had become almost a symbol of a barber-surgeon from Race Track City.

While the surgeon worked on Archduke Leopold, Amadeus went through the records, looking for which room or rooms might be leased by Gundaker von Liechtenstein.

Upstairs, word had reached the chief of protocol for the Habsburgs that Leo had shown up drunk and been taken to the basement to keep him out of trouble. He decided that Ferdinand III should not be informed. Things were tense enough in the royal family and he didn't want the emperor distracted at such an important occasion attended by so many great nobles. He directed that the lesser staff should handle the matter, whatever it was, without disturbing the guests or the wedding party.

"But...!"

"You heard me. Handle it, and I don't want to hear about it till the wedding is over and the guests have left."

"Here it is!" Amadeus shouted. He had found it. Gundaker had rented a twenty by twenty room for apples? That didn't seem right. Then he looked over at Archduke Leopold and began to get a really bad feeling. "Wake the archduke," he told the doctor.

"I'd rather not, Count von Eisenberg. I've taped the ribs, but it would be better if he was kept still."

Amadeus looked at the record book, and back at the archduke. "Wake him! It's important."

The doctor shrugged, reached into his bag, and pulled out a small bottle. He opened the bottle and waved it under the archduke's nose. Even from where he was, Amadeus got a whiff of ammonia. The archduke's head came up and he almost made the doctor spill his bottle, but apparently it wasn't an uncommon reaction. The doctor got the bottle away without spilling any of it.

Archduke Leopold looked around, blearily.

"What's in Gundaker's room?" Amadeus asked.

"A bomb, I think."

"It wouldn't do them any good," said one of the guards, pointing at the ceiling. "That's a foot of concrete up there. No bomb is going to do more than scratch it."

"Maybe, but I think we'd better have a look."

"If you want," said the guard.

The doctor helped Leopold to his feet, and they headed for the room.

The room was dark and full of barrels. Amadeus, Leo, the guard and the doctor looked around the room, lighting it with Coleman lanterns. The barrels were marked to indicate that they held apples, but Leo didn't believe that for a moment. He had barely escaped from his guards after Father Lamormaini told him that he was destined to become the Holy Roman Emperor.

"You think these are full of gunpowder?" Amadeus asked.

"Yes. This is the storeroom that Gundaker leased from Karl."

The guard, who had assured them that they were safe from any sort of bomb, was suddenly looking a lot less confident.

Leo turned to him. "Go upstairs and get everyone out of the building." The guard nodded and left.

Leo looked at Amadeus. "What time is it?"

Amadeus didn't own a watch. They were expensive, and though Amadeus was wealthy, he didn't particularly like them.

The doctor pulled a small clock from his bag. "I have one forty-five. But this thing could be off by five minutes either way. Why?"

"Because Lamormaini said that my brother would be dust by two o'clock."

The doctor swallowed.

"Be on your way, Doctor. You have done all that you could."

The doctor looked at Leopold, then turned and left. He was running by the time he was out the door.

With the doctor and the guard gone, Leo could hear a clicking. It wasn't the same as the grandfather clock, but it was close enough. "You hear the ticking?" he asked.

"Over there." Amadeus pointed. "I think that's a battery. Like in the emperor's 240Z."

Leo followed his gaze and blanched. It was a battery. They went over and looked.

The battery was hooked to something, and that something was hooked with wires to one of the barrels.

"Amadeus, how much do you know about electronics?"

"Very little, Your Grace."

"I don't know much, either. Would you mind running up to the first floor and asking Sonny Fortney to come down here?"

While Amadeus was gone, Leo had ample opportunity to examine the device. There were two wires leading from the battery. One of them went straight into the stack of barrels, so there was no way to know where it ended. The other went to a clock. It was an unusual clock. Instead of a face that showed twelve hours, this clock's face showed twenty-four, half in white and half in black. The thing had three hands, just like the grandfather clock, but two of them were bent out away from the face. To the third was attached a wire, and it was very close to a stud that was over the 14. It was giving off a clicking sound and as he watched, what must be the second hand hit the 24 and the minute hand moved. Leo wasn't sure, but he thought the hour hand had moved a fraction as well. And at the stud at the 14, an attached wire went off around a barrel. A barrel that Leopold was almost sure was full of gunpowder.

Leo was wondering where Sonny Fortney was as the second hand made its orbit and when the minute hand moved again he began to get really worried. Also he was feeling more than a little woozy and his side hurt a lot. He really didn't want to be sitting here unconscious when the bomb went off.

Amadeus ran up the stairs to the first floor and was lost in the milling crowd. The whole first floor of the uncompleted tower was packed with people. The wedding party, the wedding guests and Sonny Fortney would be at the other end of the hall with his family and the Wendells. No one was making any move to leave. He wondered what the hell was going on and where the guard had disappeared to.

The guard was arguing with the third undercaptain, who had gotten his orders from the steward and wasn't convinced by the hysterical ramblings of a guard who had probably been paid by the archduke to interrupt the wedding. By now, the guard was almost hoping the place would blow up.

Amadeus looked around for anyone he knew who might know something about electricity. There was no one. Then he saw Dr. Faust looking at one of the unused light sockets that were built into the columns in the main foyer. "Herr Doctor Faust!"

Amadeus ran up to the man, who was looking confused and a little concerned.

"I need you to come with me." Amadeus still wondered if he should be shouting at everyone to get out, but he wasn't sure, so he didn't.

"Well, all right," said Dr. Faust, looking back at the light fixture.

"Now, Doctor! It's urgent." He grabbed the doctor's arm and pulled him along toward the staircase leading to the basement.

"What is going on, Count von Eisenberg?"

"What do you know about electrics?"

"You mean electronics. Quite a bit. Why?"

The minute hand was now getting close to the 24 and the hour hand was almost touching the stud. Leo assumed that bad things would happen when the hour hand reached the stud. He pulled the steel knife out of the scabbard at his side, thinking to place it between the dial and the moving handle, so that they couldn't touch.

There was a sound in the distance. Leo turned still holding his knife. "Herr Fortney?"

"No. I couldn't find him," Amadeus shouted back and Leo turned back to the ticking device, knife in hand. "I brought Dr. Faust instead. He knows about electrics."

"Please hurry, Herr Doctor. I don't think there is much time for delay."

Dr. Faust and Amadeus came running up, and Leo pointed with his knife. "I think that when the hour hand reaches the stud, something bad will happen."

Panting, Dr. Faust looked at the device and after a moment nodded. Leo offered the the doctor the knife. "You can keep them separate with this."

Dr. Faust looked at the knife and blanched. Then he reached down with his hand, grabbed one of the wires, and yanked it free.

"Was that all it took?" Leo asked, feeling disappointed. "From the books, they are supposed to take some sort of specially trained experts to disarm?"

"That's because up-time they used antitampering devices. Lots of wires, and if you pulled the wrong one, the bomb went off. But, Your Grace, iron and steel are excellent conductors. Putting your knife blade in between the two wires would have been as bad as touching them together."

Leo fainted then. He would forever after claim that it was from blood loss.

"Just something I thought you should know, in case something like this ever comes up again," Dr. Faust said to the unconscious archduke.

Mike Stearns stood on one of the balconies that overlooked the milling crowd of colorfully dressed people. It was early afternoon and the electric lights glittered from the masses of jewels women wore, as well as the pommels of dress swords worn by the men.

He was standing on the mezzanine taking a breather from the dancing, wishing with all his might that Rebecca was here. Partly just so she could rescue him from what seemed like hordes of females who all wanted their chance to dance with the Prince of Germany.

He heard a soft step behind him and turned his head to see Ferdinand III, Emperor of Austria-Hungary, walk up to him. He was accompanied by his brother-in-law Fernando, the King in the Low Countries.

So. The heads of two of the three Habsburg houses. As often happened at royal weddings, business would be conducted. Mike was not surprised, of course. It was the main reason he'd come.

"Glittering crowd down there, Your Majesties."

Ferdinand nodded. "Glittering, it certainly is, and your young ladies are providing a lot of the glitter." He stepped nearer the rail and stared out over the crowd. Fernando joined him.

Mike followed the route Ferdinand's eyes took. Sarah Wendell and Prince Karl Eusebius von Liechtenstein were dancing through the concrete trees. A waltz, needless to say. An early version of the dance had already existed, but the Ring of Fire had made waltzes the rage of European courts in general—and the Austrian court in particular.

Judy Wendell and Millicent Anne Barnes were holding court nearby, surrounded by a bevy of soon-to-be-disappointed suitors. Gabrielle Ugolini seemed to be a bit at a loss, and waiting for her escort, Herr Doctor Faust.

By now, Mike had been briefed on the romances of the various Barbies. Moses Abrabanel was dancing with Susan Logsden, and Carla Barclay was dancing with some young count whose name Mike hadn't caught. Trudi von Bachmerin was dancing with Jack Pfeifer. Mike didn't see Hayley and wondered where Amadeus had gotten to.

The music was from a record player with electrical amplification. People of every station were chatting around the edges of the dance area.

Mike tried to hide a grin. "Four years ago, someone I knew said that there wasn't a single thing that would do his soul more good than seeing a young woman in a wedding dress walk down the aisle. The man's dead now, but he was right at the time and he's still right. We've seen a lot of weddings these last four years."

"And to think there are some who consider you barbarians."

The dry tone of Ferdinand's voice made Mike turn to look at him. He put a questioning look on his face.

Ferdinand smiled. "You have, after all, made quite a bit of headway. Using tactics well known to my family."

"Oh, yes," Mike agreed. "'Let others wage wars. You, fortunate Austria, wage marriage.'"

"Close enough," the emperor of Austria-Hungary agreed. He gestured toward a nearby door that Mike assumed led to a room where privacy was to be found. "Would you accompany us?"

"Of course."

Sarah carried a traditional bouquet and was preparing for the traditional bouquet toss.

Judy did her best to stay well away from the toss, Millicent at her side.

The bouquet contained myrtle leaves, for good luck. Brides were traditionally considered lucky and some variation of the bouquet toss had been in custom for many years. At this point, the last thing Judy wanted was to catch a bouquet. Weddings seemed to be catching or something. Everywhere she turned, some young man was staring at her with puppydog eyes, practically begging for her attention.

"I'm looking forward to getting back to Magdeburg," Millicent muttered.

"Same here," Judy whispered. "Let's get farther back. The last thing I want is these boys getting ideas. I'm getting enough proposals, without them thinking I'm next."

They didn't make it quite far enough away. Almost as soon as Judy and Millicent turned back to watch, Sarah launched her bouquet.

"Ah . . . drat."

Millicent sighed. "Can't let it hit the floor, can you? It's a rule. You know. Like the flag."

Judy stared over the bouquet she'd had to catch. At the group of more-than-willing boys. "You wish," she muttered at them, just as a bloody Archduke Leopold staggered onto the dance floor, accompanied by Amadeus and Herr Doctor Faust.

Epilogue

It took a short time for Emperor Ferdinand to realize that his little brother wasn't just drunk and that Leopold was wounded.

After that, things got organized quickly. Troops were sent to collect Father Lamormaini. A scourge of the Spanish faction of the Austro-Hungarian court would follow over the next few weeks. But from that moment the support of the Austrian court—and that of the Netherlands—for Pope Urban was set in stone.

It wasn't nearly so well documented that Gundaker had been involved. Yes, he had rented the storeroom, but he could have done it at the request of Lamormaini without knowing for what use was intended. At least, that was Karl's less-than-convincing argument.

Maximilian von Liechtenstein was not happy. He and his wife had both been at the wedding. If the bomb had gone off, he would have been blown up with everyone else.

Troops were sent to Liechtenstein House, where they failed to find Prince Gundaker. They did find a set of books that, on close examination, suggested that Gundaker had gotten away with a lot of silver and more than a little gold.

"The only direction I think we can be sure he doesn't run," said Maximilian, "is toward his wife's lands."

A more serious question was who else was involved. Hartmann von Liechtenstein, Gundaker's son, was out of town on business for his father, but they didn't know whether he was involved. It wouldn't have been hard for Gundaker to send him off without telling him the reason. Gundaker's daughters were in attendance, both of them with their husbands, which pretty much cleared them of any involvement.

But how many of the staff at Liechtenstein house were involved was an open question. Not everyone had been at the wedding.

Mike Stearns returned to Bohemia two days after the wedding. He needed to get back anyway, since the moment for his intervention in the siege of Dresden was approaching. But he wouldn't have stayed much longer in any event.

Some diplomatic negotiations require weeks and months. Others are tentative affairs, more in the way of opening channels and establishing possibilities than coming to any decisions—or even advancing any definite proposals. But he was quite satisfied with the outcome. The friendly neutrality—reasonably friendly, anyway—of the Netherlands was further solidified, and the Austrian attitude had clearly been shifted in that direction.

The impact of the Barbies on Austria's finances and social attitudes had been considerable, more so than he would have imagined ahead of time. Granted, Mike had reservations about the Austrian way of fitting Americans—some Americans, at least— into their aristocratic view of the world. *Von Up-time, indeed!* Fricking ridiculous.

But it was better than fighting another war. Besides, given some time, that ridiculous notion would probably prove to be just another lever for prying the seventeenth century toward civilized attitudes. Mike had never suffered from the notion that progress was simple and invariably straightforward.

Meanwhile, life went on. Archduke Leopold was the hero of the hour, his reputation rescued. He didn't, however, attempt to kiss, touch, or otherwise approach Her Serene Highness Judith Elaine Wendell von Up-time. There were, after all, other girls. Most of them not nearly so quick with a knee.

Cast of Characters

Abrabanel, Rebecca Leader of the Fourth of July Party; wife of Mike Stearns.

Abrabanel, Moses Financier in Vienna, advisor to Ferdinand III

Abrabanel, Uriel Financial advisor to King Albrecht

Anna Serving girl at Liechtenstein house, later buys bra

Babbel, Friedrich Spy sent to Grantville by Father Lamormaini

Barnes, Millicent Anne Member of the Barbie Consortium

Barclay, Carla Anne Daughter of Peter, friend of Hayley Fortney

Barclay, Marina Wife of Peter, defector

Barclay, Peter Defector to Vienna from Grantville

Bartley, David Financier in USE, soldier

Bates, Brandy Fiancée, then wife of Prince Vladimir Gorchakov

Drugeth, Janos Hungarian nobleman; friend and adviser of Ferdinand III.

Eberle, Annemarie Housekeeper for Fortney family, spy

Emerson, Victoria Maureen "Vicky" — Member of the Barbie Consortium

Farkas, Adorján — Agent for Gundaker von Liechtenstein

Faust, Hertel — Doctor of natural philosophy, tutor for Brandon Fortney

Ferdinand III — Emperor of Austria

Ferdinand II of Austria — Holy Roman Emperor, deceased

Fernando I — King in the Netherlands

Fortney, Andrew "Sonny" — Mechanic hired by Janoszi

Fortney, Brandon — Son of Sonny and Dana

Fortney, Dana — Wife of Sonny

Fortney, Hayley Alma — Daughter of Sonny and Dana, Barbie Consortium member

Frederic William — Elector of Brandenburg, Gustav Adolf's brother-in-law

Gandelmo, Josef — Tutor and assistant of Karl Eusebius

Gorchakov, Vladimir — Prince of Russia, husband of Brandy Bates

Gundelfinger, Helene — Vice-President of the State of Thuringia-Franconia; leader of the Fourth of July Party.

Hass, Johannes — Concrete patent owner in Vienna

Higgins, Delia — Owner of Higgins Hotel in Grantville, grandmother of David Bartley

Janoszi, Istvan — Austrian agent in Grantville

John George I — Elector of Saxony

Koell, Johannes — Bookkeeper to von Liechtenstein family

Lamormaini, Wilhelm Germain — Catholic priest, confessor to Ferdinand II

Lang, Karl — Thief of silver from bank

Leopold Wilhelm	Archduke of Austria
Logsden, Susan Elizabeth	Member of the Barbie Consortium
Maria Anna of Spain, "Mariana"	Empress of Austria-Hungary, wife of Ferdinand III
Mason, Heather	Member of the Barbie Consortium, in Grantville
Mazzare, Larry	Cardinal-Protector of the USE
Montilla	Priest in Vienna
Nasi, Francisco	Mike Stearns' chief spymaster
Nadasdy, Pal	Advisor to Ferdinand II and Ferdinand III
Piazza, Edward "Ed"	President of the State of Thuringia-Franconia; leader of the Fourth of July Party.
Pappenheim, Gottfried	General and military advisor to King Albrecht of Bohemia
Pfeifer, Jakusch "Jack"	Law student in Vienna, becomes Fortney's lawyer
Richter, Maria Margaretha "Gretchen"	Leader of the Committees of Correspondence; wife of Jeff Higgins.
Roth, Judith	Wife of Morris
Roth, Morris	Advisor to King Albrecht
Sanderlin, Gayleen	Wife of Ron Sanderlin
Sanderlin, Bob	Uncle of Ron Sanderlin
Sanderlin, Ron	Sells car to Ferdinand III, moves to Austria with family as mechanic
Stearns, Michael "Mike"	Former prime Minister of the United States of Europe; now a major general in command of the 3rd Division, USE Army; husband of Rebecca Abrabanel.
Traugott, Franz	Teller at bank

Urban VIII	Pope
Ugolini, Gabrielle Carlina	Member of the Barbie Consortium
Vasa, Gustav II Adolf	King of Sweden; Emperor of the United States of Europe; also known as Gustavus Adolphus.
Vianetti, Marco	Archduke Leopold's personal guard
von Bachmerin, Gertrude "Trudi"	Down-time member of the Barbie Consortium
von Debrecen, Márton	Son-in-law of Peter von Eisenberg, widower due to execution of his wife Polyxena by Maximilian of Bavaria
von Eisenberg, Amadeus	Son of Peter von Eisenberg
von Eisenberg, Peter	Advisor to Ferdinand II and Ferdinand III
von Eisenberg, Sophia	Wife of Peter von Eisenberg and mother of Amadeus
von Friesen, Erwin	Chief guard for race track
von Kesmark, Rudolph	Young man of Vienna
von Liechtenstein, Gundaker	Court prince of Austria, uncle to Karl Eusebius
von Liechtenstein, Karl Eusebius	Court prince of Austria, called "the Ken Doll" by members of the Barbie Consortium
von Liechtenstein, Maximilian	Court prince of Austria, uncle to Karl Eusebius
von Meklau, Julian	Friend of Amadeus von Eisenberg
von Teschen, Elizabeth Lukretia, "Aunt Beth"	Ruling duchess of Cieszyn in Silesia, aunt to Karl Eusebius, estranged wife of Gundaker
von Trauttmansdorff, Maximilian	Advisor to Ferdinand II and Ferdinand III
von Wallenstein, Albrecht	King of Bohemia

Wendell, Fletcher	Secretary of the Treasury of USE, father of Judith and Sarah Wendell,
Wendell, Judith (Judy the Elder)	Wife of Fletcher Wendell and mother of Judith and Sarah
Wendell, Judith Elaine (Judy the Younger)	Barbie Consortium member
Wendell, Sarah	Fiancée of Karl Eusebius von Liechtenstein, and economic expert
Walker, Coleman	Head of the Federal Reserve Bank of the USE
Zwikel, Georg Bartholomaeus	Spy-master of Austria-Hungary